She-Rain

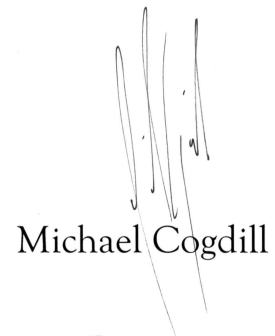

Michael Cogdill

NEW YORK

She-Rain

by Michael Cogdill

ISBN 978-1-60037-702-0 (paperback)
Library of Congress Control Number: 2009935678

Published by:

MORGAN · JAMES

THE ENTREPRENEURIAL PUBLISHER ™
www.morganjamespublishing.com

Morgan James Publishing, LLC
1225 Franklin Ave. Ste 325
Garden City, NY 11530-1693
Toll Free 800-485-4943
www.MorganJamesPublishing.com

Cover Design:
Megan Johnson
Johnson2Design
johnson2design.com

Interior Design:
Bonnie Bushman
bbushman@bresnan.net

Author Photo:
Ted Meadows

She-Rain Defined

S craps of fog, adrift on the ridges of Appalachia. It appears as lacy mist blown off the clouds of a high-mountain rainy day. The expression comes from the lexicon of folklore. I heard it during my early boyhood from my grandmother, Dovie Ella Crowe Keys, who adored and seemed to draw peace from the sight of it. "A little tear off a heaven gown. Fine as it can be. A little lace off the rain." I can hear the joy of her voice on the words. To this day, the sight of it reminds me, beautifully, of her.

Preface

She-Rain grew into an allegorical novel from writing about my first memory. Only a few brush strokes of it remain, yet they so clearly mark my mind, no time will erase them. Just shy of four- years-old, I watched my father bloody my mother with an unmerciful beating, pinning her to the floor in a rage fueled by his early alcoholism. The blood and violence of those few moments come onto these pages so vividly a dear friend of mine literally had to put the story down for a moment. So I feel the need to assure you this story thrives on hope. It became my homage to looking at the heavens on a clear night: Even the most faraway stars always draw the eyes from darkness to high and beautiful light.

My parents' marriage found redemption — and my father embraced sobriety — many years after that first memory, and only when I broke the chains of denial that strangled the relationship and everyone in it. When I finally refused to live with my father's destruction — daring to believe I was made to live in peace and in pursuit of big dreams — my father hit bottom. A mighty low bottom, witnessed by my mother, with me no longer there to enable him. And, thankfully, he bounced. When I abandoned him, my father began his climb into the beautiful man I and so many loved for years. The man whose spirit I adore — and forgive — to this day. Mine is a family history of addiction, running even into opiates of the early 20th century. I set out here to prove a life doesn't have to live down to the worst of its surroundings or upbringing. Each of us holds possibilities that can change the world for the far greater, and it's never too late to let them shine.

People tell me She-Rain entertains as a wild tale of fiction but also improves them — a notion I find deeply humbling and inspiring at once. The writing of it became an act of faithful self-help — a sweet tonic. People even without a backdrop of addiction have drawn healing and inspiration from it. For this I am deeply thankful.

I pray *She-Rain* sheds on your life the same romance and adventure I found in writing it, but my desire reaches beyond the enjoyment of a surprising yarn. As this story climbs from darkness to its constellation of hope, I want it to help break chains of old fears, menace, and low-expectations that may hold you back, even now. May *She-Rain* energize you to heal and to thrive.

As you pass through this story, you'll trace footsteps through my imagination. *She-Rain* is a work of fiction, though distilled from deeply human realities suffered — and celebrated — around the world. On these pages, names, characters, places and the goings on exist solely as I have imagined them into the narrative. Certain locales such as Marshal dwell near to what you'll find on a map, but they merely represent my mind's utter re-creation of place and time. The roads of *She-Rain* lead to no actual outposts. Yet the ageless beauty of North Carolina and Rhode Island is a thriving reality, open to us all. As is the greatness of human potential found here. Only the divine can imagine such finery as that.

"No one has ever measured,
not even poets,
how much the heart can hold."

Zelda Fitzgerald

Prologue

God's coat landed softer than leaves falling to a pond.

Along about sunset on the sixth day, there in my Granny's imagination of holy creation.

"Along about rockin' chair twilight, I reckon." She always spoke of it through a little half-smile. "Good Lord coulda just caught a whiff off heaven's cornbread and dropped His big work coat right here. Let it pile up into mountains so fine they wet my eyes. Narry thing says it didn't happen that way. I reckon there's no sin dreamin' how God might've done it. Set your mind on a right pretty place. It'll soften down the hardest time."

Granny's mind loved to wander in such three-cent theology, off to that million-dollar view. To her the rise and fall of North Carolina mountain blue might have been creation's Almighty accident. The lost coat of God. Truth is I believed that as much as I did her other stories: Talk of Indians eating yellow jackets or folks hearing death warnings spoken out loud on the wind.

I never gave her an argument about it until a summer night – having slipped off from the commotion at home again – lying in a lantern glow, watching her bare feet sway Pap's rocking chair against their porch. The rest of the house dark with sleep.

"Ain't it some no-account God, lets a work coat flop up in a big, cloud-high pile?" I little more than whispered it, glancing off to the fireflies speckling the dark. "You know what Pap says. Says religion that ain't in the Bible ain't nothin' but a big pile of stable bottom. Says some days the church needs a good muckin' out worse than both his barns. I sure do believe me some of that."

Granny huffed a laugh and nudged a foot to my head where I reclined on that porch. I turned to see her wave a hand as if Pap's ideas were gnats to swat.

1

"Awww, pee on him. He don't know ever'thing. His own grandmama believed Indians and Israelites was pert near the same folk, but that don't make it so. He chaps my flour-white fanny sometimes." Frustration and adoration ran together on the words.

The same hand that swatted the thought of him patted the fray-edged little Bible in her lap. It seemed as much a part of my Granny as her fingernails. She spoke with surety, as if the dark itself might nod an, "Amen."

"Frankie, the word of God's like a deepwater pond. There's a lot more to it than what you see. Same with these mountains. Green as a frog in the spring. Hell-fire red come October. Drab as stove ash by Christmas. But climb up high and look at 'em. Off a ways. They're always that holy blue. Blue as dungaree britches. Pert near all the fine blues in this world. That ain't a thing but God's own doin', Frankie. Just like you, sweet boy. And just like the good parts of your daddy. We'll see his soul as the good Lord does one day. Good Lord'll see to it, don't you worry. Your mama's more than woman enough to stand him down. Good Lord's on her side and yours."

In her own soft way, she preached herself into a near doze. Nodding away under the low summer choir of crickets and frogs off in the woods. I lay still at her feet, letting her gospel on mountains and things of the Almighty sift through my own thoughts. Wondering why heaven cursed her daughter to give me birth in the four-room timber cabin that seemed my jailhouse, a short walk through a tobacco field and a low ridge away. Why Ma's eyes looked forever ripe for a storm that never would quite come. Whether any good God knew the way to a piece of North Carolina so deep in hollows and scarps my father thought it "two axe handles and a slingshot north of hell."

Through the dark, there soon dawned to me what seemed the most worthy idea of my life. There on my grandparents' farmhouse porch, with the moths pinging at that dim lantern, I chose for myself the title of bastard. Let the idea of bastardom soak into me, as indigo takes to cotton, easing me into the choice not to have a father anymore. I vowed to think of him only as Frank from then on, the notion of the blood we shared just a stain to live with and hide. Surely no one could blame me. Even Granny, so kind she would cry for days over a hurt dog, had long ago said he changed like "a storm-beat butterfly working backwards into a worm."

In a few minutes she half-roused and ushered me to set off for home. She kissed my forehead and crept away toward Pap in their bed, in quiet care not to wake the rest of the house. I soon swung the lantern's amber light over the path that was often my shortcut escape. Through the warm dark and the cinnamon ferns, I let Granny's thinking take some finer form in my own.

"God Almighty made this ground, He sure enough did," I thought. "Dropped His coat and just left it to rot. Not carin' much to touch it again. Not carin' who might smother in it."

Walking the stand of woods dividing our farms, I drew up the idea that I might worship a piece of that ground. Any red clay used to form the walls of my blood-daddy's grave might turn holy in my view. Holy blue-mountain ground, with its shovel-dug hole, red and black as hell. A fine little patch to plow the man under.

Quiet as a barn cat, I slipped with that thought back through the moonlit open window to my straw-tick bed. Stripped and lay there, longing for the smell of coffin flowers and fresh-turned dirt. The feel of an axe splitting a man. A touch of fingertip to the chiseling of his name in stone. All of it cleaving to my mind the way a hot day takes to the churchyard tomb rocks just up the road. It seemed a fine bedtime companion, the idea of no daddy, ever before or behind me. The thought quieted the echo of how he had rattled the nails of the house that night in another opium fit at my mother. I regretted it, but a moment of hating her passed over me. A wondering how she could share a bed with him now not twenty steps away.

Then I hated myself for being the child who bound them, and one still too small to leave. I was hardly ten-years-old, shorter than the stakes on Granny's grapevines, still climbing trees and awing at the stars. Drifting toward some taut sleep, I thought myself no more than a fleck of human dust settled on her blue mountain dream. Sightless of any through trail beyond it. As blind to her God as her God seemed to me.

Down near slumber came a final rummaging for some boyhood solace. Granny always warned not to sleep without finding a sweetening for my dreams, and the choice fell again to a girl – a distant neighbor, of times much harder than mine. She, as ragged and beautiful as Granny's God-coat. It might as well have been a bed of crushed laurel blossoms, where my mind brought itself to rest in thoughts of her. Hoping I might dream of her. A dream light enough to crest mountains where they reached clouds. Carry a girl and a boy way out beyond the cold of hollows and family gore. Lying amid those wishes, drifting off in the thought of her, no such dream would fully come.

I know it makes as much sense to question why the heavens let any child go hungry, or lonesome. But these years from that night, I can still wonder: Is it not some divine cruelty, fogging us off from any sight of the beauty that might await us in this life? Why must children, hearts new to this world, live in a blind? Not even a snatch of view at the good that can come of them. I suppose, perhaps, it's to sugar us with surprise when we land upon a life not even a child's heart could dream.

I have long since managed to catch a ride to the living of such a beautiful life. Lifted to it by the hands of tender souls, each as stout as sun drawing water, who've carried me far off from the crests of Granny's daydream creation. Even my Granny's imagination, in all its extravagance, might strain to believe her grandson's present view and place in the world. This station of my life, from where I write to you now, would make her mighty proud.

My best times lie behind me, though in portions they will bloom again as you and I trace that path that brought me here. Our passage is bound to stretch your power of belief, perhaps even your faith as you have known it, as much as parts of this story will drench my face in the *breakage of heart. Along its course, some unholy ghosts hold secrets you may think unseemly to tell. But I must, as a calling, for I am reminded that hard times can merely floor cathedrals in the human heart. I am called to let you know who taught me this.*

Oscar Wilde, who might wilt like a rose in whiskey above these pages to come, posed a question that ought to shadow each word as I write it. He asked, "Who, being loved, is poor?" The just-discovered letters spread before me now — each an unforeseen stream of the rarest grace — prove I am a man of the most uncommon riches. An old man now, fresh from the hardest of goodbyes, about to speak of unthinkable things so long hidden. Yet I find myself again at the dawn of sweet young times. Even as I mourn, longing for the mere brush of the hand I've just had to let go, my inner boy thrives. Braced by women, whose letters attest that I am surely among the most well-loved men in the world. Such a love I can never deserve.

Reader, I must caution, we will make our way through some black swale, yet with bearings set for lush ground. An Eden, where hearts see their wreckage mended. Where they are forgiven for feeling too much for one lifetime. We are bound for a graceful view of what is possible in a human life. A firmament of living lights this tobacco field boy scarcely believed he would see.

But you will catch the final vista without me. By the end of this tale's telling, I'll be gone, leaving the last memory to a fine woman's hand. I trust she will see you on to the beauty I have promised. A shore, brimming with good.

You will judge it for yourself. Weigh what all this reveals in you. Far from where we now begin — just a scattering of days after that night on Granny's porch.

A summer afternoon that still haunts this boy, long ago shaken from the coat of her God.

August 10, 1921

Mathison County, North Carolina

The screen door landed in bouncing slams, hard as a swung bed slat. Ma stepping in from sweeping the dirt backyard and garnering the armload of split wood I had forgotten. Stooped as much by timeless worry as boundless work. She fed the stove fire, announced the bread nearly done, and stepped to the table just in time to see the okra fall.

It tumbled from his mouth like little sling-shot creek rocks, bouncing off his pants to the floor. He ignored the droppings to keep eating her fried okra with the posture of a dead man refusing to lie down. Grimy hands, trembling as I had never seen them, clawed the little pieces straight from a heavy glass bowl the color of a faded pine top. The smack of his chew made me think of a mealy apple in a mule's mouth.

I sat within range of him at the oak table, fresh from evening chores of milking and carrying in water, and worked at pretending not to see. Feigning calm. Trying to venture my mind elsewhere, as every three of four loads of his food took a washing down with the pickling juice from a jar of banana peppers. Each so hot the slightest finger touch off one would burn an eye for an hour. His taste for stinging hot pepper with just about anything, even a stem of rhubarb once on a bet, made pepper juice an orthodox beverage at our evening meal. Creases of his face flowed with streams of it like slug trail, easing off his chin.

In the throes of a drunk, or even the craving of one, his manners seldom rose far above a steer's. But hands in place of his fork struck me as more fearsome than usual. Worth the risk of escape. I slipped from the hardwood chair and sat on the floor, figuring to eat after whatever was about to happen. I had barely settled into a pool of light from the open window above when the noise of Ma's feet came suddenly near, out of nowhere. Her hand urging at my back, hard and anxious and gentle at once.

"Raise up, now. Raise up. Get ready to eat."

The door slammed again. Bouncing in rhythm to her feet drumming the porch. My mother deemed the waste of food a sin, but straining to the window I saw her toss his fallen okra onto the yard for any animal to take in the night. She wore a tan apron over a gray work dress, whose hem swished as if it had nerves. A scatter of chickens flitted out of her way.

"Time to eat, now. Didn't you hear your mama?"

He strangled on the command, but it let off a sound no less like thunder. His voice held its usual effect of setting a fire to my insides.

"Stay up off that nasty floor. I ain't got money to pay out for doctorin', and we ain't got no yeller root to fix you neither. You get up off that cold floor now, boy. I ain't sayin' it again."

None of us had been cold since the usual blackberry winter chill snap in May.

He carried on with some more bark and growl about cold floors making children sick, even as he sat in a flowing sweat, shirtless under bib overalls, sodden in the August steam of a room surely measuring better than eighty degrees. For me a scolding from an ox would have held more sense and sway.

I got up, though. The sound and nearness of him plowed through and raised me. What surely seemed a boy's growing respect was really no more than a little weed of fear. I brought my rear to the edge of the chair, facing away from him, bare feet and every muscle bracing to run through the angels. I had roused the angels.

They floated in the window's twilight steam. Traces of white, smaller than a gnat, light as morning fog against my hand. A mother's angels. To me, worthless dust. Only the stirred fragments of lint my folks carried home on clothing and hair. White soot off the jobs they worked in the high brick stockade of a cotton mill on the river in Marshal. The town stood as the Mathison County seat, with a patina of hard work and fenced-in living on most everything. I knew Ma's angels rose off 80-square — cloth made eighty threads to the square inch — woven thirty-five-cents-for-the-hour, twelve-hours to the shift. Dust of the air, given life by a mother trying to gather a scrap or two of peace into her boy's mind. I hadn't wanted to disappoint either of us by speaking out loud the truth that I believed in angels about as much as I thought a man could eat smoke.

"Look at heaven's angels, come down to keep a look after you and me."

Ma had spoken of them the first time a few days before, on my birthday, a Sunday, when we shared the supper table and the cabin's twilight alone. The fresh-bath smell of quinine came off her dark curls and swollen hands. She had made pepper cornbread and apple cake, and worked extra hard at shucking any husk of gloom — trying to give me some celebration of turning ten.

"Heaven's watchin' little boys. Your granddaddy prayed them angels in here when he hammered this place up a long time back. They're here lookin' after us. Them angels is still right here to see if you're good so the Lord'll know. We'll pray and be thankful when we see 'em. We got cause to be thankful. Plenty got it worse than us."

The morning of that birthday had just about made me believe that a prayer could find heaven's ear. In his cow barn my granddaddy, Pap (Woody Pap Warren to most folks), had reached into his overall pocket and handed me his old four-cent apple-wood pipe, mostly worn out but still shiny on its silver ferrule. He said he had ordered it in 1902 from Sears, Roebuck. The months of begging I invested finally brought the gift, which I had received with an awe fit for rabbit tobacco's Holy Grail. "Now don't brag much to your mama or your granny about it," Pap had said with a grin, trying to whittle off my worries. "They might set both our backsides to smokin' when they see it. But it beats that corncob thing you been draggin' around. And don't set your hair or nothin' else afire neither. Else you'll smoke bald and we'll never hear the end of it."

Now, these days later at my parents' table, thought of that birthday dimmed, and with it the warm barn-wood feeling of the grandfather I adored. All pressed down under the slosh and groan just behind me. Ma had slung the okra and disappeared — and wondering where she had gone, I claimed the brawn a boy can draw from a pipe. The mere feel of it in my breast pocket quashed enough worry that I dared pull it out, hoping to act like a man. I waved the black bowl through the floating angels, thinking how reliably they would burn.

"Turn 'round to this table now, boy. Drop that damned infernal pipe and turn 'round here."

This time the noise off him cracked louder against the inside of my head. When the greasy hand whapped the chair behind my dungarees he might as well have pulled a rusty saw from my private parts to the roof of my mouth. I pocketed the pipe and pulled myself onto the oak bottom in one motion, never thinking about Granny's honey jar. Not until the thud it made. My elbow had nudged it off against the floor. No breakage. Not one drop spilled. Just enough racket to rile his ill temper worse than fire set to a hornet's nest.

"Well, see, dammit? Dammit to all hell, your mess. Damn your wastin' mess to hell...."

He leapt into rant, slamming his chair to the wall, a storm of the hottest talk rising with him. I sat, near paralysis, in the rain of his indictments. He accused the honey jar of motherly incest, called the whole house an excrement pile and himself the damnedest man ever damned. He paced, declaring himself damned by God, whom he damned in return, all of which brought him in a short circle of damnations to me — where I hoped against the brimstone of it all that Ma would stay out, cool down, not come in the house.

"That's a mess your Ma'll have to clean up, and we ain't got food for wastin'."

I had dared stoop from the chair, and reach for the jar, when his hand came, full of shakes but closing, sharp and hard as a blacksmith pincher to the back of my neck. Every boyhood ideal of how home ought to feel crashing to the floor under him. I dropped to the floor almost by instinct, the way I had seen a possum curl itself, still and quiet against a barking dog. The grip tightened, rage and spittle coming like hot coals from his mouth only inches now from my face. I balled my body tighter, more the way a caterpillar curls. The weight of him pushed my cheek, scalding into a crack between the floorboards. I couldn't help, then, but make a sound. A stream of yells, cut loose and soon mingling with hers.

"Frank! Frank, you quit. What are you doin' to my young'un...."

I figure Ma had walked on to the springhouse for butter and to calm. She must have heard the commotion from the yard because the sound of running and the screen door came nearly at once, trailed by the shrieks off her, hot as crackling fire. Still under his hand, I heard myself beg him to stop.

Something in her defense of me hit him like a leather riding strap. He let me go. A chair landed, flesh-splitting hard, against my head. On his way to pinning my mother against the floor, he threw another of the green bowls from the table against the only piece of our furniture I ever heard my mother speak of with pride. A little corner dining chest took the bowl into its glass-door belly, and the crash screamed ruin. The guts of her bric-a-brac fused with greasy beans we called leather-breeches in the shattering. I crouched against my own slamming pulse under the table.

"Lord, Frank, stop. Lord, quit it, Frank," her voice strangling under his weight.

"I'll learn you. You come knockin' at me."

The hands rise to my memory. One wrapping her throat against the wood floor, the other chopping at her face, fisted, knuckles like ball-peen hammer tips, each blow rocking her head, screams flaying together, rising from both of them. When she raised her abdomen trying to throw him, the gray dress went above her underwear. His legs pushed it higher, tightening the straddle. Like some mad farrier astride the horse leg that just kicked him.

"Stop it. Lord, please quit it." The words wept out of her, weaker now. "Please Lord, get him to quit."

The sound of her surrender may have lifted me. Or perhaps it was her blood where it landed on the floor that fastened me into rage.

I emerged from under the table, throbbing where his fingers had squeezed my neck, blood from the chair-wound draining to my mouth. He spewed on.

"I know what you've done, turnin' yourself up to men. Little bastard. He ought be mine, but he ain't, is he? Is he?"

The largest shard of that broken bowl found its way to my hands from the broken dining chest. I barely recall running to retrieve it. One side dull, the other razor sharp, and the weight of it good as I took cat steps behind him. His blows cut more of my mother's blood loose. The sweet warmth of it flew off his backhands onto me where I raised the bowl shard above my head, near enough now to feel a breeze from his swipe.

"Shut up. Shut up, shut up, shut your mouth."

"You're killin' me, Frank, yer killlinnnnn' meeee." Then only huffs of crying.

"I'm the one bein' killed." He beat her more. Fatigue holding no power.

Every muscle in me tightened, like a young tree bent by wind, straining to uncoil. The glass shard shook above my head. Twice I started to swing it into the back of his, but stopped. The knocks at her face turning synchronous now with his words — so familiar the very walls might have spoken.

"I don't do nothin' but work and you handin' out money and ever'thing else to that bunch of your family. I'm sick to death, Dovie. I'm sick to death."

All of it raised courage larger than a child should know. I closed my eyes. Every sinew pulled back to fire the shard into him two-handed hard — when the noise came.

A crack.

Then roar.

It came like thunder, but there was none. Heaving, dense as lead. Rain. A vertical freshet. No crescendo of drops building to downpour. This rain fell in an instant avalanche so thick it felt like number one buckshot, cloud-blasted and beating the roof shakes and tin coverings until they wailed like a thousand men on fire.

"Lord. Lord, them apples. Let's get them apples 'fore they ruin in this wet."

The downpour stopped him. As if it reached an unseen arm against both of his.

I dropped the piece of glass in retreat, dashed under the table and turned around just in time to see him roll off my mother. She lay disguised as death, awash in blood and half-nakedness.

"Come on, Frankie, help me get 'em in," he yelled, and bounced out of the room through the kitchen, out that slamming door, quick as a fox behind a squirrel. The rage had disappeared as fast as the rain had come.

Boot sound vanished off the porch.

I raised myself to the window to watch him splash through the mercury-colored downpour toward a rack fashioned onto the backyard beside the smokehouse. He had rigged it with straight-back chairs lashed to the corners of an old sheet. It bulged to the ground by now with soggy apple pieces from last year's crop, left to dry in the August sun for barter or fried pies. Instead of grabbing it up on arrival he jumped over it, I suppose figuring I ran dutifully behind him, braced to haul in the fruit while he tended to business far more critical. Every step tossed mud as if the ground were watery chocolate. He disappeared up the path toward the spring alone. The hens had gotten out of the rain.

No more than fifteen seconds passed before back down the path he ran, harder now, his tin lunch box in one hand and two small glass bottles, both open, clutched to his chest as if they held the cure for death. At the window I ducked down on his approach to the porch, though able to watch him gently lay the cargo out of the rain and turn back toward the rack. He yanked the sheet corners into a dripping sack and turned for cover, the sheet plowing ground behind him.

He'd practically escaped the worst of the downpour when the hunk of white flint rock that was our back porch step betrayed him. Hardly a touch of his foot slipped him into a fall so catastrophic his shoulder blades, neck and head all slammed the sopping ground at once — the thud akin to a dull axe on a stump. Some of the fruit sailed loose to rain on him like shriveled brown hail. He kicked the kick of a new baby, gave the heavens some cuss, then crawled onto the wood slats of the porch just as the rain turned to drizzle, dying nearly as fast as it came alive.

A rush of her breath and the smell of blood came virtually as one at my back. I suppose a fear of finding her cold had kept me from turning to check on Ma. A few seconds had brought her to me at that window, simmering toward boil, of hands and voice. She spun me into the red spatter of the apron. Yanked me deep into it and cradled my head there, I suppose to guard a boy's ears.

"You get. Get from here, Frank Locke. Get the hell from here and don't come back in this damned house. Off to hell with you. You go to hell." It came as no weepy flow. She set off a horn at him. Her rare profanity flew through the window screen with steel force.

"I'm up now and I'll not take another swipe from you. To hell with you, Frank. To hell with you. And that's where you'll take your next meal if'n you come at me again."

She pulled my face up into her bosom under the window. Her heart a thunder. I resisted the guardian suffocation but she held, oak strong. Her chin rested on my head, and I swallowed as many as I could until my sobs finally spilled out. Roiling into her. Our trembling melded into one another.

"It's fine, honey, we're fine now." She whispered, as much to herself as me, "Lord, Lord Jesus, thank you. You musta seen me. Call me a fool for believin' that sweepin' the ground brings a rain, but you musta seen. Lord, it's a miracle he didn't kill me and you both, honey. What a God's miracle of a rain."

She backed me out of her chest for a look.

"Lord God, sweetie, you hurt? Where you hurt? Where'd he hurt you?"

"I ain't hurt none."

"Lord, you are bleedin'. You are too bleedin'. Lord, damn him. Damn him."

Her sodden eyes raked me up and down for injuries after her thumb stung the seeping knot on my forehead. She studied and rubbed it clean, sweeping at my hair and mashing my face in search of, I suppose now, some regular aspect of boyhood.

Her face had held strong against the drubbing. Only the mouth showed the start of the swelling this time. Bread-mold blue as I had seen it before. The shudders that often follow tears sagged into a moment's smile, I suppose to encourage the child in the room. She sniffed and wiped nose blood, fast flowing to both lips still atremble. Swipe marks and swellings covered her, hair to throat, though I had expected her to look much more like the inside of a watermelon.

"Come on, now."

A quick glance beyond through the glass pulled her away from the window, me in tow by the arm, across the greasy floor into my room. We arrived before my thoughts could fully blossom into what she might have seen in the yard.

"Listen now." The whisper would hardly move a spider web. "I want you to keep them clothes on and get under that bed. Crawl under right now and don't move." She shook me at the shoulders. Her long fingers some people praised as a rare mark of her elegance tightening more by the word.

"Wedge that door shut and say your prayers, say 'em over and over, and don't move. Get under. I'll be right back. Don't you dare open this door, no matter. You hear?"

The argument that followed went faster than squirrels wrestling on a tree.

"Where you goin'? How come I can't go?"

"'Cause you can't. Hush now."

"But where you goin'?" I had an idea.

"Not far. I'll be right back."

"Don't leave me here. Not with him worked up." A shuddering rode my ribs up into my throat. Her eyes flooded again.

"Don't now, Frankie. Do's I say. You hear? Your daddy ain't gonna hurt you none."

"He ain't my daddy." The tears emerged. "He ain't no kinda daddy and I ain't callin' him one."

"Lord, honey, hush now. Hush. I ain't goin' far." I broke her embrace to crawl under the bed, pressing my back against the familiar sag, surprised when she turned out of the door instead of chasing me with calm.

"Don't matter none what you hear, don't you move. Now come out and wedge this door and crawl back under and just wait."

She paused to hear the wedge thud security against the wood door bottom and told me I was a good boy. Her stepping away then made me alone. My behind pressed two dimples of defiance into the mattress top just in time to feel her slam the front door and run off the porch.

A cricket chirped, hidden somewhere in the sparse room, and I thought to look for it but sat still on the bed, almost serene in the failing light, looking at the wedge. It was a broad wedge under a knot-hard door.

Both trusty as stone.

A lot more so, I thought, than any of that old superstition talk about it soon raining after somebody sweeps the ground.

"Is she a girl or a bird? Bet she can't fly. You fly, bird girl? Let's see them tailfeathers, bird gal."

So went some of the mockery of what Granny named my mother. Dovie Evelyn Warren. That first name for the cooing doves heard by an old midwife walking to the birth.

Perhaps in some revenge against the teasing Ma endured through childhood they had agreed, shortly before my arrival, I must wear my father's name – Monroe Franklin Locke. I never heard Ma utter regret of it.

She instead reminisced to me about a fable of a man I could no more believe in than see. A long blade of an orphan boy, left to raise himself, strong as a ridge of hardwood, quiet as the pasture balds he walked to court her. He had filled her hands with wildflowers and store-bought stick candy she figured he took a jip for in trade. Granny had told her she liked the sound of it – Monroe Franklin Locke – and reminded Ma she'd been courted by men who answered to Fatback, Coontrack and Henbone, the latter infamous for what smelled like wood smoke and wet dog cologne.

She said my father looked like a giant matchstick in overalls the first time she saw him. A teenage rail standing at the Barlow knives of Mackey's store in Marshal – so gauzed up about the head his face stayed hidden except for the green of his eyes, blazing through the clean bandage white. She said a grin came up in those eyes when they first met hers. He couldn't speak much for the injury and bandage, so they wrote "hellos" to one another in chicken feed dust on the counter. She first.

"Hurt much?"

"Nope."

She said his finger shook some as he scribed the "p" backwards. He erased the whole word, and put it down the right way.

13

"You lie, sinner," she wrote back, laughing, wiping the whole thing clean in a sudden attack of modesty.

They thus anointed the store as a point of rendezvous, and themselves a topic of its front porch gossip. Arie Blevins, described by Granny as a hard wire of a woman as attached to that porch as the floor nails, put out the early word there'd be a marriage. She'd overheard the bird girl telling a friend how, when she first touched even the bandage on his head and caught sight of those moss-colored eyes, she felt a stealing of her breath.

calm rose through the house and settled soon into parts of me. Noiseless but for the cricket, still calling my fingers to its legs. That and the trickle draining the last of the downpour off the roof shakes. Whittling or marbles with imaginary friends might fill such solitude for most ten-year-old boys waiting for the usual playgrounds or work places to dry.

I kept my bed seat and let my mind hang more doubts on Ma's miracle. Questions about whether the rain had actually been some act of God grew to the conclusion that, regardless of why it happened, the sudden shower had swindled me out of throwing Frank the good sharp whack he had long deserved. I whispered to myself.

"Them angels of hers wouldn't never have stopped him from killin' me if I'd missed killin' him."

A short daydream of that bowl shard slicing against his head vanished with the first smell of the smoke.

An undeniable hint of burning oozed under the door, otherwise I might have thought the bed afire. The shower after a day's summer sun made the whole room sweat. The drafty walls, like much of the tiny timber house, were papered up in catalog pages and pieces of yellowing newsprint — able to hold out some winter cold but soaking in the wet heat of August. The whole place normally steamed like a kettle nearly to a boil in such weather, but the smoke smell seemed to heat it to unbearable. I had been scolded about matches and rough play near kerosene lamps because the walls, even a little damp, could burn faster than hay at Halloween. When the smell soon thickened to a faint white flow under the door I pulled away the wedge and eased out, half-expecting an eyeful of fire.

The house stood dusky and calm. A few toe steps brought me to the kitchen and the well-fueled "Acme King" woodstove, whose fire Ma had stoked and forgotten. A towel she had tossed on the top during the commotion burned openly until I beat it with a broom, and from inside, the iron stove choked on what I knew now to be burning cornbread. I used another dishtowel to open the door, then made the error of dousing the towel in a bucket of water on the floor. When I touched it to the iron skillet, a scalding stung through the wet cloth into my hand. Fire trailed the pan where I dropped it to the floor. I gave it some mild cuss and a good stomping out.

This brought some panic to dull the pain. It rose with the choking smoke.

He's heard the noise, I thought, and if he sees a hot pan branding the floor he's liable to use it on me. As investment in good luck, I stomped the pan's remains a bit more and hooked a fork to drag the smoking crust of a skillet to a hiding place under a cabinet in the tiny kitchen. A glance of caution out the back door. Nothing. Wiping the black from the floor wood and stowing the mess, I figured the risk of escape trumped Ma's orders to hide under the bed. I knew exactly where I wanted to be.

The smoke with the late day's heat fevered the place. Seeming to choke off the last of its air. I made way through the house, pausing at the front door for some reconnaissance, and again at front porch corner. Then moved with a fast creep along the wall, like a possum caught out in daylight, thinking about my last sighting of him on the back porch in the rain. A pause at the rear corner. Nothing but quiet. The porch and yard lay lonesome to my left and, to my right, at thirty yards at least, stood a hickory nut tree as familiar as the inside of my mouth. Up it, waited my hideaway stash. I could run for it from here.

A light stride splashed me through grass and dark mud to the rope hanging hidden down the side away from the yard. It was Ma's tree, planted by Granny to honor her birth and manured early so it grew to a high hulk of shade mostly unnecessary in the mountain hollow. I climbed fast, though careful not to rustle myself noticed. Damp overalls clung to my legs stronger than cold molasses on a spoon and fought me on every memorized move through the branches to that secreted place.

The boards and an old flour tin I had wedged above them felt cool as creek water after the rain. I had long ago navigated the limbs to hammer and tie five pieces of scrap barn lumber onto a fork at least forty feet up. The half-rotten rope made the climb easier and could be pulled up for security. Through the camouflage of leaves lay a wide view of rooftop and yard and part of a corn and bean field to the far left. To my right revealed the smoke house, the spring, then a tree thicket rising almost vertically up the ridge behind the house. This hideout and I were acquainted long enough now that a horseshoe I jammed for luck between a limb and the trunk had begun to grow into the wood.

I took care to open the tin without sound. It held a few stolen wood matches in a box, a homemade slingshot, some rock-hard hickory nut ammo, rabbit tobacco rolled in an old Bull Durham pouch, three Pepsi Colas saved up from egg-selling trips with Pap, and my corncob pipe he had replaced with the birthday gift still in my pocket. I opened a Pepsi, then pulled out the new pipe to load for a smoke.

"I'd just as soon kiss the devil on the mouth as encourage young'uns with tobaccer," Granny had long protested, but she tolerated it because Pap assured her it settled me — especially when there'd been some teasing or row about my crazy daddy.

The match was slow but finally struck off my thumbnail, and I sat satisfied, bare feet dangling, to watch the yard and think on where he might be. Where I suspected Ma went and how it might end this time. A sip off that Pepsi every three or so puffs raised a swirl of sweet, warm gas, mingling with the moldy leaf so deep into my head it tasted of purest relief.

The ground below kept still and nearly silent, except for a bobwhite quail calling to its namesake. Dangling my legs had braced the feeling of solid bones back into me. Only a few moments amid that tree dissolved the trembling. I sat in steady oneness with the boards under my backside.

I kept surveillance of the yard and studied the house a bit. It stood now in the hollow's full twilight shade. A little box of a cabin, sodden from rain yet somehow thirsting for help. It sagged, crooked all over, covered in a skin of unpainted timbers, nested together years before by Pap's good labor. Recalling my view now, it seemed held together by the very hands of neglect. The corners drooped worse than death, some of the silver-gray boards curling at the edges and ends. The whole of it rancid-looking. A catfish lying days under the sun might stand a better chance at a new life.

"I oughtta fix it up," I thought slightly out loud, the last of the smoke easing out my nose. "Sneak off some scrap lumber from out behind Mackey's store and at least hammer up better what's hangin'. If we had a finer house, he wouldn't fuss so much about Pap and the rest of the family havin' a better one."

A door slam broke that idea as if it were a dry sprig. Yanked me back to the danger at hand. The bobwhite fluttered away, chased by a muttering on the ground.

Frank was back, talking to himself again.

The usual subjects took the hottest parts of it. Staggering out of the smokehouse, burbling a low-boil whose higher parts rose to my hearing in the tree, he called for the very scald of hell to land on Ulysses and Mattie Tickman. He had long ago metamorphosed my uncle's name into "Useless," and claimed my Aunt Mattie (my mother's older sister), deserved the title twice for, "Allowin' that fool's hand to touch either ham of her chair-crackin' hind end."

"Hell bound you are, Useless. Hell bound and oughtta fry. You and that damned infernal woman, keepin' us in this mess."

He came out shaking his head and bound for the outhouse, not quite directly under me. I drew up both legs and stilled. Nearly whittled myself into the tree wood. Breathless.

One hand and arm held the lunch box and two little bottles. In the other swung his semi-precious newspaper. The trembling seen at the table had faded some. He looked more the man a town wouldn't talk so much about, though the old jaw scar appeared to deepen as he reached the shadows. Had the wound been fresh, his chosen tonic taken in that smokehouse would have calmed the hurt away.

"If you stay 'round long enough, Useless Tickman, I'll put a right fit ass whippin' on you. Right fit the whippin' you deserve. Dove deserves better than both of us. She ought have better than me."

With that note to self, spoken aloud, he reached and pulled open the old outhouse door, no more than fifteen feet from the trunk of my tree. Still breathless, I watched the top hinge. Thinking it might hold. Then watched it make good on weeks of threat. Its last nail finally popped out. The door dropped against his forehead with flawless aim and marvelous thud. His box, both bottles, the newspaper, and the remaining threads of Monroe Franklin Locke, Senior's self-control fell harder than a dropped load of firewood.

The ensuing rage of fist clout and outhouse wrestle came with a blast of white-hot profanities. If his tongue were fire, the tree's highest limbs would have caught the cinders. All of it burning into my deepest nerve a conflict — whether to laugh or cry. In one or two breaths he railed the little paintless toilet full of fornication talk and doubtful paternity, shrill as any revival preacher. With every blow and kick, he called on the Almighty to rain the damnedest of damnings on the only stand of private bodily relief we had, save the woods.

It turned then to another blood-knuckled fit of outhouse pugilism that finally sent both off their foundations into a tumble of unintelligible roar to the wet ground. Some closeby hollyhock blossoms took some of the worst of the landing. I saw the little edifice smack his head as it rolled and pinned him splay-legged to the mud, a corner of it smashing his crotch so hard even my young loins recoiled. He paused as if dead, moaned, grunted, cussed. Cussed more, worming from under it and crawling out as if in triumph that his little gray-wood enemy would need his help to rise. He let fly one more kick. Then the vanquished outhouse might as well have been my Aunt Mattie herself, lain at his staggering feet on the clay ground.

"Lyin' fat-ass laziness. Good for nothin'...." Those became the cleaner parts.

I still had not moved more than to blink. He dusted at himself, suddenly appreciating the row's high level of sticking filth, then soared back into fury. Fast around the little plank-board commode that hadn't moved when the house fell over, aiming his tongue at the Tickmans again.

"Big as a steam engine with pert near half the sense...."

I couldn't articulate it at the time, but if a devil could compose liturgy, what I next heard amounted to hell's high church. New rites of the worst vulgarity ever spoken in all of blasphemy. Hardly a sanitary word. He grew tired a moment, stooped to pick up the bottles where they spilled. Checked them back into the lunch box with the others, caught some breath, then squatted into a final rant. The usual threadbare comparison. Mattie reminded him of a steam locomotive that derailed after a downpour near the cotton mill four years before. I'll leave you to imagine how he colored it blue.

"Just sits, wailin' her whistle 'til somebody comes pullin' her out of her own mess. Fat iron mule. All the manfolk in this county could shovel her a fat bellyful, but hell no, that won't move her. Woman ain't nothin' but a whinin', lazy, loud-mouthed, commode-smotherin', pan-handlin', cast iron mule. Poppin' out young'uns faster than any cow drops fanny patties."

He stomped off through the yard toward the spring, the sermon I had so often heard nearing the final point, which he muttered aloud on the way.

"And that poor excuse for a man she married, worse than she is. Lazier. Lazy *and* dumb."

I couldn't quite hear the final line but knew it by heart. A classic at our supper table.

"That Useless is so dumb if he was a hummin'bird he'd surely suck a mule's butt for a mornin' glory."

He plodded on, a little gimped in his crust of mud, toward another place I knew he loved to hide. He had long ago anointed the dark cavern of dung smell between the chicken house and a clay bank behind it as his backyard den, apparently thinking it cleverly private. Children, though, have a sense rivaling a good dog's nose for the ways and things adults believe they can hide from the world.

My exploration of the yard around my seventh year first acquainted me with his under-the-henhouse stash of bottled bootleg laudanum. Usually stowed alongside that lunch box full of the things that had turned both arms and most of his life into red infection. Finding it made sense of the talk around church, school, and town — how that Frank Locke and certain others loved opium as well as rain loves a river. Any bottled tonic of paregoric — bought from itinerant bootleggers, scammed from doctors, even once sold as colic cure for babies — held power to turn a grown man into a demon addict. My father's habit, the scar caved into the side of his face, and mysteries of his upbringing composed the perfect alchemy for gossip — a drug of its own, so craved by the tongues of human pride.

Some normal breath came back to me as he re-scattered chickens and disappeared around the corner of their house. I could imagine what came next, having slipped a few times to peer around that corner to watch. At times he had the compound in a form he could merely drink. But I figured by now he squatted to open the lunch box, confident of solitude, wrapping a string from it around his arm, yanking it tight with his teeth. Almost in one motion he poured some liquid from a surviving bottle into a spoon, dropped in the white dust of a crushed pill from a little glass jar, struck a match with his thumbnail and heated the mixture. From the spoon he drew an amount into an old glass syringe and jabbed the backwater narcotic into his arm. Soon tumbling over into a heap of man-tears, familiar by now. I knew he lay there in the chicken dung, fermenting in the last reaches of the day's sun. The ritual of it almost tolerable compared to the time I saw him slice the liquid into himself. That day, a year or so before, he had used a jagged medicine dropper in the absence of a needle, blood streaming to rapid drip off the shakes of his hand.

The memory of it now turned my eyes away, up into the limbs and the late-day sky, in colors of dark blue and sun fire. I lay down on those tree boards, finishing the smoke and drink, my right arm curved as a pillow, resolving to think of something other than him. Trying not to wonder whether Ma intended to return or was gone for good this time to Granny and Pap's, where I could finally follow.

Calming into something nearer to normal boyhood, my thoughts roamed to a fine someone. A time not long before. A place just below me.

The end of our backyard. Out beyond the smoke and chicken houses where the spring signaled the beginning of high, steep woods. That's where she first spooked me so hard I thought I might pee ice water.

Suspended in the tree's camouflage I soon lost myself in the memory of it — and of her.

About five months earlier. I had knelt sharpening a pocketknife on a whetstone, lost in the watching of some bugs, when she stepped out of the woods, quiet as a cloud, and yelled, "You, boo!" behind my right ear. Mary Lizbeth Hunter — who took honors as the most peculiar, gossip-maligned and mysterious child in our high blue world.

From my perch in the tree, I could see where it had happened. The sight drawing me into a long daydream, beyond the hens pecking the now-quiet yard, toward that time. I might have given a couple of my fingers in exchange for her stepping out of those woods to let me live in it again.

"Whatcha doin', lil' Locke?" she had said. "You know that there knife wouldn't have done you a licka good if I'd been a bear sneakin' up on you outta these woods."

"Sweet mother of Moses, girl, you pert near scared me dead," I said from my backside, looking up at a child my age but about a head taller. "I oughtta whip you for such."

"Naw, they ain't no use in that. I ain't been whipped much yet. And ain't plannin' on takin' anybody's whippin'."

She grinned and asked me for a drink, which I gave her in a gourd from the spring, my heart still slamming my breastbone.

"I hate askin', given you shared a bite of your meal the other day. That was awful fine, what you did," she said, looking everywhere but at me. "Reckon you've forgot about it, but I ain't."

I had not been able to forget. I had done it just a few days before that afternoon of her spooking me. Mary Lizbeth came to school sporadically always in the same appearance — the very picture of a full-sized, corncob rag doll. The kind discarded and left for a dog to drag around. Her usual clothing consisted of an old long dress and a pair of worn out boots made for men. All of it, and often all the visible rest of her, the color of a creek bottom — where I suspected her clothes took their washing in water muddied from hard rain. The dress seemed to change only with the seasons, aided come fall only by an old quilted-up sweater unfit for the cold. She stayed apart from most people, sat at the back of the schoolroom, far off from groups at lunch, and practiced a habit that became mockery for fellow children, and talk around town. Each day Mary Lizbeth ate her noon meal from a burlap sack drawn up around her cheeks to hide its contents. It became apparent to anyone as smart as a dog that she did this out of shame. The most wicked and dim-minded of our peers used to laugh and claim Satan had fathered her, that she toted Eve's devil apple in that sack. That day of our sharing, I'm not sure what caused me to approach with a piece of my granny's cornbread. But I made the offer and she accepted with a smile wide as a sunset, eating the bread and crumbs with both hands. She had put down the burlap sack, and I saw what so many wondered about. A hard soda biscuit, mostly lard, wrapped around a thick white hunk of fatback. That moment I knew why Mary Lizbeth felt as ashamed of her food as the reasons she had to bring it.

That she would sneak some gratitude down to me at that spring came as utter surprise.

"Been meanin' to drop down the ridge and see you. My mama says I oughtta give a thank you to anybody what shows a kindness. It was a good cornbread, too. Since what happened with my daddy, she ain't been fit for much in the way a cookin' or work a'tall."

I remember asking why I didn't see her more at school, instantly regretful of seeming to pry.

"I help farm a little patch, tend goats, and do me a lotta walkin'. I go all over. Get me up what nuts or roots or what have you I can find to trade, whilst I build my legs for a long walk outta here. Mama says I don't gotta stay 'round these parts once I'm grown, so I reckon to be ready to light out down the road one day. Climbin' around this place makes a good stout girl, so you watch your threatenin' to give me a lickin'. My mama vowed she'd give me her last one better'n a year ago. There'll not be another."

She paced as she talked, swinging a little switch hand-to-hand, surveying the backyard, but she finally caught my stare where it sought her eyes. Wrapped in the ruddy flush of her face, nearly hidden under a wilderness of dark hair, they shone like new spring leaves in a quiet stream, so green you longed to touch them through the water, to see if they're real. Likely the finest sight I thought my own eyes would ever let into my mind. A snatching glance at them warmed me with the notion that girls lived among us for reasons far above the common work and knocking around seen where I lived.

"You're mighty welcome for that bread, girl. Weren't nothin' much."

I wrestled to my feet, dusted off a little and spoke through my nerves again.

"And you're welcome 'round here anytime. How far you live?"

The question fell unanswered. She threw a light swat into my arm, paced more, fixing not quite a glare onto me.

"Frankie, I take a right fine shine to you. Not ashamed to say so. That's all you'll be needin' to know today, I reckon."

She smiled a white grin, and I knew it gleamed from sticks of wood. Mary Lizbeth made habit of chewing twigs broken off sweet birch trees. Gnawed at one as she looked at me. "God's tooth-wand," Granny called them. A wilderness brush for the mouth.

"Might take a shine to your cornbread, too. I was so hungry that day my head hurt. I am right thankful to you, boy. Right thankful's what I am."

Her eyes pooled to their brim, then flooded over. Just a drop or two, onto the dark lashes then over her cheeks to a slight tremble on her mouth. My eyes flooded at the sight, but I fought it, looking fast to the dark ground. A quick turn and she climbed back into the woods, swiping at her face, never looking around.

"Gotta get home 'fore dark. Got a good walk up ahead of me. Maybe we'll take to walkin' up in here sometime. You and me."

Off into where the trees turned almost black, her long sapling limbs and oversize boots hiked away, too soon gone.

The memory of that day held clear as the springwater I had given her, sweet as the mingling of tobacco-Pepsi now in my mouth. I reclined into its afterglow now, trying to hold to thoughts of her, lapsing away from the cruel parts of the afternoon I was in. Wondering again how far up onto that ridge she lived. How she had found her way down it to me, through woods and laurel thickets dense and dark as old molasses. A touch of shame emerged. That secreted regret of being a boy a bit afraid to trek so far into such woods where a girl made herself at home.

The tree felt so sure I rubbed at the swelling wound on my head and didn't bother thinking what next to do. Safe enough that I had rolled over on the boards to take in the sky. The red-streaked-blue grayed low again in places beyond the high limbs, dimmed by clouds moving like pipe smoke. A little wind hushed through the woods, blew down over the yard below. Enough to belly-flip leaves and move the limbs that held me. A thunder, slung from far off, settled on its heels and raised thought of whether Ma heard the warning of it where she had run. Whether she'd found Pap where I suspected the rain had caught him pulling corn in a patch below his tobacco field.

My grandfather possessed the calm of a dove, a faith fit for Sinai's burning bush, and the patience of all evolution. Which at times enraged my mother, for he never raised his quills beyond giving Frank one long talking-to in a cow barn. I'll confess that sprawling in that tree, watching the wren-colored clouds flow together, drew up my own regrets about the man's forgiving way. Disappointment that Pap, with reasons aplenty, would not kill him. I had once stood with a shotgun to my father's face where he'd fallen into a stupor at the table. Bracing myself for the noise and red-clotted filth of blowing him to his end. Pap's own words, in his talks to me after Frank's pitching of fits, had drawn my finger off the trigger.

"You've seen wicked, son. You've seen it's catchin'," he loved to say. "Your daddy sure caught it good, but you don't have to. Use your eyes, son. He's showin' you what not to do. See in your mind what you want him to be. Then you be that. Leave him to the good Lord and me. You keep back when he's riled. You come to me, and bring your mama with you. But don't you catch the wrong off him."

The mellowing words — fitted together with the high speckle of his George Washington forehead, and the blue outflow like sun through stained glass from his eyes — made my Pap a soul-snare without escape. People in town and around the mill called him the last gentleman farmer the county would know. In my tree, resting against the thought of him, I stole a bit of hope that Frank would never tear the good of him down. That the thrashing my mother had just taken would fail again to crack him. I recall just forming the thought of climbing down and running myself to find the man when the noise broke in. The first creaks of the wagon from the front of the house. The jangle of it climbing over the roof and up my way.

It roused me for a quick check on Frank. Nothing. Only chickens and a quiet yard. I figured by now he was no more than a hump of overalls behind that henhouse, bound for no cotton mill work tonight. I downed the Pepsi, hammered out the pipe and secured the tin, making ready for what I suspected would come up soon.

The swinging bang of the front screen door. Then another. After time for four or five passes through the cabin, came another bang. She missed me in the house even faster than I guessed.

"Frankie. Where you at, Frankie?"

My mother shot out the back door, yelling to herself, Granny joining soon after.

"Lord, Ma, he's took him, oh, Lord God, Jesus. Frankie! Where'd you go, Frankie?" She screamed the latter running in circles around the yard. Granny chased, calling as she went, "Frank. Frank. Frankie," the volume rising toward the end in the way she called me to a meal at their house.

Before I could answer, a parade of clamoring Tickmans came pouring from the back door, my name bawling off their little mouths. I remember thinking it sounded like a choir of locusts directed by the devil.

"Frankie, Frankie, Frankie."

The four of them, Eb the oldest at my age of ten, down to Margie, waddling at barely five, played around and fought loudly on the backyard dirt as the two women found the hidden pile of opium stupor that was Frank.

"Where's Frankie? What have you done?" My mother rolled him out, straddled him, and cried the words over and over into his face, finally wailing fists onto him with Granny wrestling to stop her. He moaned and mumbled and otherwise lay helpless as a mound of quilts. The children had gone from shrieks to an audience of quiet awe.

I knew it my calling to climb down. Surely, somehow, but no — no way. No way I could do it with a quiet enough to keep Ma, Granny, and that gaggle of my cousins from learning of my hideaway. I stood and wedged my tin box as high and out of sight as I could above the boards and started down, trying for cat silence. At about halfway down Eb's eyes found me and the yelling commenced again.

"Yonder he is, climbin'. Looks like a three-legged squirrel!"

That brought the lot of them running toward my now-publicized sanctuary. They came fast and this time with loud chorus of the two women, "Lord, there he is, Lord God, praise Jesus," Ma cried. You might have thought I were an angel in the rapture of their living Baptist Savior, descending some holy tree of life.

"Sweet holy Jesus, Frankie, sweet Jesus you scared me to death. What'd he do to you? Why didn't you stay in that house like I said?" She seized me into a hard hug.

Granny joined in, nearly strangling me with relief, as I caught a look at Eb. He stood a few feet away, shining a grin nearly as wide as his forehead, his chest and backside thrust out. These were the lines of his father, infamous for a tail-swinging strut. My cousin, Ebenezer, stood a little taller than I, a good-sized boy, but clearly cut from peculiar loins. His swagger seemed to say, "I'd fight you if I didn't care so much about looking dandy enough to borrow your mother's Sunday shoes." Some thought he'd simply grown up with so many girls he forgot how to live as a boy. I knew better.

"Was you skeered, Frankie? What run you up that tree, you little possum boy?"

He began to laugh and dance around with his little sisters, who took up his mindless cackle of, "Possum boy, possum boy. Frankie's a lil' possum boy." I defied a longing to choke him, even though it felt as right and satisfying as water to thirst.

"Hush that mouth, Eb. Shut it," Granny turned and yelled. The pack of them then scurried back and calmed.

"He's took a knock on the head, Dovie, but he ain't bad hurt," she said, looking back at me, hair pulled like gray wool off the tan of her face, her dress briny from pickling spice. Both women raked their hands over me, polishing the knot the chair had left. "He's right as rain, Dove," Granny said, trying to ease my mother's fingers off the little head wound.

"Holy sweet Jesus, sweet holy Jesus." Ma kept up the words inches from my face, where I stared back at the swelling parts of hers.

"I ain't hurt none." I let it fly so the gaggle of kids a few feet behind her would hear.

"Git him some clothes and let's go, Dove. Let's get before my temper turns." Granny stood, hard and straight. She turned to the backyard as if to guard us.

Ma held a hand over her crying as she made fast toward the back of the house and inside. I cut Eb a look that threw the very scythe of intended murder into him, while the entire party of us walked to the wagon around front. I would drive the mules. Granny's rare change of demeanor had blown a new air of manliness into me. Gave the feel of walking a foot taller. She didn't need it but I offered her little frame a hand to board the seat while she tried to chasten down the children's rousing high singing of Eb's new possum boy song, which he led in his usual defiance. The little glee club loaded itself into the wagon bed and bleated on until Ma emerged out the front with a small wad of clothing stuffed into a pillowcase, which she used to swing a smack at Eb's greasy head, drawing a satisfying yelp.

"I ain't afraid to whoop you, Eb. Your mama ain't here to pet you now."

Her voice sounded tight as mandolin string. The feel of it, and I imagine the sight of her face, helped throw a load of quiet onto that wagon. Frank wouldn't have heard thunder by then in his stupor among the hens.

Ma boarded the seat, Granny between us, and sat rigid and seething. The day's wrath seeming to drive itself through her into the wood below. I called the mules as Pap had taught, "Git up now, git," and we all rolled through dirt ruts up toward the old church. Our nearest neighbor. Any who opted against the shortcut path and took the two-mile road between our place and my grandparents' farm had to pass the little house of Baptist religion and its boneyard garden to the side.

The voiceless creak and clop of that wagon seemed to draw Granny back to herself.

"I've seen him in that church, Dove. Frank knows about the Lord, and maybe they're gettin' back on terms."

She pointed out toward the old sanctuary's gray patina we would soon draw near — the hammered-up steeple rising on our cresting of the hill that would make the cabin and farm disappear behind us. "I seen him just sittin' in one a them back pews one evenin'. He ain't lost to no devil yet."

Ma sat silent, fixed on the road ahead.

The wagon rocked us through what turned into a canyon of trees, the reins sturdy with authority in my hands — the two women crammed muggy against me, children prattling and dangling legs off the back. The wind had died, thickening the wet air with the coming of night, and a mild thunder reported off the far mountain walls. My pants might as well have been dipped in honey.

I looked back a final time to see the house drop from sight. It looked the way I pictured an ocean might swallow a boat. The land seemed to gulp the place, and for a moment my mind could see the house and its drunken captain under the weight of more water than a daydream can hold — about a mile down, under an ocean of imagination, forever gone.

Then there was just the view of the girls on the back flanking Eb, a last bit of that day glowing off his oily head, both sisters swatting and flapping at the swarming gnats around it, and him fighting all of them with swats of his own. The boy lived an obsession with his skin and hair, doting on and slicking at both, using every homemade material he could concoct to call lotion or pomade. He had read the world "luster" on one of his mother's practically futile beauty salves and decided he would not live without luster of his own making. Getting that glance at the bugs teeming over him, I grinned a little vengeance, recalling the time he combed his hair full of Pap's sorghum and Granny's lard, compounded together. It had turned his entirety into a barn-dance feast for a swarm of yellow jackets. They buzzed and stung and otherwise assailed him until he finally thrust his head under the well pump behind the house we were headed to now. People had teased him ever since about drawing bugs so well you could stand him off somewhere to keep them away from you.

"What's that you combed in your hair this mornin', Eb? Why not just slick it down in some kerosene and let me fire off a match?"

I had barely uttered it, and he had just turned to crack un-wise, when the sting came, hard enough to redden the skin under my overalls. Surely bruising my mother's hand. She reached across Granny and gave another smack on the same leg.

"Hush up, Frankie. I'll not have you provokin' him or any of the rest."

"Dove, now don't, Dove," Granny spoke in defense of both of us. "They're just young'uns, and they ain't gonna fight none now."

Then she turned on Eb.

"You keep shut, Ebenezer."

"I ain't said nothin'. He started it up."

"Never you mind. Just keep quiet, all of you. This is not time for your shine-cuttin'."

Granny rubbed the place on my leg and looked at Ma, who cried again as the wagon rolled within full sight of the church. A gray clapboard hump off to the right, matching the weathered headstones scattered about that cemetery yard. Granny's hand left me for the bosom of her faded work dress, the apron still on, pulling out the little New Testament cherished there as though losing it would mean death. The sweat-stains of it much older than I, the pages cleaving in tatters to their black leather hide. Her scarce three years of schooling and decades on the third row of preaching helped her teach herself to read it, nearly to memorization. She opened and searched it.

"Here. Right here. John 9, verse 7."

"I ain't in a mind for Bible readin' right now." Ma's reply welled up from a certain resolve. Trembling at its edge. Granny ignored her.

"Jesus spat on dirt and made clay to heal a blind man. Right yonder it is. 'He anointed the eyes of the blind man with the clay.' You know if the holy Jesus can make a miracle outta dirt, then by Jesus a man like Frank Locke ain't too far gone, Dove. We just gotta pray like Reverend Piles said."

Ma broke through in quivers. As the mules yanked us by it, I looked to see her glaring at the church's front door.

"Don't talk to me about any preacher. He's the very one that did nothin' for any one of us. Us livin' this close to his church, and I told you what he said. Tellin' me it's not the Lord's will for a woman to go leavin' her husband, even for a day or two. That he was awful sorry Frank had turned out like he did. He's awful damned sorry, for sure. Stop this wagon, Frankie."

She turned and pointed back, as if the white-knobbed door might hear.

"I'm sorry too, Reverend. I'm powerful sorry you wouldn't even come and talk to him, you little yellow coward dog. I'm sorry you didn't see fit to help me put a roof over my boy's head for the Sunday night when I run up here afraid his daddy might kill the both of us. Get him drunked up on that devil-dust and come at you. *You'll* be the one sorry then, Mr. God's man. You can fall off to hell. Straight off to hell with you!"

The screaming of it trailed into heaves and sobs, stunning the wagon tail's cargo into a hush. Granny reached around her. I stared ahead and counted my pulse where it hammered up through ribs to the knot on my face.

"Dove, we ain't givin' up. I could kill him, too. God knows Frank's had it hard. And God knows I want to kill him sometimes. Him and some more. I'm bound to raise my foot so far up some fannies it might take a horse to pull my leg out. Good Lord's all that keeps me from it. And it's like I've told you. Just 'cause you love a man don't mean you can live with him. Don't mean you have to. I don't care what narry preacher says. If you'd leave the worst of him to the Almighty he might straighten up. We'll *make* room. You don't have to go back. You could pray for him on the moon and get heard. If *he* was on the moon he might not be safe from me right this minute, seein' you this way."

I slowed the mules on this rare raising of Granny's ire, seeing my mother's head weeping down now in a cradle of her own mother's upturned arms. If I had thought it would work, I might have prayed for Ma to take my grandmother's little tantrum as some inerrant gospel. Praying Frank Locke, in his dripping sorrows, would never plead her back into his favor again.

We had passed the church into deep shadows of the coming dark when I turned for a look. A check on where Eb and I had bedeviled that little house of worship not more than two weeks before. The women beside me had calmed into dull talk of Ulysses, Mattie, and poor mental health, so with the wagon creeping away I shot a glance at the evidence. Back toward the clay stains and a piece of wood that did not belong. A patch, still there, as if the church had an eye put out on its westward face. Signs of our conspiracy, and how well mischief can unite two boys who often live sworn to civil war.

It had happened on a Sunday. We had joined the more than three dozen who streamed in to the musty summer dankness of services that morning. Ma and I walked to meet Granny, Pap and my squirming mass of cousins, all attending the church by family tradition. Because he lived with them, I let Eb do the talking. And without surprise he convinced Granny he and I should begin to worship as young men — off to ourselves to ponder matters gospel and eternal, a few rows toward the front of our regular family pew. Her eyes glowed with rare skepticism, but she apparently couldn't resist the idea that we desired to spend the hour and a half closer to the altar of the Almighty. Neither Granny, nor Ma, nor any of the worshippers knew how we had armed ourselves, and that we wanted only an arms-reach proximity to the front-pew place of prayer taken reliably by Miss Clara Ponder.

She lived near town, a spinster, devout as a rapture angel, quiet as a cemetery. Always dark of clothing and topped by a petite head of white hair, pulled so tightly into a bun her face wore the expression of a woman in a constant windstorm. By all sight, she lived a kind life made largely out of church, a sewing business, and an avocation of attending funerals — all in deliberate avoidance of contact with children as she minded her business. She did not deserve to have a pair of ten-year-old demons sit behind her, pull a harvest of wiggling Catawba worms from their pockets, and secret their squirm onto her dress collar and the top of that bun. The timing just right. The worms crept to their bidding and launched her off that pew into shouts and a spray of head and neck flagellation just as The Reverend Piles sharpened his voice to a high point about the sin of failing to praise Jesus out loud every day.

Some in that little sanctuary, its windows in the purple-painted glory of poor man's stained glass, clearly deemed her happy with the Holy Spirit. So they joined, raising arms and "Amens" in high approval. The room's every eye having most assuredly turned on Miss Ponder's batting and smacking at herself — finally so hard the bun of hair collapsed into a long white shower a few feet from the pulpit. The worms had held sway, livening her into a jig resembling the dancing The Reverend Piles so vociferously deplored. He raised his voice and the cadence of the preaching again, rejoined by another spray of "Amens" from behind us. Miss Ponder, virtually scarlet with humiliation, lit herself onto the pew, raking and clawing at the hair, whose order she finally restored by stuffing it down the back of her dress — where, beyond question, innocent worms had gone to die.

By then Eb and I had straightened ourselves, surely resembling a couple of seated little pitchforks, gazing pious attention up at The Reverend Piles — the explosive that is repressed laughter disarmed now by the chill of knowing we had gone much too far. Barely a month before he had baptized us together in the puckering cold of Panther Creek, the singing of "Shall We Gather at the River?" still fresh in my head. I believe Eb and I shared a remorse. It mingled penance with the fear of having disappointed God just enough to make all of glory madder than the wet hens of hell. I noticed several grown men in the choir proving less successful than we at stifling a grin.

After the benediction, Miss Ponder gave us no glance as she tucked chin and joined the flow toward the door. Eb and I trailed, as far arrear as we could, whispering a plan to duck under the preacher's handshakes and slouch into the churchyard as if fresh from the dullest of services. I knew it bound to fail when Pap cut an eye back at me. But the feel of imminent hanging came with the squeeze of hot fingers at the back of my neck. The reverend's wife, a round woman with tall hair and a voice rich and deep as pasture weeds, announced her husband would like a moment of fellowship with us behind the church after greetings. She snapped us around for a spine-pinching escort through the back doors and down the steps, speaking assurances our families would wait. The three of us soon stood silent in the shade of the church's hind wall. Eb had turned the color of sour milk, when it ripens to the odor of death.

Draping a dark suit onto the limbs of a young dogwood tree would approximate the figure cut by The Reverend Everett Piles. The black Holy Bible under his small arm looked the size of a bass drum. His boots wore a spit-shine almost miraculously defiant of the reddish ground the rest of us seemed to track in everywhere. After what seemed a year of our attempted indifference, he rounded the corner and stood over us, barely taller than Eb — little blue eyes burning over a black mustache so heavy he seemed always to peer from behind a fence. He pointed his chicken bone of a finger in Eb's face, even while talking directly at me.

"I'll not have it, boys. Not in my church."

Both of us looked at the ground, only to feel skeleton fingertips lift our chins hard to his face.

"This is my church, boys, and I'll have no such evil in it. You didn't think I saw what you did, but I saw. I can always see what little sinners such as yourselves is up to, and I'm here to tell the both of you such little sinners will not find welcome. Not in my church."

His breath soiled us. Long, spitty and curling of vowel, coming from a face flushing the color of weak beet juice.

"I know where both of you boys come from. I know the loins and the precise kinda evil you spring from. My church will not take such in. Not such evil as you. God's word says I ought tan the both of you. Do you know that?"

He raised the Bible and pounded a finger into it with the pointing hand.

"This worda God tells me to resist evildoers and so I shall. You boys remember that and tell your filth-hearted daddies I'll not have such evil in my Lord's house here. And you boys don't forget it neither. You two might be some of the worst I've ever heard tell of. But the Lord's judgment is righteous and true. You tell your daddies that one. You go tell."

With that he spun and made for the corner, off toward his black lacquered buggy, ordering his wall of womanhood to follow. He had given neither of us a gnat-sized opening to say we were sorry. Never spoke Miss Ponder's name. Nor a word's regret of her disgrace.

Eb and I broke for the other corner, and climbed the hill to meet the women in our lives, who'd received full report of our deeds. That afternoon we each took a lashing of tongues and a hickory switch — our Pap objecting to the latter. Granny wiped moisture from her eyes with every thrash of it to our bared legs. My mother had gone home for sleep before a graveyard shift at the mill, leaving me at Granny and Pap's place. Frank was to work the same, swilling any paregoric at hand to ease him through, trying not to take so much it leveled him again.

After lunch Eb and I commiserated about the morning, which logically hatched into a plan. Under guise of a Sunday creek swim, we strolled back to the church, gathering every kind of rock and dirt clod we could find into burlap sacks and seething like two kettles on to boil.

"It weren't *his* church to start with," Eb said and I gave it an amen. "I reckon it belongs to God A'mighty, but if he aims to steal it, well then Rev. Piles is gonna need that paint job he keeps askin' for. Some men's bound to paint her, time we're done with her."

I turned a little gutless on him at first, but my cousin could shine a near hypnotic get-away-with-anything grin. By the time we got close to it, the church stood alone in the shade and the bug-song of thick woods, the faint rush of the creek behind it the only other sound. To ensure some anonymity, given the severity of our morning crime, we decided to peer through the front windows. The only ones not opaque with purple paint. Neither expected what we saw.

On the front pew, the very pew chosen each Sunday by Miss Ponder to hear The Reverend Piles, sat the man our tiny world knew as my father. I recall he had gone off walking early that morning, calling the house too hot for sleep. Now he sat like furniture, surely in a swelter, facing the front of the church and the large nailed-up cross on its far wall. A violet-colored light streamed off the windows. Gave the lone congregant nearly a look of belonging.

"We gonna scare the hellfire, yellowwater pee outta him, Frankie," Eb whispered. Then he quietly laughed, his breath smelling of fried squash and snuff. "Come on. Let's give the sumbitch a fright so good he'll think the holy end of time is come."

"Whipped so hard we need another bee-hind is what we'll get. They'll make saddles outta our loins is how hard we'll get whipped. You do as you please. I'm walkin' on to my house."

I could hardly breathe the words aloud for the very knife of fear pushing in. It came to the hilt on mere sight of the head hanging mildly down above that pew. The squared, close-shaven hair of Frank Locke, Senior. Unmistakable.

"When are you gonna quit actin' like such a little mama's girl fool?" An odd question I thought from a boy who, that day, had confessed to dressing his hair down in what smelled like boot black, then coating half his body in one of those mail order toilet waters trying to kill the stench.

"Maybe you oughtta suck a rubber nipple 'stead of them pipes you're always makin'," he said. "Quit bein' skeered and come on."

"Hey, I ain't the one smellin' like Granny's Sunday bosom. And I gotta live with him."

Eb ignored that. Sprang from our crouch under the window, down the wood steps on the tips of his boots, and across the side yard toward the woods — the bag of ammunition rumbling off his leg. I followed, shaking my head, though tending to agree that my mother treated me too much like a baby. My insides felt heavy as the sack in my hand.

We positioned down in a blind of laurel, in its deep, long-leaf camouflage. Eb went over a rapid-escape plan, drew out ammo, and commenced a three count. The first salvo of clods sailed like Gatlin gun lead.

They left in seconds. Clod after rock after clod, fired hard from Eb's left hand, mine from the right — the ammo sounding off the little house of worship in staccato thuds and pops almost as satisfying as Christmas candy to a couple of ten-year-old soldiers, whose only general was the devil of boyhood.

Until the crash. We had talked of it. Hit only the boards. Avoid glass. But one of those purple-painted windows exploded in noise that seemed to split the sanctuary in two.

Not a word was exchanged between us. I believe by the time it struck Eb that we had most certainly roused God and the devil into equal fury, we had run forty yards in opposite directions, sprinting like deer. I plunged deep into the screen of the hardwood thicket, up toward the creek pool where The Reverend Piles had baptized us. Fear and guilt doing harder battle than my naked feet splitting the shallow cold water. Any thought of Ebenezer's well-being falling like the spray. I ran until I reached the quiet eddy upstream where the baptizing always happened, veering to its worn path, then cutting through more woods to our steep dirt road, which carried me, still running, to home. Up the rope, the boards nailed into that backyard tree felt sure as iron. My heart's thump finally waned into thoughts of burying Ebenezer Tickman in at least three shallow graves.

The reliving of it ended there. Now, in the creak and chatter of the wagon, that memory of only days ago flushed me with what felt like a sadness many years old. I took one final glance. Where the church still wore clay weep-marks, and that piece of wood covered where we had broken some earthly glass of God. The blasphemy of it having been talked about all over. Eb and I, after the mild beating I had given him, vowed to die with the secret and never to speak of it again. The mules seemed to drive themselves as I stared at the marks, back through the gathering dark, expecting Eb might turn and contact my eyes. But he sat in the bug-swarm oblivion, prattling and dangling on with his sisters, looking more innocent than they. Ever their sport and distraction.

I turned back to driving. We rolled under tree cover, downhill and across a little sideless wood bridge near the connection to the main road, Panther Creek chattering below. The voice and scent of its flow like balm on the evening air. A thin vapor ghosted above the water, not quite to the wheels. The wagon rocked Ma's curly head in Granny's lap now, dark hair brushed by hands notably long and graceful for an elderly farm woman. The beating had pulped my mother's face enough that she hid to guard the feelings of others, especially the children. Granny's left arm wrapped my shoulder as I turned the mules to start climbing the nearly one mile of little rutted dirt road leading to Granny and Pap's farm and our crowded beds for the night.

"Don't a creek smell good in summertime?"

Granny's voice crept into the wet air, the feel of it now soft dove-down.

"Smells like watermelon rind. And makes a fine song of itself. Singin' through these mountains. Dear Lord, hear me like I hear that water. Love us into somethin' fit for you."

I clenched my teeth trying to stop it, but it came. A tear cut its way free from one eye and pushed down through the day's grime to my chin. A tighter clench failed to stop another one.

"Not me. I ain't fit for any church and Frank Locke ain't neither, Granny. He ain't nothin' but dirt, and I ain't far above him. But I ain't havin' him as my daddy no more. Ain't havin' no doin's with him. If the only kinda daddy I can have ain't much of nothin' but dirt, then I'll not have me one. Not him."

We whispered to each other now.

"Frankie, don't talk like that, honey. It ain't right or good for you. The good Lord loves you and the rest of us, includin' your daddy. I just as soon hang the hateful out of him, too. But that ain't all of him. I've seen the God parts of him. You rest your mind off that hateful business. I'll help you tomorrow. We'll go to the pocket. Sit and talk and not give up on ourself."

Far up into woods behind their farm, Granny knew a rocky little place she described as "the pocket of God." The view from it calming as any liquor might have been to her mind. From my seat on that wagon, near the weeping jostle of my mother's head in her lap, any joy of the place seemed distant as the stars.

I gave the mules a little slap to speed them against darkness and the rumble off a low, dark cloud to the north.

"Granny, I ain't givin' up. I just ain't right for a thing to do with that church business. And I hate me this place. Just as soon slap any God makin' me live in it. I'd take myself outta here if I could, Granny. Take out and be gone, and miss you and Ma and some of the rest, but I'd be gone if I could." The crying had me now, tightening like rope. She pulled me closer.

"Shhhh, now. No more. Don't you get vain with God's name, son. We need you here. We need us a young, strong man like you. All of us. Your mama and daddy, too."

I pulled away.

"Don't call him that. I'll not have that dung-mound called my daddy or pa or nothin' like it. No more."

I tried again to push the crying down. Squeezed leather into my hands, but the throat clot grew. Granny spoke up.

"You listen now, to me and your Pap. Don't he always say you don't have to be what you don't want? You be whatever's best. He never was for that cotton mill or any of you workin' in it. Hemmin' people up in all them metal machines before they finish school, and payin' just enough money to get people hooked on workin' for it. And the whole time makin' one man rich as Solomon was wise. Folks here ain't dirt, and they ought not be farmed like it. That's what's hurt your daddy. You ain't dirt, so don't you aim to start talkin' and livin' 'neath yourself. I'll be mad, now, if you keep up thinkin' such as that. I'll be mad and tell your Pap. Then you'll be in for a barn sermon."

Granny had a way of turning firm talk into a place of ease. But she soon returned to the topic I wanted to crush, horse-kick hard.

"And I'm tellin' you again, I saw your daddy 'fore you did. You know I get mad as a hornet at him, but I'll not lie down with any part of hatin' on him. You can't rest in such. We just gotta pray. You can pray for him from my house, outta his way, anytime. The Lord loves him, and we'll keep tryin'."

"Granny, if any God loves on him, then I don't want that God lovin' me. I don't want no part off that kinda lovin.' And if your God A'mighty loves so much then I don't understand why we're all in this wagon in the shape we're in."

"Hush now. Hush that talk and shame on you. Come on."

Her arm let me go for a grab at the leather. Ma stiffened but never fully roused off her lap as Granny gave the mules a smack of the reins, spurred by my heresy — her eyes and jaw set on a vista place we both loved, little more than a hundred yards up that road toward the rising moon. A pair of soot-black crows raised a late-day fuss in some high limbs above us when we reached it.

The wire of a road between our patch of ground and Granny and Pap's place rose out of a hollow and along a little ledge that seemed threshold to the world. Just a little stone gap. A narrow opening of the tree curtain, looking out onto folds of blue, draping further than you believe an eye can reach. I could never pass without pause to look at it. One of the longest sights I figured ever to see. Granny seized my hand, with a stare fixed on mountains spread at our feet. Off where they layered into veils of cloud mist, stretched to the clearing sky and its early shaving of what would rise as an almost full moon. Its pewter light strong through the red remains of the rainstorm nearly spent.

Ma lay quiet as we rolled to a stop a few feet off the road, better than sixty miles of ridgetops, and a sheer drop, before us.

"That ain't nothin' but holy, and you know it, Frankie. That's straight off the Lord's back, a sight like that."

Granny whispered, cutting a look to me. She hushed the silly clatter on the wagon bed, then sailed her eyes back off into the view. Such a vista always turned my Granny's eyes alive and new again. They looked like little gray-blue bird feathers molted onto a bed of soft leather. "We all ought be thankful we're here. Alive in such a place."

Her voice turned light as the fog off the river, where it ran beside railroad tracks to town, neither quite in sight below.

"Like I've told you. My Bibles don't say it, but it just looks forever like a coat of our God, honey. If we're filth on that coat, then I reckon that's a filth I wish to be."

She pulled my head to her chest, and we sat in the quiet a moment. Watched the denim layers brighten under the moonrise. Soon she pointed again.

"And look, Frankie. Look at the she-rain. Yonder it goes. A little tear off a heaven gown. Fine as it can be. A little lace off the rain."

In the rise of crickets and peep frogs, Granny spread out her mountain mystic view of things again, and the whole wagon treated it as sacred for a moment. She'd often speak of how a little scrap of fog tears from a rain cloud. Floats on the waves of blue ridge as if a wisp off a bride. Granny and others called it she-rain, I suppose for its womanly drape, white as wedding gown. Common legend, though Granny took the vision further. Said she-rain was like us all — little scraps torn off into the world, given to the wind, and meant to find a paradise. As she saw things, no human scrap of this life is made for the trash. Even the most ragged are fit to beautify somewhere. Fit for some quilting into the finery of creation.

"You gotta trust enough to live like rain, honey. That rain'll find its ocean no matter where it falls. Drift off yonder, she-rain. Drift on. 'Til the Lord takes you home."

None of us in that wagon had ever seen the ocean apart from what we imagined. Though Granny seemed to harbor a mind's eye longing for it.

The moon emerged enormous, the whole view in its light, and to my eyes Granny's great blue coat still looked no better than Pap's old work shirt, drooped on a scarecrow in his lower corn patch. Every thread abandoned to weather, the owner not caring to touch it again.

But her talk of she-rain, this time, raised an idea. That a little scatter of fog was surely a fine thing to be. I thought of some school ridicule I had witnessed from our peerage, and of my classmate who took it. Mary Lizbeth, labelled a bastard simply because of a daddy long gone. Scandalized in town by the notion a man never abandons a child without believing her veins and heart are wet with another man's blood. She seemed peaceful and fine with the taunts, almost happily living torn off from the father who did the leaving. I thought of how I might live far off, maybe where that moon had come from, happy as a bastard who didn't get called a linthead boy anymore. Never having to help shoulder Frank Locke's load of fresh-raised hell again. It would beat the consequence of killing him, too. Of caring enough to bother.

That moment saw me reborn. Re-evangelized into my own faith of hallowed bastardom, its creed more clear than when the thought first emerged to me on Granny's porch those few nights before. I committed anew to live as I had seen my sweet girl live — bracing to bend the hinges on hell's gate if that's what it took to break free of this place one day. Even if it meant missing the hand that had just let go of mine. Granny's palm felt virtually identical to the leather reins. She had given them to me again.

"Let's go now. Gonna be plumb dark by the time we git home. I worry about Mattie with that baby, scared of a storm as she is."

Granny seemed frustrated no one had stirred to agree with her sermonette. She pointed for me to drive on.

"And we don't want no boogie man gittin' us in this moon-shine dark."

At this a thought came up, and fast. I had nurtured and rehearsed in my mind what I was about to say more times than I knew how to count, never letting it emerge into words. But this time it came with a voice, strong as a crackling fire in its fullest flower.

"I reckon I'd just as soon come live with you and Pap all the time, Granny. Reckon you're right. We ain't gotta stay with him, and him beatin' and carryin' on. It makes Pap mad enough for cussin.' I heard it. If us livin' with Frank makes Pap cuss I want no more part of it."

Toward the end, a boyhood crying threatened to twist itself around me again. Some hard quiet, as real and strong as wire, surrounded all of us — even the young girls to the back. The mules clopped on toward the turn to my grandparents' farm. Pap had left that morning for an overnight egg-selling trip to the doctors of Asheville. I had forgotten he wasn't there. Granny had been the farm's only refuge my mother could find after Frank showed the worst of himself this time.

Into that quiet, Ma roused herself, every word a tremor.

"I am not leavin' my house, or my land or my life and givin' it over to him for wastin', Frankie. I ain't leavin' what your Pap worked for. What I've worked for. Your daddy ain't runnin' me off."

Turning the mules into a drape of woods that ended in a thriving tobacco field below the farmhouse, I cocked my mind to risk it. A firing back of the first rebuke my mother had ever heard from me. It was ripe to come — when one of the urchins spoke up. Her words reminding the entire wagon that Eb possessed a touch of his father's braggart soul and his mother's strapping tongue.

In that instant, from behind us, with the wagon wheels finding their ruts and the mules nearly home to their barn, Marie Kate said it. I thought she'd gone to sleep, but the small, rascal voice from that wagon bed said the thing that put a pair of ten-year-old cousins at odds with nearly their entire family and a large portion of the town. It flew out and hovered like a buzzard. The only topic she could have raised that would, the next day, cause my Pap to wilt me by saying I had disappointed him. That he thought I was more of a gentleman. Kate's little words flushed my head with blood. Caused me to discard any shavings of faith that I could belong to anybody's religion ever again. And they heaved into me a deeply nested vow to strangle Ebenezer Tickman until I reached the very bones of his neck. Even if I were to hang for it.

He couldn't reach her in time. She let it fly with full childish volume, up spinning in a dance and cackle. Just a hint of her mother's shrill.

"Look yonder at that moon, Eb. Reckon you and possum boy might hit that thang with a rock? Reckon it might crack good like that church winnder-light you fellers broke? When you scared the yeller fire outta Uncle Frank?"

P{.eople thought she fell for him in equal parts — love, sympathy and expectation. Monroe Franklin Locke, Senior lived as a rough-cut, almost overly polite, mystery of a boy carved out of the hills. In the town and the family's view, he could grow through the work chinks and calluses — if not that jaw scar — and fit himself into some fine way of life.*

Before the wedding, Pap bought him a Sears, Roebuck shirt, linen collar and dark jacket, all too big. Ma wore a gown Granny made from material Pap bartered for, and The Reverend Piles married them in a snowstorm on the shortest day of the year. Long after, people talked of how the storm had beaten some coat of white onto the little Baptist Church, how they wanted its graying clapboards painted to look like the Locke wedding day, and how no one could remember a day any colder.

I confess to wishing for the Monroe Franklin Locke of my grandparents' memory. The man my mother described as crying silent tears of joy into my face on the day of my birth departed for France and the World War when I was five. He returned two years later, hacked down by more than the saw blades of battle. Some foul habits and a feel of permanent loss came home with him, taking their place with a rank and violent history the man carried over there. To hear Pap talk, it didn't matter how mad he made you, feeling sorry for him was a snare without escape.

By the time he returned in his uniform, Ma's sister, Mattie, had made a near profession out of breeding. So prolifically, my grandparents voiced what seemed an Old Testament obligation to nest the entire litter of them — including the sire, Ulysses — into their home, lest the county take and divide the Tickman family, or the whole of them make nest together in the woods. Granny deemed Mattie delicate-minded, afraid that setting her free might mean her baby daughter would be lost to the world. So the Tickmans made themselves more at home on the farm than Granny and Pap ever had time.

Frank took cotton mill and road work, saw the growing lot of Tickmans living off another couple's work and land, and simmered a constant loathing. Intoxication reliably fueled it to boil over. Opium fits aside, he and my mother managed to agree Mattie never broke a sweat

40

without either wallowing under "Useless" or birthing him a child. She eventually bore him six who survived and one stillborn, whom she demanded to have photographed. The midwife stood grim and pale, holding the little corpse on the red dirt front yard of the house, for a now yellowing picture few but Mattie ever wanted to view. Ulysses groaned about being cursed with a body too fragile for work — though it managed that regular procreation — and travel that included jumping railcars and throwing off sundry stolen goods he would then go back to collect from the tracksides. This usually happened after Pap misplaced his large store of patience and threatened expulsion unless Ulysses shouldered some help for the family. Frank argued with Pap for putting up with him, saying if it hadn't been for that career as a railway thief (and part-time work as the town's panhandling liar), "Useless" truly would have been as "useless as tits on a boar hog."

August 3, 1929

T he church stood almost the same. Darker gray maybe, with the sag deepening on the steps. But its side yard lay full of eight years' change, through which we walked in a thick heat that enveloped the afternoon. The sun warmed a stone for my Pap Woody, Woodfin Lloyd Warren, who lay in a sinking grave, put there by a fast death some said came before he even hit the floor of the Marshal saw mill. I was with him and will never forget feeling the floor move when he collapsed. The men ran to swarm over him, saying, "Oh, Lordy," and yelling his name into his ears as though he were deaf instead of gone.

My Granny, May Ella Warren, known to the entire town as Granny Ella, lay in the grave beside him, found dead in her bed by a grandchild barely ten months later. Townspeople said her heart had broken after Pap's had failed — and that it was no wonder for either of them. Just a snatching sight of her tombstone next to his made me wrestle back water trying to rise to my eyes.

And no more than ten yards from them, near enough to the church to make his bones tremble with ideas of mischief, lay the piece of cemetery where all of us had buried my cousin Ebenezer, years before. He lay beside his stillborn sister, who lay remembered only by a creek stone engraved, "Baby Tickman," green now with moss and weeds since Granny died.

Eb had drowned on a swimming adventure little better than a month after Pap took both of us around to Miss Ponder's little red house in town and compelled two apologies more painful than any spanking would have been after that worm assault given her in church. He had jumped, trembling in his drawers, from the highest reachable part of the north rail trestle into the French Broad River. He climbed and did it defying warnings from me and four other boys who had just survived a stinging thirty-foot drop together from one of the lower supports, our testicles lodging some place behind our eyes. When Eb finally found his nerve, he landed with a wind-

42

taking smack, spray falling where he failed to rise. Screaming panic and diving under the muddy cold, we finally pulled him out, his skin already milky, resembling the feel of an earthworm. Charitable women of the church bought him a tombstone and had it engraved, "Ebenezer Louis Tickman, Dancing with the Angels," which evoked in me the notion of angel Eb still throwing rocks, giving sass, and preening his head. Teaching the whole of heaven lessons in homespun pomades and the uses of worms, bugs and frogs for the entertainment value in giving someone hell.

Standing there gazing at his marker, I recalled Miss Ponder had attended the funeral, telling people she had given Eb homemade grape juice after he had carried stove wood to her house without being asked. He had stayed to talk with her on the porch. I remembered how The Reverend Piles had started the funeral sermon on Jesus raising Lazarus, letting it drift on to a hurl of sharp points about the fires of hell and how easily they would lap at any of us of any age if we weren't perfectly careful. I missed that sermon's very conclusion. Pap had taken my shoulder in his hand and walked me out of the church, through the wash of tears and wailing, to wait out the remaining service beside the little grave. There, on that ground I gazed at now, we had cried some together, and he had talked his soft way into me.

"Not your fault, son. Heaven knows it, and I want you knowin' it, too." He reached behind his coat into the blue of the overalls and pulled out his gold-filled pocket watch and chain — bought by a good tobacco year — the image of a steam locomotive ornate on its cover. "When I'm gone, this here is yours. You make sure and get it." As he let me hold it, the case threw a warming glint into my eyes.

In the heat of the present afternoon, and in my nearness to manhood at eighteen years now, I retraced all of it. How light Pap's broad hand felt on my back, my head sagging toward the red clay hole. The arms of my mind naturally reached for the sight of Eb in the little felt-covered coffin. How still and clean and pale he looked in the blue flannel shirt. I remembered that, to my eyes of the same age, a gaze at his corpse felt like looking into a mirror I couldn't quite believe.

Now, stouter and taller, with a two-day growth of beard, I knelt over Eb's grave wanting desperately to trade places with him, wherever he may be. I rose from placing the last of the blue wildflowers Ma had picked from a little pasture near our yard. Eb's blossoms slipped into a Dr. Pepper bottle he might have used for snuff-spit. It's water and the drooping flowers, still weighted with some dew, catching sun now on the hot headstone.

"Shame on them. Shame on ever' one."

Twenty feet away Ma stood near the road, facing me, digging at the ground with her eyes. Fixed on an unmarked grave much of Marshal, North Carolina and its surroundings had filled and decorated with speculation and sanctimony and righteous sympathies. Some anger stretched and tightened down the corners of her mouth, her gaze boring far into that grave, with a longing and sadness real as a shovel handle.

"It's a shame. A disgrace, you layin' here without even your name for respect. And people sayin' whatever, and won't even bother to buy you a rock."

She clearly intended on keeping it to herself, but my mother's voice allowed me to hear the change in her heart. She had, more than once, joined the chorus of ill talk about the woman in that grave. Though perhaps the pile of withering man we had left on the cabin porch a few minutes before reminded her of Marshal's ever-rising din of whisper and gossip about us, the household of Frank Locke, Senior.

"Come on, Frankie. Let's get this over with. If I get any hotter I'm bound to lose my temper 'fore I get there."

With that she turned from the unmarked grave toward a little green Ford pickup truck, chugging an idle into the dust of the roadside. The sky blue cotton dress chosen for work that night swung on her frame as if someone had dressed it onto a tall stalk of corn and held it up to a breeze. The dark mane of pulled-back hair like silks against her back.

I followed her across the unkempt grass and slid behind the wheel, moist in the overalls I had worn to the mill that morning, each of us soaked in the familiar dread of what lay immediately behind and ahead of us. The feel of it filled the little metal cockpit like choking smoke.

"I'm right close to the end of what I'll put up with, Ma. And I'll put 'em outta here. Put 'em all out," I said, steering the truck past the church down toward the bridge, dust rising into a clay cloud behind us.

A reach into my pocket revealed the watch Pap had promised me. I held it to her face.

"It's just like Pap said. You take it when I'm gone. He told me that, and I did it. If I hadn't, you know whose pocket this watch would be in. First thing I did when he died was wade into that house to Granny and told her, and she give it to me with narry a question."

Ma's head jostled with the truck. Her eyes blank as a trout's and aimed straight ahead. In the Ford's rattling silence we passed Granny's beloved vista place, the ridges veiled in light blue haze. The truck rolled beyond the farm turn-off and headed on for town.

"And she didn't give the big farm to neither one of us." Her voice finally came, sounding as hard as the steering wheel I had often held with hand and forehead and thought of how far the truck might carry me if I allowed. Through two switchback curves, I throttled it on down the steep road's tiny cutting through trees toward the river bridge.

"Ma, I don't mean a disrespect, but you're talkin' about a woman who said a voice in a thunderstorm told her Aunt Mattie was to have a stillborn. I know the child was born dead, but we both know that voice was in her mind. Narry a bit of it real. Now we just come from what is. Granny and Pap went to them graves wantin' you and me on that farm they made. Us and not that Tickman children machine — makin' 'em faster than I can drink a Pepsi Cola. That's what's real. That's the truth, and you know it. Truth is they'd both smile to see you and me on that farm, instead of who's wreckin' it now."

This minor tantrum had threatened to overflow me for a long while. Ma kept staring ahead, seeming to see a thousand miles beyond the summer's green, then spoke without looking at me.

"The truth of what a body feels and what we have to live with ain't always the same."

Her voice quaked and rose.

"What your Granny and your Pap wanted ain't near what any of us got. We might just as well live with that."

Fury came fast. Flooded my head, then the wet air. Cocooned there within her reach, I heard myself yell at my mother for the first time. Pounding the wheel so hard I all but took us off the wood bridge into the slow river twenty feet below.

"All I know is, we're the ones makin' a livin' for these people, and look how they thank us. You know why we're in this truck and not a mule cart, Ma. You know why Granny give you money for this truck after Pap died. To keep Useless Tickman's fingers off it. So we could make a better livin' outta Pap's farm — and here we ain't got room to live on it. Pap hid money for this truck for years — and me knowin' about every dollar of it. So we wouldn't have to kill ourselves in that cotton mill he despised. And here we are a tryin' to work two farms and two mill jobs and feedin' that Useless rat nest that takes the best of it. I'm tellin' you, Ma, if Granny'd died first, Pap woulda put them out. He put up with that bunch for her. And I'm right big enough now to send the whole lot of 'em down this road for good, packin' their drawers on their fannies. Hell, we bought the drawers they all wearin' right now."

She kept the quiet stare another moment before she finally turned on me.

"Look at little Frank. Listen to him. You keep tellin' people you don't have a daddy and right off you go soundin' just like 'im."

A gloom came up in her eyes and poured out. Sweat shone from her hairline to her neck and trembled on the sun-brown above her mouth.

"Your grandaddy wanted many a time to put your daddy outta our house and off our land. He and your Granny knew better than you how mean he can be. But they knew how it had been for him. What he's come from, and God help me, so do I."

She wept now, and I slowed the drive, with the truck almost to main street.

"Now they both made me promise not to give up all my life. Not on family, no matter the looks of it. I promised, and I aim to keep it. I'll turn on the better part of this town, but not my promise or my good Lord. Not as long as I believe He wants me here. And don't you think I ain't wondered what I'm doin' here. Many a time if it wasn't for you, I'd done been gone, a long time back. Just said, 'Lord, I'm sorry,' and made myself so gone they'd never find me to bury around here. Not that anybody might care."

She whimpered with a swing of her face back toward the windshield, seeing Marshal come into earshot and view. Both of us quieted, I suppose out of a fear someone might hear a morsel of this conversation and share it for all to chew on. I slowed the little truck more amid the pedestrians, remembering how Granny had favored me once with a sermon about thankfully living the truth of where God put us. As a young boy I had responded that if a body shouldn't run and hide from some of the truth, then why did she and other ladies waste money on toilet water and lacy girdles? And why did I like it so much staying with her rather than the meanest man I knew? Granny had paused, clearly a little perturbed, said Christ never ran from Golgotha, then prattled away about the heat, "curdling her milk."

I stopped the truck as near as I could to Mackey's store and turned all the gentility I could gather toward the figure I barely recognized beside me.

"Ma, I'm powerful sorry I got mad. I'm just tired of livin' like we are. Like them. Just please don't ask me to talk him off a fit again. Never again. I'm through beggin' Frank to straighten up and live right. It's too late for such. I don't care how much he shows up cryin' after one of his fits. I don't care how many times he waits for you, wailin' outside church or holds your hand comin' from work. I don't care. I ain't beggin' him again to stay off that needle."

"Don't then. I ain't askin' you to. Don't do no good anyhow."

My mother's entire aspect changed. Hardened, holding back rage with a dam of false calm. Before I could speak again, the door slammed. She had gotten out and left me to catch up, turning herself into the store through the pleasantries from townsfolk commonly seated on the porch out front. For Ma that day, three old farmers and the babble of Miss Hensley, with her gaggle of apple dolls for sale, might as well have been part of the floorboards. On the way in I nodded some hellos, met with meek smiles and faces scrawled with that patronizing sympathy that comes when people are grateful they aren't you.

We shopped in virtual silence, treating the task as joyless work for no money. I followed Ma, holding a wooden crate. We made our way over the oiled floors, avoiding human contact and the fishing tackle I loved and could afford were it not for the obligation felt toward the place and people we and the merchandise were headed to next. When we reached the counter, Pap's watch told me we had spent better than thirty minutes filling the crate full of our family obligation. The math in my head said four dollars of my hard-earned, coins-an-hour mill money — plus the promised trade of three of my chickens and some fresh milk I drew that morning — were about to be spent on it as well.

Mackey stood near the door, his khaki apron speckled with tobacco burns from self-rolled cigarettes, making us wait while he finished saying goodbye to Hattie Martin. He cooed over her famously cheerful, bowlegged grand-toddler, Sara Jane. "You purdy thing, Saree Jane. Purdy, purdy girl. And sweet to boot. Come see me again real soon. We'll flirt some more." After the screen door slammed behind them, Mackey made way toward us, grinning and muttering about how Sara Jane was, "sweet as Necco candy but so bowlegged she couldn't trap a dog in a ditch." After which he added, "God bless her heart. Sweet child, sweet child."

Mackey carried his usual air of ancient-but-endless youth, his body so long and thin Granny had said he looked, "made outta fence wire." Though nothing about Mackey appeared unwell. Unlike certain of our neighbors who bent under life and looked apt to break, Mackey walked with the vigor of a teenager. Stood straight and sound as a poplar trunk. He chattered a joy toward everyone, never condescended to any, and reached out of his way to smile and laugh with the few folks of darker color who lived among us. He drew whispered criticism for that, though his college education and the clout of extending generous credit helped stave off much hostile talk. Not that Mackey gave off a whiff of caring what people said. Conversing with him, folks did well to get in a word. His tongue worked with the speed of possessing a mind of its own, the sound of him seeming nearly able to rattle the dead to wake.

"They good gracious, God A'mighty, Miss Dove, it's a fine day to lay my eyes on you. How you farin', my love?"

He let a grin shine onto us across the counter.

"I'm fine, I reckon," was her merely polite answer, looking down, rifling dress pockets for money. "You doin' all right?" Her face had turned ashen, and to a sadness that might break a chisel.

"I'm above ground. Above ground, better than I deserve, and then some, Miss Dove. Finer than frog hair, I reckon, by God, especially for the shape I'm in. You don't get to my age without just a bein' thankful you're not pushin' dandelions in the churchyard."

That's when he turned to me — eyes vivid and quick behind tiny wire spectacles. The whole of him aglow with mischief.

"They good Lordy. God A'mighty, Frankie, you're gettin' big, son. Growin' up right outta the floor before my eyes, by God. God A'mighty. Bet the gals swarm you like crows on a biscuit scrap, by God."

Mackey's tone could prick a thorn of humor through even the most callused heart. I caught even Ma turning up her mouth corners, just a hint, as he carried on.

"Them gals swarmin' you, like the man you are? My oh my God, Frankie, good to see you, boy." He turned a sudden quiet onto me — leaned over the counter. "You know you're sorta spoke for 'round here, you know that, don't you? By God, you and me both know what young lady's turned sweet as a swarmed honeycomb on you. And God A'mighty knows she's sharp as a bee's butt, that one is. Fine flower to look at, she is, too. Draws a lotta lookin' herself. You know who I'm a speakin' of. Oh, Miss Dove, how proud you must be. Surely must be."

Having smiled all over Ma, he moved his white-whiskered face so near mine I could smell his tobacco. The whisper amounted to a shout.

"If any of these other boys around tries makin' time with her, just don't you forget she takes a shine to you. And you hear me on this, son. There's not a word fit for truth to any talk you hear about her. Don't ever forget, you won that girl's eye by who you are, not what you got. She told me. You don't owe any man a fight, nor any woman a fuss. And I don't wanna hear tell of you lickin' any of 'em. That includes lickin' their tailfeathers, you hear?"

The squint of his eyes wrung an inescapable caring over me. Even as I looked down the feel of it made me regret a thing I had already done that day. As if a shame of that very morning lay scrawled on my face, in language he might read. My retort came as some mumbled nonsense, embarrassment, and feigned interest in my pockets. To my relief, the colossal sound of an even larger woman pulled Mackey away.

"What you doin' to that man-child, Mista Mackey, now? Good sweet Lawd knows he don't want none of that sugar off you."

An explosion of laughter pealed into the room and certainly out to the street, Mackey joining in, crackling the place full of the mirth that seemed to follow a woman the town knew as Big Miss Ed.

Margie Edna Clover was her unworn formal name. She stood on oddly small feet that carried a mountain of chestnut-brown female brawn from just outside Marshal. She was stout enough to work as a farm hand, renowned for cleaning houses and diapers for the prominent Asheville doctors — both arms ever braced to hug a neck, whether that neck wanted hugging or not. She had stepped up to the counter beside Ma, a sack of what smelled like strong onions dangling from one shoulder and a bag of rice thrown over the other.

"Why, God A'mighty, Ed. I have to smooch somebody. You won't smooch with me." Mackey's answer raised another wave of joys off both. "Ed, don't spread scandal now. I'm just teachin' one a my favorite boys about the evils of kissin' tail and shovelin' guano, that's all."

She cocked back her head and wrinkled her nose. "They law, Mista Mackey, what you had in your mouth. At least you did spit it out and didn't swaller it."

Another blast of laughter sailed through the store until Ed noticed Ma stood immune to it and shaking out the small huffs that precede bawling. Their fun politely retired. Ed had sensed heartache emanating from a woman known for ache, and she answered it instantly and without shame. The rice and onion sacks thudded onto the counter as she grabbed my mother into a smothering embrace — the darkness of Ed's great arms smacking from her short-sleeve dress against Ma's back. My mother's face suddenly burrowed into what was, doubtless, the county's largest bosom — and rather than hugging her back Ma merely wilted. Big Miss Ed whispered, in a way soft and loud at once.

"Miss Locke, honey, how you gettin' along? I am so sorry about carryin' on here and cuttin' a big shine and not lovin' on you. That sweetie of a mama you had ain't here to love you, but I am. Me and that fine boy yonder. Lawd, we unmarried girls can shake the bushes and never find so fine a man."

Ma surprised me by finally returning the hug, pressing herself deeper into Miss Edna's abundance, the great openness of it absorbing her head and the seepage of a bawling that had broken through. That day Ma's body — more so than usual — had turned into a hard vessel, a rigid trap for a soul, but Ed's clutch squeezed some out. Tears flowed from both women now.

"You cry good, now. Don't shush it back. Mercy, Lawd, Miss Dove, you done nothin' worth whatever's botherin' you so. You go on and let it out on ol' Ed. I am powerful sorry what the Lawd sees fit to let you go through. But you just remember what Big Ed say. Don't believe what you see. Believe what you feel. And you goin' to leave here feelin' loved by Big Ed, praise the good sweet Lawd. The boy yonder had better love on you too, or I'm goin' to haul off and get 'im. Get 'im and give 'im a whompin' so hard it smokes his hams."

She grinned and winked at me, while stroking my mother's black hair. Mackey had turned away, on a pretext of fetching some sacks, and he turned back wiping a glisten from his cheekbones. He then seized a moment to thrust himself back into my face, whispering between sniffs.

"Frankie, you just remember son. There's not a man around worth hatin'. Don't let any man yank you down low enough to where you go off and despise him. 'Cause when you do, you've gone and lost any fight worth pickin'. You remember that, son. Remember that, and be sweet to that girl of yours."

"Yessir, I will," I said, convinced more than ever now he knew my every thought and every move of that day and any other. I had looked for her the moment I set foot in the store, but the girl on each of our minds wasn't there, which made for me a crucible of mingled gladness and sorrow. This day already overflowed with embarrassments — notions the town knew every secret about us. By now I figured the one I had revealed to Frank that morning had made its way across more than a few lips.

Mackey wiped his face some more. He had noticed customers beginning to congregate, so he raised a bit of jollity as a kind distraction. The room had grown mercilessly hot. Clothing cleaved wet and heavy all the more.

"Why, good God, Ed, you're gonna love that woman plumb half to death. She knows this town loves her. Now, Miss Dove, don't you suffocate in all that lovin'. I don't want the law in here pickin' up Ed for killin' somebody with love."

They shared a weep-mingled laugh as Ma pulled away, both women dabbing and straightening themselves. I noticed Nell Waters, a tiny sprig of middle-aged, unmarried bitterness — standing near and cutting a look of disgust over her hawkish curl of a nose — as if Miss Ed's dark color were some grime that might rub off. I shot back a look fierce enough that it turned her head away.

"It'll be fine, now, Miss Dovie. Hush. You need anything, I'm around," was Ed's final whisper to my mother in my hearing.

"I know, and I'm right obliged to you," Ma said, with some life returning to her voice. Miss Ed said a few refrains of, "God bless, y'all," and left the sacks to go back into the store, shaking a fist and laughing at Mackey for letting her forget the paraffin she needed for canning. They laughed again and she disappeared, singing "Palms of Victory" in a near baritone.

"She's a darlin' woman, Miss Dove. Darlin' woman. And so are you," Mackey said, returning to the transaction of business with Ma. The other customers hovered closer, so he went out of his way to deflect any stares and humiliation off her. Mackey was as reliable as burlap. Most everyone commented with wonder how a man surely nearing ninety-years-old could run such an enterprise. The time he spent at the University of North Carolina had not cleansed his tongue of the mountain-speak that made people contented with him — he clearly made sure of that. Yet many took even his mundane words as some high gospel. Even in witness to his adoration of Big Miss Ed, I never saw a soul dare challenge him.

"You want some horehound? Have plenty today. How 'bout a plug of tobaccer, Frankie? Hell, I guess you don't need it. You're raisin' your own chew. Please pardon my profanity, ma'am."

I said, "No, thank you." People always marveled that I grew a tobacco crop but despised the flavor of chewing it.

"Don't need none of that," was Ma's reply. "Where I'm headed they do well to eat."

Mackey drew near her again, voice low but loud enough so others near could hear. I supposed he wanted eavesdroppers to hear of Ma's charitable nature in payoff for their craning and gawking at some creature of the pathetic.

"Well, I understand, Miss Dove. She hasn't been in here for a good spell, your sister hasn't. I don't know what the children might eat without you and the boy. Might do well to live on mast like animals."

Ma said nothing outside settling how much she owed him until Mackey addressed me again, eyes glistening a kind intelligence over the tiny spectacles riding the rump of his nose.

"Frankie, the school people surely do miss you. Miss Evans was in here the other day and askin' if ever I saw you. Said our girl we've been speakin' about reminded her about you not long back. The girl's talkin' mighty sweet about you. She's wearin' you around on her thoughts, son, mind and soul. I hear your church people ask about all of you folk, too. The Baptists miss seein' you around church, 'specially with you livin' so near."

Talk of the girl again flushed a thrill through my blood.

"Wasn't my idea, him leavin' school. If I had my way he'd live at school and be more than I ever could." Ma's voice rose a little from its low bog. She had stayed mired in reticence or monotone for weeks now.

Having not set foot across the threshold of school for far more than two years, and church for more than three, I doubted what either of them said. I turned my eyes from Mackey to a gaze at nothing on the dark wood floor.

"Gotta work. Got spinnin' work at the mill and all I can do with two farms."

After he mentioned willingness to buy more of my eggs and salted butter — that the mill workers loved it — we said the most polite goodbyes our moods would allow. Ma and I loaded the groceries into the truck bed with hurry, trying to look too busy to speak to anyone who may ask about us. I cranked the Ford to life and was ready to turn out on the street when Mackey appeared at Ma's window, speaking to her just loudly enough to let the engine drown out his words to any longing ears nearby.

"Sweet, I didn't want to raise a word of it in the store. He was yellin'. Yellin' somethin' terrible, and they had no choice. Word is Frank got into some fracas with the shift foreman again, and they tossed him in the calaboose. Course you probably know by now."

Mackey took off his glasses and wiped his sweating forehead with the tail of his apron. He looked up the street and continued.

"I hate it, Miss Dove. High sheriff himself came and picked him up outta the street yonder, with a few people lookin', just after daylight. It had ended up in fists yonder in front of the depot. I hate what that stuff does to him. And I just want you to know we at the Methodist Church, we'll help. We'll do all we can."

Ma never looked at him. She kept the forward stare, as if she had died but hadn't lain down yet. Her face began to blush with anger.

"I thank you. We all thank you," she said, seeming to gaze off to some far place even time can't reach.

"Well, you all take good care now. Take care and take no meanness. And just so you know, I'll give her no more credit. Neither of 'em. But Miss Dove you oughtta know they have some help comin' and goin', that sister and brother-in-law you keep buyin' for. Day or so back, some ladies of our church came in askin' me about settin' up an account for some poor. Said our preacher heard the Tickman children were wild, runnin' naked and hungry without tendin' from a weak-minded mama and no-account daddy, gone most times."

He put his head back into the window, sweat glistening again like tiny ball bearings on his bald head.

"But Miss Dove, I see him. I see that Ulysses. Some afternoons in my store tryin' to trade canned goods for a Nehi drink, or tobaccer or what have you. Nonsense stuff that's no use to anybody but him. Seein' the back of this truck, I reckon some of the canned goods he's come tradin' are most likely yours you'd given to his own children in times past."

Ma lowered her head, lips thin now, stiff as wood. Mackey carried on.

"I'll tell you, my daddy believed in helpin' all souls. Said even a seed dropped from a bird's hind end can grow into a tree. But that Tickman is not helpin' grow his own self, much less that gaggle of his."

He paused another moment, the rich, sweet smell of the store drifting off him. Ma said nothing, still facing the floor.

"I just thought I'd tell you, 'cause you deserve to know."

With that Mackey withdrew his head, hit the truck door as he might pat comfort to someone's back, and I lurched the little Ford's wheels into the dirt street, around toward the place we had to go. Along with the sundries just bought at Mackey's, a box of canning jars full of my mother's put-up sausage and snap beans clanged reminder from the truck bed of what we may find. I tried working my mind away from any thought of where we were bound.

Mackey's confession seemed to fill the truck with steam — a seething that scalded at my insides. To guard Ma's nerves I kept it in, half-expecting a fury to rupture out of her. Rolling past the fuel station, the funeral home, and then the Methodist sanctuary on our left near the river, she just rode — eyes set far beyond the glass again, limp now, as if any lingering life in her had faded like colored cloth under the sun.

The added truth of that morning is both of us drooped under fatigue. Before Ma claimed a headache so sickening she needed taking home, we had worked part of the mill's graveyard shift, only a few hours of nap to brace us before the sheriff had come knocking official news of Frank's arrest against our front door.

I drove on now, with my secret of that same morning weighing a hard hurt against my own head. I thought of what Ma could not and must never know as she rocked beside me now. What Mackey couldn't tell her because only the two Frank Lockes who had ridden this very street in this same little Ford early that morning knew of it. I tried to push it out, but the memory pressed its mass further into me — smothering my mind the way a heavy body marks a corn-shuck mattress.

Sheriff Ernest Long had banged on our door at dawn that morning. It had jarred me, for not knowing the exact whereabouts of the man we lived with always gave me sleep no better than a nervous dog's. Ma spoke to him through the door, and from my bed I had heard the sheriff tell of the big row at the mill and mutually bloody mouths, and how the courthouse wanted no more to do with Frank Locke. "Just come fetch him, ma'am." I could picture the sheriff shaking the disgust from his head as he went on to explain throwing out Frank's lunch box and, "the dope in it." To this day, I wonder why he hadn't just loaded him into the county truck and hauled him up the mountain to our front porch. Perhaps he wanted to give us the opportunity to say, just keep the devil in jail — knuckle bumps, needle marks, raised hell, and all.

"Frankie, you go, honey." She had pleaded, muffled, arms around me in the bed, her wet cheek against mine. "I'll just rile him if I go. You go and talk to him. He'll listen to you. He loves you, deep in, Frankie. You're about the only one he loves most times now."

She cried more, and I had said nothing, pulling on the same clothes I wore now and driving off in the truck barefoot, the early sun revealing a quarter of seven on Pap's pocket watch. As I wiped the sleep from my face, a plan rose to mind. The trip had offered an opportunity as real as the breaking day ahead.

I loaded pouch tobacco into my pipe with the hand not driving as I followed the sheriff through the fresh morning to the courthouse, where the jailer — known as Coontrack McElhaney — stood above the human slump I had come to retrieve. He sat knees-up, head hanging toward the curb, likely hauled out to prevent another clean up of vomit. Coontrack walked away as I stopped the truck. He seemed disappointed Frank failed to provoke him enough to warrant a drubbing or shooting by law enforcement. Sheriff Long never slowed, but drove his big drooping hat on past the courthouse, I suppose back to his bed, leaving me to gather up the man who had denied all of us — Coontrack included — a bit more sleep.

"You come to fetch me home?"

The words dragged like a plow through mud.

He had spoken looking up at me with eyes resembling a pair of green-swirled marbles, milky with wear. Blood crusted under his nose, and a cut swelled his lower lip. The red of it seemed out of place, for he appeared more apt to ooze a liquid the color of ashes. The infamous scar appearing deeper than normal into his jaw, dark hair matting the weathered granite of his forehead. This man most of the county knew and kindly regretted as my dope-hungry father trembled under my glare, which without doubt seemed hateful enough to wilt stone.

There was no defeating the recalling of it all, as Ma and I made the turn out of town and onto the little bridge. I silently retraced what I had done next with Frank that morning. The Ford's rattle and the river's voice failed to drown the memory I knew I would never kill.

"No, I did not come to fetch you. I drove down here 'cause I like livin' without sleep and I love smellin' somebody's puke."

The whole of it punctured regret into me.

I had jerked him off the curb, helped by my mother's bloodline — which had pushed my height a good two inches above his. I thought about the bed but heaved him into the truck's cab, where he rode in a groaning sag with me up the main street into the cool of that morning. All of it seemed distant, blunt and surreal now with Ma beside me on that same seat. But reliving what I did with him, the fulfillment of my secret, felt as real as a nail tip.

I remembered thinking I should feel more like a man as I drove him that morning, striking a stick match against its box and lighting the pipe without looking at him. Silence, but for the engine rattle. All the teaching about forgiveness and the Golden Rule muscled into me by the tongues of my grandparents might as well have been the smoke, rising off my breath into nowhere. Keeping the Ford at creeping speed, I chewed at the pipe's tip — then grabbed at him some with my eyes, hoping he would glance up and say something to get me started. He looked only at his feet and drew breath that seemed as fast and shallow as a frightened bird's.

"Just you and me, ain't it?" I had finally spoken, looking down the nearly empty street, seeing only a scatter of people, a few wandering town dogs, and our destination not far ahead. "Just the two of us, and you without that box. Ain't you gonna get awful hungry now without that lunch box you carry 'round? That mess you guard like it holds your next breath? You don't gotta needle stuck some place I don't know about, do you?"

He answered my mockery more stoutly than I expected, never looking up.

"Son, just turn 'round and run me up the street to the café. She's 'bout to open. Let's go get some leftover cornbread 'n' coffee. I ain't had a thang to eat, and Miss Ann'll give us some. I got a lil' money."

His clarity daunted me a little. He was more sober and sturdy than he looked, even in spittle and nose slime.

"That so? Well, I ain't hungry, and I ain't gonna ask where you been for three days 'cause I reckon I know. And I ain't gonna ask where your box went, neither, but you can bet there ain't one at home. I tossed every infernal needle you had hid. Tossed 'em down the privy. And you ain't goin' nowhere but where I'm goin' to take you. Got me a little somethin' I been wantin' to show you."

He never asked what, trembling some now, resting his head against the glass. Everything but the stench about him turned humble.

"Frankie, son, I'm sorry. I am right damn sorry. Sorry's 'bout all I am." He sobbed a little, still looking at his feet. "Please help your daddy. Help me."

My teeth nearly ground off the pipe tip as I stopped him.

"You're soon to find out how sorry you are. How sorry everybody is about you." The finger I pointed at him felt as hard as a knife blade. I calmed a little and drove on.

"Know what I can't figure out? I can't figure why it is pert near everybody I ever cared anything for is layin' in a cemetery I have to pass by every day a my life. Everyone of 'em layin' with the worms, and here you are lookin' fit for a grave. Fit for it, but alive, and havin' earned more than one buryin'. And yet right here you are, still drawin' breath when the devil could use your help. Why you suppose it is Granny and Pap and plenty other fine people is layin' dead and you're still here in my face? Why is that? Reckon I don't know, but it makes me mad as hell."

Neither of us spoke again as I drove past the turn-off up to our house and on toward the town's outer reach. I turned into the yard of an old, mostly abandoned livery stable, its shake roof swayed like a horse's back. The owner was known for dissipating himself and his dying business into the same vapor of opiates and liquor wafting beside me now. So into his breach had stepped a stonecutter, Willard Cross, whose business needed some storage not too far from the funeral home opened not long ago near Mackey's store. The old stable stood as the perfect low-rent bargain to house a product few wanted and no one would steal. Cross's new location, with its history of animal waste, had helped spark my idea.

I stopped out front — and with a voice as flat as the Ford's metal dash warned my passenger not to move — then got out, peeled open the big door, and drove us deep into the blackness of the place. He said nothing as I lit the kerosene lantern I kept tied in the truck bed and pulled the door closed. The only other light squeezed in through the clapboards. Slivers of the morning, cutting their way down onto three mules swishing flies and stench a few yards from the truck. Otherwise, only quiet and darkness and my plan.

My feet squished through the soft richness of the stable floor to his side of the truck, where I rested my pipe on the top. I threw open the door.

"Get out."

He looked up as if my words had scalded his face, his mouth seeming to melt, tears rattling loose and running. With a groan, he yielded to my grab of his shoulder. I threw him with my free hand against the truck fender — him squinting, mouth gaped open now, the lantern raised almost near enough to singe his dark brows. My mind was like a locomotive finally on a downhill run, its fire chilled only by the truth that killing him now would belie our purpose in coming here. He was to know my secret, long ago ordered and kept by exchange of money.

"As I see it, one of us is goin' to that church boneyard near the house right soon. Maybe both of us. And I don't aim for folks strollin' through it to see Frank Locke carved more than once on a rock in the ground."

By the hair I pulled back his head, its skin yellow under the light, moving my body against the rattle of his. He wept now, hard.

"Frankie, quit now. I'm sick. Please take me on home, son." The wetness of crying dissolved the blood crust and the rest of his goo to flow again.

"Shut up. Shut up about home. Far as I'm concerned you ain't got but one home to make, and it's in the ground." I pulled his head back harder still, my voice tight as barbed wire. He sobbed on as I dragged him by his hair now, feet barely shuffling, through the lantern glow to the swept-clean rear of the building where I had paid for the work ordered weeks ago. It lay, covered by a heap of dusty burlap tarp, where the old stonecutter had let me inspect the craft of it.

"Now here's what's goin' to happen. I figure you put me to enough shame while you're alive, me havin' to live with your name like a rope around me every place I go. So I bought you and me a gift. Paid ol' Mr. Cross with my own money to make it."

I pulled off the burlap and pushed his head down to smack against the hard thickness of the rock, then strafed his face against the sharp, hand-chiseled lettering.

"Read it. You like readin' so much. Read it!" I yelled now, jerking at him with each word as he cried on. With the other hand I lowered the lamplight to glow off the gray simplicity of the words in stone.

Nobody

Born: Somebody   *Died:* Manure

"See it? It's done. And it'll mark your grave, right soon I expect. Then I won't have to fret about folks seein' my name on it. I ain't callin' you daddy when you're above ground, and I'll not have the ground that holds your bones carry my name when I'm shed of you. Not if I can help it. And I'm through carin' how much people say 'bout you growin' up hard and gettin' gassed overseas. I'm right near as done with you as I can get."

I raised his face to mine, his body still as yielded to my hands as a sack of potatoes.

"I'm sorry, boy. Mighty sorry." Sobs heaved and choked him now.

"Shut up." I let go of his hair, put the lantern down and slapped him with my open hand. I slapped him again, hard, then again, and again — the feel of it like a board against his jaw, the hollow of the scar popping each time — until he finally fell from sight to the ground. I grabbed him up, my mind still fast and unsatisfied, dragged him back toward the truck and the mules, threw him down and pressed his face into a fairly fresh pat of manure.

"Remember the only time Granny ever smacked you? You was accusin' Ma of goin' 'round with some man. Some lie you cooked up, liquored up on that devil-dust. Granny and me come in from pickin' blackberries. Walked right in on you raisin' hell, and she hit you, and I loved it. I loved it 'til she cried regret of it later. I's no more than ten and I thought, well he's made the both of 'em cry now — Ma and Granny. You got no idea how many times I wanted to kill you just for that. Ma's talked me out of it more than once." Toward the end, the steel of the words began a melt into weeping rage.

"I worship your mama. I worship her 'n' you both. I can't get no sorrier than I am."

He begged me to let him up. I pushed his face harder against the ground, then yanked his head by the hair. Into the lantern glow. He came off the soak of animal waste the same man — but in shades of more shame than I intended — the look of it running deep beyond the blackness of waste. Surrendered to my hands, he glanced at me with a scrawl in his eye, a dishonor written indelibly there, addressed to both of us. What had been done would live in him, and I would die unable to forget it. I collapsed into sobs on top of him, the swish and breath of the mules warm above us.

A few more words finally poured out, sodden with regret, intended more as confession for my ears than his.

"Pap told me one time he hoped none of us ever gets what we rightly deserve. Reckon he was thinkin' about you and me."

With that, I picked up the wreckage of Frank Locke, Senior by his shirt and the seat of his pants and helped the squalor of him into the bed of the truck — noticing he had two of the Asheville newspapers he loved to read rolled and stuffed into his back pockets, part of a broken syringe poking out of one. My assault, combined with his usual intoxicant, seemed to chase him into a walking coma — both legs shaky as twigs in the wind, eyes closed, his face the sculpture of an agony no word will quite fit. I wiped the worst of the manure from both of us with newspaper, re-covered the tomb rock, and said no more. Hoping death did not grant the souls of my grandparents a vision of what I had done.

He had failed to give me the fight I wanted. Offered no violence as reason to annihilate him by some feigned accident or self-defense. I felt a sudden sadness as real as a steel bit in my mouth about this man I hated so completely. It haunted me almost out loud as I hauled him out of town, wiping tears, up the winding switchback road — speeding up past the church and cemetery, to the dry dirt front yard of our house. I dragged him feet first from the truck bed and practically carried his staggering limbs, again by the slack seat of his pants, through the scatter of pecking

chickens up to the porch, where I let him drop fairly quietly onto the boards like a
bag of feed. He lay in a crumple of shaking and sickness, and I took a knee to whisper
to him, figuring not to wake Ma, likely sleeping just to the other side of the wall.

Some of my regret and sadness had solidified into hickory-stout loathing again
on the short trip.

"This is as far as I'm takin' you. And I'm warnin' you now, this ain't gonna go
much longer. This place was give to you, and Pap always said he had good reason for
not puttin' you off it. So I reckon I won't neither, not yet. But if you ever come even
holdin' your mouth like you'll raise a loud word, much less a hand, at my ma again,
it won't matter how much cryin' and honeysuckle-sweet you spread around after.
'Cause I'll be sure to kill and bury you myself. So help me I'll do it, Frank, and pray
not to see you in hell."

I gave him a shake, rolled him to face the wall, and left him.

Around the house waited some quiet distraction — the milking of my cows I
had already waited too late in the day to do, stowing the jars in the cool of the
springhouse for later travel. After that I pulled a few corn ears from the patch below
the barn, ate a bowl of cold hominy on a back porch rocking chair, and thought
about how the ocean must look. Imagined some places far off that had occupied my
dreams since the days of my tree-board hiding place, now rotting away. A fitful nap,
forced on me by exhaustion, came and went. I hadn't opened Ma's door, figuring her
worn out enough to be safely numb with slumber.

An hour later, my face and hands clean from the cool of lye soap and springwater,
she woke me, her face pale but fresh with ignorance of the morning's events. She
asked why he had flopped up asleep on the porch and why hadn't I put him to sleep
in the old front-room rocker he loved. I said no more than he smelled too much like
pasture to bring in the house and that I had advised him to stay out. Ma ended it
with that and carried on, officious as an autumn squirrel, with what had to be done.
We had nearly to step over him to pick the cemetery flowers near the yard and leave
on our present journey of the usual family charity. He had not moved from where I
had left him, and I refused a look back as we had rolled away. The sight of him had
seemed to shatter something in my mother worse than usual.

Nearly three hours now after I had picked him up from the sheriff and hauled
him to that old livery, our destination lay not far ahead of where I steered the little
Ford back up from Mackey's that morning. My secret battering of Frank stowed in
my memory, safe enough from Ma, who sat still oddly mute and glaring ahead. What
I had allowed myself to do, what it might mean, loitered in my head nearly all the way
to the turn off toward what had been Granny and Pap's farm and our expected storm

of Tickmans in need. But in the curve just before the farm's rutted driveway, coming
off the mountain, appeared a sight that yanked the day's haunt off me. I straightened
myself, feeling some color wash through me again.

In her wagon, no doubt full of homemade apple butter or goat milk to barter at
Mackey's, rode Mary Lizbeth Hunter, driving a surrey behind the single black horse
she had bottle-raised. She said nothing. Never slowed. But her large eyes smiled their
green life through the truck glass into mine, the gaze seeming to vibrate through
me like chords of a music only she and I could hear. I knew, however, that mothers
hear what we think they can not, and somehow see the unknowable parts of their
children's lives. When I finally put my eyes back on the road, having nearly missed
the turn to the farm, Ma sat staring so far into me I felt she could see all the way to
the secret parts of my adolescence.

"You see the mess we're in? Well, this is what marryin' too awful quick will
get you."

I kept driving through the trees up the driveway as she spoke, and denied her
eyes their chance at burning into mine like a branding iron.

"Me and Mattie didn't have no better sense than get messed up with what we
thought was love. That girl's the last thing you oughtta have on your mind, 'specially
with all that's gone on with that one and her poor mama."

She turned away to the window and began talking as much to herself as to me.

"The evil that put her mama in the ground is still runnin' loose and lyin'. Him
not carin' a bit what he done to that woman or the poor girl, I reckon. God forgive
me. Hush, Dovie. Hush or you'll say worse and regret yourself."

My mother had witnessed what she spoke about through the too-often blind eyes
of gossip that regularly peered through the mill, café, Mackey's store, and most of the
churches around us. More than most, my mother seemed sympathetic to what had
brought Mary Lizbeth's mother to that unmarked grave in the churchyard near our
house. And as I had witnessed again that very morning, Ma seemed oddly connected
to that grave, often putting a single flower on it to join another one usually there.
And sympathies notwithstanding, knowing the history that helped put that woman
in the ground seemed to make my mother more afraid for — and of — Mary Lizbeth.
That, and one look at the girl.

For Mary Lizbeth Hunter had grown. Adolescence came early and pushed her
through the dirt crusts of her tomboy wanderings, out into a full-bloom adulthood.
She lived with the independence of any man but so undeniably curved into dark-
haired womanhood she formed the very letters of scandal — even apart from her

mother's own reputation for drawing the eyes of men. From the narrow hollow that was still her home above our one-street town, Mary Lizbeth had evolved to a lush fullness, of muscle and mind, that strained against the confines of her place in the world. Like a mountain laurel flower trying to blossom inside a bottle. Pink-white petals pressing soft but determined against the glass. The shared nectar of that bottle had recently become another of my secrets — *our* secret from the entire town. An elixir keeping some deep part of me alive, and I hoped Ma couldn't see far enough into either of us to find it out.

If she could see that far into me, my mother would have found a simple truth: Thoughts of Mary Lizbeth had ghosted nearly my every thought for years. Shadowed my movements and bettered me through the depths of our times. Seeing her in that wagon raised in me a longing to spring from the moving truck, fall into the softness of her in that wagon, and roll in her direction forever. But I could not. Not with what lay ahead. The dreaming of her would have to suffice. That one filament's worth of a look would do for now.

I drove on up the driveway, past the blackberry briars growing over the shortcut walking path I used to take between our place and a visit with Granny and Pap as a boy. The little truck eased Ma and the load of food across a tiny bridge spanning a branch that rounded the property. In front of us, splayed full of my work trying to maintain it, lay the farm every member of the Locke household felt had somehow been stolen.

The little patch of steep hollow we lived in lay like a wrinkled scrap compared to this quilt of a farm Granny and Pap had made, and left, a mile away. A small vale: Two little squares of hay field, a tobacco patch, corn and some other row crops, a small orchard of apple and cherry trees, and a pasture long empty since I evacuated the cows and mules to our place where I could tend them. The yard held Granny's grapevines, bent now with purple despite the children, and the weed-strangled patch where she had grown strawberries that seemed as big as baseballs. The place held two small barns, an empty chicken house, and a palace of potential, I thought. My grandparents had pieced together a life far better than survival from the dirt of it, and I vowed to Granny I'd wear my hands to the bone holding some farming together on it — keeping weeds and Tickman neglect from overgrowing it.

And just beyond our trail of Ford dust stood the house, at the foot of a mountain above the fields. A whitewashed wood with a deep porch. It once seemed nearly able to smile a welcome at me, a peace solid as the boards. But the expression had changed — the house seeming somehow angry and hurt at the same time now — as though someone had kicked it in the shins that held it up.

The truck's noise had no doubt announced us as I pulled to a stop onto the clay yard, dry and red as fire under August drought. As the engine rattled to a quiet, my mother's hand reached to squeeze my arm, pulling at my attention before I could get out. I suppose events of the morning kept me from looking at her.

"Frankie, you know I'd rather take pneumonee as go in here. And I'm sorry for draggin' you up here again. We're just stayin' a minute. I can't stand no more than that. We'll see that them kids has enough to eat, then we're joustling outta here. And I'll help you lay tobaccer sticks down yonder after you get a nap."

Her hand joined mine on the steering wheel. The pat of it softer than expected, her words on a quiet tear-flow again.

"You're all I've got, honey. You're all I've got. If it weren't for you I would surely have wanted the Lord to take me, a long time back."

Silence. I looked at the squeeze of her hand against mine.

"I miss 'em. God, I miss both of 'em. All of 'em, " I said, gazing then through the glass at Granny's honeybee boxes up in the trees on the west ridge.

I don't know why it took me so long, or why thoughts of dead family suddenly resurrected the pleasure of it, but at that moment I realized my pipe was gone. Pap's gift to me, so opposed by the women and flush with the aroma of manhood. It had fallen. Placed by my hand on top of the truck where I had left it to deal with Frank, no doubt now it lay on the floor of old man Cross's place. My free hand reached to the breast pocket of my overalls. Empty. Then my own tears nearly overflowed their brink. I suppose Ma thought I had simply reached for my heart.

"I miss 'em too, Frankie. God knows I do, and I ain't gonna let some no-account take this place forever. You'll have it, honey. You'll have it 'cause that's what Granny and Pap wants, I know."

"Let's get done with this," I said, in a tone colder than I wanted.

I pulled away and got out of the truck, mad at losing something so intimately my grandfather's the touch of it could nearly conjure his voice: "Work hard, mind your biz'ness, and when you get hurt pray for somebody worse off than you." The vista in front of me seemed to echo him.

Outside the truck now, I just stood and took in the air of his place — the smells of living land under the threat of rain creeping just beyond the ridgetops, all of it seeming to carry his breath. The feel of the place was calm, but for a wind flipping the tree leaves to their lighter green underside and bending the corn and tobacco in the little valley below us. Four months earlier, in that field where Pap long ago had begun teaching Eb and me to grow Burley leaf, Frank had helped me set this year's tobacco crop. He had kept himself clean nearly a year from his second trip on the train to a sanitarium in Kentucky — the first one paid for years back by my grandparents, determined to see him pulled from opium's mire — this latest funded by my mother, convinced the three of us together could dull his paregoric-craving for good. The view before me echoed him as well.

"Frankie, son, we'll make us a tobaccer dollar that'll make your Pap's soul prouder than any patch in heaven. We'll run some irrigation to his corn patch and be in biz'ness."

I recalled how lightly Frank talked and laughed that day, standing in the softness and aroma of newly turned ground, half-joking about Ulysses being, "so lazy the flies think he's dead." But he had turned off serious and misty after that. Patting his near skeletal hand against my shoulder. "We'll make somethin' of this farm 'cause of you, Frankie. You're as much like your grandpap, it's like he's a standin' here with me right now. Finest man ever made, he was. He's what I want you to be, son."

"Well, I'm workin' like he did," was my response. "This ain't no garden of Eden. Somebody's gotta bust a clod to feed us."

His sobriety of that time — like the family tales of his charms and hardships and even heroism — I found about as reliable as talk of people one day rising from the dead. So far my cynicism had proven correct all around. He had managed to shun the wallow of opium just long enough at times to infuse us with bleakest disappointment when he poured its cruelty into himself again. Frank lapsing onto that needle proved as predictable as the coming of midnight. As reliable as I was lonesome now, looking down on corn and beans I needed to hoe. Hay to cut and weeds in need of Pap's swing blade. I looked at the tobacco, whose proceeds I could save toward my goal of leaving here, if I could somehow get it in the barn and off to market in time against the weather. All virtually by myself, though Mary Lizbeth pledged to help.

Bleak though it sounds, the solitude of this moment freshened my mind some. A sprinkle of rain, just a light curtain of it, had settled across the dust of the yard and sent Ma into some hurry. She had said no more, picking up a box from the truck bed and going on in without me. I lifted another, full of store-bought cornmeal and a bucket of lard tucked around her canned goods, and started up the steps.

Near the top, in no rush to flee the little storm's early spray, I thought I saw him. Just a glimpse. Ebenezer, as young as the day he died, but mature somehow, and grave of face — standing on the porch glancing a sorrow toward me that covered his normal look of wry devilling. Only a thought. Just a snatching of one. Then gone like lightning. Never there, I thought, as I climbed the steps missing him and wondering how his survival might have changed the steps my mother and I had taken this day.

The insides of the house greeted me on the porch, even four feet from the door. A riot of stench, noise and irritations no balm would cure. A gaggle of children raising themselves and hell at the same time, in a squalor so fetid with indifference it might send some pigs looking for better wallow. My boots had barely crossed the threshold when Ma's favorite of the nieces, five-year-old Ada Mae, ran toward me, throwing off an ear-cutting scream about stick candy.

"Uncle Frankie, you bring me some? You bring me candy?"

The child was dirty as a wet dog rolled in dirt, and otherwise covered only in her philosophy that life in summer was best-lived completely naked. A younger brother, Obidiah, trailed her, his diaper about to trail him, and the whole of it looked and smelled worse than the last time Ma and I had been summoned here, three weeks earlier — again by the oldest girl, Marie Kate, the same child who betrayed the window breaking of Eb and me. The humiliation typically fell to her to walk the overgrowing path to our house and tell us her daddy had gone off again and that the entire lot — all the surviving six of them — was hungry toward starvation. Though this time, more than usual, the house seemed to spin with chaos — a circus, with strung wires of stiff hanging laundry from inside the kitchen out the door to the back porch, children acrobatic against the furniture and walls as if they had been caged indoors. I was sure if we dug into the graves right now, we'd find my Granny and Pap lying facedown. And if the Bible meant what it said about a resurrection of the dead, what was about to happen might bring the two of them high out of the ground.

"Where in heaven's name did you get money to buy this?"

Ma commenced the yelling just as the screen door hit my backside. I had heard her drop the box hard in the kitchen, and soon saw her chasing her sister, both coming toward me, Mattie sprinting like a cat two steps ahead of a fox. As if we had somehow surprised the entire household.

"Leave me be, and let me see sweet Frankie. Fine lookin' man."

She nearly sprang to me, arms open, mouth smooching, bosom rumbling large in a yellowed and variously stained housecoat that emitted from an arm's distance the aroma of old sweat and cooking poke salad that grew wild out back. I turned my head just before the muddy-cornered snuff lips would have smothered mine. Their wet press against my cheek irrefutable evidence that either the absent man of this house lived utterly dead from the neck up or that each child here proved a modern miracle of immaculate conception.

"Gimme sugar and hug my neck, sweet man. You look mighty fine. Lawd have mercy you are a beautiful thing." Her brown eyes filled with tears, gazing upward and hollow as I smothered in cleavage, arms, and the reek of it all. The heavy wood box of food nearly fell from my grip.

"My Ebenezer woulda been stout as you by now. A stout, good lookin' sweet boy."

That's all the molestation of me she could manage this time. Ma had reached us on a stride so hostile she seemed a one-woman wrestling match against several of the Ten Commandments. She held a container of contraband in either hand. Her face seemed hard as oak.

"This is what you buy with the help people gives you? Where'd you get such? Why are you sendin' after me sayin' you're all hungry? And don't tell me you ain't a gettin' help, 'cause I know you are."

Ma spun Mattie off me somehow without dropping what occupied either hand. Rain came louder on the tin roof.

"Where'd you get Grove Tonic? And who's drinkin' it?"

An inch from Mattie's nose Ma held a half-consumed bottle of "Grove's Tasteless Chill Tonic" — an apothecary product that promised to make babies fat, though most assumed it also capable of getting adults intoxicated. For that reason Mackey would not carry it in his store.

"Dove, me and these young'uns got to have laxative. That's all that is, and I pert near have to choke it down ever' one of 'em."

Ma had just moved in closer on her when we heard the first of the noise. A series of four metallic pops from above us. Much too heavy for rain. No squirrel or bird made such a sound. I figured it the rock-throwing work of the now-oldest boy, James Paul, about twelve, carrying on Eb's boyhood high jinks. Ma ignored it, raising the other hand into her sister's face while Mattie nudged all of us toward the front door.

"Well, tell me what help this devil-dust is to your house?"

Opposite the Grove bottle, my mother held up, in a quake of fury, a little yellow-wrapped tin. "Society Snuff" the brand name, a woman of Elizabethan refinement printed on its paper label as assurance of a quality female dip and spit. Just as the two sisters came nose to nose, another of the children appeared to confirm suspicions of what Mattie tended to buy with whatever money happened through the door.

Thomas Howard, three-years-old and barely able to speak — yet hopelessly addicted to tobacco — pulled at the tail of my mother's dress with one hand and his lower lip with the other. The remnants of snuff-dips-past drooled from the corners onto his brown-spattered shirt. He was conditioned to react to any adult's touch of that can.

"'Nuff. Gimme dip 'nuff," he implored my mother, yanking the dress now, his crying joining that of at least two more children in the house.

Ma knew of, and often railed against, the toddler's taste for snuff and Mattie's tendency to shovel it into him as a pacifier. Though today would bring no helpless warnings. I thought I heard another of those metallic pops above my head just as my mother gave Thomas Howard a moment's survey, then carried on toward shouting hell loose from its foundations.

"Mattie, what in the cornbread hell have you fed these kids for two weeks now? Snuff? Snuff and that stinkin' poke salat I smell cookin'? Is that it?"

"Why Doveeeee, what evil you had in yer mouth, may the Lawd fergive it. I'd be ashamed if I was you, I would," Mattie cried back at her in a simpering wash of sanctimony and sadness, way overdone. I finally put down the heavy box and stood back to watch my mother flood the room, and without doubt the yard and nearby woods, with a frenzy years in the making.

"Don't you bring God into this. You sit up here on your fat hind end while I work mine off. You know what I put up with. I've tried to help you and this bunch. I feel sorry for these young'uns. But damn you and that low-down, useless, good-fer-absooooolutely nothin' man you married...."

Mattie suddenly stopped herding us toward the door and the porch and turned. "Well, Dove, I feel bad, but I can't help you married a dope drunk so fulla meanness nobody can't pray him cured. Now can I?"

And that did it. Lit the fuse to the keg that held years worth of my mother's deepest wrath. It blew out into a full row. Ma raised the hand that held that tonic bottle. Mattie appeared nearly to swoon, and yet cried out.

"Dovie, don't you! Don't you do it now!"

I reached over my aunt's shoulder to prevent fulfillment of it. Too late. The haymaker landed.

A glancing blow, yet Mattie's lip shook loose blood as that fistful of bottle withdrew. Ma flashed me a glance that married regret with a hurt that seemed deeper than a well — her body still wearing a full kit of rage and winding back toward another blow. I knocked crying Thomas Howard over into a ball of screams, grabbing the arm that was poised to crack the bottle fully against Mattie's head. No one ever expected this — not from my mother.

The back door slammed with a bang that brought Paul James running in through the hymn of childhood screams, his mother wailing a chorus of, "Lawd A'mighty, Lawd A'mighty, Lawd...." as she wilted, hands to her face, barely standing against my arm.

On the tide of this row, the rumble fully came. The popping heard before evolved to a tin-roof thunder. One a man of more faith than mine at the time might have taken as the disapproving hand of the very Almighty, smacking chastisement against the whole house. Again it came, louder, knocking all of us into a pause. For a moment the entirety of us stood reposed — utter stillness apart from child cries — the beadboard walls somehow full and empty of my grandparents at the same time. Then, the quake. The rumbling that rained down a revelation to change everything.

My position, with an armful of one woman and eyes full of the other, kept me from seeing it, but even a deaf man couldn't escape feeling the clamor. Sounding of horse hooves in stampede, something slipped and tumbled on the rain-slick tin above, flailing and slamming as it fell. A yell of dread followed. Unmistakable. My Uncle Ulysses, seeming to fight valiantly, but the bellow he let fly spoke of surrender to gravity. In one long body roll, he yawed and flipped off the edge to drop better than twenty feet with a smack against a spread of stagnant blackish mud I had seen him and the male children urinate into off the side porch to save a walk to the outhouse. The wet dirt cushioned the fall, which he punctuated with a dull, "Ummph." Then quiet.

Speculation about Ulysses had grown like weeds for years. Since Granny and Pap died his wanderings and abandonment of his family grew more common, drawing greater amounts of charity from us to his children. I had long-suspected him of hiding out around the property and had looked for him in the barns, sheds, and even the orchard. I never thought to look on the roof. That large-body thud to the ground confirmed it. That and the caterwaul. He often had not, "run off somewhere," as Mattie would accuse, but had merely crawled up and perched atop the house somehow. It made perfect sense — with the chimney to shield him, he had fast escape, reconnaissance of the property, and the illusion of fatherly absence to evoke more pity for a family naturally pitiful. Roof noise and falling formed the only weaknesses on the idea. To this day I assume he was straining to listen to the women clash inside when that quick shower of rain slipped him off to the ground.

Yelling some business about mercy of heaven, Ma had torn away from me in a run for the window he had passed on the way down. Then out the door to the porch, Mattie right behind her, screaming, "He's dead. Oh, he's kilt, oh I know he's kilt dead," wailing children in her wake, but for the youngest who sat screaming on the floor.

I remember yelling something after my mother before we all paused at the porch rail. The expectation of looking into the face of death itself soon dimmed. I saw my shirtless uncle rolling over, revealing that some part of the fall had yanked his pants south. The black hair he had Mattie trim every few days had fallen from its usual foppish pomp into a curtain that reached his eyes. But the worst of it came in a glance at what no such dirt-despising dandy ever wants revealed. As he wallowed that ground, I witnessed a steadier rain bouncing off the muddied milk-white skin of Ulysses Tickman's protruding naked backside, his sorrowing bride at full wail.

"You awright, darlin'? Oh, darlin', you are alive," she cried, the children crying on with her and the rest of us stunned to see him wallowing, windless and retching a little, trying to sit up and catch his breath where he landed — apparently more alive than he was embarrassed. He held plenty of life and soon would likely regret it.

"You lazy, low-down man-sow."

With Mattie crying toward swoon again, Ma poured a fit of perfect hysteria on him. Such that I had never witnessed from her. Ulysses had rolled completely to face her, his backside now at rest in the mud. Then he fired back, not seeming to care how the fall of his pants exposed most of his natural plumbing as well.

"I ain't goin' to lay here and take..." he coughed a little as his wind came back, "...and take any mouth off you, Dovie. I ain't asked you for nothin'. Mattie! Marie Kate! Come down here and help Daddy outta this mud."

"I got me some help for you!" Ma screamed it on the run, waving off my try at grabbing her. We all chased her to the steps, then off the porch, around where Ulysses sat still trying to gather himself and shake the hurt. Mattie stammered behind, crying and yelling, "Lawd A'mighty, Lawd A'mighty, help us," the children still bellowing after her.

"Ma, leave him be. Just leave him and let's go on," I implored in pursuit. Within the same thin, dark-haired rail of a body seemed to co-exist my mother and some animal boiling rabid, deaf and blind to reason.

He huffed and panted and raised his hand as if to stop her from jumping on him, making no gesture of hauling his cheeks from the ground. I quickly saw he had fallen only feet from the chopping block and woodpile, an iron wedge and maul lying perilously near his landing. Ma had just started to scream some more vitriol into him when he interrupted with the unnatural calm of one denying his own disgrace.

"Dove, now, let's have no improper talk that ain't right 'tween decent, God-fearin' folk. Now I was just up on that roof a seein' if I could climb a ladder well 'nough to work for the railroad again. Jimmy Paul's off a huntin' right now, tryin' to help his daddy feed his family. We're a tryin'...."

"Shut up. Shut your lyin' mouth." Ma seemed to cool a bit, down to a more composed inferno, pacing and jousting at him with the bottle still in her grip.

"Jimmy Paul come runnin' in the house when you fell. He's right here all along, likely watchin' out for you, you lyin' fool. Just more lies...." She turned and looked for the boy, but I had seen him go. He had taken off down the driveway, running barefoot and nearly rabbit fast away from the house through the rain, which had slacked but still wet us all.

"Lies and more lies, is all you know to tell ...." Ma moved on him, pushed into his face. Mattie sang off some more, "Lawd A'mighty, Lawd, Lawd," grabbing at her chest, pacing behind us, pulling back the assembly of crying children, who had begun scattering back onto the porch or standing off as if something else might happen. Ma turned and yelled back, "Shut yourself. Hush it, now."

"Ma, let's go on now, come on," I pleaded with her, ignored again. Ulysses tried the same, nesting his cheeks further into the urine smell, groaning, holding his side, and holding forth in a ministerial way I knew she despised.

"No. No now. Dovie you just lay back them tailfeathers and quit hollerin' in fronta them lil' chaps. Such hollerin' ain't proper 'tween ladies and gentlemen." He glanced around at the audience, groaned for sympathy, then preened, "And, I'd be right thankful if y'all might turn away 'til a man could draw his butt-biscuits outta this muck without showin' hisself."

This finished setting my mother's tongue afire.

"Frank's right on one thing. You are too lazy to find your own butt with both hands." She yelled so hard it rattled her. He fired back, his calm draining away.

"Well, now see, Mattie, how she talks? Such talk from a woman what pretends herself a Christian lady about town. Come up here dartin' around, showin' her tail, and in front of these young chaps." He finally began to seize the pants back north over his bared southern spheres. "I'd be right ashamed if I's a woman. I would. Such vulgarity ought not show itself here no more."

That lit the fuse to the rest of her. What had thus far been a mere spitting of regrettable words exploded into rapid-fire row. Ma yelling, "Shut up!" and more, over and over at him, bending two feet from his face at times, Mattie groping at her and imploring all heaven to intervene. Ma waved her white-grip fist around the bottle at his nose, which finally had the effect of blushing him. She and Ulysses then launched into a duel of pointed fingers and noses nearly as swords.

"Listen woman...." "Shut up...." "You hush up...." "I'll take none of your sass...." "I'll sass you all I please...." "Hush woman...." "I'll not hush...." "Hell you won't...." "I've fed you and them young'uns with money I don't have 'til I'm sick...." "Git offa my place, Dovie...." "Your place? This ain't no more your place than you're a lumberjack." "Well, we're a livin' just fine on it, like your own ma wanted...." "I oughtta kick you and your crack fulla stinkin' mud off my mama 'n' daddy's place for good." "That's it. You've sassed me your last...." "Have I? Well, it's high time you got told out loud what all creation knows. That you're about too lazy to draw your own breath. Frank's right about that."

About there in the barrage I moved to carry my mother away, feet kicking if need be, when Mattie, grooming each syllable with sneering pride, threw on the fuel that finally pushed her older sister to full ferocity.

"Lawdy Dove, quit now. Just 'cause you married a fool don't mean you gotta right comin' up here talkin' such and takin' yourself out on us. Just 'cause you're jealous I married me a Christian man."

Mattie dared move close again, clearly vitalized with the notion that some pity would rule, holding her mouth as if the wound were mortal, then yelling for the first time in this battle.

"She done hit me, darlin'! Don't you go provokin' her, now. Up here carryin' on like some Jezebel and showin' her tail end. She's lost her cotton-pickin' mind is what she has."

At that thought, Ma broke down, without even a splinter's warning, as if something inside her had collapsed under weight and fire. She turned to lunge at Mattie, who let fly a hail of of, "Have mercy, dear Gawd," her brown eyes as big as dinner plates. My hands caught my mother's raised arms. As fast as I could blink I stood between them, both railing and crying, but Ma lost in screams. So dense they still bind to my heart and pinch it across the years.

"No. No, I'll have none of that!"

His voice came before I saw him — over Ma's shoulder. Perhaps he had finally caught a sight of the small ooze of blood on his wife's face or maybe Ma's delirium, spewing wild onto Mattie, brought him up. Something made my uncle madder than a swatted hornet. She had shocked me already, but I never expected to witness what came next from a woman the entire community deemed too peaceable and tolerant for her own good.

In all the squalling between the two women, with me flailing to pull my mother away, Ulysses Tickman came up behind her. Risen fast from the mud. One hand pulling at his canvas pants, the other reaching toward Ma.

From somewhere I heard Marie Kate yell, "No, Daddy, now, no!" over the din of the crying women who flanked me. In a moment's time, my mother lay on the ground — shoved there for her own good by me as I rushed him after he grabbed at her and missed.

He and I thudded together into the mud, neither yet throwing blows but wrestling hard. We had rolled only seconds when it raised itself. High, even above the children crying and Mattie's wailing to heaven. It was a woman's howl — sounding as if it boiled up from the blood-deep place where she had stored every hurt that ever cut its way into her. Ulysses had just rolled atop me, stinking of an outhouse and huffing something about the two of us calming down. I felt him about to let me go, then through his thick limbs I felt the throb. I hadn't seen the log splitter yet, but it had found its way. Ringing cast iron hard against his head. The eyes, what I could see of them from so near, flipped to white. A deep, sighing groan sounded like rocks tumbling down in his throat. Spittle flowed out as he fell, my mother crumpling over him, swinging the simple black wedge five more times. Her screaming came unbridled by language or any bit of control. At least two more swipes of its iron weight chunked his skull, and he lay still — blood creeping from his nose, ears and the side of his head, pooling to red waste on the richness of the ground. My mother dropped herself beside him.

"Lawd God, Lawdy, Lawd Jeeesus," became the row's final words. Then sobs — akin to the last smoke from a smolder — rose off the human debris of it all. Mattie wept and whisked hair from the wound and spoke to him as if her husband, in his stillness, could hear. I expected the crying would rise into a conniption, but Mattie just stayed near him, her voice an unintelligible softness of denial and panic. Ma had rolled herself a few feet away, hysteria fading. Just sitting up, glaring at the tremble of her hands, my uncle lying near in a mangle of blood and calm. Mattie whimpered, having gathered tiny Obidiah against her leg, where he sniveled and fussed. Wind and a pair of crows cawing up in the woods were the only other sounds. The cries of children should have joined, but we were alone. Shocked to near paralysis, I glanced around for them. For other witnesses. None. Even Marie Kate, aged into premature womanhood by cotton mill work to help feed the enormous family she had not borne, had abandoned the yard. I had seen none of them run, except for James Paul. Two women, two men, and a toddler shared this ground alone, shackled by a piece of time unbreakable. The next one to escape would need a maneuver. Some idea, some lie, capable of slipping us free of these last few seconds we couldn't change. I had scarcely absorbed the clash of it all when such a lie poured into my thinking.

"Say I did it. It was me, you hear?"

The next moment I remember, I whispered that against my mother's cheek, trying to coax her into standing.

"Me, you hear? Ma, you have to tell the sheriff I did it. It was me. I killed him."

She felt twice as heavy as Eb's corpse when we lifted it from the river the day he drowned. I eased her back down onto the mud. Her eyes kept locked straight ahead, venturing to some far-off nowhere, empty. I pulled her face to mine but the eyes wouldn't hold me. Wouldn't look. I held my mother, but Ma felt long gone. Awake, yet not there.

"Don't say a word but what I said. You hear? Do it, Ma. Just do as I say."

I turned from her and ran. With dread tightening every sinew and strangling all the decency that should have kept me there, I lit out up the hill toward where the farm ceased and a high wilderness began. Hard as a teenage boy's heart will allow, the wind a roar in my head, I ran up the grade. So fast the moist earth might as well have been fire under my soles, aiming for Pap's toolshed beside the cow barn, laying out the plan as my tracks went down.

Panic can pull hard — strong as any wire and choking the urge to look back or turn around. Past Granny's bees and under the low-limbed apple trees too-little tended, my boots squished and slipped against the sweet fermented orchard ground, rotten apples no match for the yen practically yanking me toward Granny's path. I rounded the shed corner, thinking I might step in for an axe to help cut my way, but bailed fast into the familiar opening in the treeline. Fog from the rain leached into what amounted to a cathedral of hardwoods. The mountain dwarfed the farm from there, rising steep under its covers of green, Granny's trail a foot-wide climb of tree roots, moss-carpet logs, and memories of the times we had made the trip together since I was five. I never slowed, rushing through leaves, then, further up, hearing the steps turn mute against the loamy decay of centuries — the running carrying me higher off the bloody wreckage of Granny and Pap's backyard. Both lungs already feeling like two bags of hot stove coals.

No thought of fatigue came along, and shame had yet to catch up with me. The huff of this run felt more like the breath of freedom than the smother of exile. I wanted to run. Had cultivated the desire for years. I had put up with enough of what Granny might call, "a dung hill so stinkin' it wouldn't grow a blossom," that clambering up the mountainside felt like a legal right.

Through beech and black oak trees dripping cool vestige of rain, I carried on, hardly slowed, bound next for Granny's pocket — a place she called sacred. The edge of her world. The wooded hollow darkened, but for strands of light sifted by trees. Climbing it saw me trying to clear thought of his blood. Scour its red and all that lay behind from my mind and think beyond the ridge ahead. Rounding the mountainside where the woods thickened to a near curtain, exhausted now nearly to vomiting, I caught the sound of it. A rush. Relief. I was near the cliff — the doorway to her gorge. Through it rambled a stream of water that fell from that ledge near Granny's little stone pocket, an accent on her great coat of God. I could hear it, even through the wheeze of breath and a gush of storm wind through the limbs above.

Reaching the waterfall and the pocket's finery demanded a downward climb. I hunched to rest a moment at its entry: A gap between two blue-green mountains, giving vista to misted layers, the scarps hazed by the stormy day. And just below — flowing over gray-speckled rock, worn slick — ran that water toward its drop.

The aroma of it freshened and pulled at me. I followed, barely catching breath, figuring to carry on and die on those rocks or in the woods, rather than drown in the refuse of where I had been. I climbed the familiar perils of a ledge, as Granny had, into a channel of steep laurel hells, toward the place where she adored to sit and take in the sweet breath of mountain water flow. But the rock underfoot fit the feel of that day. An angry second-guessing rubbed hard at my insides. Why, again, hadn't Ma left that gaggle of Tickmans alone — simply taken leave, throwing any thought of them into the mud? A touch of shame managed to catch me, indicting my present plan as a dreadful wrong, but the callus was thick. I had taken to the wild just as Ma stepped into her most desperate hour, and yet my heart held some of the blame against her. The only surprise came in how I managed to keep my dishonor from breaking that heart wide open as I skidded down rock onto Granny's little ledge of solace — utterly alone in my plot finally to climb out and be gone.

Or so I thought.

"Reckon you'll think I'm plumb cat-walkin' crazy."

Her voice startled me so, my chest felt like it caged a flapping crow.

"I ain't crazy."

On the outer ledge beside the falls, I spun to find her. Only the haunting of my dead Granny herself could have spoken more a surprise. Twenty feet away — her knees and dress drawn to her chin, shins in her hands, underwear planted against the cold moss and lichen of solid rock — she crouched in a shiver, barely out of breath. Marie Kate had run ahead of me out of the backyard, up the path I had deemed mine and Granny's alone.

The near-emaciated frame of her was so drawn and gaunt she appeared a mere scrap of humanity, blown into that little cleft of rock by the uproar just behind us. The water rolled off no more than six inches from her seat, a whispery flow, in no apparent hurry or dread as it fell its forty feet to more rocks below us. She showed no fear, though only a slip away from certain death. The pocket wasn't quite a cave. More a covered rock porch, whose streaked granite opening caught the noise of the water's crash and turned it into a soothing hush. As she spoke to me, Marie Kate never took her eyes off the shelf where that water took its leap to fall.

"Reckon you're bound to think the lot of 'em has done run me batty when I tell you what I'm a gonna tell you, but I heard it. I swear I did, and I ain't crazy."

She said all that before I could find a thing to say or catch breath to say it — my lungs still wind starved and shock very much at the helm of my thoughts. I managed to grunt a response.

"What the devil you doin' up here? Where'd you come from, Kate? Heard what? What'd you hear? I gotta go."

She answered, the rocky drop still a magnet to her eyes. She appeared as detached and fearless and surrendered as that falling water. As if neither of us had just witnessed the shatter of her father's skull. A low roll of thunder sounded from the other side of the mountaintop.

"'Fore I left for work yesterday, I's on my way up here, Frankie. I'd just board-washed a tub of clothes and listened to them two carry on 'bout not havin' nothin', fussin' on and raisin' ever' kinda Cain 'bout certain colored folk a havin' more than we got."

She finally glanced my way without looking at me, the reddish hair falling in strands of droop. A deep gray showed under the eyes. Her stare, vacant and unreachable as clouds, then returned to the fall of water.

"They was actin' like I wasn't even 'round the place, much less bringin' in money from the mill to feed a few of us." She turned shivery and tearful. "I had to get gone for a minute. I was on my way to come up here just to listen to the water. Calm myself a little. When I left the house, I was so fulla blues I was near crazy, I suspect, and when I pulled the back door shut I said out loud to myself, I said, 'Lordy, how much more? How much longer do I have to live in such as this?' That's when I heard it. A voice come to me."

Her eyes turned and caught mine, determined to have me believe.

"You'll think I'm crazy, Frankie. But I heard it. Clear as that creek noise and just as loud, from over my shoulder, right at that back door, come this voice — a woman's voice. It answered me, plain as you a standin' here right now. That voice said to me, 'Not long.' Clear as can be. 'Not long,' she said. 'Not long.' I turned to look but they wasn't nobody there. Just me and the house boards."

She turned and talked toward the waterfall again.

"Reckon whoever was doin' that talkin' knew what my daddy had comin' today."

Her entire aspect sat in a pale, chiseled absence of regret about what just happened to him. She even sounded a bit freshened and relieved, each word carried on a tone flat and even, as if straight from a sawmill.

"You can't say nothin' about what just happened, Kate." I finally found my voice as I moved a couple of steps nearer to her. "You gotta keep quiet 'bout Ma. I'm sorry 'bout what happened back yonder."

She said nothing, but what she did next rinsed through me a feeling I was living this moment apart from the world — as if this whole day might dwell only in a dream. My cousin reached behind herself into the shadow of that cleft and then skidded Pap's little hatchet toward my feet. Sharp as the axe I had in mind at the shed, yet a quicker weapon in the hand.

"I grabbed it outta the house 'fore I come runnin' up here," she said, barely moving. "I had made me some plans for that little hatchet a long time back, so I had it hid and figured I might need it in them woods yonder after I used it on him. But sittin' here, I figure I ain't fit for runnin' off in no woods, Frankie. You go on now, if that's what you want. I ain't tellin' nothin'. People think I'm sorta dumb 'cause I don't say much anyhow. I ain't sayin' narry word but that my daddy come hard at your mama, nigh to killin' her. I ain't sayin' another thing. Lessen they ask me if he got what was comin' to him, which he did."

Her voice stayed hard. No tears even near. My heart had barely slowed. I picked up the hatchet and walked to her, putting my hand against the top of her head while I wondered what she had been through that I didn't know. I could think of nothing more to say, so this came out.

"Kate, tell the sheriff I did it. I did it, far as anybody knows, Kate. I did it defendin' Ma. He ain't gonna chase me for too awful long if I did it for her." Tears rose, and I strangled them back. She went on.

"Quit your frettin' on it, Frankie." She looked up at me again, a bit less detached from that day we were living. "You and your Ma put food in my mouth 'fore I could earn my own. They'd a been the whole lot of us hungry a lotta the time without you and Aunt Dove. I ain't a gonna forget it, neither. That part I'll not forget."

"I'm goin' on, Kate. You be good. Be good 'n' get outta that mill, quick as you can."

"I said quit your fret. Git on, Frankie. You gonna be just fine if you get over that mountain. Ever' one of us will. Ain't nobody would a blamed you for takin' a wedge to your own daddy's head a long time back."

Our talk against the rush of that creek and a quickening wind lasted little more than a few minutes, but amounted to more than we had spoken to one another in years. This vine of a teenage girl and I had shared a cotton mill spinning room and a farm in silent desperation. Thoughts of escape kept hidden, never passing between us until now. Hearing her had pierced my insides with a calm I failed to decipher, even with the part about voices from the vacant air. More of Granny's nonsense, I figured. I had not figured on the confession that would part us.

Just as I knelt to pat her arm and run on, she bolted up, making her way across the rock face toward the path leading home, turning to look down once more onto me and the spread of the falls.

"Reckon he'll not come slippin' into my bed again, Frankie. He'll not lay his heavy stinkin' self atop me again."

The words felt dense and strong as maple. This girl, bent for years under an onus stout enough to break most men, seemed suddenly lithe and straight and unrepentant.

"My chicken-scratch excuse for a daddy ain't havin' his way with me no more — and Ma knowin what he's done to me on that straw-tick. Reckon I'm done with him now. It's all done but the buryin'."

Her eyes livened, and the look of them seemed to drop strands of gratitude into mine. No celebrating gladness but a glance of sheer relief, the blue stare of her still vacant with shock.

"I killed that man with my mind more times than both a us together can count, Frankie. Reckon Aunt Dove's a better woman than I am. She kilt him just once and kept his own blood-kin daughter from doin' it whilst he snored. I don't have to take to them woods now, Frankie. I'd just as soon take my chances in town." Her face wore some flush by now. "I been fixin' to leave for better 'n' four years, but I ain't a leavin' them young'uns in a mess with nobody fit to care for 'em. This fix I'm in won't be so bad now. Go on, Frankie. Go. You'll find your way through them woods as good as Granny taught the both of us. Get on now, and don't fret it no more. I'll make it work out fine. Fine for us both."

Marie Kate then turned for the climb, back toward the trail leading down the mountain to the place we each had fled, the sway of that red hair the only gesture of a goodbye.

"Sheriff might get every barkin' hound he can find after me, Kate. Make it sound good."

That became my shout after her, likely futile against the wind. I stood in the lonesomeness for a moment, so filled with what the day had brought the total of it slammed a hurt against my head. Yet the grief and fear would help sling me to the wild.

Kate's words had just exceeded my every notion of her father as a scoundrel. A sliver of joy at his death ran through me, followed by a shame-thought of Pap's disapproval and heartbreak at it all. The thought of that man always made me a better one. Stouter. He would disapprove of the run, yet the return of low thunder, akin to some avalanche of rocks no one could see, finally turned me around to go.

In the squeal of mosquitoes and flies drawn to sweat, I took in one final look at the vista from Granny's pocket. The gorge she had spoken of as if it held the very body warmth of her Creator lay hard and terrible in beauty — and was now the only escape I saw from this day. My climb through it surely my mother's only way out of her fix down the mountain. The final look at it reminded me Granny's faith had a place in this world. A sweep and fall of ancient ground — all some portion of her highest church, high with reverence in smoky blue mountain walls. She had told me of its legends, it's hallowed Cherokee, and how such a holy place had killed the strongest of men. How some had never returned from a venture into these mountains. On this very rock, we had talked of mysteries: Who was Lot's wife, why people and times had to die, why life came scarce and hard for some folks while for others it stretched into a long day's leisure. Taking in this same view long ago with me, she had spoken of the biblical Mary, blessed among women, God's favored girl — yet fated to suffer near their boy, see him dead and buried. "Lord sees us through the best and the worst," she said. In her fingers that day she had held a tiny leaf, marveling that a God bigger than the sky could make — and know the place of — a thing that gentle and small.

I started my climb out of her pocket with hardly a grain of my grandmother's faith in things divine. Thoughts fixed on the river and how to get off to a place of hiding, knowing that any dwelling now on what — and whom — I had left would not allow me to go. I had run the hatchet handle through a belt loop, letting it flap some security against my leg. Then I skidded down off the rock, climbing into battle with the first of the laurel hells. The vine trunks thrashed me as if they carried an old malice. By the time I reached the waterfall's landing, I regretted having not jumped off the edge above to finish this journey and myself against the rocks. Had I not feared such dying would feel more like stone than a pillow, my story would have ended unwritten there.

I climbed on, further than I had ever gone on foot behind the farm and the mountain above it, down toward the house-sized boulders — my frame one foot-slip away from a bloody end. The place felt more like doom's weed patch than any sort of Eden by the time I reached the poplars that stood a hundred feet out east of the creek. I had caught enough breath to run, as much as the land would allow, gratefully out of the blade and tangle of laurel. I aimed eastward, gulping air and climbing scarps until a sheer crag forced me to ford a creek into a stand of hemlock. The ground leveled some and turned wet, bogging my boots along a stretch where the water widened and relaxed. After better than four miles, I suppose — crossing a glade of fern, and slipping on the moss of rotting trees over a short ridge — I came down into a patch of little green umbrellas I did not know were a kind of trillium, thick and surreal near the black ground. Bending to rest a moment, I took in their quiet, reminded I already stood far out of reach of the waterfall's familiar din.

"Poorest fool in the world," I thought out loud. "That's what I am now."

Pap's truck, my tobacco plants, the land of two small but worthy farms, the dropped pipe and the Barlow knife Pap had given (left on my night table) — all of it was gone. Gone with my mill job — the clack and sweat of the spinning room more lost with every step I had taken away. All left behind with my hidden money and a soft place to lay my head. Gone. More so by the stride.

The early running set my mind on those material goods, I suppose, to filter out the abandoned faces. It gave emotional survival, keeping my mother's rare flash of joy and Mary Lizbeth's little white grin out of my mind's view. At that stage, dwelling on the loss of them would have stalled the ruse, turned me back. Grief over leaving them tried to muscle its way in, but I couldn't give it room. Not yet. I did indulge a thought about Frank — a warming revenge of finally taking flight from him. Yet even that nearly broke my heart down.

Now in a reliable hike, still forming thoughts on how the trip should end, I learned the August tree cover, hardly allowing light to the forest floor, would not hold off hail. A harder storm, threatening all day, finally poured down in a blinding rant. Roared and tore through the woods shortly after I took a drink from a deepening stretch of the eastward creek I followed. I had just formed a cup from a leaf of Little Sweet Betsy plant — taking some of Granny's teaching about living in the woods. She never told me, though, how thoroughly hailstones can feel like a legion of bees, riled against a fugitive fool enough to run full-stride through their sting. Blowing the higher treetops nearly horizontal, the squall threw a hail fit that turned the air whitish green and into a roar. I stopped under a scrub of rhododendron, its refuge nearly useless against the pelt of ice and rain under thunder. A strike of lightning would show me mercy, I thought.

The cloudburst came and went in a hurry, the clangor of its residue still rolling fresh and cold from the leaves, when I decided I must run again — venturing upward now into an easier patch of hardwood, the swollen creek soon fifty yards below. The soaking weighted my clothes into the feel of carrying armor.

Cresting the ridge revealed more of the same — layers of scarp, one looking steeper than the next, daunting me almost to turn around. I paused a moment. Wiped sweat and caught some breath. Tried to think practicalities.

"Marie Kate'll not do me wrong," I thought, pulling out a mouthful of spiderweb taken in the trees. "She'll tell just enough to save us. Sheriff is sure to give up quick when he figures I killed a useless man who was makin' harm for my mama. Kate and me together can keep him off her. This is the right thing to do, and Mary Lizbeth is bound to forgive it."

I had often pondered loading the truck and making for the coast. I had money stowed. But for every misery running me off — drudgery of the mill, Frank, the Tickmans and all — I had greater reasons to stay: The care of Ma, as much as she would allow, and the aching for another filament's worth of time in the renewal of that emerging woman I knew as Mary L. On that ridgetop, the feel of parting from them finally came, and with force. They already felt permanently gone. I stood in regret of failing to carry my mother out of her life with Frank. Regret, too, of not coaxing Mary L. into that truck to start anew somewhere. I had been too much the coward, deadened by not living. Realizing that raised a new resolve — make the run lead to some new life that would fit me bravely into theirs, or die in the trying.

The sun had emerged, reddening high clouds, when I stepped off that mountain spine toward the layers of green-to-blue wild, sensing a glow of heat blushing through my insides. A feel of panic at the falling light perhaps, or simply the adrenaline of the day — I don't know which. The look of things brought on the urgency to run again, as far as the ridges and daylight would allow. Yet exhaustion and the moist air held some sway. I remember feeling like a clump of lard strained out of hell's own dishwater.

Softened by its fall through the thickness of woods, the sun kept me eastward. I climbed over more ridgelines, crawling at times through a sopping molder of steep ground, looking for the French Broad river from every high place before the day passed any further toward dark. I figured the river would guide me out.

The river's first sighting came thanks to the rant of some crows, where they harassed a falcon near a high jut of rock. They helped me notice it, and I climbed for it, homing to their noise, knowing I could drop down the ridge later to find a creek that was surely river-bound. The way up was nearly as steep as a tree, sodden with old leaves and decay. Wet, black muck soon covered nearly every hair and thread of me. The hatchet came out to help cut and claw me through some vines toward the stone shelf, two hundred yards above. By the time I reached it, expecting snakebite all the way, the day had turned to shadows and my every muscle into rags. Chopping vines and sapling trunks, I cleared a way onto the little perch of rock and its assurance I was comfortably alone. A look back at where I had been revealed no rustling, not even the faintest sound of a sheriff's posse. Only some lingering commotion of those birds, soon to calm.

The river failed to appear from that little knob, but it spread a swath of far greater rock and altitude up the mountainside. A short survey of it brought me in sight of what looked like a great mouth with a protruding lip — a high perch, fit for sighting a long view. To reach it I had only to scrape and bleed my way another steep thirty yards over a solid slick of hard gray, worn by centuries and oiled green with a scattering of moss. From near it a few scrub hardwoods managed to find oasis enough to grow. Hoisting myself up by the handle of their trunks, nearly slipping to plunge off that mountain's high ledge a time or two, I reached the opening of a tiny cave, just deep enough to give pause about entering its gloom.

I rested on that lip for awhile, raw and beyond tired. Nearly five hours worth of thrash and stumble through boondocks lay behind. The storm rain had pooled in a few lower places but sun had returned enough to leave the rock warm against my collapse. The cliff — and the enormous view off it — seemed older than Granny's imagination or her Holy Bible could tell. I reclined on it, still as death a moment or two, watching clouds turn from white and red to gray straight above, feeling the last of the dusk harden the dirt taken on during the run thus far. The hatchet, some canvas-like work pants and a simple cotton shirt were my only luggage — the whole of me lousy now with ticks, grime and briars. That and Pap's watch. I rose to my elbows and pulled its shine from a pocket into the earthy funk of my hand. Twenty minutes after eight.

The rock rose a few easy steps from the cave mouth to a top, and I soon made it a crow's nest to surveil for that river. Sure enough there. Across the wrinkled blue far below and beyond, some amber light glinted off what at first appeared a strand of metal, barely visible in the mountain folds to my left. It was the curvy French Broad, surging on its eastward run, never to tire, and paralleled by train rails bound next for Asheville. I knew I could thread myself to those tracks and on to that greater town, scam some means of earning my way into a worthy life and figure out how to fix what I had left. In the doing of it, I might go on to the coast and the sea of my daydreaming. A place so blue it hurt marvelously to think of it, so large and different I had no vocabulary to wrap around how the imagining of it made me feel. Surely the towns around it would welcome one who's willing to work, help him find some peace and a fine home, fit for the love he would call to his side. It was new and necessary, whatever existed downstream from that river, whose flow lay better than a five mile hike into tomorrow. The sun's rise on the next day would surely make for some better living than the one just now dying away.

Watching the final colors of this day disappear mingled all possibilities with the sorrow the last hours had brought. The horizon darkened into a haint — the great silhouette of a man lying corpse-like, his stillness drawn by the line of mountain crests that were my goal to pass. I turned away, stepping back down to sip like an animal from the little pools of rainwater on rock, more sore than hungry, then surveying my room for the night. One look tempted me to sleep under the stars.

The little cave held true mystery, deep beyond what any daylight had seen for centuries. Not the mere overhang of a boulder that formed Granny's little creek-side pocket. This place startled with its reminders of her story about the woman folks called "Crazy Nance" — old and so poor and desperate and ignorant she walked her toddling granddaughter into these mountains one day and rocked her up in a cave to keep from feeding her. Just walled off the opening with stones and whatever brush she could find, deserting the child to wither into a death overflowing with hunger, thirst, and no hope of fleeing the dark. Dogs scented out the corpse two weeks after Nance began lying about the girl's absence. I stood in the dusk thinking about the wilt and crease of the old woman's face I had seen in an old newspaper photograph taken shortly after her arrest. I thought of how she had finally confessed to her ruse about meeting a dark-dressed stranger on a road and kindly giving him the child to raise. How she had built prison time for baby killing but had gotten out and was still living, well into her nineties, not far from where the little girl perished, better than three miles from the nearest neighbor. If "Crazy Nance" could live through that, then maybe I could survive this day and at least one night in an open little cave. Without venturing so far that I couldn't see the last of the twilight, I crawled into its chops, desperate to meet up with some rest.

The day came so cold the air felt breakable. The coldest day even the grayest heads could recall, talking of it for weeks. A pack of us had piled on Pap's mule wagon, the children smothered in quilts and shivers and a show of good faith. We were party to the goodbye.

Everything outdoors shone silvery white, all the trees wrapped and crackling in the shimmer of frozen January rain atop a snow. Cloth wrapped about the faces kept the ride quiet under the low winter noise. It seemed every branch, twig, and roadside weed crunched against the lightest wind. A feel of frailty came off it, yet I loved the blank white. The way it made that trip to town feel as new as Christmas morning that day we hauled Frank to the Marshal depot. Pap was paying his way.

The railroad trip to a sanitarium in Kentucky would dull his longings for the opium. That sums up the hope we carried. Eb's drowning the summer before had revived the notion Frank could thrive as a gentleman. His too-often vinegar of a temper had turned sweet as honey, flowing about the mourners even before the funeral. Rattling sick with withdrawal, he had volunteered to sit up with the child-corpse at Granny and Pap's house, hugged crying women, and vowed – full of trembles and soft talk – that he would shrug that needle off himself. Only days after we heard Eb's little coffin hit the grave bottom, Frank lapsed into his habit, but he managed to emerge often enough to brace Pap with hope he wanted better.

"If that sanitar'um can get me slacked off, I'll whip this thing, and both of them bootleggers, and I'll not go back. I'd ruther die than live like this. I love y'all, ever' one."

He said as much even as the locomotive blew its last boarding whistle into the cold. With some clothes, money, and his newspapers bound in a pillowcase, he shivered and cried with Ma and Granny hugging him. I stood as a doubting boy, back against the coarse warmth of Pap's coat that smelled of his pipe smoke. The two men shook hands for awhile, Pap saying only, "God's will be done, son. God's will be done. Don't think on money. I'm here to help you." Frank placed his hand on my head, weeping, then boarded the train. We stood freezing until the sound of it disappeared.

After three peaceful weeks around our farms, he returned, eyes clear as a winter night. He took regular meals, talked himself back into work as a sweeper in the cotton mill, and generally behaved himself long enough to make me eventually despise the fact I could not quite hate him. The disappointment of watching opium snare him again seemed to hurt Pap the most.

Gathering my other reasons, I hated Frank for that. Mercifully, Pap died before having to watch him try and fail on his own, too many more times to count.

R est and I could get reacquainted in that cave, I thought, even if it held room for only one. The mouth of it opened more than four feet, the top protruding as if the rock face had buck teeth. The stone gullet narrowed, which I discovered by cracking my head and cursing in the dark. Yet the cave ran deep — black as iron only a few feet in. I crawled back near the mouth, thinking the place felt dank enough to make Lazarus the dead feel at home. Its knobby rock floor fit the day. I reclined on it, craving even the light of a match in the clammy air, and thinking that panic and running had become fine friends that afternoon. They had carried my mind just out ahead of stillness, where guilt and worry have their way.

No dream of escaping my life ever held the possibility of abandoning my mother as I had. But into that cold dark came a tinge of feeling she helped cause this run. I lay suddenly furious with her, letting the weight of it press me deeper into shame. Why had she lost control of herself over him? Why throw such a fit over Useless, of all reasons? Why hadn't we run off the whole Tickman clan long ago? Why hadn't either of us slung a wood splitter against Frank years back? My mind stumbled around in this awhile, then ran into another hard stand of facts: There would be no forgetting a line of Ma's face from that afternoon. Her wail would stay fresh as a new wound in my head. And yet making my bed at the mouth of that cave, I was able to miss Mary Lizbeth as much as I lamented the worst of that day. Perhaps more.

And that became too much. A weeping tore through me. Unstoppable. It boiled off the cave walls and surely flew out into the gathering night. A cry born of places sodden in gore. It quieted only when my strength was spent. Fatigue forced a shadow of sleep to come on. More the oblivion of wear than any slumber, but it was enough to dim my thoughts for awhile.

I woke to a thicker dark. It would have been black, but for a spill of moonlight near the cave's entry. The worries of lying in rough country and with no real tools of survival wanted to dawn on me, but I pushed them back, scrambling on hands and knees toward enough light to read Pap's watch. Eleven minutes after two.

"Lord, what a fit he would have, seein' this mess," I thought. "Pap would want me thinkin' on Ma now. What shape's she in?" I couldn't stop a thought about the red seepage from Ulysses Tickman's head on the ground.

"Lord, God, just in case you are for real, I'm mighty sorry. Sorry for all of it."

I remember whispering that, following it with an out-loud confession that I had little idea what I was doing. Absent a real plan — the night squalling with noises that seemed to out-number the stars — I lay reminded again of how these mountains had killed better men who had carried guns into them.

The only touch of relief came in gathering to mind a few shards of good times. Granny surrounded all of us with reminder that dwelling on the smallest bit of good can ease the hardest trouble. "Help shuck your worries right off. See you off to a right gentle place," she'd say. In the cave's scatter of moonlight, I let a thought crawl from under the crush of the day, out toward a memory stouter than any dream. I had lived it barely three months before, and it came back to me as real as the mineral stench of damp rock in that shelter for the night. So strained a mind, I suppose, will finally seize some rest in the nearest softness it can find.

As odd and even callous as it may seem for my circumstance, that memory rose full of music. Strings. Guitar and mandolin atop the thump of an upright bass, all draped in an alto voice on the verge of soprano, light and soft as cotton yarn. The sound of her stroking the air of a long wooden roomful of Mathison County celebration.

It was the mill's plank-built recreation hall. Ma had practically begged me to clean up and attend Marshal's tradition of Saturday singing on the river. I had dressed in a new white shirt, pressed pants and the pair of like-new seal calf boots Pap had bought through mail order just before he died. For awhile I had walked around the solitude of the main street, taking in the spillage of string music from the hall. I may never have wandered in had the call of her name, and soon her music, not flowed from the windows. From the stage, under a hang of dim, naked lightbulbs, she held me and the rest of that rough-hewn room in the words of "Wildwood Flower." Letting the song soar through the smoke and cedar smell of the room, every note nearly a fingertip raising the hair on my arms. Most of the audience stood rapt — some just staring wonderment at her. Mr. Mackey had introduced her, insisting she rise to the stage to sing "Wildwood Flower" as he had caught her humming and singing it in his store.

"It's like I hired us an angel for a stock girl, by God." He announced it to laughter and applause. "God bless us, this gal is some kinda sweet spectacle."

She had protested she couldn't keep up with the band. Turns out the band, Alton Harris and the Sweet Valley Boys, went nearly dim trying to share the stage with my Mary Lizbeth Hunter.

"Oh, I'll twine with my mingles and waving black hair
With the roses so red and the lilies so fair
And the myrtles so bright with emerald dew
The pale and the leader and eyes look like blue.

Oh I'll dance, I will sing and my laugh shall be gay
I will charm ev'ry heart, in his crown I will sway
When I woke from my dreaming, idols were clay
All portions of love then had all flown away."

The song, much older than both of us combined, seemed to compose itself from within her.

"Oh he taught me to love him and promised to love
And to cherish me over all others above
How my heart now is wond'ring misery can tell
He's left me no warning, no words of farewell.

Oh he taught me to love him and called me his flow'r
That was blooming to cheer him through life's dreary hour
Oh, I'm longing to see him through life's dark hour
He's gone and neglected this pale wildwood flower."

She finished, with reddened cheeks and to a lasting applause, Mackey and several other men and women letting fly whistles shrill enough nearly to threaten the windows. Some of the people who cheered had spoken ill of Mary Lizbeth within my hearing before. Though I saw in more than a few moist eyes some hint they understood a small part of her now. I kept failing to grasp what she saw in me. Why she ever wrapped the honeysuckle of her fondness around such a wobbly post of a boy as Frank Locke, Junior.

Another tune — "Old Joe Clark," I believe — enlivened the room to some dancing on strains of Jess Harris, barely twelve-years-old, sawing his daddy's fiddle so hard he surely put rosin in his little red eyebrows. I sat in the back and talked with Edith Handley, a hefty, sweet widow with what appeared a luxurious set of graying female sideburns, grown from her peculiar way of hair combing. With every sighting of me, she always rushed to compliment my late Granny's gift for crochet, offering condolence even this long after we had buried her. That some young man bothered to listen to her prattle on a moment had bent the creases of her face into near elation. They wilted into a touch of disappointment as she looked past me, seeing someone over my shoulder.

"Beg pardon, Miss Handley. I need to distract Mr. Locke here a minute."

I turned to find Mary L.'s face, still ruddy with the remains of her performance, still demurring its applause.

"Why, you surely can," Miss Handley said, her grin wry and yellow and satisfied that someone would laugh with her. "He better suits a gal with some green in her bones, 'stead of an old stump like me."

"Oh, hush now. I'll not keep him. Just want to borrow a minute's worth of him," came Mary Lizbeth's reply. She gripped my arm and hoisted me to nestle against the long walking skirt and what looked like a man's shirt she wore.

"If you won't ask me to dance, Frank, then I'll get to it myself," she spoke at my ear, just over the noise. Her eyes had come at me clear and light as rainwater, happier than I had seen them in awhile.

"How was it you told me your Pap asked your Granny to dance? I believe somethin' like this."

She backed up a step and curved a pose of chivalry.

"My dearest Mr. Locke, reckon I can borrow your frame for this struggle?"

She widened a smile. Miss Handley launched a high cackle.

"Boy, I'd get to lendin' her that frame if I was you. If I's a boy young like you and a girl that purdy grinned so at me, I'd dance 'til I died and the birds picked me clean."

I yearned for dancing that night about as much as I hungered to join the droning flies at the dance party's back-wall pie table. I went along for the mere feel of Mary L.'s perfect hand. We meandered and I stepped on her through two numbers, saying I agreed with Mackey. "No angel ever let off a finer piece of a song as what we heard from you." She smiled and asked when Miss Handley and I were to wed.

This nearly tore a scrap of laughter out of me but I yanked it back. "I got no time or inclination for any weddin' business," was my overly grim reply, and I instantly regretted the coarse way it came out. Her face stiffened but took no hint of anger. My equally loutish apology came with the end of the secular music. Hats came off for the spiritual songs of the night. Mary Lizbeth's breath came again to my ear.

"I'd like to go now, please, 'fore they get me singin' again. Come with me." Her whisper landed balmy and low. "Let me go out first. You follow about forty paces behind me. I don't want folks talkin'."

Certain I had at least disappointed her, I obeyed. She slipped out the door. I tried to follow in nonchalance, feeling subtle as a bear crossing the room. Just before I reached the door, even over the chords of "Amazing Grace" that had calmed the party, I heard the first gesture of a mouth known to run like March wind. Leo had been waiting.

Leo Blount stood as usual, a large stockyard of a boy whose people owned rich bottomland and grew the largest crop of tobacco in several counties. He swaggered a confidence born of the family money and a frame fit for moving houses. His blond-to-the-eyebrows head, considered handsome by some girls, blended into the neck, giving him the look of a bleached bull, and the similarities ran amok from there. Some of my former schoolmates not many years back had him persuaded that lightning bugs glow because they've sat on the moon.

He waited until I stepped into the May twilight of the porch to launch the full ambush.

"You and Miss Mary Magdalene have a fine time tergether now. Want me to come along, Frankie boy? I hear yer lady friend yonder craves herself somethin' nearer to a man than a boy. More than one man, I reckon, just like her mama. My mama says that gal of yers ain't nuttin' but a Magdalene whore, right straight from the Bible."

I had stopped with my back to him by the time he uttered my name. Mary Lizbeth came running back and yanked at my hand. "Come on, Frankie. Pay him no mind and come on." She shot a grave look of attempted calm at me, but the air around us might as well have turned red. I spoke even before I spun myself into his face, each word low, taut as the twist of fence wire.

"You might give me a whippin', Leo, but if you say another word about this woman, I'll see you bleed right here and now. If I have to crack my own head to do it. So help me."

I must have glared jags at him. He stood a good four inches above me but a little stunned, eyes as vacant as a church on Monday. I waited, braced to duck the metal-hard swipe I expected my next comment would draw.

"Resta these girls around — they're sure to love you after I knock you in the teeth so hard your grin'll look like your butt."

I stiffened more. He moved to shove me. Mary Lizbeth, faster than a match strike it seemed, nudged me out of his face and muscled herself up into it. Pushing her face so close his head thumped off the wall. My reach to pull her back only provoked a tough whisking away of my hand.

"Maybe your mama oughtta turn some of her talkin' time into readin' time with that Bible, Leo. She might come to learn Mary Magadalene showed up at the crucifixion, long after Peter went off swearin' and ever' other man scattered. Don't know about hers, but that's what my mother's Bible talks about. And don't you know that floutin' the friends of Christ might set you on a fast train to hell? Especially the dead. Keep carryin' on, Leo. I feel a warm breeze offa you already. And by the way. Your breath's fit for the part of my goats I have to shovel. You might take a brush to that mouth once a month or so."

He stood quiet as a corpse, his mind seeming to wear itself out trying to keep pace with her. I tried to cut another glare into him as she turned reaching for my hand and dragging me stumbling from the porch to the street, but his eyes never left her. He just leaned against the wall, as if her upbraiding were a windstorm. His mouth gaped so far it could hold a bird's nest.

With no more than four steps under us, Leo came to himself. His voice spilling into the street with the chatter of some people about to come through the door beside him.

"Least my daddy ain't some lint-headed dope dog with a big hole off in the side of his head. Your daddy ain't nuttin' but a dirty drunkard dog. Bet he'd lick hisself if he could."

I tore free. Turned and sprang, seeing him move just as fast toward me. The brawl would have started at the edge of the porch, but my feet betrayed me. Loose gravel and gravity dropped me chest-down in a goo of old rain mud, hardened just enough to stick to my good clothes. Rage seethed, from my head to my left shoe, whose toe I dug into the dirt, braced to uncoil my full force onto him. It would have looked like a fox attacking livestock, but her voice stopped both of us.

"Now Leo, would your fine mother approve a such?"

Mary Lizbeth had darted between us again, fast, but as calm as sunrise, her neck bending up to his altitude. I huffed, cussed, kept the foot flexed to jump from the muck, as she put legs under a scolding that was bound to follow him home.

"Leo, now, we can not have a woman as fine as your mother disappointed by such carryin' on in her boy. We can't have a fisticuff. Why, your mother would swoon, like the queen she is. The talk that came from your mouth is not suited to the child a such a woman."

From my mire I could see an opening. The perfect angle to spear my body through his mid-parts hard enough to drop the whole hulk of him onto that wall. I hadn't thought much beyond that. She kept talking, and I could see his eyes darting to the high mounds of her chest. Leo seemed confused, trying to absorb her flesh and her words at the same time, his mouth still a cavern.

"Leo, do you know what an adulteress is?"

"Adult-ress? Not rightly," he said, smiling now, still pulling at her dress with his stare.

Every muscle I had seemed to tighten toward a sudden move. But to Leo I might as well have been on my hands and knees in the next county.

"I reckon it sounds like a woman what growed up real good and full-like." His grin widened. The leer thrown onto her grew dirtier still.

What came next confirmed what I had long known. Mary Lizbeth's mind was as abundant and finely drawn as her profile, and a good deal stronger than the combined mental powers of the two young men in her life at that moment. More composed than any lawyer, she washed him down in a sea of her own smarts, and he fell into it, bemused and headlong.

"Well, no. That's not quite right, Leo. You see, some words fit only the rarest of ladies. The mature and high Christians of us. Now, it's almost Sunday. And it's time you did this. When you sit down to Sunday dinner in front of your people tomorrow, you raise your glass right after they say the blessin'. You tell your entire family you want to honor your fine mother. You say, 'Here's to my mother, the gentlest and most generous of ladies, and the finest Christian adulteress in ten counties.' And when they ask you where you heard such a word, actin' all surprised that you know it, you tell 'em it just came from a lady who's been on your mother's mind and the lips a her prayers."

Leo's smile had dissolved into the hypnotic mystery of a mind overwhelmed.

"Can you say adulteress correctly for me, Leo?"

Mary Lizbeth carved out the words with the authority of a schoolteacher, insulting him and his mother with such grace he thought it all a compliment.

"Why, yessum, I reckon. Adult-er-ess." His chest thrust out as if he thought he had won her.

"Mighty fine. Now don't leave it out. It's a grown-up word. And your people'll be mighty proud, hearin' you make such a lovin' use of it. They're bound to be."

With that, she glided off the porch, gave me a fairly stern wink as she passed, gesturing that I was to follow. And so I pulled off the ground, out of the sucking mud. To my back rose some laughter, leaking from the gallery of eavesdroppers Leo couldn't see. I ached to hurl a promise of murder onto him, half-expecting him to run out and tackle me in the row I feared and wanted at once. Nothing. After no more than four steps, I turned back to hurl an insult of the large buttocks genre, noting his mother might pull up a couple of chairs and discuss matters adulteress sometime. With hardly a syllable out of my mouth, Mary Lizbeth seized me with, "Shut ups," and cut my arm nearly in two, yanking me down the street. My salvo would have gone to waste, anyway. Leo was suddenly out of sight.

"I'm a takin' you home before you get the both of us killed," she said as we climbed onto her wagon. She urged the horse away and down mainstreet toward the bridge, the wagon jangling into the dusk. In the humiliation's afterglow, my ill temper and my tongue soon got together again and beat the gentleman in me senseless.

"You didn't have to get in on my fuss back yonder. I woulda got my licks in on that dull blade. I woulda took me a fist and dotted one of them eyes of his."

Mary L. answered kindly, which made me regret my harsh self even more.

"That 'dull blade' mighta made a dot outta you. He's bigger than that horse, and not worth a wink's worth of your time or mine. I'm just disappointed in how I acted."

The reference to my losing the fight just made me mad all over again, so I quieted into a sulk and felt small for a few hundred yards, and she said nothing more. No sound but the August evening bugs and the horse and wagon on the switchback curves leading up the road. I planned to get out at the turn to my house and walk on home, lest both feet find my mouth again. But just before we reached it, I let fly another regrettable round of commentary. This time reducing my dignity to a speck of chicken feed.

"I don't need narry girl defendin' me, that's all I meant. That's all I'm sayin'. I've took care a myself this long. Reckon I'll be fine without a girl doin' my arguin' or my fightin'."

Instead of raising her hackles, my bleating pride caused Mary Lizbeth to confirm herself a fine-hearted grown woman at the age of seventeen. She stopped the wagon and pulled my defiant chin toward her face, cupping it in fingers hardened by work but somehow velvety in their deeper parts.

"Well, now, what happened back yonder makes both of us able to defend one another now, does it not? I'm not sayin' a thing about you, Frankie, 'cept I don't want you hurt. I just wish I hadn't showed him my tailfeathers. That's all. I know better than to fool around in a head like Leo's. He'll talk and make other folks talk — even more than the ones that heard me."

"Well, let 'em go. Let everyone of 'em talk," I said, fixed on the regret washing now onto her dark lashes. "Gossip's like a clock. It's gonna go 'round no matter what. Even in your sleep. Ain't no sense tryin' to stop it. Fact is, you shut Leo's bean hole for him. Shut him up good before I lit into him."

Parts of that felt about as courtly and romantic as a mouthful of stale cornmeal, though the words did swab me with a mild pride — a feeling I had done something modestly wise. Like some of her goodness — and a touch of her recent polish — had somehow flowed over to my side. Traveling home without her I would have fumed and dreamed of taking a stick to Leo. Now, I had all but forgotten him since her hand had reached out to mine. It had been awhile since I swelled with the notion I had actually said something in the vicinity of halfway not stupid.

"Well, I said too much," Mary Lizbeth nearly whispered, squeezing my hand hard. "My mama always said when your heart breaks, let some love out or get out. I shoulda just walked away and dragged you with me."

"Leo ain't deservin' of no kinda love. Not a talkin' about you or your mama the way he did. He ain't gotta right, and I'll not have it." I caught myself nearly at a shout, echoing through the trees.

"Hush now." She put those same fingers to my lips. "Shush and listen." Even in the near dark, her eyes appeared to glow into mine. Still wet enough to fill a Mason jar. The first falling drop brought a flood.

"All the times you've come up to my place to help butcher a pig or haul me some thing I needed or we went fishin' or what have you — not a one a those times did we ever talk about what happened to my mama. You know why, Frankie? 'Cause you stayed polite enough not to go pryin', askin' me if the town talk is true."

The truth was, every moment she had just described, regardless of the chore that had drawn me to it, had bathed me warm with a thrill at being simply near her — any thoughts of prying and gossip drowning under the elation. She turned, rein-strapped the horse, kept driving and talked on.

"You will never know what it means to me, Frankie, havin' a fella not care if my mama lived honorable in her life or died a proper death. And I never brought it up when we's together, 'cause it felt good for a little while, just livin' a life fulla you instead of what all's happened to me and Mama and all people say. You got no idea, young Mr. Locke, what you've done for me, do you?"

They flowed like tiny creek water now, drenching her sleeve. She swiped the tears, leaned against me and lay wet fingers against my face. The brushing touch, a trace of her salt tang in my nose, the moistening air of coming night — all of it stilled me, including, with good fortune, my tongue. I couldn't seem to take in the fullness of how good it felt to live that moment beside her.

"Frankie, ever since you thought enough to offer a piece off your mother's bread-makin' to that little pile of filth I was in the schoolyard, I have chosen you, Frankie Locke. You had little choice in that. I chose you. Put you down into my bones. Made you every bit a part of me as the legs that grew under me. Nobody, includin' my mama, could tell me a child couldn't love another one with all the love a heart can make, 'cause I did. And I still do. You got no idea, Frankie. And I can't find the words to tell you about that kinda love, other than to say you pulled me out of a trash hole. Mind and all. You did it, and right then I chose you to be loved the resta life by me. I never thought I'd love somebody more than I did you in that schoolyard, with you takin' all that tongue off the rest for givin' me a bite to eat. But I do. I do love somebody more. Somehow I love *you* more now than I did then, Frankie. I'll not lie and keep it to myself. And no matter how mad you get, I'd rather die than see somethin' bad happen to you."

On her embrace I took the reins, letting the horse clop on, and pulled her into my left arm. We sat against each other, her crying as she had over every word, until I pulled back the horse at the turn that would have taken me up past the church and home. Mary Lizbeth reached again for the reins.

"You're not goin' home with that street dirt all over you. Not after defendin' me. You're comin' home with me." She smiled at me, wiping at her face, and I paused, finally mustering some words, if not wisdom.

"Let's go, 'fore it gets plumb dark."

Satisfied I hadn't kicked *both* feet into my mouth again, I kept watch on the surety of leather in her small hands. Her urging of that horse pressed us up the road, long past that turn to the place of my birth, moving toward the ramshackle place where Mary Lizbeth Hunter had come into the world. The tiny cabin — center of townsfolk speculation and imagination — where she had been left by two parents to raise herself into the world.

Mary Lizbeth flowed tears much of the way up that mountainside, and I found keeping my mouth shut the best cloth to absorb what came with them. Through the better than three miles of tree-canyon road, which narrowed to little more than a trail toward her place, a history of her I didn't fully know poured into the early night's balm. I had heard only hints of it and the lies peopled gabbed.

"Frankie, my daddy didn't show the decency to slip away in the night. He made us watch. Made us watch him leave." She took my hand. "He just told her one mornin' he couldn't live with us anymore and left on a horse with my mama runnin', grabbin' at him and the horse, too. She'd nearly took a hoof to her head. Lord, how she screamed after him, draggin' at his leg on that horse and beggin' him not to go. I's no more than four, cryin' after her 'til she finally fell on the road, and he disappeared. Not one snatch of a look back."

In all our times together, we had yet to talk about it. The brief story I would finally view through the eyes of the child who had lived it. It was the truth of a young mother abandoned and broken from the inside out. Her fierceness of independence kept company with bouts of the most grim brooding and oddity. She tended to wander, sometimes half-dressed, into town, acting like a mute — or just cutting herself away from life, disappearing for long swaths of time into that cabin. Going weeks with hardly a gesture toward her own child.

"Mama managed to scratch out a little food from a garden, trade a little goat's milk for some cheap meat, but she'd take no charity, Frankie. Lest it just show up in the middle of the night, which sometimes it did. I took to wanderin' these hills just lookin' for somethin' to eat sometimes — just like some little Indian. I could hunt with a homemade blowgun and a slingshot by the time I was six."

I knew most of this already, but she had turned talkative and I adored to listen, no matter the content. Mary Lizbeth went on to say she might have taken permanently to the wild, were it not for the mill school teacher, Miss Evans, riding up personally to take to school what she deemed an intensely bright child nearly lost in a crust of dirt. "Sometimes the lunch Mama put in that burlap bag I carried to school was nothin' but a handful of chestnuts I had gathered myself. Mama sometimes would come to herself, cry and make me promise not to tell how hungry we got. And I was never to speak of that anonymous box of food that would appear on the porch on some mornin's."

I felt her on the verge of speaking of the town's harlotry talk and the mystery of the time just before her mother died, but we had pulled into the yard of the tiny cabin. I had given little thought to how I might get home, and I didn't much care. Listening to her seemed the finest gift I had ever given anyone, and the journey's end struck me as a perfect time to test my untrained legs as a gentleman. And I ventured far beyond their vigor, jumping off and running to her side.

"Miss Hunter, would you kindly allow me to help you down off your carriage?"

I offered up my hand. She smiled and pretended to need it.

"Why, Mr. Locke, I'm most pleased and honored."

I helped her off the wagon, eventually with both my hands wrapping her waist. It felt like touching some rare and sacred place.

"And call me Mary L., kind sir," she said as her boots touched the ground. The thick heels raised her slightly above my height.

With my inner places molten now by just the touch of her, I proved an eternal truth. That a boy's adolescence, deep within him, amounts to no more than a whiskey party of devils. They will stoke fires bound to smoke up his good sense and scorch him with red-hot embarrassments. Let an attractive woman come within four hundred yards and the party roars. I will forever despise those demons for convincing me the timing was right to bow. But bow I did, then dropped to one knee, kissed Mary Lizbeth on the hand and, needing only a suit of armor to complete the nonsense, I capped it all by opening my mouth again.

"A pleasure, ma'am, havin' my frame borrowed by a fine lady such as yourself. And it were no struggle a'tall, dancin' with you. You sure are a powerful fine specimen of a woman. Lady, I mean."

With the feel of the words reminding me of a comment Pap might have made at the stockyard, I was certain no man ever said — or did — a more foolish thing to court a woman. The whole of it seemed a bouquet of poison ivy. I braced for a bath of laughter, but she just smiled and pulled me up, placing my hands on her waist again, and moved so close her breath kissed my mouth.

"Let's go in the house, Mr. Locke. You could use a bit of fresh'nin'."

She moved from me, and I tied the horse, figuring it a waste of time to put him away, for I would soon need a ride home.

Through darkness collecting fast in the thick woods, a final gesture of sun glowed against the little cabin, which I had visited fairly often but never entered. Every other time I had been there helping her with some chore or just chatting about little things that would lead to a tapping kiss or two, we had never plumbed the wells of what hurt us. My contempt for my home life never rose to conversation. We had become each other's relief, I suppose, and resolved to put off any taint of that as long as we could.

Now on her porch, I should have resolved to remain upright. Soon following her by the hand, my left toe stubbed a risen board, which sent me faltering nearly to stand on my face. "Don't break your neck, boy" she said, laughing. "It's gonna get darker 'til I find the light."

She unlatched the door and we stepped into the cabin's steamy black. It smelled just faintly of old wood and kerosene mingling with a sweetness I failed to identify, other than it reminded me of how purple grapes taste. I heard no fewer than three door bolts, one of them a chain, being latched behind me. "Light's comin'," she said. Soon an oil lamp's glow dissolved away enough dark to reveal a room that didn't fit the splintery exterior. Homemade quilts and crochet-work draped all over, even from the walls. The furnishings sparse, old and hard, but softened by neatness and little canning jars full of fern fronds to freshen the eating table and rock hearth. Against the chimney stood an axe that appeared new and never outdoors, and beside it two homemade dolls. A boy and girl in formal-looking clothes. On the table, beside the light, an orange butterfly with dark spots lay displayed atop a little glass egg timer. It looked like a perfect work of art that had never been alive.

I could barely see her from where she bustled around and spoke near the kitchen off the back.

"Hand me the clothes."

The realization she meant mine doused heat through me. "I'm fine," was my retort, as one might reject an offered tin of coffee.

"Don't get all bashful on me, now. You don't work with the dead and not see just about all there is to be seen."

That reminded me I stood in the home of a notoriously tireless prodigy of a girl, who had been a woman most of her life. Instead of quitting school as I had, she was about to finish. When that teacher, Miss Evans, needed help putting out the town's little newsletter, she recruited Mary Lizbeth. Mackey took her in to work as well, claiming the store needed a young female touch to stock womanly goods. Mary Lizbeth studied, worked those part-time jobs, made a considerable garden every season, tended and milked her late mother's goats, canned and traded tomatoes, okra, and corn with mill people too strained by work to grow much. And amid all that, lately, she had taken on one more chore. When Lem Bookman, the funeral director, had asked Mackey who might assist with the laying out of female bodies, doing hair and such, Mary Lizbeth accepted the job and the added gossip about a girl living alone and being into too much. For some people in the town, both the women of this cabin just seemed disgraceful somehow, even the eldest in her grave.

"I'll give you all that's dirty, but I'll need somethin' to put on."

"Well, there is plenty of dirt on your fine self, thanks to that Leo." I could feel the smile in her voice. She threw me an off-white quilt that smelled faintly of dried fruit. Behind it came a wet washrag rubbed in store-bought soap. "I'll not look while you wash up. Now throw the clothes. I'll not get 'em overly wet. I'm just gonna shake the worst of the mud out."

I retired to a corner, as far out of the light as I could get, and obeyed, stripping to my underwear and buffing off my face and hands with the rag. Keeping the clothes nearby, I had just wrapped the quilt around myself when I felt her behind me. Turning around revealed what looked like a living statue — Mary Lizbeth's long tan neck flowing toward shoulders barely covered by the white abundance of a man's shirt, more draped over her than worn, the tail of it meeting her bare legs at the knees.

"Are you ashamed of yourself to be in this place with me, Frankie?" She gave me no chance to answer. "I sure hope not, 'cause this place feels a lot more like home with you in it."

Her arms slid around my neck. Before I kissed her, she pulled back.

"It occurs to me there has never been a decent man under this roof, Mr. Locke, 'til you. Not one decent man 'til you. I am mighty glad you're the man of this house right now. It has surely hurt for one."

With that came only the third kiss of a girl in my life. Everyone of them had been shared with this same girl, but this moment differed. For a young woman, her words may seem aggressive and lascivious on this page — they surely would to the town of that day — but her eyes held only an overflow of lonesomeness. She had given in to its sweep and flow, and I eagerly joined her.

I had first kissed Mary Lizbeth far better than a year ago, in a setting that amounted to a strangling chain around the neck of romance. I had come around on a freezing day to help her kill, scald, scrape and carve a pig she had raised — all skills my Pap had taught me. Soon after the worst of the gore — when we had merely meat and no image of an animal — I turned and kissed her wind-chapped face. My move doubtless as graceful as a three-legged dog, yet she surprised me by kissing in return, and on the mouth that day. It was so cold the air felt blue, but she tasted of July — some briny, warm sweetness I could not quite believe. It surprised me much the way I always lived in awe that honeysuckle flowers grow their nectar from what has recently been hard winter ground.

This night felt different. The kiss felt new. Fresh as a sip from a good spring.

Every movement, even the slightest, quenched a deep longing in both of us. The tangling of hands, then mine across her private places — all of it finer than a thousand favorite tastes rinsing through a mind.

The kerosene lamp filled the room with the color of sun through honey — the cabin's features dim through the dusk heat. Just enough light for our eyes to sketch each other without fully seeing. It felt as if we yearned each other downward, her arms wrapping my neck, mine bracing her about the middle. The kiss lasted to our knees when her lips gave way to a sigh that reached her breath to my tasting. I spun with her, falling backward, feeling her pour over me, the quilt open and under us now, her long lines stronger than the muscle of river current, both of us still in some salty skim from the sweat of the dance and the warm-weather ride. She rolled under me, legs and arms and all of us knotting together, and in her soft clefts I hid myself from every other awareness of the world. Every kiss a tremble, the chagrin of nakedness against a girl I had known most of my life quietly drowning in the dampening heat of her.

The breath grew. Heavy wordless speech. Gusts of her breath, feeling stout as storm wind against my face. Then on my chest. Her hair splayed its darkness over me, soft as the brush of a thousand moth wings.

Without very much trying we together carved my body into hers. She shrilled a high sigh, a note almost of pain but in confluence with joy, as she rose again, her legs wrapping the low part of me, and we barely had to move. The gold of lamplight revealed her looking onto me, mouth open, body slowly yielding to the depth of where we joined. Her hands joined mine against her thighs, mostly covered by the fallen flow of her shirt. Suspension. Just before the taut portions of each of us gave way. Motion. Her mouth wider, eyes closed now. The sound again. Not quite pain. Then a smile came to its full bloom. The one I have placed above the mantle of my mind to hang through this lifetime. Mary Lizbeth's perfect, sweet-birch-scrubbed smile bit into her lower lip with a force that pushed us so deep into one another, no one would ever bury me without a large part of her.

I lifted her with my lower half, at my very brim, when she raised to fall across me, her pulse a force against my own. Her breathing quieted, cottony across my face now. I lay in a blind of her — covered in hair, muscle, and easing heartbeat.

The rest we took soon found its way to that place where the gentleman should say things tender and enduring. I kept silent and absorbed the light flickering off the roof planks, thinking how it seemed to glow the color of the woman atop me. Any word, even a sliver of thought from beyond the cabin, would intrude on the bliss of hardly discerning my limbs from hers.

I soon learned the rock that had been our friendship lay forever changed. Opening to each other as we had amounted to cracking open a geode, letting light spill in and out. The translucence of its insides much more fragile and complex than the surface. Feeling Mary Lizbeth's nakedness shudder against me confirmed we would never see only the surface of one another again.

"Hold onto me, Frankie. Please." She slurred a little, her face wet again at the cleft of my neck. She had hidden it against the rub of my hand across her hair. For the first time since we were children, when I gave her a bit of food every school day, I felt like the stronger one.

"Frankie, I'm sorry. So sorry and 'shamed of myself. I know what you must think of me. You must think it's all true."

She raised her eyes to mine before I could speak, revealing a sadness suddenly reflecting the day we buried her mother.

"Frankie, you have to believe me. God's my witness, a stack of the world's Bibles under my hand, you are the first. You are the only man I ever had in here." She looked down again. "I'm too 'shamed to show you, but I could prove it to you. You have to believe me, Frankie. Believe me, and please don't quit your care for me. Even though you're yet to tell me you love me back, I believe you do. And 'cause you do, I'm beggin' please, don't tell a soul about this. It'll only fire up more of what Leo said. I hear it nearly wherever I go, and it's wrong. Please, Frankie."

Her crying tried to rattle contagiously into me, but I fought it.

"Sweet, I ain't sayin' a thing. Narry one thing."

I was about to say more when she gestured toward the shirt. Without falling fully away it had gathered about our lower reaches and crept between us where we twined. She reached for it with an urgency I found worrisome. "I'll be back," she said, raising herself off me.

"Come back now. Come on back." I could muster no better plea as she nearly disappeared outside the lamplight. She finished wrapping her lower body in the shirt on the way, not looking back. "I'm not goin' far. Lay still. Or light the stove. I'll bring us a bite to eat." Her words came in soft waves from the dark where she busied herself in the cabin's back side. I heard the wooden shuffle of chiffarobe drawers, then the back door clack, and she was gone on a goodbye of, "Be back, sweet boy."

I lay on the now quilted floor, my man-boy eyes still deep with the impress of her bare form. The entirety of naked womanhood too much for them. But they had managed to read the dark red message written on that white cotton shirt. The light had offered only a glimpse, but it was a simple truth composed in a streak of blood. The view of it as dim as my knowledge of female matters, but clear enough to say what we had done had indeed been the first time — and for both of us. Any notion of otherwise would not enter my mind, apart from fear and guilt I had done something horribly wrong and harmful to her. My mother's warnings about the dangers posed by girls would not fit the woman who lived in this place. Not that I tried terribly much to make Mary Lizbeth wear them.

The thought of somehow cheering her broke the spell of caring what Ma might think. Resisting the urge to stammer around outside to look for her, I opted to obey, fumbling around the cabin — wrapped sweating in the quilt, stubbing more toes and nearly dropping the lamp before finding some kindling and matches to fire the stove. I planned to cook up this late meal she had in mind, making myself into a show of devoted help. But time soon set off alarm. When Pap's watch, ever in my pocket, revealed she'd been gone at least twenty minutes, a fright came on.

Just before I launched an expedition of rescue, some feet scraped the back porch. She came in carrying another lit lamp. I ran to her from the place where I had nearly worn a rut in the floor. "Sweet God, girl, I's scared witless for you. Where'd you go?" I said, fearing my relief failed to land as gently as it should. Having shaken some of the dirt and reek from the clothes I had never given her to beat clean, I had dressed and worked my hair down with my hands — the whole of me surely resembling trampled ground.

"Did you give up on me? Didn't mean to stay gone a dog's age, but I thought I'd give us a speck of privacy. No girl wants a man to see her fix up."

She carried a little hand mirror and comb in one hand, having dressed someplace outside the cabin in a simple dress, bluish-gray, crisp from a clothesline. The dark hair was swept back and bundled into a wide spray. In the other hand, a little metal bucket dangled with some eggs and canned homemade sausage sealed in wax. Her voice held its usual light, which had drawn me to life more than once. Yet joining it was the omen of a woman with weight on her mind. Far off her full state of, "I'm better than all right."

"I missed you and was about to come lookin'," I said. "I'm ready to do us some cookin'." I supposed the best way to deal with my own nerves and foolery was pretend they didn't exist, even as they surrounded me, as real as the walls.

"Cookin'? That a fact?" She grinned but let it melt quickly away. "In a minute. The fire'll wait. I wanna show you somethin', Frankie."

She put down the bucket and led me by her lamp into the dark of the cabin's north corner, where the light fell on a bed that had been made so long the blue and white quilt on it held dust. It was a corn-shuck mattress, holding a body form that did not appear recent — the imprint deep enough to hold a shadow under the light. Mary Lizbeth looked down at it as one might gaze at a holy place.

"On the floor where we were, Frankie. I make a quilt-pallet and sleep there. I've gotten used to it." She took my hand tightly in hers without looking up. "Nobody's been on this bed since my mama died, Frankie." The light aspect of her dimmed. She turned shaky as a leaf against hard wind. "It's time I told somebody what happened to her. What truly happened. And time I stopped treatin' this bed like someplace she'll come back to one day."

With that, Mary Lizbeth began unraveling one of the fattest yarns of speculation and gossip the town and mountains around it had twisted together in our lifetimes. The focus of it the only man more revolting to me than Frank Locke, Senior.

"He looked to me like a devil dipped in coal dust." That's how she began describing the man who had stolen his way into town. The initials A.C. amounted to the only name he would give, and the infamy of him spread into the steepest and outermost fringes of life around Marshal, soon after he scared some hooky-playing school children wading in a creek below the depot. They told of a starved-looking creature in a black coat, dragging his left leg as if it were dead. The lank of him bent under a wooden box strung for carrying on his back. He had, without doubt, rolled out of a freight car, made a camp near that branch, and loitered about town asking for jobs "a crippled man might do." In a grimy flopping hat that had once been tan, he hobbled around, grinning a yellowy creep all over people. Under a straggling curtain of dark hair his face came off boyish enough to give a whiff of innocence, but a complete look at him told of something wretched and hard, parts greasy as an old frying pan. Yet it was his left eye that sent children running. It wore a skim the color of bloody milk from some injury or disease and gave the impression it had soaked up the vistas of hell. Some days, as talk went around town, he'd show up around Mackey's store porch claiming the first World War had chewed him up. Other times he claimed polio of the spine killed his leg. Regardless, the choice of whether to pity, despise or run off A.C. became a town conundrum.

"He started followin' us," Mary Lizbeth said, still staring down at that bed. "If I went to town with Mama, which didn't happen that often, he was somehow around, wherever we'd go, grinnin' and askin' if we had any knives that needed sharpenin' or carpentry done. One time he slipped up on us and stroked my hair outside Mackey's, and that just sent Mama into a fit, slappin' at him. He just laughed and ran off, vowin' to marry one of us some day."

I knew that shooing A.C. away, as if he were some common animal pest, became a chore to many. He clung to a habit of appearing at clotheslines to caress women's undergarments as they dried. He would stand in yards, stroking the cloth that held private female places, letting it waft onto his face, hurrying away that foul leg after he lingered long enough to get caught. People would chase him off with Mason jars and anything else they could find to throw.

His voice drawled the sound of a much larger and older man. The words slurred together, though I never saw him take a hard drink. My only real conversation with A.C. happened on one of my boyhood Saturdays as I led a little jenny mule through town, trailing a homemade wood cart full of the new Nehi Cola drinks I had just bought at Mackey's. A.C. had stepped from behind Mamie Walter's boarding house, undoubtedly a reliable place for a handout and panty-stroking.

"Yo, boy. How's 'bout lettin' a po' ol' boy have one a them dopesy-colas offa you." The sudden sight of that milky eye above tatters of beard and dirt and the dark coat startled me into handing him a bottle of grape Nehi without a word. "Why, now, that is awwwful gen'rous, boy. You're a mighty good boy. More power to yuh," he had said, stumbling off behind Mamie's place, the stink of urine lingering after.

More than the notorious panhandling and loitering around female laundry, the grin had always shot a chill through me. Even as a boy, I understood why railing women would chase him and swing broomsticks, and I wondered why most men merely made sport of mocking and laughing at him. I suppose A.C. gave the town the same lightweight creep that makes Halloween fun — full of tales and mystery and what seems a harmless stunt. What Mary Lizbeth was about to describe had changed everything, though. It had stopped the laughter at A.C. and set off a symphony of gossip. Only Mary L., her dead mother, and one other knew the full story. I was about to join them.

"I never thought he meant real harm, Frankie. Never thought he could get up here, and to this day, damned if I know how he did."

She glanced into my eyes a gravity I had never seen on her before.

"Come here."

She pulled me to sit with her on the bed, in what felt like some hallowed way. "Frankie, you know how I used to be as a girl. I walked all over and lived off the woods and I was nasty 'cause I never thought about takin' a bath when Mama would take to this bed for weeks. She just couldn't get herself up, and would lay here and cry and sleep and sometimes just stare at no place a thousand miles off, with me feedin' her a bit of meat when I could get it, or some oat gruel with wild chestnuts in it when I could get her to take it. She'd been barely out of this bed for better part of a month when I came off the ridge behind this cabin with a sack fulla squirrels I'd killed with a slingshot. I was thinkin' how I'd roast 'em with some pole beans somebody had just left in pity on our porch. I'd been gone a good spell. Too long, I thought. I walked with a bad notion in my bones that evenin', Frankie, and I knew why as soon as I came in first sight of this roof. I could hear it, from way up in the woods."

She spoke by then in a smolder of remembering — the vacancy in her eyes detectable even in the lamplight. I said nothing as she went on.

"I ran into that back door, thinkin' all the way some animal had gotten in here to her. Lord, Frankie, she had already screamed until she nearly couldn't. She squalled and fought at him with her fists and feet, but he held her down. That's how I came in and found it all. He had her stripped down nearly bare, wallowin' all over her. On this bed, him holdin' her down yellin' for her to hush up and her kickin', and the sight knocked me dumb. Froze me. I took and threw the biggest and hardest thing I could grab. A little iron pot from the kitchen. It landed right between his shoulders, so hard he fell off her to his knees. Then he turned on me."

Hearing this aloud felt like walking from a foggy dawn into the fullness of day. Each word a new clarity of her — a schooling in what a heart can bear — wedding us to a trust for life, no matter things to come. I held both her hands now in part to ease myself, soon to learn there was no brace stout enough for what would follow.

"You'd never think that stiff leg of his could bring him up through the woods as fast as it did. He came huffin', yankin' up his britches after me, carryin' on about not meanin' harm. I just ran, Frankie. Ran right outta one of my mis-matched shoes. I never even dropped that squirrel bag. They beat dead against my leg. I climbed on and pulled away some, but he kept comin'. Me knowin' I could beat him on foot. But I was scared crazy."

Heaving sobs had taken her.

"I never planned the harm I did. Never, Frankie." One set of her fingers set my hand free and dug into my leg. "I's just a girl. And I knew what I'd seen amounted to some awful wickedness my mama never wanted, Frankie. And if he'd do such to a woman not fit to feed herself half the time, Lord only knew what he had comin' to me."

She caught some heavy breath, shuddered, then lifted out a load of grief and guilt the hearts of many men could not carry as ably as she had since that childhood day.

"I let him stay close. Led him straight up the ridge out back."

Mary Lizbeth had lured A.C. into giving chase, his usual gimp in a fast drag. Upward through the tree-bristled ridge behind that cabin, the child had led him. I imagined her in the chill sweat wetting her clothes — every root, ledge and pathway mapped in her mind.

"I shook all over, but I had my wits. Lord, don't let me ever get that scared again. I was so scared it tasted bitter in my mouth. I had to keep him close enough so he'd stay after me. So he wouldn't give up and go back. And he kept on, huffin' and beggin' all this guile about just wantin' to sit with me a minute. How I was the one he'd come to the house looking for. Sayin' he had a sweet candy little girls wanted, right in his shirt pocket. And me runnin' on outta this hollow up toward the one place I had in my head."

She told of the ground steepening toward the crest — nearly a straight vertical rise. So much so they climbed exposed tree roots to cross it, wrestling the undergrowth. He drew near enough to take a grab at her foot. The grip failed to hold.

"I tossed that sack a squirrels at him. He was so close I smelled the sweat off him, so I hurled that sack. It thumped him square in the face, but barely staggered him. I figured on gettin' him lost, Frankie. Lost in some woods I knew so well I'd named some of the trees. Get him lost long enough so I could run back and get Mama in the wagon and down into town, but I couldn't get out ahead. So I hatched me an idea, and damned if he didn't follow me right into it."

Her idea had risen from an old and enigmatic place she had long ago made into a playground, nearly a mile above the cabin. She composed a bit, stiffened, as she described climbing into a clearing, where the ground leveled out hard, A.C. slowing but still behind her.

"I grabbed a hand fulla rocks and chucked 'em down at him. The littlest rocks you ever saw, Frankie. Dirt you couldn't kill a butterfly with, but I hauled off and I flung it at him. He's no more than ten feet down that ledge and climbin'. Pieces of it flew straight as a jack pine and caught the top of his head. Didn't even addle him. But it gave me some run time."

I have never ventured to see this now-awful place. Her talk of it formed the image of a bald of split rock, rimmed in trees, slanting westward to a long and nearly sheer drop, then railroad tracks below. That bald held the place she intended to hide out of his reach. It became one neither of us would ever fully escape.

"Frankie, anybody ever tells you a girl child can't set sights on doin' a man harm, don't you believe it. But I never planned on it endin' the way it did."

She told me of the mystifying crack in the place. The ground that formed that bald lay split, deep into a zigzag of narrows that a child could traverse. But a man might trap himself in the clean break. Slip and tangle himself long enough to buy her some escape. Centuries had passed since a force stouter than a child's imagination had chiseled it open. Mary Lizbeth had played in and around its dangers for years. She knew the way down into its ledge work.

"The crack was my only hope, short of a fistfight with him. He had to be near to climbing out of the woods, but I never looked back. I ran to that crack and slid myself in."

I imagined its cold near-entrapment. She told me of fighting not to make a breath sound, listening for him, already better than four feet down.

"When I looked up, he was already there, callin' me."

Her voice curled into a mocking disgust.

"'Hear now, girlie. Come on out. I'm jus' a po' ol' boy what don't mean harm.' Frankie, it was like he could sniff me out. Like I was bacon and he was a dog."

She said he thrust his face down at her, trying to catch her and his breath at once.

"I'll never shake it," she said. "The way he oozed down at me. Sayin' I was his little gal. That I needed a good stout hand. I figured he couldn't reach me. But before I could climb on down, he took a swipe and I felt the wind off it. He strained and grabbed down at my hair, and I let out a yell. I mean I bawled, and tried to wedge deeper into that rock, thinkin' I was bound to fall to its bottom. And he got agitated. Carryin' on about a demon gal. I don't know why, but I've reckoned he reached too far in after me then. Next thing I knew, he fell. So close his head grazed my leg. And I'll never forget the racket he made. A crack sound fit for a big wood fire. He let out a wail I never knew any man could have in him. Made the verge of vomit come to my mouth."

Grazing rock on the way down, A.C. had fallen, floundering into a twist. "He let off a yowl," as she recalled it, "like some scared little boy." She had watched his head bounce and scour off the side before the narrows caught him, trapped, no more than four feet below her. Most of his lower parts — the hampered leg — had disappeared into a dangle out of sight. The breakage sound had come from the better leg, wrenched upward and broken behind to his back, grotesque in its bend.

"It would've been a mercy for him to run off the edge and meet the train tracks," she said, with both my hands in hers. "Better to fall all that way than get trapped the way he did. He nearly got me, but that rock just about tore his good leg off him in two pieces."

Even then, she jolted at the noise that rose off him. I could nearly hear it myself. A scalding of the air from a man hopelessly dropped into what surely felt like a tomb. I've always pictured him as some human rag doll contorted by a child. The thought of it — of her seeing and having to live with it — bristles my nerves to this very hour. That, and how Mary Lizbeth trembled, nearly shaking the bed, as the reliving of what followed A.C.'s fall poured from her mouth onto my chest — the heat of her breath dissolving into the muggy dark. She judged it a miracle he had failed to pull her down with him.

"Listenin' to him cry that way just sent nails through me, Frankie. I clawed my way up and out, and that's when I caught the full sight, lookin' back in. That snapped leg, and him just about hangin' by the bloody skin, and Lord how he cried, Frankie. Lord God A'mighty knows I never wanted such."

"Mary L., don't tell me no more. They ain't no use in it," I said, trying to pull her eyes to mine. She glared on at the dying lamplight, the oil nearly gone. Most of the room had turned to black ink but for the fading lamp and a touch of moon, sifted by trees and the kitchen window.

"I left him, Frankie. Just left him to hang and scream. I's all tangled up in cryin' the whole way back down to the house, scared witless of where I'd been and what I'd find where I was headed. I ran the whole way, fell hard once on the steepest part. I flew in that back door with that same feelin' of some terrible sight. That's when I found her. Her and a house fulla chickens. They'd come in the open back door, peckin' and trackin' blood...."

For the worst of the recollection's flow, Mary Lizbeth wrapped my shoulders in her arms and burrowed her head into my neck. The release of it yanked hard at both of us, for the whole town knew the surface of the news about to come.

"She was gone, Frankie. Down at the edge of this corn-shuck bed. Just thrown down, nearly naked. Disgraced, and gone. There was blood all over, Frankie. Blood smell and all that red all over her. He'd opened a little Barlow knife on her, and when I knocked him with that pot, he musta sliced at her. That or she did it. She mighta picked it up and dug it into her own throat, Frankie. We can't tell. But I know it was too much for her to take, what he'd done, and I figure she was sick about lettin' him get after me. I found that knife in her left hand. And there was no takin' it back, no matter what happened. My mama was gone, Frankie. Nearly cold by the time I got back. Finally all the way gone."

"Hush now, Mary L. Quiet," I whispered through her hair. She wept out of control for a time, then pulled away, wiping at some renewed calm that had found its way over the look of her. She sat up and looked at me again.

"Frankie, now you know for yourself there's not a gnat's worth of truth to any of it — all what people's said about her. Some folks go and flout somebody with their religion when that somebody just looks like she's sinned worse than they have. Mama's mind was in no shape for livin', much less for carryin' the ugly talk around. All of it started with one or two tongues, waggin' on about Mama sellin' herself — and me — for money. All some people saw was a woman with a fine-drawn form and a weak mind, and they made sport of talkin' up nonsense. I don't know what tomcats they figured did the buyin' of what they thought she sold, but they sure loved to carry on about slatterns who knew no better way to eat than to sell theirselves. And one of 'em a child. For the longest, I never knew what all of it meant. She tried to keep it off me."

At the sharing of this, Mary Lizbeth seemed to surge a tranquility that comes from telling a truth too long held back. I winced back tears and glanced off, determined not to let them wash away the feeling I was some worthy man of the house. We lay back on the bed, silent for a moment — as if two parts of a single broken heart, resolute to heal. She was composed, almost herself again.

"I wiped the blood off her face, best I could, held her and cried all over her awhile. Then I quit cryin', and I went to work. Ran to the spring and fetched water. I stripped her and washed her clean, and sopped up as much blood off the floor as I could find rags to hold. Then I picked her up myself. She was limp and heavy as wet clothes, and I'll never forget the sound. The last wind of her breath came out while I pulled her — gentle as I could — onto this bed we're layin' on, Frankie. I straightened her, and the more I worked, puttin' on the best dress she had and fixin' back her hair, the more my insides boiled."

The small-handed grip, so mild most of the time, clamped my left hand as she went on, telling me I had to know this. The two of us, on our backs now, lay cast off to the full advantage of the room's near dark. She dwelled as much in the recollection as in our time.

"Some night was comin' on when I left this house. I left out that back door, same way he chased me. Right outta this room full of my dead mama's quiet, past goats that needed tendin' and everything that had been our life in this place. I walked, calm as could be. And my head fulla somethin' I started thinkin' on while I soaked up her blood. I went to the shed barn and got down a rope, and I went straight for one metal can I couldn't get off my mind. It was so heavy I doubted I could carry it, but I did. I came back to that kitchen porch, wipin' the slop from my nose but not cryin' so much anymore. I soaked one of the blood rags in some pickle brine. Soaked it good, then fetched a box a matches off the stove and stuffed my pocket with it. I took a long drink outta the spring, and that's when I set out walkin', back up the ridge. Me with that rope slung over one shoulder, swingin' that pickle rag in my hand, and that heavy can jostlin' against my leg. It nearly pullin' my arm outta the joint. Straight back the way I'd led him, I carried all of it with never a thought to turn around. By the time I hit the steepest part of the climb, I could hear A.C. bawlin' again."

The lamp's last glimmer had died of fuel thirst by now, the spillage of moon just enough to chill me with the notion the cabin walls had stood around the corpse, and that the very bed we lay on had held it. Mary L. rested her hand on my arm now, telling of her walk back up that scarp, the salty blood smell on her clothes, with red streaming down both legs — her own blood from where the rocks had gnawed into her knees.

"I wanted to see him. I looked down at him and just listened, Frankie. Listened to him moan and mutter about his daddy and make no sense, apart from hurtin' about as bad as a man can. It was a terrible thing to look on, him all smotherin' and that leg all scraped back and twisted. No way out. If he coulda gone on through, he mighta hit the ledge under it, then dropped what felt like a mile into the treetops below that big rock break. No such mercy. And do you know what? It made me glad, Frankie. I sat on that crack ledge and bounced my feet for a minute, listenin' to him beg me, all meek like. 'Lord, please, gal, go git help. Lord help.' Just hearin' him hurt made some part of me feel a tinge better. I am so sorry for that now."

I stroked her face. "Mary L., you ain't gotta tell me this. It don't matter," I said, thinking of nothing else to comfort her while I waited, in some fear, to hear the rest. She said again I had to know and confessed on, nearly as if I weren't there.

"I tied the pickle-juiced rag to the end a that rope and let it down to him. Dropped it on his head and he managed to reach up and grab it. 'Take a drink,' I hollered. 'Take you a good long soak in it.'"

I know now these were the acts of a child fractured by trauma, but at that time, hearing her recite what she had done jarred me nearly into fear of the woman with whom I shared that bed. She told me how her head felt hot on the trip back up the mountain. How it had spun full of a day's meanness and panic and her mother's years of tirade about devils who had crucified Christ. From all that, Mary Lizbeth's mind had forged a justice that day. An answer to atrocity in overflow. That afternoon had brought forth a little girl's revenge, born of her mother's fascination with Roman soldiers offering vinegar to the dying Jesus and deserving the same they had given. Deserving their own hell. She had sat on the rock's edge and had given the only devil she could see that day his own dose of brine. What she gave him next might have shaken chills through a hangman.

"He knocked away that pickle brine rag and squalled out a yell. Sounded just like a child fresh from a whippin', and then he cussed me. And, Frankie, that's when I took that can to him."

My wondering about why she had trudged a heavy can of water back up that steep ridge melted now against the truth. It was a can of lamp oil, likely from some of the charity- minded who thought to help a suffering mother and child.

"I soaked him in it. Poured that can almost empty. Listened to him scream and cuss and beg. I had pulled that rag up and soaked the rope in kerosene 'fore I poured it — made what I thought might be a fine wick, which I dropped on him and started strikin' matches to it. It scares me witless how good I felt listenin' to him beg and pitch a fit. I soon figured out that rope wouldn't burn enough, so I went lookin' for some leaves or whatever. And that's when I found his hat, back on the trail. Don't know how I had missed it. God, how it reeked of him. He had quit hollerin' so much by the time I carried it back onto that rock. I sopped up what was left of my kerosene, balled it up some and tied it to that rope. I lit that hat afire and let the burnin' stink of it down, real slow, right on him. He bawled — dear God, how he bawled."

She paused and rolled to me, pressed her face back to my chest, squeezing me nearly breathless and drawing her knees up — curling into a living ball of crying shame.

"The noise he made reminded me of the last time I saw my daddy. That day I watched Mama beg him not to leave, and him shakin' her off that horse without a look back. And that's when I blamed him. Just then, standin' on that rock with my mama newly dead, I thought it was all my daddy's fault. About the time A.C.'s shirt whooshed into fire, I just knew I hated my own daddy more. I blamed him for Mama breakin' down the way she did. My daddy not bein' here had let that awful little animal of a man do what he did to her. And that's when I tried to stop it. My daddy had set his own fire of lonesome against Mama, and I didn't want to be meaner than he was. So I started to yank up that rope. But I was way late. He was on fire, Frankie. Screamin'. When that hat hit that kerosene it was done. Fire ran up in his hair, and the smell doubled me over sick. All I could do was run. Turn and run, sorry as I ever thought I could be. I thought to pour water on him but that ridgetop is dry. I looked back just before the trail, and all I saw was a gray smoke curlin' outta that rock break with the worst misery you ever heard, Frankie. I couldn't do a thing but run on. Run back to my dead mama, feelin' like a smear of outhouse dirt."

Mary Lizbeth quaked against my neck by then, her embrace and confession twining into a force near suffocation.

"Frankie, I burned that man alive. Burned him, and I was nothin' but a child, and I pray you won't hate me for it. Don't put me in a hell of not lovin' me for what I've done. Sometimes I still feel like a born devil. Please don't leave me for it, Frankie."

"I ain't goin'. Hush now. I don't wanna be anyplace but where I am."

"I just lost my mind," she said. "Just took leave of my better part. That's all there is to it. I should never have wanted him to die the way he did, but I was crazy mad."

She drew back. Paused a moment. Some of the moon tried to seep between us, though its light failed to show me her eyes. I could feel her trying to read me through the prevailing dark.

"What A.C. did was the ugliest thing I thought I'd ever seen. But my mother's mind died way before she bled to death. She withered for a long time. And it told me plenty about the meanest kinda evil on earth, Frankie. It's not gettin' mad or hatin' somebody. The meanest thing a soul can do is just not care. Make a soul feel she's no better than dust and hard ground. My daddy did it ever' day he didn't come back. So I suppose he's just as sorry a man as the one I killed. And now I trust you with it, Frankie. You can't speak a word of this. I trust you to keep it. And keep sighted on some better part of me. The part that loves you 'til I ache, boy. You had to know all this, and now you do, and I pray what I've done won't lay me in your dust. Miss Evans said it woulda been a miracle for me not to let some meanness carry me back and do that man harm. And she said there'd been enough miracles that day. She claims I'm one of 'em, and I ought to live up to it. Frankie, I need you to help me in that. Help me feel like a lady who's forgivable."

The knowledge that Miss Evans knew of this rang like a spoken gunshot in my head. It hit me with envy that I wasn't the first and only. I held Mary Lizbeth for a time in some quiet awe. No thought would compose into clear words, though I held to the notion that if a hand could condemn her for burning A.C., it might as well point at me. Attack my every fantasy of Frank Locke, Senior lying still in his coffin. Since boyhood I had cultivated thoughts of a bloody death for him. How death would sand the coarse parts of him off my life. I had long felt deserving of torment for such thinking and was sure my guilt glowed as hot as Mary L's.

Her crying throbbed down to a state of near collapse — that priceless and curative rest of setting free agony too long held. For a long while we talked of what happened next — of the hours and days after she turned away from the smoke and anguish of A.C. and that gap of rock. Her manner eased, but still flooded the room with a candor as real as the dark. She told about the chill of lying sleepless beside her mother's cold body that first night, expecting heaven to smite her dead for fiery murder. She had stayed in the cabin two days, hungry and dehydrating from a vigil, drawn to simple gazing at her mother's face. She said the expression — even in the color of cinders — sent an odd peace running through her. I still shudder to imagine the wreckage of it. Mary L. in the company of a gory dead woman she had loved and shielded with childhood care. A mother finally fully gone.

I lay with her also trying to figure how she had hidden such a secret behind a life that spilled joy into the world. No one would have guessed the true scandal. I remember kissing her hand before I asked why she had dared tell Miss Evans. She raised from the bed — her long curls in silhouette against that moonlit kitchen window across the room.

"I had sense enough to take some help, Frankie. No sense allowin' death to get contagious. I was young and shocked, but not a fool," she said. "The lady cared for me."

I knew they shared a two-way communion in that care. The reek of the corpse and the dishonor of the flies it drew had finally sent the child walking down the mountain and through the town. She appeared at the cotton mill schoolhouse — a bloody and stinking twig, widening every eye. She walked to our class door and said only, "Mama's dead. I need help." As a boy who had yet to quit the school, I had witnessed part of that. That and the funeral — hearing only rumor of its cause until now.

Since then Mary Lizbeth had lived a prodigy's life, between the cabin, Mackey's store and Miss Evans' home in town — where that kind woman tutored her, deeming her a gifted child worthy of shelter from schoolhouse clatter. The whole county talked about a child left with a putrefying corpse and a floor full of blood. People carried theories the death was a homicide. Some guessed it the suicide of a woman overcome with the shame of harlotry, presuming A.C. had disappeared from town without killing her. They supposed he had gotten what he ultimately wanted: A wallow with the town's most peculiar woman who was imagined its only whore.

Mary L. splayed across me again, the grief slackening, as she claimed Miss Evans didn't know this part.

"I never went back up that ridge 'til a year after we buried my mama, Frankie. I went tremblin', but I had to go. I carried a handful of wild ferns and some dogwood flowers I knew where to find. Part of the rope was still draped across that rock, the can was where I let it lie, but apart from a splatter of black down where I left him, A.C. was gone. Best I can tell, he rotted off down into that crack, and I guess animals dragged off the bones. I started to climb down toward the ledge to see, but I didn't have it in me. I left the blossoms and ferns at the edge, and I've never been back."

"Why'd you never speak up for your Ma when folks accused her the way they have? I couldn't stand it, listenin' to what you've put up with."

It was the only other question I would ask during Mary Lizbeth's confession to me. The answer brought light back to the room. She rose and felt around for a big Bible on the hearth. Feeling her way again through the night, she filled and lit the lamp and returned, wiping at her eyes.

"It's time I let you see one more thing, Mr. Locke," she said, thumbing the pages.

"Plenty of folks have looked at me and seen what they wanted. But you see more than they see. Always have."

She plunked the book open onto the bed and carefully pulled away a red maple leaf that had been pressed and conserved as a bookmark over First Corinthians, chapter 13, the words underlined in heavy pencil. Standing over me, she recited out loud.

"'Though I speak with the tongues of men and of angels, but have not love, I have become sounding brass or a clanging cymbal. And though I have the gift of prophecy, and understand all mysteries and all knowledge, and though I have all faith, so that I could remove mountains, but have not love, I am nothing.'"

"Frankie, Mama always wanted me to read this Bible, but Miss Evans set me to doin' it, and out loud. This is one of the first things she read to me the few times I slept at her place after Mama died, and it reminded me of you. Reminded me of all the times you were sweet to me. Back when we were too little to understand how much it could mean. So I've read this piece nearly every night, marked with this leaf. You know where this leaf came from?"

She gave no time to guess.

"I picked it up not long after you first fed me in the schoolyard, Frankie. It was the most perfect color of red I'd ever seen, and I kept it because I wanted to keep the way you made me feel. This leaf reminds me about the best love in the world. The kind that loves what it can't see and never minds the fits people raise. I love my mama that same way. And in quiet. I keep her off other people's tongues, the best

I can, 'cause gossip tongues don't have eyes for the truth. They won't honor who she was, no matter what. So I keep her to myself. Just the way I keep this leaf in Corinthians. And you in me. Miss Evans always says, 'No matter what a body's done, you'll not stop the good Lord from lovin' the soul in it.' I will never get over the way you've loved all over mine. And the way you're doin' it right now."

She misted again.

"You are God's man for my days, Frankie, you know that? I figure if there's a God who might love my daddy and A.C. and even me, with all I've thought and done, then God can will himself to live in human hands."

A smile cracked its way through. She slackened her own sorrow.

"I've been mostly on my own since I was a sprout, and never would have made it without some fine hands reachin' to me. I believe there's some stout God in your hands. Yours and Miss Evans', too."

With that, hers took mine into a hard squeeze.

"That lady taught me a prayer, and it helps me live with myself. Said she learned it from a grandmother who'd taught slaves how to read."

The idea of prayer didn't rouse me much, but I nodded to hear it because it would come from her. That, and my fascination with Miss Olivia Evans. She had sprung from Alabama's lingering cotton plantation refinement. The bearing of a queen seemed to breeze off every step. The woman stood more than six feet, if the measurement took in the stand of gray-streaked black hair, wound above a face cut in patrician angles. The skin looked flawless as a formal teacup, even in older age. In school most of us could scarcely believe her tales of luxuriant upbringing — full of milk baths, and chocolate from across the ocean. Her drawl resembled ours as much as a lit pipe smells of smoked ham. When she spoke, long ribbons of Alabama light seemed to stream into the air. As a young teacher, Olivia Evans had brought some of her daddy's money to the mountains on a mission to shine light into isolated minds. When she found Mary Lizbeth, the mission expanded from teaching children to the attempted raising of one, even with Mary L. vowing to live most of her time in that cabin.

Facing me now on the bed, Mary L. closed her eyes without a bow of her head to recite. I sat watching her, taking it in, brimming with the thrill of hearing her more than any words thrown toward heaven.

"'Lord, alive in my heart, I make a mess of your quarters. Help me sweep the rooms of my soul down clean again. Forgive my thoughts that won't wipe their feet. And for your graceful broom, taken to my filthy parts, I thank you. Amen and amen.'"

"That's right sweet," was my only review as her eyes opened onto me. It seemed the best — and the safest — my faithless heart could manage. Her aspect had turned hopeful, and I wanted it to stay as she talked on.

"When Miss Evans started takin' me down to the Presbyterian Church, I was scared. I figured it a matter of time before I made the walls shake down and fingers of the devil would wrap my neck. And she seemed to know it. One day when I was sick with a cold at her place, she told me the Lord has more use for love than religion. She told me to say that prayer to remind myself I can never get too low to be loved. I've said it so much now, it's nearly carved onto my tongue. It's my little poem of grace. And you are my graceful boy, Frank Locke."

Hearing that balled up my mind as if it were tangled trot line. What I knew about grace amounted to Ma's friend, Gracie Parris, a farm woman known to challenge boys to contests of spit distance. Her mouth could manage a tobacco gob nearly the size of a kitten. I thanked Mary L. for the compliment, called the prayer sweet again, and kept silent — figuring not to complicate the moment with my ideas that any part of that church business could protect a man about as well as Eb's rabbit's foot had defended him against drowning.

And then, I was alone on the bed. Mary Lizbeth, having restored that leaf to the Bible, was suddenly gone. She sprang to the porch and brought in a crock of water and we drank from the same cup. Her body draped beside me again, long enough to wipe her eyes, then mine, and let fly a touch of laughter.

"I can sure light up a room, can't I? Even with a light on, it seems blacker than a well bottom in here." She touched a kiss to my neck and spoke with it there. "You're never gonna want to come in here again, me carryin' on this way. But I'm thankful you did."

I let her mouth linger, then spoke, pulling her weight onto myself.

"Mary L., neither one of us has had it easy. But you've took what would have killed three men and made some good livin' out of it, and this whole county can't believe it. That's the whole reason folks carry on so much about you. They can't believe some orphan girl that shoulda starved half to death growed up to be just about the most handsome and smartest thing ever to set her feet to ground."

I was stroking her face, deeming myself courtly, when she raised off my chest and gave it a sounding hand thump.

"'Handsome'? What woman do you think wants to hear she's 'handsome'? I am not your Granny, boy, Lord rest her. You'd better be glad I take so fine a shine to you." She rapped my chest again where her head had lain. "And what do you mean by, 'just about the most handsome and smartest'? And, who you callin' a 'thing'?"

I suppose the sudden lightening of mood testifies to the peace our childhood times had made with hardship. Fresh on the heels of all she had told me, Mary Lizbeth and I wrestled around on that bed, laughing after I surrendered to her punishment. We kissed some more before I got up vowing, again, to cook for her. In the dim light, groping to fire up the other lamp, I skinned both shins over a chair and crashed headfirst to the floor. That broke a dam of laughter from both of us, and it flooded the tiny home. We wiped different tears as she helped me up. Late adolescence had won the night.

Working together, we fried eggs and sausage on the woodstove and ate them in lamplight. We talked of train rides and far-off places, then lay in rapt quiet, near slumber, on the bed. Judging from the experience, the tiny mattress had lost the sacrosanct gloom of her mother's final hours above ground. Mary Lizbeth announced she would no longer take to the floor-pallet of quilts, where she had slept since her mother died, unable to rest on the bed. She claimed I had made the bed new. A home. I felt some achievement, hearing that.

I pondered spending the night, but feared somehow scandalizing her and taking a reprimand from Ma, so I left for home, a quarter before Pap's watch hit midnight. The mule was still hitched, so Mary Lizbeth drove me the three miles down to the cut-off to the old farm that held my bed, the bright half-moon the only light keeping us on the road. On the way she talked of wanting me to leave the mill and join her with Miss Evans in the private tutoring. How I could finish school while helping her teach the younger children who needed it. I answered with piles of cliché, filling the muggy night with inflated argot of farming and thread-spinning and the good business of tobacco. Anything I could think of to expand my manhood in the view of this woman I knew no ten men could deserve. We arrived at the cut-off surrounded by optimistic talk, the time alone together a fine armor — secure around both of us, on guard of our dreams. I savored all of it. Everything drifting into my nose from the night and the woman beside me, her hand and forearm moist against mine. In the slowing clops and scrapes of the horse, some thought of what shape Frank might be in when I got home penetrated the moment. Dug its dull edge back into my mind. But the sound of Mary Lizbeth's last whispers proved more than a balm for the wound.

"Thank you, again, Mr. Locke, for seein' a lady to home." The words floated from her perch on the wagon seat. I remember thinking her every word came out rich and gentle as baking aroma. I had gotten down, and she bent to kiss me. I held a long time on her tiny mouth before I pulled away, taking her face in my hands and pressing my mouth to her forehead. Few chalices of communion wine ever witnessed such a reverence.

"You gonna be well, gettin' home?" I asked, squeezing both hands in mine.

"I'll be fine, sweet boy. I'll be more than just fine. You get up that road quick, now. And if you dream a sweet dream, tell it before breakfast so it'll come true. Dream one for me, you hear? Dream a sweet one for the both of us."

I vowed to see her tomorrow, detesting the moment our fingers parted, and stood listening, waiting for the wagon's jangle to dim after the dark absorbed the last sight of her. The clack of the wagon faded to reveal the place where she had left me — the creek whispering under the little wood crossroads bridge, the cool of it rising into a bouquet of mountain water and wet earth reaching deep into my head. I stood a moment, proving a truth about darkness. It will draw fear from children, and even men who live tossed in its mystery, yet the primacy of the blackest night will bow. It holds no power under the memory's light of a woman, ever fresh in the heart of a boy, no matter his years. I live that proof even now.

Thinking of how little she really needed me, I set out walking under tree-limb shadows cast by that half-moon. On the way, sniffing my shoulders, sleeves and hands for the slightest aroma of her. The rustle and buzz of the woods never even threatened fright, for my mind still drew life from Mary L.'s breath. She dwelt as much inside of me now as she did on a wagon rattling on the road home.

I paused at the churchyard cemetery — its tomb rocks a hushed thicket of hoary grays. Not even the murk of death could cloud the clear joy I had taken in this night. A brief pondering of Mary Lizbeth's mother, Corrina Mae Hunter — asleep in unmarked clay just off the road — made me swear a silent oath to a dutiful life. A vow to earn the precious gift that shattered woman had given the world. I understood now why Mary Lizbeth had long ago told me she wanted no marker for her mother's grave, even though Mackey offered to raise one. It would raise more hurtful babble than blessed thought. In my view, Mary Lizbeth lived as her mother's monument. No stone would hold so fine an epitaph.

I dared not step in, but stood looking at that cemetery as never before. Let the quiet pool in my eyes and float an old memory of when so many folks busied themselves with the burying of Miss Hunter in that still-unlabelled grave. The same grave Ma so often dug at with her eyes. The Presbyterian Church women, kindly talking of how they were slain with sympathy, had gone around collecting money to buy Mary Lizbeth's mother one of the finer caskets, full of soft bedding and satins. Even as a child on the day of the funeral, watching Mary L. sob against the dark dress of Miss Evans, I had thought of how much too late the comfort of townsfolk had come.

With the moon nearly straight overhead now, thinning the dark, the grave markers invited my thoughts beneath the grass. Deep into the well-dressed world of rotting humanity reclined under my feet. It was, I thought, the most foolish thing I had ever heard of — wrapping hard wood and soft cloth around the dead, especially those who had possessed so little in life. Every stitch lying damp and cold in the dark, each thread counting for a kindness left undone. The whole of it serving only to ease the worst kind of guilt among those of us still above ground. I stood thinking of how I had never seen Eb look nearly so polished as he did in the clothing and box bought for his tomb. And to this very night, I regretted never telling him he, as a boy, amounted to the only true man of his household — even if he had needled my nerves worse than a blister.

In that thought, I vowed it to myself again. I swore to make some part of me count for some scrap of goodness among the living. I would live as well as I could before I lay down there in that silken hush of the dead. The woman I already longed for had shown me to the path.

I carried that idea on up the road, through the dim pewter-color light and the gentle drowse of night woods, and tried to recall her eyes. At the dance, Mary Lizbeth's mildly drooping gaze had very nearly glowed, bright green and warm, giving off the look of still water reflecting early June trees. Any recollection of the near row outside the party and what folks might say — all that faded in my head like photographs under summer sun. Leo's nattering bulk amounted to no more than a bit of paper blowing around a chicken yard. It didn't matter that Mary Lizbeth's wile had kept his knuckle bumps off me. My mind overflowed with her — so much so I'd fight ten men his size to win her. Though I confess — I did entertain the idea of Leo home alone, ponderous in his bed and maybe full of wonder toward his sleep, thinking about just the right time to seize upon Mary L.'s advice and regale his mother in the title: "Adulteress." I was sure he would try it, all fluffed out and rooster-proud until he felt the smack. I loved Mary L. all the more for that one.

Walking the final quarter mile to the house, not knowing what I might find, I felt a touch of sympathy pierce through me. The opiate that had gnawed Frank down to a scatter of bones must feel in some way as good as what I had known this night — the thrall of a woman, who held me under her influence even now. I didn't have the words at the time, but knew I wanted nothing more than to yield to the yen of her, soak in her depths, slay the worst of myself to bring her joy. If opium felt half as sweet as Mary Lizbeth, it was nearly a shame to hate Frank for wanting another dose.

Twenty yards beyond the flint rock step, I could just make out Frank on the porch. The moon wouldn't reach that far but the front window carried faint light from the back of the house, enough to silhouette his head, slung back over a chair top. I paused just off the boards, taking in the emaciated whole of him. His devotion to laudanum, in any form he could scam it, by then had left him the human equivalent — most times — of an old laying hen. In such a state — all droops and sags and reek — I found him, asleep in a rocking chair. He adored that porch. A few times we had sat there together in warm afternoons and talked of the professional baseball he had read about in the Asheville paper. Now he slumbered on it, looking like a ghost of the nearly starved. Even in that humid night, my mother, with no small care, had tucked an old sheet about him again — holding off what she called, "chill of the dew." I remember thinking no one else in ten counties — save the bootleggers — would have drawn near enough to him.

Rather than roust him I tiptoed around the house, took off my boots, jammed in my shirttail and slipped through the back door, expecting the reprimand a boy earns from his first time catting around half the night. My mother, with her face sideways on a pillow of her crossed arms, sat at the kitchen table in a waste of kerosene light, her breath in the slow tempo of deep sleep. Yet no more than three of my sock-footed steps woke her. She seemed to feel me in the room.

"Lord, Frankie, honey, what time is it? You had me scared half to death," she whispered, relief and anger creeping all over her. She sat behind a newspaper spread full of dried corn she'd been working toward hominy.

"I'm fine. Wore out," I said, trying to keep moving toward my bed. "Ain't fit for a thing but sleep, which is where I'm goin'."

There was no escape.

"Where you been, Frankie? I lit out hollerin' for you like some fool up the road when it got to be ten o'clock. I's afraid some varmint carried you off. I was about to go jostlin' out toward town in the truck a lookin' for you." She spoke in a prickly hush. I was louder in changing the subject.

"Why's he asleep on the porch, all wrapped up again like some orphan baby left at Christmastime? And how'd that winnder get broke?" I pointed toward the pane of hanging glass shards behind her.

"He never meant it. Never meant to do it, Frankie, now, he's been quiet. He just stumbled out of his chair at supper, is all. He ain't far off from leavin' this world, honey." With that she looked down, sadness and disgust wrestling for their places alongside the sympathy in her voice. "Shush now. Don't wake him up. Your daddy's not a well man. He ain't well a'tall." She stood, pulling back her hair, and stepped around the table toward me. "And the last thing I need to worry about is you, Frankie. Please don't you start layin' out of a night on me. Not with some mess of filth."

That chafed, and hard. I wasn't sure whether she aimed the filth indictment at certain delinquent boys, with whom I mostly cultivated a mutual loathing, or at some imaginary harlot from the dance. I pointed toward the front of the house in a raised whisper.

"He's the only worry you got, Ma. No sense frettin' over me, 'cause I know better than make myself into some damned fool pig. That damned devil people call my daddy would gag a maggot on a dung wagon. And if I catch him foolin' with you again, I'm gonna put me an axe in him enough times I'll have to dig ten holes to bury the pieces of his nasty hind end. Nobody would miss him but them three or four dope hounds hangin' around that road crew at the river, pretendin' to work. I oughtta kill every damned one of 'em. And myself, too. Nobody would miss me, neither."

Setting foot back into that house had shattered the spell of where I had been. I know, now, I pulled out that suicide talk just to cut loose some pity for myself. Seeing Frank, then that window, and hearing Ma defend him had set my tongue into a hard swing at her. Just as fast came a shot of guilt, pushed by the disappointment that covered Ma's look back at me, and the notion Mary Lizbeth would have shared it, fresh from our kiss up the road. It all washed my insides in a cold regret, which incited my mother to speak a truth I could not deny.

"Well, just look right here. Your daddy at his worst." Her voice crept out wobbly but determined. "Right here he stands, right in front of me." A finger point came nigh to my nose. "Only difference is, your daddy ain't so mean when he ain't all jagged up, wantin' that dope. God, don't be like that, honey. You ain't gotta be like the worst place your daddy ever lived."

Arms slipped around me. Forgiving. Ma's face pressed into my shirt. Held there, as if its nearness might soften the hammer of my heart.

I realized the fit I had thrown had emerged in a voice I longed to silence forever. The tiny kitchen's walls might as well have spat the echo of Frank. His rage had bounced off them, yet from my mouth. In a back room of my mind, I had feared somehow becoming him. For years I had fought to keep him out of me — Granny, Pap, and Ma herself lending aid and reassurance. Standing now with my hands around my saddened mother, I felt Frank Locke, Senior's worst demon had won. He and I occupied the same piece of human clay after all. Together we formed a sinking grave my mother could not escape, even before she died.

Just after I grunted some apologies, she arrived. A nearly unidentifiable woman seemed to take possession of Ma's being. From my shirt drew back a face defiant of the usual melancholy. My mother, suddenly different. The change proved a woman's heart is no simple creation, marked only by lines of where it's been broken. It is drawn more in pages of music, every kind of harmony and disharmony in lyrical highs and lows. A symphony far above words. Never fully mastered.

Ma moved away from me faster than she had come, her mood suddenly much lighter. She raised her bottom onto the table, rested back on the heels of her hands and swung her feet, jaunty as a child with an all-day sucker. Her mouth and eyes turned up a mildly derisive smile. She stared at me.

Before then, apart from some photographs, I had never seen my mother resemble the person people enjoyed remembering out loud. It was very nearly not the Dovie Locke I knew, looking at me from that table. Instead, she seemed the faraway girl, who had been Granny's tall and slender pride — bright and lithe, with an elegant bearing that rose through the early pictures. She draped in front of me, suddenly not so stooped and worn. I stood flummoxed, then tried to make a point without flying back into the rant.

"Well, ain't nothin' but some hard worryin' to be done around here still," I said, wanting to turn toward my bed but held, a little frightened, by the change in her.

She looked through me a moment.

"Know what your Pap used to say, Frankie. He used to say, 'Keepin' worry in your head is like hoardin' change in a pocket. Gives you somethin' to hang onto. Gives you somethin' to do, to jangle around, but after awhile it just weighs you down. Don't do a bit of good for you 'til you get rid of it and let it go.'"

I stood thinking Ma lecturing on worry was akin to a prize milk cow complaining about the stink of a mule. She stared on at me, twisting her head, and said, "Come here a minute."

I complied until her feet rose to stop and hold me. From this girlish repose her eyes seemed to magnify the toss of my hair and the crumple of my clothes. Her feet grabbed and pulled me closer. She rose toward me, shining hints of a grin into my eyes. She gave the shirt a sniff and rub.

"I'm tryin' to figure which little snot-nosed girl you've been loved up with tonight at that music party." The grin fully evolved, then vanished. "Don't matter much, long as you don't plant your corn in somebody's field before you're big enough to raise it. And don't say you don't know what I mean."

I said I did and tried pulling away, still in some wonder at this spirit who now occupied the often reticent and lately grim woman who had raised me.

"Sit down a minute." Her foot shoved me toward a chair, quietly enough not to penetrate the slumber on the porch. I sat and she talked and I felt like I heard my mother for the first time.

She talked of a father — and in many respects, a mother — I had never known. How Frank Locke had suffered more, worked harder, and deep down possessed more uncommon intelligence than any man she had known. How the war denied him the chance to show a son the heart that had won his mother's. She reminded me of how he had grown up with the scar on his face, wearing it and the scorn of the world "strong as a bull and gentle as a little bird." In cadence with the swing of her feet, still seated atop the meal table, my mother reclaimed a man. He lived in her voice, untouched by the trenches and stings of France. A man unmarred by the injustice of Ulysses and Mattie Tickman, the calluses of road, mill, and farm work, and times that chafe and harden from the inside out. For her, in those moments, he was but a boy, full of prospect, whose feet of clay had yet to stumble and break him down.

My mother, through that reliving of him, rose from the mire of her life, lifting herself into tender and young love again. She talked a long while, until fatigue of her shift at work that previous day faded some of the wonder. But it had made her briefly new. I had sat in silence, buoyed by the marvel of it, until we hugged and she urged both of us to our beds, never hinting that Frank — in his current form — should take rest anyplace but the porch where she had tucked him.

I lay awake until the first motions of dawn were but a nod or two away, pondering what the night had brought. I dropped toward slumber, finally awake to what brought on Ma's change. On my shirt, she had caught whiff of no girl, but the spice of young womanhood — unmistakable and fresh on the shirt and now scenting the days of her boy. The change was somehow her way to say, with due maternal caution, "Atta boy, son. Don't lose the glory." Rather than retreating into some jealous place, my mother had instead chosen for herself — for a small spate of that nighttime — the dwellings of the same youth. Into it, I drifted to rest, the arc of Mary L.'s form as real against my memory as the moon shadows and quiet far-off lightning had been on my walk home from her.

The reliving of it all felt more wakeful than dreamlike. I came from the recollection, stiff and tired, to the opening of my present day — the memory of that night with Mary L. the only rest and comfort I had known. Miles off from my own straw bed, the rock a hard certainty under my frame, I had only nodded toward occasional sleep in the mouth of a cave.

Oblivion and the snatching of a dream had proven kind but mortal friends, dying just as we got to know and care for one another. Into dank vapors of that ancient little cavern where I had paused on the run, the hardest of thought re-emerged. Before I had even opened my eyes, the memory of Ma splitting my uncle's head tore its way in. Reality had rousted me. Whether I had fallen into full dream or merely let my mind dwell on those memories in fitful sleep, I don't know. Didn't matter. I lay fully awake in the wilds, far from Mary L. — she and my mother and every fruit of my life utterly deserted behind me. I had run, a coward, straight into a snare, and I had no idea the mettle I would need to escape. Nor the bliss to come. Through the cave's mouth flowed early threads of sunrise — that morning after my mother had lost her wits. It was up to me, now, to keep mine.

T he rocks and the river steamed from the rain of an August storm. It had come hard and fast off the heat of the day, but we waited it out. Leaving cane-pole lines in the water, we had climbed the bank to take leaky shelter under the trestle. The sun returned, drew more steam off the river eddy and warmed the sand where we squatted again, mildly wet, to finish the first time my father took me fishing. I was seven. He was still my daddy to me.

"You're fixin' to get a bite," I said, digging naked heels into the wet grit. "You'll get one. Pap says they bite after rain." I drew out his line and mine and re-cast two nearly drowned crickets – pluck – into the quiet water. The bobbers rested into a faint drift. An island rose forty yards beyond, and beyond that the majority of the river ran fast. Our place was still, but for a few yammering crows and the patter of lingering drops through the trees.

"I'll just get hung. All I ever get is hung, and draw in some stick or what-have-you," was his reply, his eyes fastened to the water, looking beyond the afternoon. "If you get hung, I'll wade in," I said. "I've waded with Pap to save a hook. My feet know the bottom." I wanted to draw him back to me, even then feeling his need for calm.

He had been fine before the thunder. Bought me a red-topped cork bobber and some gum at Mackey's before we parked the wagon and walked the rail tracks to the path that wound down to the little beach. He had kept his hand atop my head, the palm covering my hair most of the way. We had talked of cornmeal catfish and watermelon and I had laughed when he imitated the crickets with is tongue and pretended to belch just for fun. I felt myself the boy of a strong man.

I believe he never would have left if that thunder hadn't come. Something in the thunder and rain turned him. Cast him off from me and the fishing place. The voices from the trestle pulled him even further away.

"You boys doin' any good?" One of them yelled down, another one yelling on the heels of it, "Ain't no fish in yonder. I done peed in 'at river too many times offa this bridge." They laughed, *and the barbs of it stuck in me. They were four men of the ilk a small boy had already heard more than a few adults describe as, "No-account and fit for nothin' but filth." Four men who seemed to wander up out of nowhere. Soon to be five.*

"You stay right yonder, Frankie. Don't you move. Jus' watch them poles. I'll be right back." My father yelled that down from the trestle. I don't even recall him saying anything before he climbed away from me to reach them. "Be right back, son. You be a good boy," he yelled again, and they disappeared off the bridge into the woods.

I knew he was wrong to leave me. I didn't so much fear the bears, snakes and human wickedness I had heard talk of from adults. Just the feel of his absence. The fact he had gone quivered through my stomach. He stayed gone so long the sun turned the clouds crimson before it abandoned the sky to the blue-gray verges of dark. The moon had emerged by the time I pulled in the lines and set out alone up the path to the tracks. I was nearly to the wagon, trembling in a near run, when I heard him call from behind me, wobbly but alone. Coming near, I could see the light in his eyes had taken cover again, and the old scar of his jaw seemed deeper than before. I never asked where he had been.

On our way home he told me not to tell Ma about the men, and I did not. I wanted only some supper and to hear the crickets off in the night through my window and to feel the stillness of my bed. From the bed I heard Ma argue with him about things I didn't fully understand, and about having a child out at such an hour. A door soon slammed the debate into their room of the tiny home, and the voices muted some. The night drowned out the rest. To the summer night sounds I drifted to sleep, gratefully alone.

At the first stirrings of waking up, I was pretty near certain I had drowsed a couple of months away in that cave. The night — even after the heat that followed the storm — had turned the place chill. Fog mingling with the new light. I came to my senses in shivers. The cave's mouth seemed to have exhaled August and breathed in some damp wind of October, nearly enough to convince me a shoe-mouth-deep snow had fallen in summer. But it was only that aspect of cold that emits from damp rock and shattered nerves.

I came to my senses awash in the feelings not of a teenage man but of a little boy. Fear replaced the adrenaline that had braced me the day before. My body had drawn into a fetal ball, my mind grappling for any thought apart from Ma's face and the ooze of my uncle's head where she had hit him before I took flight. Every awful thing I had ever felt in my life before she had clouted him with that steel wedge suddenly felt like treasure. I would have run myself face-first into another childhood with Frank Locke, Senior if it meant Ma had not killed my uncle and I had not taken off into the woods. There was no knowing how many coon hunters, Indian foragers or other outliers had reclined in this cave before I came. But I awoke to a surety that no one so deep in wallows of failure or quite so useless to the world had ever taken its shelter.

The first touch of full sun finally drew me out. It began warming the cave floor and pressed through my sweat-sodden clothes. Some of the self-pity and sadness seemed to dry away. I checked Pap's watch — nearly seven o'clock — gave it some winding, then felt the August morning heat against my hands and pant legs as I crawled out across rock into the rising day.

It was too early for the high clack and whine of cicadas through the trees. A near silence met me that morning. Not even a breeze. But for a few chittering birds, the view lay quiet as a painting. The last of a storm fog had awakened from its settlement among the trees below me, some of it already climbing the ridgelines against the indigo spread of mountains. With it along the ridges came some of Granny's she-rain, scattered like lace. Little scraps broken off the clouds to drift alone, wherever the day might take them. Seeing it propped me up with the thought of her. How I had never seen Granny truly afraid. Heartbroken, she had sometimes been — but always lighter than fear it seemed — never letting it gain a full grip to pull her down.

The view was hard wilderness, daunting as any dark, at least to any reasonable mind. But in my thinking, I could walk it. The forest thicket in mottled greens spread an invitation beneath me, the miles of it rising eventually out of the mist to those blue high places, layered to horizon and the eastward glow of sunrise. It was not all the tangle of vine and spindly hardwood that rimmed the cave and rock ledge. Though just beyond my feet, the ground sloped toward a drop of at least eighty feet. A survey of that somehow failed to remind me of the myriad ways the mountain woods could kill and rot a man before anyone came near to finding him. Yet I had emerged aching from the rock mouth determined to go on.

Only a few moments in that sun brought on a sweat, which drew the hum of nettlesome bees, which the Cherokee had been known to eat. Granny and Pap talked of Indians gathering an entire honeycomb to roast — stingers, wings and all — as part of a meal. My grandparents would make table conversation of it just to watch finicky children recoil into gratitude for what had been placed before them on a Sunday plate. Right now — better than fifteen hours from my last mouth of food — I could have swallowed bees by the spoonful. Three plates of Granny's day-cooked soup beans and her fresh cornbread would have made a good trade for Pap's watch.

It was, doubtless, the hunger that helped goad me to risk the rock face with little hesitation. And I knew I had to go, helped along by the recollections — dreams, if they were that — of the night before. They stirred fresh in my thinking. That first night with Mary Lizbeth — my mind glowed full of it still. Remembering such things numbed the sting of the trauma that brought me to this place. One might think such a flood of good memory might sober a boy and urge him back home, to make confessions and the best of what had been the worst day of his family's life. But there was no going back. Standing now in a shower of that hot morning, running was all I could do. To become the man who would free his mother from the entanglement of cracking a man's head was reason enough to go. To find, beyond those scarps, a way to grow into Mary L.'s affections was reason, too. Ma had broken down — truly retreated from me. This worried me. I could not afford such weakness, especially if the sheriff held any sympathy at all for the man the entire town knew as my "Uncle Useless." Would the law pursue anyone for the death of such a man? For killing him in defense? I couldn't allow myself to dwell on it. The hunger was too loud. My stomach, as quiet as this very dawn for hours, had started a groan that might win a hollering contest. It was joined by the hunger to get myself safely faraway.

I stepped to the ledge to study the view to my left — northeastward — picking up through the glare the slimmest sight of the river, winding into the folds. The same touch of it seen better in the dying light of the evening before. I scuttled around the rock, rinsing my hands and face in a pool of rainwater, drinking some from my palms, and then looking for a way down into those woods toward that river, nearly absent any thought of the people and affairs behind me. Practical thinking tried to come — trying to fuse with regret of abandoning family and love — but I allowed little room to consider the corn and tobacco that would stand untended. Or the money hidden in a place known only to me. The mill would sweat and clang and swelter in cotton dust without me, and I would take relief in my absence from it. Frank Locke, Senior, what was left of him, might wonder what became of his only boy. He might finally have to regret the loss of Ma now, for she may finally abandon him to his opiate foolery. There was no escaping the notion I wanted to go. Wanted to go and bring all this on. Go far off, for now at least. Even amid missing Mary L. and Ma so much it hurt already, there was liberty to be tasted, and love to be earned.

Having found a place where the cliff was more a rocky ladder of rhododendron vine and scrub pine than a sheer drop, I began climbing down, deeper into the tameless woods, Pap's little hatchet slung through my belt loop. "It oughtta be little different from climbing down off Granny's stone pocket the day before," I thought out loud. "Just a lot more of it." I climbed knowing every move bent the steely honor of my grandfather, who would disapprove of all this. By now he surely lay tired from rolling in his grave.

The rappelling, in a sheer will to cleave against the rock, began well enough. I made respectable time for the first thirty feet or so, until the work deteriorated into a wrestling match with a mountain. The cliff grew steeper than calculated, and eventually it held me in its nether crags, jagged enough to tear shirt, pants and skin, the sun full against all of it. "Now, see? See what you're doin'? Not a thing but skinnin' the hide off your bones, and for what? Get back on home and tend to your Ma and that good girl, son. Please go on back." I could nearly hear Pap saying it, his face mad and hurt at the same time, telling me I had done the very thing that would most wound the two women I loved.

By now there was no climbing out, so my limbs and occasionally my chin skidded further down, as tenderly as the rock and gravity would allow. The cliff was as sharp and unforgiving as misery and panic. Rather than dwell on what might happen, I tried to focus merely on drawing breath and surviving the next move. One glimpse skyward brought into view a buzzard, soaring in silent ease along an updraft against the watery blue. The flapless wings cast a wider span than I was tall. If such a bird could feel mirth, that buzzard had a right to split itself with laughter, watching a boy try to perch where hardly any fowl could find footing.

Nearing the bottom, and stabilized by some better traction on the rock, a faster escape plan again took form. I would simply walk the woods to the river and let some good wheels take me on. The plan was sparse, just a few strokes of imagination, but it seemed possible enough for a stout boy who could survive this cliff. Some part of me knew it was folly. A plan entailing nothing less dangerous than a full-speed steam train — but it gave me hope, so I kept it. Let it cover the stains of my present circumstances, while I imagined how I could carry it out — even against terrible odds. I would surely find it no harder on the body than the scrape of this mica-flecked cliff.

I thought I was nearly off the steepest stretch, having wrestled rock, dirt and vines for about an hour, when I felt the sickening fulfillment of dread. A foot snapped loose from a rotting stump on that mountain face. The force yanked me into a spinning skid, slashing into the trees below. After falling what seemed like five minutes I crashed, blessedly, onto a wet, loamy place of shade — nearly tail first, the hatchet handle burying itself into unwelcoming body parts. The pain fired down my legs, then it bloomed and rose back into my groin. Eb, instantly balling into hoots of laughter, had once yanked up a strand of barbed wire fence into my upper thighs just as I tried to crawl over it. Skidding down this rock hurt a hundred barbs worse. Enough to raise thoughts of A.C.'s fragile carcass — how it must have looked days after he collapsed, freshly burned, into his cranny of rock. I was sure the hatchet blade had found blood and bone enough to leave me for the maggots.

A natural burst of roll, thrash, and the gripping of my groin followed. I writhed on the now leveler ground until some of the pain died, then explored myself for blood and flesh pulp. I found no alarming amount of it, and then lay coiled for a moment's relief. The trip down had coaxed the hatchet handle up into my manhood seeds, but with force enough to tear away the belt loop. Instead of chopping me into a gelding, the money edge of the blade found only dirt at the bottom. We had landed separately, the hatchet and I, and soon we both came volcanically off the ground.

I rose, swearing fire. Not the delicate profanities that speckle a whisper after a toe is stubbed. This was flame-cured wrath — melting every manacle that holds back rage. A scorching of the quiet blasted out of me — in every foul declaration and blasphemy of Jesus a soul my age could keep molten in his core. Had they been steel balls, the words would have crackled off that rock in a hail of sparks thick enough to set the woods to roaring fire. And with this squandering of breath came wasted motion. I finally stopped the fit, heaving and panting, having swung the hatchet's hammer side at least fifty times into the foot of that ledge. Apart from little white chink marks on some rock, the mountain had not moved. Yet it had conquered me. I crumpled to the ground, deep in tree cover, sweating toward dehydration, profanely hot — thinking only that Granny would say, only half-chortling, "You know, God's earth never felt a single lick a that, but it sure wore you slap out."

I sat a few minutes in wheezing self-disgust, regretting the foolishness and realizing that my fit had, at times, sounded like prayer. I had begged the Almighty — in a sacrilege fit for setting wet tinder on fire — to damn the entirety of my predicament, and me as well, if it weren't too much to ask. I felt a notion that some God, somewhere, sympathized. He was surely mad at me, I thought, but I figured no God could exist who didn't understand why living so near disaster raises a boy's hackles high. I supposed it was the nighest thing to acknowledgment — actual conversation — any higher power and I had shared in years. I asked for no help, though, feeling it prudent not to stretch the divine nerves any closer toward breaking.

A glance up the unclimbable precipice and then out into the downsloping trees invited my mind to rest now in a reality: There was no going back. Even if some sentimental boyishness — a child longing for his mother or girlfriend or some mix of the two — had tried to intrude, it could never help me back up that rock toward home. I sat in the fit's afterglow for a minute, letting it cool to a smolder, while I looked into what lay ahead.

A slight breeze stirred the upper limbs. Otherwise, quiet. The only other sensations were the smell of wet earth smeared about the moist air and the sense that everything was utterly different from here. The little stone porch had given me a vista of woods that, while enormous, looked decipherable. Being dropped into the trees, however, offered the feeling I had been sucked into some verdant ocean. I sat looking into a throng of trunks — beech, poplar, hickory, patches of pine. From the ground they blended eventually into an unfathomable dark, even in midday. A few bands of sun penetrated the high canopy and relaxed in little bright beds on the undergrowth, but otherwise the trees stood thick, allowing no more than thirty yards of clear view. I rose, wiped off a little, picked up the hatchet, longed for water then resolved not to think about it, and set off walking — hiking the downhill grade that steepened from where the rock had dropped me.

The river's position was my only compass. I knew it flowed with those rail tracks to my left. The simplest reason told me a northeast hike would reach them. I checked Pap's watch. By calculations I had plenty of time to hit the four o'clock Marshal-to-Asheville train, which I would somehow board. That is about as far as I could think into the plan or any other part of the future by then. Since my awakening in the cave, hunger, exhaustion and a quiet terror had dulled reasonable thought down to near torpor. Climbing the woodland slopes became a second-nature act of will. My mind wandered randomly about the present, working at not falling into the past.

The journey proved fairly easy for the first two hours. The deep-shaded land offered few obstacles, apart from gnarls of rock, occasional steepness that had to be crawled, and the falter over some hidden limb. I listened at times for some rustle of creek water to drink or maybe even the river itself. A light wind and the pierce of crow caw were the only sounds for a long while.

The walking saw me fall twice, but turned dull enough to lead to some wondering: Why had I taken so long to know things were bad enough to excuse leaving? And why did things get so tangled up so fast they set me tromping around such an infernal wild? Why didn't I just load what money and hope I could gather and take off in the truck long ago?

I ultimately concluded, with every talent that attends adolescent nonsense, this was not the fault of my bleeding uncle, or even Frank. This mess before me was somehow my mother's doing. I thought it was the error of a woman caught in a fit of love-fired foolery. I resented her for refusing to leave a life that killed by the scratch of worry and the claw of humiliation. So I slogged along and merely resented her for a time for making me love her, my every step accounting for a time she had desperately begged me: "Talk to him, honey. Please go talk to your daddy. He'll listen to you. Talkin' to you calms him down." Thinking of how I had let her talk me out of thrashing him — one time in particular — after he had given her a smack or a harsh word made me madder still. There was no reason for me to stay, other than Ma and Mary Lizbeth, and the latter could not be considered — for any thought of hurting or disappointing Mary L. was strangling to me. Contemplating the fact I was placing Mary L. above Ma in the pecking order of the heart then bounced again off the fact I had discarded them both. The whole of my mind spun into a maelstrom of self-loathing.

The chiming trickle of a creek floating through a patch of beech trees eventually led me to take a diversion, following the promise of a much-needed drink. It led downward through the whisk and lash of saplings to the face, and finally to a fern clearing, where the tiny branch pooled, plain and still as glass above its brown pebble bottom. The cold sips of water eased the hunger and restored my clarity a bit, which renewed the longing to make the river in time to execute the rickety plan. Pap's watch told me there was a moment to rest, so I took a seat on some nearly boggy ground, easing my back against a fallen log, which lay under a soft blanketing of a moss so green it seemed to give off light — brighter than any enamel. For better than three hours that day I had traversed a bona fide jungle of hemlock and sumac, maple and giant oak trees, occasional vines thick with barbs. All of it made me lousy with minor wounds. The threats posed by snakes or surprise of a bear or merely getting forever lost had whispered on, but I allowed this tiny oasis to have its way a moment. From my seat against that log, I could nearly feel Granny's touch.

She would have loved the tiny glade, its twitter of living things and the spangled light on its floor. "Ain't never been a diamond that shines like God's green creation."

It was as if her very words breezed off the little stream that fell sluicing over rocks, seemingly from nowhere. I had turkey-hunted in mountain woods with Pap, sawed timber and played along ridges near home, but until this moment it seemed I had never truly felt the place. It surrounded me now in the scent and color of some Eden — life forever springing out of death, as if nothing could prevail against beauty. Sitting there seemed to lift the angst off me. I fancied Mary Lizbeth and Ma and the sheriff all understanding I had justly defended my mother and myself in killing a man, and that to flee was only the temporary and necessary work of a hero. But more than that, the little patch of delicate ground, scattered with red huckleberry and filigreed leaves, eased my fear of dying and being buried, and going rancid in the dross of a mountain floor. A body could do far worse than die in such a place as this. I didn't understand this feeling of detachment from life, but it sent my guilt and fretfulness to a grave for a time. I accepted the gift of it.

I got up and carried on, nearly torn in two by hunger but somehow grateful. The flow of that little creek would lead me to the river, I felt sure. I followed its thread down a ridge of thin but abundant maple trunks, the grade no steeper than Pap's cornfield, which rose like a leafy wall between Granny's apple trees and the tobacco field I had abandoned. Suddenly, inner senses raised the smell of fresh cut corn into my mouth. Followed by the firm sensation of a sliced July tomato. Trailing that — reminiscence of the velvety hair across the back of Mary Lizbeth's neck and the supple bow of her lower spine, felt but once by my hands yet a thousand times by recollection. My imagination brimmed with thoughts far afield of the craggy ridge I was descending, which eventually fetched reality to settle on me again. When and how would I find a bite to eat? "You're pert near the brightest bloomin' fool what ever walked," I said out loud to myself, the woods, and the nattering harvest of flying bugs around me. The killing could be explained if I walked the tracks back to town and got on with my life of tobacco and the mill. Considering a reunion with food and the comforts of all things womanly had all but turned me around to trace my way back home by the time I found the river.

The watch hands said almost ten minutes after three when I heard the first motions of it. The hum of fast water. Navigating a few hundred more yards of not quite vertical forest brought me sweating onto a sunny ledge of more stone. At least three hundred feet below, carved along the base of the mountain, the shine of rail tracks curved out of sight in both directions. And just beyond them, the rush that was the early part of the narrows — a deep vein of the French Broad River, manic with speed. If a river could hold adrenaline, the earth's great gland of it had to thrive near this stretch. Granny, during a train ride along it, once turned her head away, saying that piece of fast water made her toenails hurt. In a swell of recent rain, it nearly had that effect as it roared up at me. On the other side rose another sheer cliff of trees. I stood alone within a place nearly as wild as my ideas.

Mosquitoes had thrived along my journey, and near the water their whine grew more frequent about my head, joining the swarming gnats, fascinated with my eyes. I swatted and sat a moment on the rock, finally in some open sunlight — enough to tell me the day was dropping fast into the drowsy quiet that speaks of too late to begin what can't soon be done.

But from the woods my mind was emerging into a dawn. It was as if I had hiked in some blind rote of rhythmic numbness — apart from that time just spent in the moss glade. The river leaping below seemed to wash my sight back into me, fresh in the flow of distilled possibility. My mind, in its newfound clarity, could fully appreciate the three animal kills I had found that day — just sprays of bird feathers and squirrel fur and bone in near-perfect circles, left by a fox or bobcat, perhaps a hawk. There had been the large rustling off in the timber — shadows of creatures aware of me first. It dawned on me, standing on this cliff, that I could have walked only a few feet from surprising a she-bear with cubs or a mountain lion, braced to thrash me. The traversing of such distance — fifteen miles perhaps — evinced itself in the ache of muscle. My lungs hurt and my head throbbed. Yet I felt propped by a miracle of survival. I'm not quite sure but believe I must have run a large part of the trip, as best the topography would allow. Watching the sun on the river, I thought about how far the light had traveled to glint off the current and warm this tiny clearing. How something so delicate as light could thrive all the way from the heavens was a wonder. The idea forced some good blood back into my head and legs.

Ignorance and foolery kept me in stout company as well. They kept beating back healthy fear. There was the matter of getting down off this cliff, near enough to the rails in time to fasten myself to that late train to Asheville. In the pastures of reason and good sense, my plan already drew flies. But I was confident, and there was some time. The warm spot of rock on tired bones and the cooling drone of the river had their way. I lay back a moment, trying not to think of food. This naturally raised the thought of Granny's common words when hunger gnawed hard: "They law, I could eat a dozen eggs and a whole ham of meat. Maybe a jam sam'wich — jam two pieces of bread together and I'll make believe about meat." It was a comfort just having the thought of her along, even lying famished for the taste of anything — even a spoonful of lard.

I sat resting and hearing the river, noting how the hum felt akin to the cotton mill. Whitewater and weaving machines spread nearly the same rush around the air. The whir soon filled me again with Pap's disapproval. He would hate this predicament of mine nearly as much as he despised that mill. I believe he could not have mustered a greater hatred for the very chapel of the devil.

"Young folk and women with children in their baby britches — they ought not be in such a place as that," he'd say, even after child labor was technically outlawed. "The young ought be in school raisin' theirselves outta ignorance instead of raisin' a sweat in some rich man's wool weavin' house."

Any attempt to correct him on the wool point, saying we worked in cotton, only roused him more. "I reckon it don't matter much what sort of field a mule plows, he's doin' it with a bit in his mouth. And with a man's hand on the rein. He's bent to a man's will. And I'll tell you another thing. I've seen borrowed farm animals treated better than some of them poor, hollow-eyed mill people. Biggest thing separatin' mill hands and chattle slaves of the old cotton fields is a few cents on the hour. Gettin' shed of that whole cotton-pickin' place would do these mountains nothin' but good."

I lay nearly able to hear him, eyes closed, wondering how a man whose soul was about as rough as worn flannel could rankle up so much bile about a mill, and yet he never would once curse the members of our own family who might get tossed out of hell. The totality of that mill was the greater evil to my grandfather. As he saw it, everyone who fell for the fast and steady little pay of the place eventually fell out of it, worthless as chaff. "This farm *will* take a rest. The land, my spine and the good Lord know when I ought ease back a little. That dad-blamed stinkin' cotton house won't rest for a soul. And it won't weep for narry a one who keels over, tired to death from keepin' it alive. Place has cut the fingers and toes off little boys and girls. And it makes a grown man into two hundred pounds of nothin'."

Adoring him as I did, some part of me often seethed when Pap riled himself over the mill, for it seemed wasted outrage. There was no time or energy for such now.

The few minutes rest on the rock turned my spine even more into the feel of wood, yet a look at the watch raised me into aching motion. A check of the cliffs along the tracks below settled my eyes on a goal. The hatchet helped cut my passage back into the woods and down through a steep place, so dense with spindly jack pines the visibility was three feet, then nearly black. My heading was eastward, off the high stone cliff toward a tiny perch that would very nearly let a boy lying facedown reach over and brush his fingers against the tops of the train cars. There was no winning a footrace with a steam train at full speed — that was clear. I had resolved to catch my ride, somehow, on the train's back, preferring the hazard of falling clean off to the peril of rolling under its wheels. I knew they had sliced more than a few stout men apart from their limbs and souls.

From the faraway and high Continental Divide the water below flowed west-southwest, eventually to the Mississippi River rather than the Atlantic. The rush of it grew louder as I descended the thicket.

Having reached a semblance of clearing, living wildlife emerged. First, a deer — large for a doe — sprang up the ridge, then turned to set her eyes into mine. They stared for what seemed longer than her natural suspicion should allow. The moment held us each startled until she turned away up the crag, the whiteness of her tail quick to soak into the shading of woods. I stood hungry enough to eat her raw, though such a thought barely entered the moment. The sight of her had a calming effect on my mind until twenty feet more or so brought me nearly boot-first onto the back of a copperhead snake. It sunned fat against the tiny ledge that was my destination. The snake sensed me and iced my veins as it coiled. I stood still, hearing a low groan of its motion barely audible against the river sound. We were in each other's way, for that ledge seemed the ideal place from which to drop myself onto the spine of a freight car. I backed up slowly, and soon some handfuls of rocky dirt sent the snake gliding mad off into cover, trailing a reminder that every part of this wilderness amounted to ground where I did not fully belong.

My heart's thump eased a bit as I stepped fully onto the ledge. It was a precipice no wider than three feet. Just a gnarled rock step missed by dynamite, which decades earlier had cut the way for the railroad, lying better than twenty feet below my toes. The gravel corridor, slightly curving, was barely level enough to fit the polished span of tracks before the land dropped again through trees, another twenty feet or so, to the thrust of river.

Behind me grew a curtain of blackberry briars, competing with a little stand of pokeweed. "Poke salat," as Granny called it, wild-growing and rising into little white blossoms, fecund with dark purple berries by late summer. I knew the berries carried poison, but the leaves could be boiled into greens, similar to collards. Boiled poke gave off a stench so thick it had muscle. Granny and others shared a taste for such greens that eluded me. But hunger will flout taste. I broke off a few leaves, rolled them into tight balls in my hands and choked them down as one might take aspirin without drink. The color lingered on my palms, and within minutes the leaves — helped by the day's heat — began wrestling my insides into a knotted hold only a good vomit can untie.

Between my feet dangling off the step, I threw it up — heaving and slavering onto the tracks far below. All the while, amid gags, monitoring my watch. It told of a train surely about due to pass beneath me. I strained to catch hearing of it. Nothing. Only the violence of river and some cooing doves off in the windless trees. I tried to put my thoughts far off from nausea but found only some final regrets. Truth was,

Pap rarely got riled about the mill or anything else, so I was sorry to have coddled such hateful memory of a man who in death still felt to me like a warm blanket in winter. A few words of his voice in that moment would have been worth my final breath, which I sat bracing to draw. His voice or Granny's would have eased my heart. If spirits can see into dwellings of the living, I thought, the leathery goodness of my grandfolks had surely been torn by a disappointment in me by now. Ma and Mary Lizbeth would never forgive me for taking leave, regardless of why I thought it a decent thing to do. So much retch and brooding quickly wilted me into a droop of sleeve-wiping tears, which I indulged on that little rock until the sickness faded some. The river lulled, and I let my ears reach for any whisper of comfort the air might hold. That's when they caught the first distant metal-to-metal clamor of the full-speed Marshal to Asheville train.

It grew loud in a hurry. Slobbering to my feet, craving water down to my quivering knees, I stood pondering Pap's chink-worn little hatchet. It held nearly the warmth of his very hand in mine, and — sadly — no more use for this trip. Reason said it may do harm on the jump. I stooped and placed it on the rock with a reverence of touching a loved one's body for the last time. I had little more than turned from it when the bawling hulk of the engine trudged directly under my little roost — a trail of steam and cinder rising off the stack to fog the trees. The awe of it — so much quake on wheels at fifteen miles per hour — told of some history about to be made under my heels.

I stood suddenly as yellow as that steam engine was a gleaming dark green. Cowardice might have provoked me to start climbing back home had the cars not been so near. Their height rose to within two yards of the base of the ledge. This train was short. There were but seconds to deliberate, to grit up some nerve. I groped around for the only piece of religion my dull head could clip from memory.

"'Ashes to ashes, cuss the dust, sweet Jesus Lord, mop your floors if I must. I'll tend heaven's rows, wash its chamber pots. Sweet Jesus seize my soul when this ol' body goes to rot.'"

I said out loud that prayer I had heard muttered for fun a hundred times strolling about town. Then my feet, feeling nearly as if they belonged to someone else, stepped off. Trying to anticipate the metallic speed, they let that ledge of rock go.

The short drop launched an already roiling stomach into my mouth. The steel top of a boxcar stung every bone of both feet, thudding the bass noise up through my legs. Then, nearly instantly, I fell — first onto tailbone, then spine, then head — a collapsing desperation of trying to grab a hold. Nothing. I had failed to lead the leap into the train's pace and thus never held myself on its back. Boys have stayed longer on rodeo steers.

As I flipped, the potential of those wheels dashed again to mind — just enough warning. Somehow, skidding off the edge, I managed to thrust myself apart from the shred of certain death underneath this mammoth mistake. More than fall, I spiraled off the boxcar's slope, the roar of metal and water coming up hard. Even now, the mere recollection of it lifts my belly somewhere north of my eyes. That train was the stoutest thing I had ever touched. The lumbering mass threw me to the ground, within a few yards of the shriek and bang of turning steel. My first landing felt like an omnipotent kick. Glancing off the steep cliff just under those tracks, I thumped. The blow took my wind. The angle and force of it splayed my scattering limbs through brush and into a fall that ended with a backward somersault yank, almost neck first, against the river.

Hitting water as I did felt like splashing through cast iron. Then, lost moments. No thinking to do. Only some gesture of feeling — commotion — the sensation of churning, deep through heavy cold. Even in August, the river held a chill of high-mountain creeks, which fed this dark misery that held me now. I clung to the few wits that can remain after such a bouncing drop, the current hurling my frame and head against rocks, each a smack of confusion more than hurt. The wind had been knocked so far out of me the capacity to draw breath seemed forever lost. A blessing to both lungs, for it kept me from inhaling so much of that river the rapids would surely have died with me.

I have yet to fasten my mind around exactly what, but something threw my addled thinking a line. Death surely had me by the foot when it came. The first clear thought came in a flickering memory of Eb. The shriveling cool of his little hands as I touched them after he drowned. His scamp smile flashed to mind, followed by the sense of being lunged upward, as if by the pull of rope and a shove of stout arms at once. My head broke the surface in a coughing huff for air that felt strong enough to suck a bird down my throat. The river covered any lingering rattle of the train.

Ridges nearly stacked the trees into green walls, towering toward reddening clouds. That became the first sight to my flooded eyes after I surfaced. Then downriver, a predicament no swimmer could escape. The water whitened all the more into a chute of rocks. Within seconds the burst of it carried my bobbing head to what appeared a last opportunity to reclaim any portion of control. A great dam of rock leading to a broad islet of more trees lay only a few yards ahead. To its left, the river howled down into deeper lather. To the right, the water branched, fast into darkness of woods but I figured it could prove narrow enough to escape.

The clothes were leaden, my energy only vapor in the current. I could merely will my flailing self through the gush, legs and arms little stronger than drifting cloth. Enormous rocks, a rotting tree trunk and what seemed a mile's worth of thrash later, the detour was finally taken. By then, the tantrum of rapids had turned me into a sinking rag of a boy, ushered into the calmer tine of that river fork — part of my body numb, the rest afire with hurt. Under some low, shadowing limbs, the softening current welcomed a body that seemed no longer mine. The water deepened as it stilled, and what was left of me did likewise. I recall some final striving for breath — little more than a gasp of will remained. I thought I heard a shout, some timbre of voice. Then, only surrender of breath and the cool of water where I had gone fully under. Quiet and restful and dim, that little path of river urged me down to suckle its peace. It deadened the remains of my fight. Crossing the threshold between air and pure river, I yielded to the drowning. I remember a final brush of thought that every soul I loved should know such calm. Feeling my body become river, I finally allowed myself to become mercifully gone.

The silt bottom felt soft and good. I remember the ease of it — drifting down to take marching orders on toward mysteries Eb and the horde of the dead had solved. My pain eased, as if a tight rope loosened toward freedom. I recall the most vague pulse on the river floor — a chafe of feet against sand — just before the commotion hit. A wakening. A rush of noise grew toward me through the current. A brush of fingers. Then again. Then a hand. For an instant I feared the grip of the devil's own minions, sent to drag my sorry entirety to hell. The force yanked me by the hair. Another hand came to the chin, clenching hard. Then against my kidneys, a set of knees, floundering. A whole body, throwing an urgency against mine. An upward brawl. Then, the breakage of surface into light. The body's nature to save itself by vomiting water and heaving breath at once set me into a confluence of inner fires. From at least five feet down, I had been pulled off that bottom by a grip attached to the shout heard moments before.

It had been, undeniably, the voice of a young woman, who now dragged toward shore as best she could the sopping weight of chokes and near-drowning that comprised what was left of me.

"Mercy, Jesus Christ, mercy. Help me, boy."

My face came limp against her soaking bosom. She was breathing hard, our feet a tangle along the mire of floor. My lungs resigned and, even amid this ruckus, they refused to sign back on. I rolled skyward to see some bands of sun through treetops, then all light dimmed — everything graying toward dark. She slung her arms under mine and dragged.

"Get up, boy. Get up. Help me a little. If you don't help, you'll dance with the worms."

I answered by willing my feet into some small use. Little more than water would come out of my mouth. The retching fit carried on toward blinding sickness. We staggered through shallows, finally putting the river behind us, apart from the bounty of it I spewed onto the sand. Still foaming with the earthen taste, I crumpled, sodden in my own vomit, to the ground. It was as if she had yanked me back through a veil draped between this life and what felt like warm currents beyond. Death and I had billowed against one another — with force enough so I knew dying led to no cold place. No place at all.

Flopped to the grain of that quiet piece of riverbank, I blacked out.

n the few weeks after we buried Eb my boyhood faith evolved with the speed of a manured vine, winding away from all rites of reckless fun to twine itself around every nail, board and syllable of religion I could find. Most audible belching, tobacco use, and gratuitous public spitting ended. I regularly stopped to whisper, hat-in-hand, "Excuse-me-Jesus" prayers for such infractions as knuckle-cracking or visible scratching of my private parts. Muffling even thoughts of cuss words became a sacrament – mostly futile, for to stifle profanities caused my mind only to sparkle with more profanities, which I worked, all the more in vain, to stifle. This failure I atoned for by carrying extra water and stove wood for the grieving people of Granny and Pap's place, washing my own britches for Ma, and entering the church no fewer than a dozen times a week for some contemplation befitting a hair shirt. The door was always open.

This reformation lasted until the Monday before Thanksgiving. Walking home from what was left of my schooling and some farm work with Pap, I reverently approached church to meditate, thankfully, on being above ground rather than locked in the dark of Eb's still-mounded grave. The creak of the door – and nearly my heart – stopped at the sight. It was the back of Frank Locke, Senior's head. He sat hunched on a front pew, both arms apparently folded circumspectly onto his lap. Nailed to the wall behind the choir pews a spindly cross – crudely fashioned from skinned and varnished dogwood trunks – seemed to hold a physical grip on his stare. I hadn't seen him alone here since that day Eb and I hailed rocks and mud clod terror at this place. If Frank knew someone had just stepped through the door, he never flinched to say.

It is a testament to boyish arrogance that fear eluded this moment. Some sort of murmuring chant came off him, but to hear the words required a stealthy crawling across the hardwood planks, under the windows of the outer right aisle, which I did, the whole of me as quiet as a bird hopping on a bed.

"Sorriest man what ever walked," were his first words I detected. I stopped as he carried on.

139

"Never meant a thread's worth of harm to narry a soul, Lord. Narry nothin' but do the right thing. That's all I ever wanted to do for my family, and I ain't fit for it. Ain't fit to do nothin.' Hell, I ain't fit to be, Lord. I ain't fit to live. Why'd little Eb have to go and die and me still here, ever' other minute havin' to imagine my own Frankie sleepin' dead in some box. Lord help me, Lord help me, the worst part of me you made wants to show his tail again. Sorry filth of a man I am, Lord help me, I want a shot of my dope so bad. Lord help. I'd rassle ten devils for it."

I had slipped under a pew to listen, only a few yards away, confident – somehow – he would never know my ears gathered his weepy near-whisper intended only for the room's utter quiet. Nothing could have startled me more – not even if Frank had discovered me – than the sudden opening of the door behind us, followed instantly by Rev. Pyles, stomping the center aisle and shrilling the air full of freshly raised staccato hell.

"Say there. Say, what can I help you with? This is a holy place, sir."

Frank turned and started what seemed an apologetic greeting, but the preacher snipped it off. Polished black boots had scuffed by no more than a yard from my nose, and from the pew's cover I could see the feet of both men, Frank still seated, the minister standing over him.

"So it's been you, trackin' dirt through this here church of mine. I figured if I just showed up sometime I'd catch you. I don't cotton much to trespassers on these floors of the Lord, Mr. Locke, and yes I know who you are. I know exactly who and what you are. You are the sort of evil the Lord of this sanctuary, all decent people and myself battle ever' day. Such enemies of the Lord's work, drunkards, vandals and such, they are not fit for here."

Frank stood, jangling change in his pockets, and they came nearly toe-to-toe. Any lingering worship melted in the rise of temper.

"Well, I ain't done a thing, Reverend, but come and idle here a spell and put me some quarters and nickels in that offerin' plate stack yonder when they ain't nobody else around. I reckon you don't care much for me, but I'm pert near certain you'd sweep my nickels off that floor with your own tongue. And I reckon that'd beat hearin' you go on waggin' it. If you wanna follow me out to the road, we'll finish what you come and started."

With that, Frank stepped around the preacher, turned, slammed a barrage of coinage against the floor, and stomped down the aisle. More ministerial talk chased him as money danced and scattered all over.

"Go on, Mr. Locke. Go and keep your money and your filthy ways outta my Bible church. Keep your dirty boots out, too. I'd just as soon the Lord God went without your nickel as to have to sweep up after you again. I'll be here cleanin' up your filthy mess and prayin' mercy on you, sir."

The door slammed, and Frank's boots left the steps. A few minutes of unintelligible muttering followed, then came the clank of the Reverend Pyles' key, locking me in. I had lain corpse-quiet, petrified he'd launch into money sweeping and find me. I finally fully breathed, rose, found the broom, and swept the entire sanctuary to a small dust and coin pile at that locked door. Then I leveraged the broom handle against the floor, kicked to break it in two, and arranged the pieces into a cross atop the sweepings, taking not a penny. I calmly raised a window, jumped down the ten feet no one could climb to get in, and ran across the cemetery for home — feeling the glow of recent piety turn to smoke through the November dusk. I never saw that church's insides again.

I 've long supposed the swoon that hit me came from more than the river. Falling hard from the train to a near drowning on the heels of sweltering across mountains with little water — all of it formed a trauma that finally reigned, pulling me into an oblivion I didn't know possible. I woke from it in another round of heave and gag, having been out so long that dusk had come onto the day. I remember hearing a rattling in my own breath, then the distant rush of fast water. I came to in the funk of what seemed a dozen milk cans of vomited cold river.

Her voice, at first, felt like only a shimmer of thought — some snatching off a dream, and one scarcely believed. Yet it soon confirmed I had been dragged to the wet sand by a woman's hands.

"That river beyond those trees — it's a lunatic. I imagine this feels like holy ground."

I heard this over a regiment of agonies — the wounds of the fall and a fire of the throat, all coming fully on now. A claw hammer seemed to ricochet inside my head. I rolled my face to her voice, wiping dirt and trying to see. She sat a few feet away, knees-to-chin, still drying in the last sliver of sunlight to reach the little clearing around that pool. Menswear hardly dulled the angles of her womanhood. The cement-colored britches, rolled heavily at the ankle, cleaved to her, as did the shirt of the same color, all still mildly darkened from the soak of pulling me out.

"I've fished here the majority of my life. You're the first man I've seen that river spit out. And if I hadn't fished today it would have swallowed you." I tried a climb to my feet but merely staggered, humiliated by the stupor. She came to me on her knees, hushing and urging me down, and I dropped over nearly onto her lap. Only then did I appreciate fully that I had been saved by hands the color of an October acorn.

"Just lie back another moment. Let's not finish cracking you open before I can get you home. Those scrapes will scar enough." She wiped and pressed at my face, and I surrendered to the touch, squinting up now at the points and angles of her face, taking in the tight sweep of hair partially bound behind her with what looked like cuttings off white silk. She looked me over through eyes the color of hickory nut shells — the gaze streaming shades of light I had also seen autumn sun cast through mellowing tobacco. Her face, at this first blush, brought to mind the cocoa tones of Big Miss Ed, and the few other dark-skinned people I knew. Though this woman's bearing spoke of no humanity I could fathom. The early sight of her convinced me I had died and been diverted to the heaven of the hymns that rang from Big Ed and the little church she attended just outside town. But the voice differed — as much as fine music rises above the average spoken word. The woman who pulled me out sounded like no one, light or dark, I had ever heard.

"I don't know what transpired to drop you into that water. But as my mother would say, 'I'll trust you to the God of my constitution.' There's good comfort barely twenty minutes through those trees. I'd like to reach it before dark. We can if you can walk. If not, you'll have to wait until I come back with a horse in the night. I don't need to know your origins yet. Just tell me how you are. Do you believe you can walk?"

I was struck nearly mute again by even the smallest sound of her. It showered me in awe. Each word formed in a cool precision, not so much spoken as cut by a tongue clearly honed on books and abundant minds. I had never heard anyone — no minister or teacher or even Asheville's rich who bought our farm products — distill language into so graceful a sound. She embarrassed me — enough that I resolved my thick tongue would keep mostly still.

"Reckon I had a nap," I said, groaning to my knees.

"You *had* a flirtation with the grave. I've sat here drying out, afraid your breath would quiet." She spoke on a rise to her feet, brushing off sand and retrieving her shoes from a log.

"I gotta get walkin', I reckon. Walkin' on toward my camp back yonder where I tail-busted myself right into that sorry water," I said, hacking out some more river, lightheaded and on the cusp of passing out again. "I'm powerful obliged for the help. Reckon I'll get back out this way one of these days. Get you properly thanked."

I wobbled to my feet, groping for more lies about a camp upriver, trying to form a credible tale to explain how I landed in her lap. What she was doing here and where she came from had yet to matter. I was soaked in defeat — my planning and hiking lost now to that river — and the weight of it all made me wish I had drowned. I kept looking down to avoid contact with this savior who made no recognizable sense at all to me. The ground soon seemed to come up against my knees. The little beach spun and dimmed. Her hands braced me again.

"I'll demand no thanks, but I'm going for that horse, and you need to sit while I do."

Her firm way was not unkind, yet I pushed her back.

"Just leave me be, ma'am. Mind your business. I'll make it back to my camp up yonder just fine, and we'll both get to our beds 'fore dark."

I lied about as well as I looked, and the insolence sprang from a frustration she could clearly read. She raised my face to her eyes. They neared the edge of real anger.

"Listen, I'm written into this tale of yours for some reason, as I see it, and unlike this homespun yarn you're tangled in, I'm quite real. Real and quite tired, and I'm most overdue at home. So let's settle this. Whatever the reason you intruded on me here, your need is not too much for me. I can meet it, I assure you. And if you can't muster civility, then please show the good taste of gratitude." Her finger stabbed at my chest. "I'll not live with your perishing on me. Not if I can help it. So please settle your mind, sir, and let's see how able you are. I need to get on with this. You're not alone in depending on me."

The latter part of that scold came from her shaking head a few yards down the little beach, where she assembled a stash of fishing gear — the creel stuffed with pinecones and wilting blue wildflowers. Her upbraiding seemed to sedate both of us. I finally managed to assemble some wits and stand, full of ache, beside the quiet of the water flow. It curved into thick woods toward a reunion with the whitewater beyond the island.

Streaks of late twilight fell around us as she bundled three storebought rods — of the kind afforded to people who discussed their fishing in formal clothes over fine place settings. The mystery of her frightened me a little by then. Every person of darker color I knew — most of them sharecroppers, laborers, people of work — always treated me with a humble regard far greater than I deserved. They suffered unkindness and outright scorn from whites as if these were some portion of the natural order. This woman's high manner, her finely edged mind — none of it could find a label in my thinking. She stood nearly my height, yet towered with refinement, even in damp, dirty fishing clothes. Our ages seemed nearly the same, though I was her peer on par with a wren hatching an eagle. I remember feeling ashamed even that the river had torn the boot and sock from my left foot, leaving that much of me naked to her.

"If you can stand that long, you can walk, I suppose," she said next, in full dress of gear — vest and a large hat. She motioned me to the mouth of a nearly undetectable path. "I'll lead the way. You just tell me if you need to rest. Path's pretty firm. It's shown me through the dark before. But take some care with that bare foot."

"I can't. I can't be known to nobody," came as my reply, head hanging, tears shaking to get out. I fought them, thinking all I wanted in the world at that moment was to go with her and confess everything about me. But I kept up some bravado. "I've got good reason to keep hid. If you could leave me some matches and let me borrow one of them poles, I'll be fine right here 'til I can walk on back home. Or get off to catch me another train somewheres."

It came out coarse and weak, but strong enough to agitate her again as she stepped toward me.

"That makes two of us on that point of needing to hide. You'll stay covered if you stay with me, I pledge you that. If you try that river again, you may hide in Saint Peter's arms."

She had reached me and taken my arm as a gentleman might lead a lady to a dance floor. I never looked up from the unshod foot.

"So rather than finish killing yourself, let's take ourselves a gimp through the woods. Shall we? Or would you prefer another nap here so the dark can finish falling on us?"

I stood, still looking down, silent. I could feel her stare soften in the words.

"Incidentally, you are going to have to trust me. I am going to ask some things of you. I've sat here thinking about them. Very important things. As I see you now, you have few choices but to comply. I have a weak heart for indigents, God help me, and right now you're the very child of indigence, it would seem. So, come on with me."

She nudged me forward. My mind snatched around at that latter part, but drew back only confusion. I knew of no people named "Indigent," knew for sure I was not related to any. So I took her remark with a pang of insult, just to be safe. Before we stepped from the beach into the woods she dug into a knapsack. The hand came out with a bundle of soda crackers, handed toward me. I grabbed the food without a word and tried not to resemble the devouring way of a stray dog. She turned into the woods, and I tottered behind the flop of her hat. She did not look back.

"Keep up as best you can. No more argument. I'm hungry, too, and I could pee a quarter mile, which I will not do in these woods with you."

The sudden raw candor startled me, nearly into a laugh. Finally, something familiar, yet she cloaked even pee-talk in the same finery of speech. Somehow, from her, it was not inelegant. All the more, this rendered her too much for a plain, worn mind. So I tried not to think, limping ten feet behind, listening to the whisk of our feet.

A final glance back at where she had pulled me out stirred in me a longing for some peace. The water pooled into nearly motionless calm. A sheet of glass but for swirls around rocks on the far bank and the breaks of fish nipping insects in the late afternoon. The stillness seemed to wash my nerves in a remedy of surrender to the mystery in front of me. The picture of Ulysses dressed in borrowed clothes in his funeral box managed to leach into my head. I remember thinking folks would figure a fugitive doesn't run from innocence, so I had surely spared my mother. That part was done, and there would be a chance to fix the rest of what I had left broken. Into this logic, my tired wits collapsed, as if lulled back on a soft bed. Though I resolved to keep up some walls between my secrets and this woman now ten yards ahead until I figured what to do next.

We walked into a depth of high poplar and birch wood, thick enough at times to feign the fullness of night. Yet the place felt like no wilderness. Her presence somehow made it brim with a tender feel that softenened even some of my gloom. My companion — leader as she had arranged it, walking so far ahead — stopped to pull a kerosene lamp from a sack she swung. She struck a stick match to fire it.

"Path's full of heavy roots between here and the end," she said, turning back toward me. "You'll stub that naked foot again if you don't keep up." I was sure she had not heard the vulgarities I muttered a few yards back when it happened the first time. The light glowed nearly white, and the sight of her masculine clothing tinged me with the first notion a man lived at our destination. Trying not to think about this instantly felt like working not to breathe.

"Do you possess a name?" she asked, facing me — leaving the light to swing at our knees.

"Frank Locke. Frank Locke, Junior," I said, emphasizing the "Junior" and urgently regretting the honesty. Go ahead and tell her you're an axe-killer while you confess everything else you know, I thought. Too bad you didn't twist a leg out in that river so you could kick your own hind end. I opted — as boys will — to hide stupidity behind a mask of bluster.

"Name's not important," I fired back. With a hint of furrowed brow, she turned and walked on.

"I suppose you're right about that. But calling you Frank sounds better than calling you nothing, don't you think? You can call me Sophia. I seldom hear a man speak it anymore."

A few minutes more of silent following and the path fell into steep descent, the air filling with the familiar sweetness of farm animal ground, then the sharp trace of cultivated land. As if looking out a tunnel, I soon saw a portion of it beyond the flop of her hat. It was a clearing so large darkness was far from sealing it for the night. Under a sky of perfect August sapphire, setting itself for an emerging moon, we stepped across the threshold of forest into a small orchard of apple and pear trees, in need of a mow. Below it, some patches of tomato vine, beans, and short lettuce. Sunflower and delicate beds of blossoms I did not recognize lay to the right, all of it meticulously worked. The two white barns, some high-fence pasture, and a small square of healthy corn to our left hardly entered my notice. The house at the foot of the hill, even from its back side, commanded every shred of attention I had left.

Against more woods, a hundred yards beyond us, stood the largest dwelling ever to meet my eyes, even on trips with Pap to the monied boulevards of Asheville. Three floors of white clapboard, finely trimmed — rising full of gable and arch eventually to a lightning rod standing on the roof's highest ridge. It was mountainous, very nearly shining even in the final hints of dusk, the whole place nestled in a dense remoteness of green. A dim light glowed through drapes of a window on the second floor — the only hint of inner life I could see.

"Who lives in that place?"

The question came flippantly, my simplicity of mind further simplified by awe.

"I'm quite sure you think I don't. Or perhaps you presume I clean that house." Sophia never turned around as she said it, walking on ahead. The land was flattening. She sped out of the orchard toward the backyard.

"Don't be shy or ashamed, Frank Locke, Junior. I understand misunderstanding."

I understood virtually none of this.

We veered left along the pasture, which lay rimmed in fine fencing of light whitewash, eventually coming onto a grass-center road. The house grew statelier by the step until it loomed with a bearing that very nearly called out for a salute by someone of my rank. We carried on toward it, passing more accurately minded flowerbeds, until I noticed — in the center of the great home's backyard — a small cabin of heavy square timbers. It stood dark, draped in tin roof and a husky covering of this-doesn't-belong-here. Its position caused it to seem further out of place. The cabin's front door faced away from the main house, as if the lesser felt unworthy to face even the rear of such grandeur. Its only decoration was a broad porch pouting out toward some woods and the orchard we had traversed. That porch was soon Sophia's aim.

The hat came off when her high boots hit it. Gravel mashed my shoeless foot before I made the first of three steps, and by then she was through the door, free of the fishing gear, and back out to invite me on in. The walk had snapped most of my remaining threads. Any nerve not splitting with pain or trembling for rest stood in dead minority, which is perhaps the reason my shod foot stumbled against the final step. The stub sent me scattering knees-first against the floor planks. The only thing to grab was the arm of an oak rocking chair, and the next sound was a glorious thunder of both of us against the floor. The pain provoked anger, but what broke the bindings of my self-control was the womanly laughter. Sophia's breathy attempt at stifling it only finished rousing my inner devil. I retaliated with a splendorous raining of profanity. The chair and I wrestled. I lost again.

"You're beginning to remind me of the man who built this place," she said, still chuckling while reaching to untangle me .

At that, I braced against the wall, finally disgorged my feet from the offending chair and, even with failing strength in both legs, flung the full-sized rocker with a kick. It soared, wheeling off the porch, as I lay on my side letting loose some verbal damnation to chase its tumble across the yard.

"Whoa now, sir, that is not your chair to destroy."

Sophia's amusement dimmed before the chair stopped moving.

"It's vulgar enough to rough up the place before you even get in it. But then you soil the air with a smutty mouth. How sentimental you make me feel."

She turned away toward the lantern she had put down by the door. I kept quiet, hoping shame would soon pass again.

"I didn't soak myself wading in after you only to have this place befouled. There's enough irreverence around here without some half-drowned mountain nomad hauling in more."

She crouched, insisting that I pick up the chair, which I humbly did. I caught glimpse of her eyes again in the lantern light. They cast some mix of sorrow and affection more than real anger, the expression alive with contemplations that ventured far afield of mine.

"Can you please get quietly up? We don't have all night." I quietly stewed in my own shame again.

She stood, reaching a hand, which urged me upward, then disappeared with the lantern into the cabin.

Soon two oil sconces glowed from the left wall to reveal a room so full it was hard to see anything in it. Furniture, rugs, wall hangings, some formal-looking documents. From a painting framed in dark wood, a large rust dog stared over the fat stone fireplace between the lights. Cedar and wood smoke and a faint fruit smell met me as I stepped in. Sophia lit a third lamp I thought unnecessary, one of adornments, with a big fragile-looking globe the Sears catalog might have marketed as its "very finest." The pink and white flowers on frosted glass marked the room's only female note I could see. From its light she walked immediately to a massive rolltop desk, ornate with carpentry, pulled the cover down, locked it, and pulled determinedly to make sure.

"Have a seat. Or would you like to throw one more tantrum?" She huffed a bit of laughter that spoke of a truce.

"I'm powerful sorry about that chair, ma'am. I don't mean to be the way I am," I said, looking down and shuffling to the nearest chair, sinking into a leather embrace of old comforts known by someone of larger frame. From there I watched her still-damp legs march silently past, out the open door.

"Take a spell of rest. I'll be back," she said, scuffing off the porch with the lantern.

I sat taking inventory of what seemed the richest little loghouse in either Carolina. The walls of heavy pine, hewn-down smooth, rose to a ceiling of beams and light-color beadboard. The floors lay mineral-streaked and dark under varnish and heavy rugs. A masculine patina of money overflowed every corner. It was a gentleman's home of weighty oak tables with turned legs, a huge bronze clock that said nearly a quarter of nine, a far wall full of bookcases lush with opulent bindings, with more volumes scattered atop the locked desk. Through a door to the back I could make out a high wooden sideboard that spoke of a kitchen; to the right, just enough light revealed the end of a high bed of polished wood with furnishings to match. A set of tall field glasses rested on a library table next to my seat. They stood atop a book on whose spine I recognized the name "Jane," but the last name — beginning with "E" — was an arrangement of letters above my learning. A divan of a deep blood color lazed under two open windows, whose light drapes swelled on hints of breeze. I looked it all over, nervous, finding little that made sense, wondering if I dwelt in some dream about to go dark as a grave.

A drowse nodded at my head several times in the chair until the nap caught up with me. It was dark outside when I woke, still alone. I ached all over, but curiousity enlivened me to explore. I stepped to one of the documents on the wall. "Steal the Abundance of Poverty," it simply said, in a calligraphy dark and heavy as the black frame holding it. A search for signs of who may join Sophia in living here led to an oval photograph heavily framed behind my chair. The eyes seemed alive through the glass, which curved toward me like some giant lens on the room. The subjects were a seated gentleman in formal frock coat, a black ribbon tie falling from a stiffness of high linen collar, his face warm and proud and tinged with a dram of melancholy behind tiny glasses. He wore a heavy mustache, and his graying hair was combed back, curling at the neckline. Above him stood what appeared an ivory carving of womanhood. Her left hand — long and nearly sharp with nobility — rested on his right shoulder, the length of her awash in white fabric against the velvet backdrop. Her hair formed dark waves under an ostrich-plumed hat whose crown swelled her to even greater height. Her face held a look of nearly boundless care, though the smile gave pause. Gentle, yet resolute, cast in a thin spray of hubris my mind of that time could not articulate. It reminded me of things I had heard the mill and town speak of in conversation about city refinement and the fearsomely educated.

But the picture's smallest part drew my deepest attention. She sat, no more than age four, on the man's left knee — hands folded in tiny gloves on her lap, looking out through an expression sweet yet mildly grave for a child. Her smile, just reluctant enough to seem fairly rare and nearly out of place, gave the portrait its center. The small, dark-skinned girl wore one of those costly child outfits the common people of my boyhood deemed extravagantly wrong. No person of such color — certainly no child — ever wore clothing so fine in my experience. This was the very picture of lives foreign to mine, yet the image stirred a memory. As with a scatter of candlelight in a dark room, a recognition of this man and the whole place had come to me. Scraps of story and legend talked up since my boyhood. I thusly knew the two females. That name, Sophia, since the moment she spoke it, jangled a vague recollection of old chat and whisper about town.

"I've changed a little since that day."

"Sweet Moses, girl, you scared the angels outta me," I said, jumping to find her little more than a foot behind me. She stood barefoot, placing two baskets onto the chair I had vacated.

"I came through the back door on my toes, thinking you might be asleep." Her face carried the same fragile affection as before, suspicion battling to overtake it. "Sorry about the angels. I'll try to spook your demons next time," she said, turning to the baskets.

I turned back, pointing to the photo, cleaving to my natural flair at playing ignorant.

"That you there? Who's them other people?"

"That is Julia Sophia Proctor." She stepped beside me, near the glass — a flash of longing and sadness on her face before she affected a gentle pomp. "Julia Proctor of New York, Vassar, and many fine parts of the world. The mother who has offered me the best parts of her beautiful self. Beside her there is James Thurmond Proctor." The sadness paused, giving way to a reverent smile that pined for times long gone. "Absolutely the sweetest eccentric who ever walked."

We observed a silence. She seemed in eye contact with the faces, both hands dug into the pockets of some clean, and no less masculine, khaki work pants. The damp ones were gone. She didn't seem to notice or mind my staring at her. That last name confirmed what I assumed of the people in the photograph and this place where I had come. I had staggered in the very back door of a secrecy. A family scandal, riddled with rounds of rumor, and for years. The truth is, some deep place in me had guessed her part of it from my first clear moment, seeing her on that riverbank. The legend had cooled with time. People assumed the child I saw in that portrait had surely been sent away. Yet the breathing reality of her stood two feet away from me, and in a form scarcely any of Marshal might believe.

The silence had begun to beg for words, so I spoke in what seemed a fitting tone, trying not to touch the question of the portrait's differences in skin shade. This became my sling at lightening the moment.

"Well, I reckon the feller in that picture ain't even near as big a sin-trick as some I know. I could pert near fill this here cabin with sin-tricksters you wouldn' trust to muck after a mule."

Sophia turned, quizzical, trying to make sense of it.

"I'll have to beg some pardon here, but why are we talking sins all of a sudden?"

"You said somethin' or other about that man yonder and sin-tricks."

At this circus of ignorance, Sophia managed, with both hands, to stifle an all out burst of it, but laughter prevailed. Against all politeness she used trying to smother it, out it came. I must have looked a bit like a confused dog, all twisted of head. I smiled back at her, trying to fake that I understood what I didn't come near to understanding.

"I'm sorry," she said, water covering her eyelashes only inches from my face, one of her hands on my shoulder. "I lost my civility. Ec-cen-tric. It's a word, and it means beautifully peculiar when I talk about him. And it's best he's not here to share his thoughts on sin or we'd not eat 'til midnight."

She let a grin diminish into a smile as she brushed hair off my face. The hand came with a care reaching beyond the few minutes of our relationship since the river.

"What a field of wild untended weeds you have in that head of yours. There is some rich growing ground in there, too. Don't let the weeds take it all."

At first, I understood this weed thought of hers about as well as I could reach the moon.

She turned toward the baskets.

"I imagine you feel less like a man and more like a six-foot welt, Mr. Locke. How about some food and fresh clothes? I brought a touch of remedy to go with them."

She handed me one of the baskets, weighted with dense fabric in crisp folds.

"They may be a little big, but they'll do."

A smack of her hand on the desk announced her disappearance into the kitchen, some final instructions trailing.

"I suppose you're hungry enough to eat the rugs off the floor. Tidy up while I set my table out here. You'll find soap and water in the kitchen. Put the lights out as you come."

The slam of the screen door announced I was alone. As hungry as my body must have been, my mind could not escape the effect of my last few hours. The touch of rest had only thickened me with aches and throbs — my whole body taking on a feel of pork fat left to harden in a skillet overnight. I managed my way into the kitchen, where she had carried a kerosene lamp to glow off the white plank walls. Beside an iron stove Sophia had brought a basin of lukewarm water to a table. Above it, I found the only broken thing I had seen in the cabin — on the wall, a mirror, split by a singular crack, dividing it nearly straight in half. One look into it shot back an image that shook me dazed. Frank Locke, Senior, dirtier than normal, wounded by some encounter bound to disgrace us all. Definitely Frank as the town and I knew him — the same high forehead of knotted hair, his eyes under a skim of disorder. Another second shook loose the illusion. It was my own face — in the inescapable image of Frank. Living just a few hours as fodder for wilderness had rendered me further down toward the look of him. I approached the glass to examine the scatter of gash and mud that formed what gazed back at me. The mirror's break, thin as hair, split the visage in two.

"Come eat."

Sophia suddenly peered through the screen. I had heard a clink of dishes on the covered porch.

"Come on before the bread's any colder than it was when we got here."

The mirror held me for a few moments of hand-scrubbing and finger-licks to my hair — all futile repair work. She saw this and came in, soon behind me in the reflection.

"Okay, Narcissus. Don't stand there until you wither, looking in a mirror that can't see through the dirt you're wearing."

She raised both eyebrows then vanished through the screen door.

"Come on, now. You can clean up after we eat. I do have a mirror without a break in it."

I preened another moment and then followed onto the porch, walking as if both feet raked corn-shucks off the floor. The porch took its cover from a slant roof, apparently newer than the cabin. Three lanterns hung from the eaves, drawing little clouds of insect and showering light on a table in white cloth. My lingering in the house had caused the tall candle to droop, yet it cast an undiminished elegance over the meal: A lettuce-and-onion salad mounded in a large bowl, half a cake of cornbread in a basket lined with red cloth, and next to it a cherry pie with only a slice missing. Beside the greens lay precision-cut slices of dark-orange cheese, still in the husks of heavy wax, and around it Sophia had arranged cuttings off a cured ham. Finishing the table were some stag-handle flatware and cream dinner plates next to cut glasses into which Sophia ladled water from a handled pottery crock.

"The bread and the pie aren't warm but they're fresh," she said, nodding me toward the straightback chair and joining me at the table. "I have fish stew, cold in the house. I can warm it, too. None of it made by me, so it's good."

My decline to have her go to more trouble came while taking my chair. "This is more'n fine. I suspect I ain't never seen a table dressed so fine on a porch." The mere smell of food — even after the sickness of the river — put some of my soreness to rest. I sat at the verge of devouring it to the table splinters when my hands found themselves in the coolness of hers for prayer.

"Lord, You are merciful and kind. The proof lies before us again. Bless You for remembering us, though we forget You." She paused for a moment's contemplation, deep and far afield of saying a table grace. A slight quiver came through her fingers. "Save us from ourselves, Lord. Christ be praised, amen."

She wiped her eyes and, busying herself with plating the salad, thanked me for my compliment of her table, of which I still sat in awe. "Don't think this special for you, Mr. Locke. I eat out here most nights now, usually later than this. Just me, a book, and a table fit for the occasion of having more than enough to eat. That's how

I was taught. My mother says life must be lived as fine music is played. Each note struck well, or the whole thing is noise."

"I reckon I made me a devil of a racket most of my life then," I said. "I ain't never seen such a fine spread."

She smiled and we ate together in the sepia glow and evening sounds, our only company a speckling of fireflies and the occasional scream of mosquitoes. She soon took notice that I ate with the worrisome delicacy of one unaccustomed to sharing a bowl of greens with linens, soft light and a strange woman.

"Tablecloth already has spots on it," she said, making her way into the meal with an appetite nearly as lusty as mine. "Eat, please. Nothing to fear. Worship of a table won't get you fed. Eat as though you're thankful for what's on it."

"Yes'm, thank you, I will. I'm just more used to soup beans and creasy greens than I am such as this."

The meal took a devouring as Sophia reached for another pottery container. Out of it she poured a liquid the deep red of dying roses to rest in her empty water glass. "Blackberry wine, my making. It'll make you glad you're alive no matter the day," she said, pouring for me. Mary Lizbeth fermented a similar drink of what she took from Miss Evans' cherry trees. I had tasted and detested the earthy sting of it. "Drink up," Sophia said, after a less-than-dainty pull off her glass. "Don't dare insult the fruit of the house." A melancholy smile moved across her face as I drew a sip of wine that would hardly drown a gnat, feeling the warmth more than the taste. A touch of its loamy fire rose into my head stronger than the force of tobacco. I fought back a wince. "Whole table's pert near fit for Moses, ma'am. Much obliged," I said, putting down the wine and finishing my pie without allowing myself to catch her in another stare. She snickered and raised a glass. "Well, I see more John the Baptist than Moses at this table. A rebel cut from the wilderness. Here's to eat up, clean up and settle the rest later." She finished the glass. "And may God forgive us this unholy communion."

To be polite I forced down the remaining wine in my glass, more conscious of the fact I still carried a nasty portion of that wilderness, wafting off me. I soon caught her looking at me again, the light sharp off the dark pull-back of her hair.

"There's more food in the house. No shame in hunger. I'm glad to bring it out."

"I've had aplenty," I said, trying to sustain something other than the manners of a mule. "Obliged for what I've had."

"Without meddling my way too far into your business of marching about the woods and jousting with a river, what have you had to eat since you last saw a plate?" I could tell she wanted a reply beyond nourishment.

"Had some poke salat in them woods," wiping my mouth as I said it. "Ate it raw. And I shouldn't have."

"Raw poke! *Raw* poke will kill you! Daddy used to pick some and fill this entire cabin and the yard with the stench of boiling it. Pure manure on a poison stalk. Mother wouldn't let him in the back door of the house wearing the clothes he had worn to eat it." Sophia shuddered, a near smile dissipating, as if she had said something she instantly regretted. "I would rather eat my own socks."

The final comment seemed forced and out of place. Sophia kept a look of curiosity and suspicion on me but asked no more questions. With the food soon gone, I glanced toward the great house a couple of times, trying to avoid her examination and to catch any hint of another person stirring about. There was only darkness, apart from the single lighted window. Silence took its uncomfortable place between us again, and I forced it away.

"I am powerful grateful, ma'am. Much obliged to repay if I can one day. I'll not forget what you done for me," I said, with a shyness in the way. I thought it best to say nothing more for fear of revealing too much. My mind already busied itself trying to chart an escape — perhaps even later that very night with a pair of borrowed lanterns lighting me out toward some road away from here. But exhaustion, fueled by effects of the meal, held me down. I nearly nodded into my empty plate.

"Well, you're more than welcome," she said, rattling the candle glow by clearing the table. Sophia seemed even taller than before. A hint of flowery sweetness came off her as she removed the dishes to a wooden box strung with rope handles.

"Just keep your seat. I'll do this and ask no more of you. You are welcome to a clean, quiet bed here, and you're invited to tell me why you need it — but only if you want. I'll not pry, at least not now."

She stacked the dishes, wrapping the glassware in the napkins, snuffed the candle with her fingers, then went for a bag I hadn't noticed against the wall. From it came a box of some Mexican headache powers. With them, two bottles hit the naked wood table — "Grove's Tasteless Chill Tonic" and "Strong Tincture of Arnica." She pointed to each with a physician's confidence.

"Take a good swallow of the tonic with the powders. It's beyond apparent that you hurt worse than you tell me. The Arnica will ease you, too. But you don't drink the Arnica, Mr. Raw Poke Leaves. Just rub it where it hurts — as much as you need — and try not to drown washing your face."

I tried and failed again to make sense of her. Sophisticated, yet apt to toss out some cornpone crack fit for a tobacco warehouse. All of it stupefied me, nearly as much as the way her tongue carved out such graceful diction. The more I took her in — the chestnut features framing a high refinement of young womanhood who, yet, might spit at any moment — the less any of her resembled humankind as I had ever known it. It was as if three or four people found home in a single body, each demanding to be heard.

She uncapped the tonic, opened the powders and withdrew into the cabin, her surmise about my pain hardly an exaggeration. I sat there feeling about as raw and sore as a worm yanked up by a bird. Every strand that held me together weakened by the minute. I took a mouthful of the powder, expecting the bitterness. Granny and Ma had ordered the same potion from the Sears catalog for years and pushed it down my throat when I complained of anything from a headache to constipation. The tonic chased the pungency with an ease that filled my head nearly as fast as the liquid went down. I took another drink and sat nearly dozing, slouched my head over the chair back in the failing lantern light, startled soon by a pile of cloth tossed across my lap. Nightclothes, cool to the touch and layered in folds atop a nearly new cotton shirt and pants. A belt of thick leather bound all of it. Sophia stood over me, dangling a pair of like-new boots of calf leather, shined clean.

"These are yours now." They landed with a thud beside the door. She picked up a tin water bucket and without a word walked in again. I followed as if by instinct, feeling that congealed stiffness of before begin to liquefy in my nerves, under the influence of old-timey chemicals. The thought of rest had fast become omnipotent — my only yearning, of soul and mind, trumping all thought of my suspicions about this woman, the place, or my complications in life. Nearly absentminded of how I reached it, I soon seated myself against the firm mattress of a high bed, the pile of clothing beside me. Sophia had lit a lamp on a dressing table under the open double window. Some mountain night air cooled the room through long white drapes.

"I'll give you some privacy and some trust to go with it." She leaned her bottom against a dark dresser full of bottles, brushes and womanly things. "There is fresh soap and a clean cloth with the water on the table there."

"Obliged again, ma'am. I'll be out of your way soon enough. Thankin' you with every step I take on my way."

"Well, just prove I can trust you not to steal from me. The house doors will be locked. I'd like you to be here in the morning, but if you're not, you are welcome to those clothes and the food in the bread-warming box of the cabin stove. Sleep as long as you wish. Something tells me that tonic will have its way with you. And make no mistake, I am asking you to stay here with me. I'll be most grateful if you do. You and I can help one another. Seems serendipity just might be another name for the will of God between you and me."

Serendipity sounded more to me like a sentence than a word.

We exchanged goodnights and Sophia strode off the porch. I rose to see her cross the yard toward the back door, swinging both lanterns. The second story window light of the great house had already gone dark.

Three days before our first Christmas without Eb, the air turned warm. The brittleness of winter felt coated in a spell of wayward spring, moist and utterly still under gray clouds. It came after a snow and hard freeze that had raised ice that resembled mica shards out of the ground. Fields, roads and yards melted into slicks of shoe-grabbing muck, which seemed to cling to everything – even Granny's dauntless joy.

She and bitterness usually knew little of each other, but for a short while that Christmastime after Eb died they became kindred. Granny banged around the kitchen, whispered under her breath, even cracked a broom in two over her leg when she stumbled over it in the yard. The gentle hum that normally filled her days turned into a set-jaw silence as hard as a doorframe. Frank had gone briefly and obsequiously sober – his homage to a little boy's death and the cost of the drug sanitarium, I suppose – but my Uncle Useless lay in moaning heaps of hibernation, claiming, "My heart's broke, my back's hurt, and my feet feels worse." Mattie waddled tearfully about, too broken for chores – bewailing her missing of Eb while complaining more than ever about the messes and uproar made by the pack of surviving wildcats she had already cut loose on the world. Pap and Ma seemed lost in their work and a reticent denial of it all, but Granny's hackles rose. A sense she suddenly disapproved of most of life steamed off her quiet and resounded in every move.

Then, in that odd winter warmth, she decided to get herself over it. She tied two rocking chairs across the back of her little jenny mule, Cartie, and led me off with her on the journey. "Let's go to the sittin' place. We'll sit in God's pocket and watch the creek thaw," she said. "Let's get gone, 'fore I say somethin' that'll follow me to my grave."

We trudged out of the hollow and up the tiny ridge path behind the house, Granny swinging a sackful of apples against her leg. We set the chairs out on the little stone ledge above the fall of water and rocked in the sound of it, gazing off at the leafless ridges, talking of nothing for a long while before I felt the warm leather of her hand on mine. She had a peace to say.

"Frankie, you remember when I took sick right after Eb died? I was hotter than a stove, but I still got up and swept out the whole house. Even took me a mid-night bath when you told me them church women was a comin' the next day to help look after me. I couldn't stand needin' help, Frankie. Couldn't stand the notion of them seein' my mess, and it liked to killed me. I had to go and jostle around, cleanin' up for people who was a comin' to clean up for me, and I still ain't over it. Still hackin' and wheezin' and can't get no better. Well, I'm done with such, Frankie. I'm done tryin' to force my sense into this ol' world. I reckon when the good Lord comes for me, He'll have to find me in my cobwebs and all. Reckon He'd ruther find a soul who needs help, instead of one claimin' it ain't got a cobweb a'tall."

I didn't know what to add to that, other than to ask if the Almighty might find cobwebs in her drawers the day she breathed her last. It was the unseemly thing Eb might say. And it made her laugh.

We sat rocking. She talked again of how the mountains resembled great coat shoulders and what might lay beyond. I said virtually nothing, and it all took both of us far afield of the chaos behind.

Granny's anger seemed to evaporate on our breath in the cold air, which began its return toward late afternoon. Cartie, as a mule will, decided to sit down on us twice for no reason, hauling the chairs back down the mountain — so dark had nearly come by the time we reached the house. Mattie had strung more strands of popcorn for the Christmas tree, and Granny seemed to share joy in the achievement.

Before spring warmed the air so much again, Granny would lay dying of pneumonia.

"Honey, you've been like the quiet friends of Job, the way you salved my heart. Thank you for sittin' quiet with me. You put a salve on the break in my heart," were the last words she spoke to me.

I might have slept until dark fell again had the dawn not risen damp and hot. It invaded to the skin where I lay splayed across the clean bedspread. Sleep had come within seconds after Sophia left the room and daylight found me unmoved, unwashed, and loath to see the glow of day.

I eased off the bed, stiff, with old dirt cleaving like tar — as did a touch of hangover from the remedy. Yet planning escape chased off the aches and daze. Sophia seemed an early riser, likely to check first thing on the guest out back, so I flew into motion, worried about who might join her to examine me. A check out the window. A scene of photographic quiet — the drapes of the great house still as stone, the yard skimmed with fog. I pulled Pap's watch from my pants, only to remember it had taken to the river with me. It read nine minutes to twelve — wrong and ruined. I rummaged for another clock and found one that said ten minutes to seven. Later than I wanted.

I took what Granny would call a rag bath in the basin Sophia left, then dressed in the untouched pile of clothes from the bed. I found the pants too long and the shirt too big, but cleanliness seemed a decent travel disguise for someone last seen hightailing into the woods. After being scrubbed nearly raw, my face took on some greater respectability in the split mirror, though still too remindful of Frank after a night out in the rain on a paregoric drunk. I was prickly with beard — no blade found to shave it — and the scrape and chafe of wilderness travel gave my looks an even stronger air of trouble. I thought of Mary Lizbeth's opinion that a man owed grooming to himself as much as any lady. So in desperation I borrowed Eb's notion that a man's truest beauty composes itself along a well-lubricated hairline. The nearest thing to a pomade I could quickly find was a tin of mink oil in a dresser drawer. It gave my head a high sheen and a primal funk akin to wet dog. The reek continued to bloom as I explored the cabin for a pencil and scrap of paper.

In the cabin's main room, mostly untouched by daylight, I remembered Sophia had locked the desk. But next to it a trash basket held a few scraps of heavy stationery. One sizable piece with most of the lettering ripped away contained some word fragments — something about a company and some street in what I deciphered as New York. I found a pencil on a reading table, and wrote on the back side of the scrap.

Thank you for the help you give. I'm rite greatful you would not let me die. I hope I weren't terrible much more trouble than feedin' a stray dog. Reckon there ain't a thing I can leave but a thank you. So I do. Frank.

The scrap would hold a little more of my left-hand scrawl, but I was reasonably satisfied. The faces of Ma and Mary L., my uncle's gore on the ground, the whole hash of everything that brought me here began to rise again into worries, so I put the pencil down to go rummage the kitchen. Into the cloth napkin I rolled the leftover cornbread, half of which I stuffed crumbling into my mouth. A tin of evaporated milk joined the bread in a pants pocket. From there I slipped out the cabin's front door, lodging my note in the crack with needless quiet.

The morning's fog held, but not enough to conceal my passage to the barns. I crept over the yard, climbed a fence, then broke into a sprint across the pasture of this farm, which I knew was not worked out of any necessity. I needed to borrow some transportation, knowing now the source of the money that bought it.

My entire life, much the way they rattled the grapevines about Mary L. and her mother, people had chattered and speculated about the man who founded and still ran — from nearly anonymous distance — the Marshal cotton mill. They talked of why he and his high-born wife had taken to raise a little black girl, some railing about how it didn't seem decent that the dark-color baby had last been seen in fine store-bought clothes while townsfolk of lighter color wore patched homespun. People argued about whether the adoption amounted to Christian charity, often in sharp words that mowed down friendships. And then there was the rumor of what had happened to the child, who disappeared from town as fast as she had been carried in. Had she died? Had such a death thrown the Proctor house into long and solitary mourning? Or had the storm of opinion — especially from those who didn't work in the mill — moved the Proctors to return the child where they found her? Regardless, the Proctors — faced with excoriation and scandal — had abandoned all neighbors. Jim, his wife — known as Miss Julia — and the quietly shocking infant only a few had ever seen, had retreated into the sanctuary of their wealth, leaving management of the mill to foremen who admitted even they had no direct contact with the owner.

And there I stood, looking at the backside of a great part of the Proctor fortress that cotton weaving had helped to build. The house stood on an enormous swath of land, a retreat protected by some steep ground, a single entryway, but more so by natural and cultivated forest — a thicket as green as the riches that walled the owners in. Like the Vanderbilts of the grand Biltmore House of Asheville, the Proctors also lived protected by the reverse snobbery of the poor, who believe they must avoid the rich or else risk humiliation. The deep-skinned baby helped seal the walls of this ostracism in the hearts of many, though Pap said he didn't care "what color young'un John Proctor took to raise — purple as a grape," for all he cared. He still thought that mill made a slave of every soul who worked it.

I was quite sure no one who had ever turned a scythe tongue on the Proctors had ever stood where I was about to step. This emboldened me nearly as much as it scared me half out of what were surely Mr. Proctor's pants, as I slipped into the first outbuilding — the smallest of the three. This was no true barn but more a house itself, windowless and painted white. Two doors comprised the entire rear of it, one ajar, just enough to fit my head for a look. Nothing. Too dark, apart from a glint off what looked like a curve of metal inside. I had pulled open the door an inch or two more to let in some light when the opening yapped at me. Iced my blood. A high, piercing yowl descended into a near bark, which sent my intruding head backward, rock-hard against the door wood. I staggered, braced for immediate dog attack from the black opening when a drooping hound emerged — seemingly the one from the cabin painting — yawning, stretching, and eager for company. He mellowed into a wagging sack of whines, sniffing at the bread in my pocket.

"God A'mighty. Hush up, now. Shut your beggin' dog mouth," I whispered, feeling my heart slow to a gallop from a pounding stride. I rubbed the dog's head and pulled open the door.

I knew I had to be quick. If Proctor's farm held much in the way of livestock apart from this dog and the one horse Sophia mentioned, someone would soon be up to feed, or perhaps milk. The tail slapped my leg as if the dog were showing me around as we stepped inside. The room smelled musty, foreign, nothing like any stable. A touch of cool, painted metal, smooth as ice, met my hands. The rubbery smell and curved outline I could still barely see confirmed it. The dog slept, at least part time, with a car.

I could drive her, I thought. Not much different from the truck. I skimmed a fingertip across the steel. No heavy dust. This car surely ran. It smelled of having run not long ago. How fast could I get out of here in this? The sheriff had a truck, but this would set me down the road so far my dust would settle under three rains before anyone got near me. "A car," I whispered to the dog, who still wagged and begged at my knee. "I'm gonna drive myself to some freedom, hound dog. Far as I can 'til I'm sure somebody figures killin' Useless couldn't be helped." I knew the latter was a lie and that even borrowing a car this way could send me to jail. The foolish boy in me, for a moment, ignored the pangs of both.

The next step was pushing open the doors to reveal the prize and figure some way to borrow it without waking the dead. A touch of light flooded across a long name cast in metal on the rounded hood — which was even more massive of scale in the tiny garage, where it rested at the end of fresh tracks I should have seen. A fairly youthful Cadillac, curved and brawny and black, looked to me like some momentary automotive dream. As I studied it in the light, the dog wagged eagerly for the door to open, and I felt my plans flush away on a tide of practical fear. Too loud, too criminal, too grand a feat for so small a fugitive. I had made enough trouble for myself just by running and wanted no more from temporarily stealing John Proctor's car.

"Gettin' gone's more my need than car thievery," I whispered, caressing the metal as if it could feel. "I reckon I ain't that done-for yet." Though I imagined steering the great force of her past the house, out on the road, all the way to the sound of ocean — if I could pick up enough work for the gas. Onto this came the image of Mary Lizbeth frowning on some criminal wreckage of me in handcuffs. Just the thought of her brought on a storm of longing, calmed only by the work at hand.

I hoped the dog would stay inside. He had lost interest in a ride — had begun inspecting his own underpinning — but he slipped out as I closed the door. I tried to scatter him away but he followed, dutifully quiet, up the hill through trees to the barns. Everything lay still in the dew.

A wood barricade slipped easily off a door, and my intrusion stirred movement. A rustle of straw under a long breath, then came the overpowering quiet again, apart from some crows arguing up the ridge. Light leached in on four stalls, two with horses — a big, dark stag with an assuring gray on his nose, his smaller neighbor a chestnut mare with a calm in her eyes. "Shhh, ch, ch, ch," I whispered, then rubbed and prattled at them a moment. "Say there, bud, Pap would say you're old as Mathugee (his grinning contraction of Biblical Methuselah). Say now, sweet girl, I won't hurt. Be easy now."

My horsemanship experience went more to plow mules and small jennies, but all the parts at hand were familiar enough. I searched fast for tack and was not disappointed. One wall hung with excess: Loops, halters, even some Lucas racing bridles dangling amid the combs and quarter boots. Stumbling around and noticing trough marks — indicating the animals had already been fed and watered that morning — sent me into even faster motion.

A halter bridle from that wall slipped easily over the chestnut's head. She led tamely out the door, showing larger of muscle in the full light, but trustful of face — as easy as a child's pony. I can't explain my assumption that borrowing a farm's horse — perhaps someone's cherished pet — amounted to less than stealing its car. Other than such a frantic young mind can turn dense as a black hole. I stayed honest enough not to pilfer one of three saddles perched across a wall where I found the bridle. Yet my next decision flickered off a set of wits and virtue dimmer than a snuff-dipper's grin.

A hay reaper rested against the rear of the barn, where I had led the mare for some seclusion until we got to know one another well enough for me to mount her. The reaper was recently used, given the look of a nearby field, some fairly new tracks in the weeds, and the plow harness I found hanging handy and supple inside the barn door. I had spent many a July day on such a hay rake, pulled by Pap's big gray mule, Jez. It was a simple carriage: Two big, wide-set metal wheels in front of rake tines five feet long, like some giant curving hair comb, all of it controlled from a big steel seat just above the works. It would ride nearly as well as Pap's wagon. I figured it a decent disguise. Anyone driving a hay rake on a main road would blend in as a clod-buster without any better sense. It never occurred to me that even on the fabric of our farm culture, the thing might stand a scandalized boy out — show him up like some gaudy jewel. And that was the least of the idea's flaws.

I coaxed the mare into position and rigged her to the rake in a hurried minute or two, during which I mulled designs on how best to pass the house in quiet and make for the road. I never visualized capture. Thought of some lawman taking notice of a haggard teenage boy driving a hay rake through the hustling streets of a town never pricked its way into my reasoning. I wasn't even quite sure whether to head on toward Asheville and points east or answer the inner roar of guilt and curiosity by turning back to Marshal and owning up to everything. Just as I mounted the hard seat came a twinkling of good sense. "Why didn't you just light out walkin' thirty minutes ago, 'stead of foolin' with all this?" I asked under my breath. But the hitching work was done. I refused to waste time turning my back on the pursuit of foolishness. Not knowing the mare's name, I gave her one Frank used as a generic for all plow animals. "Get up, Maude, get up," I said, shaking a decent slap of the reins out of fear she wouldn't pull. This fulfilled one of the largest mistakes of my life on any farm.

The wheels rolled a foot or two forward, then back, and with dust still rising from where the leather hit her haunches, the mare reared and launched the entire apparatus toward madness. The clang of machinery spooked the horse into an uproar. The yank of it wrenched me nearly breakneck to the ground.

"Whoa, now, whoa, no, no, no, now, no." It was all the reprimand I could manage. My feet had flown so high they nearly replaced my buttocks with the back of my head on the seat. In the sudden heave of it all, I had lost the reins.

The mare thundered around the corner of the barn with the rake and me wagging at her tail. I held the seat, howling for her to stop, as she broke into full run past the car barn and down the hill, the old dog galloping behind us, yelping to keep up. The rake bounced under a willow tree, whose limbs gave me the whipping I deserved, then the horse aimed straight for the big house. The metal wheels drummed my tailbone against that steel seat with force ringing clear to my hair. There was no telling whether the mare was truly startled, in a sprint for fun, or some of both. But she was free, in control, and fast as a larded pig chased at a county fair.

The noise only fired more steam into her heart. I had never seen a horse run so. I nearly flew off as she spun shy of the cabin and hurtled back uphill, past the barns, through the orchard, reversing again at the cusp of the woods. Downhill was much worse — rising speed — toward the house again. I gripped the rake with hands, boot tips, and every certainty that to fall off — or jump — meant bone-cracking ruin. The mare muscled us off the ridge in a near zig-zag. This set the rake into such bound and swing it felt like riding the clapper of a giant bell. Somewhere — I had lost sight of him — the dog yapped harder than ever as we jounced near the back of the house again. I heard Sophia plowing out a yell before I saw her.

"Whoa...Charlotte...Charlotte, stop...Pull her, Frank...Pull her hard."

It all sounded nearly as one word and seemed to lure the horse toward the back door of the great house as if she'd been called there. I groped hard and managed to get the reins as Sophia leaped off the back steps, shirttail flagging above her pants, a rifle in her left hand. The horse-drawn carnival passed her, and she gave chase, yelling more for the horse to stop. The mare gestured toward swinging some laps around the cabin, but Sophia's voice slowed her just enough for me to venture the risk of jumping — rather than perhaps being shot — off the seat. I remember going airborne, trying to clear the tines and wheels, then the suffocation of breath knocked faraway again, followed by rolling on grass and gravel for what seemed a half-hour.

I came to rest at the base of the cabin's rear porch where we had eaten the night before — my ribs tightening into a hard knot. Catching a breath felt like trying to draw a watermelon through a perfume sprayer. I rolled some more, then lay still, looking up and gasping at the clouds, silently urging death to come on and not loiter so near. The horse din faded behind the cabin. There was only Sophia's distant yelling before that soon quieted, and I was alone — a silent mound of fatuous boy who just wanted to die or go on back home.

A few people loved to brag and promise about one day riding out to catch sight of this Proctor place and the mysteries it held. The home, mythic in size and riches from all the surmise about it, held allure for teenagers wanting to badger the occupants with Halloween pranks, to see if it were home to mouth-lathering lunatics or just the uppity rich. One or two of the dullest minds imagined Julia Proctor some kind of highly educated witch who wanted a baby of dark color for the blackest of un-Christian ritual. The truth was, the Proctor house seemed nearly further off than the stars. It was accessible, other than the backwater way I came in, only by a narrow crevice of a driveway — an old tree-tented logging trail, winding faraway from the main river road east out of town. Scarps and sheer drops, the river and thickets so dense wild turkeys wouldn't live there, lay between Marshal and this spot. This helped secure the place, along with the fact that some people worked so hard they had little time or energy to explore where the mill profits went, much less where the boss and his family had gone. All this gave the Proctors their isolation and the babblers a banquet table for their own babble. Rolling, then, on its backyard, I grew certain my death there would become one of its well-kept secrets.

But as some of the breath eased back into me, I thought it possible a curious soul had gotten up to this farm only to turn back, pale and mum with fear from facing Sophia the scandal baby, nearly six feet tall now, fitted with a firearm. She was gone only a moment after the horse and stood now, shadowing me, aiming the rifle in my face. I knew she could kill me without fear of discovery, prosecution, or perhaps even guilt.

"This is judgment day, thief." She breathed hard but her eyes held a calm. "I have family to protect here, and I'm resolute to do it." The dog stood panting into my face. I writhed around some more, all winces and chokes, pain from the fall a hot glow in my bones. But it paled against the fear of looking at that gun's eye. The black of it glared barely a foot from my nose.

"Lord, I hurt, ma'am. I hurt. Please don't wreck me worse than what I am. I'm beggin'." I whimpered and turned away. Sophia soared into high rage.

"If I were going to shoot you for this, I would have done it by now, and I would not have aimed for your derriere either. Tell me, do you steal horses for a living? Or just for the bracing thrill of grass-staining that ass when you fall off? Are you trying to bruise one cheek black and the other blue? I can tell you, being darker won't grease you through this life any better. Open your eyes. Give some defense of yourself."

I could do little but confess in my own mind. I was a horse thief, and stupid enough to attach a rickety farm tool to sound the alarm of it. I expected any second would bring John Proctor wielding the most ill temper, and who knows what other weapon, out the back door of the big house to help Sophia rid the place of the pig child who had bitten the hand that saved and slopped him. So the pig chose to play possum. I pretended to swoon for a moment, hoping for some sympathy and to collect a thought. The performance had a peculiar effect.

"Oh, Lord God, Lord, what have I done here?" she asked. Through a clenched eye I saw her lift back the rifle and walk away, rubbing her face, head bowed. Her words carried that wrinkled feeling of someone near tears.

"I don't swindle easily, young man," she soon said, turning suddenly back to me where I lay groaning, holding my ribs and ostensibly coming to my senses. She came so near again I could almost view her cleavage through the gape of the shirt as she knelt on one knee, finger-waving my face again. Her rant began to calm.

"You test me, Mr. Locke. I'm the Samaritan who pulls you from a river at my own peril, gives you board for the night, never to pry, and these are your best thanks? Worse than a vandal." She stood again, muttering something about disobeying herself while she paced, then came back at me again, a little calmer. "Do you realize I would let you stay here as long as you needed? I require nothing from you. No answers, no forced labor, no board. I guess my largesse of last night came a little too easily for you, didn't it? I know the meal and the company weren't fancy, but they deserve better than a criminal."

"I'm sorry. I'm powerful sorry, ma'am." I began trying to raise myself, figuring confession may light my way out of this mess. I was tired of the whole matter. Shackles and a jail would have felt good.

"Ma'am, I regret takin' the horse and rake and all that. I wish they'd just killed me and got me over with. I never stole before. Nothin'. But I got desperate. I told you yesterday, I can't be known to nobody, but truth is I reckon it's gonna happen, so we might as well get on with it."

With that, I carried on, tangling truth with the lie of omission, confessing about running away from home in Marshal, from some witless family and a good mother and a brilliant girl who was bound to wonder what had become of me. I told her I had fled the law.

"Ma'am, I gotta move on 'cause somebody got hurt real bad. It was never meant to happen, but ain't a thing can be done about it now. I reckon I woulda done everything I could to get your horse and machine back here, somehow. I was taught better than all this, and I'm about as full of sorry as I can get."

By now I had pulled myself up to sit on the edge of the cabin porch, noticing the lathered mare grazing free by a rose trellis near some trees beside the cabin. I had no idea whether Sophia had calmed her or she had run herself down, but she stood happy and sweet as a new bride, the rake still attached as her train. Sophia stopped pacing the porch and took a seat beside me on the edge of the pine boards. I noticed she was barefoot, the feet long and narrow and fine, nearly the same color as the chestnut horse. She spoke in that hush that comes from restored calm, asking me if I were hurt. I said I hurt all over but would survive. Then she showed me the rifle was loaded. It was a Winchester "Take Down" — .22 caliber. Her hand seemed comfortable and satisfied to hold it.

"Do you know where this gun came from? I didn't yank it off a wall when I heard all the uproar out here. It's kept locked in a cabinet in that house. Not easily retrieved."

By now a fear shot through me, wondering whether she lived here by herself, having shot everyone else — for she and I seemed utterly alone on this place.

"I didn't entirely trust you last night, so I slept with this rifle." She sat oddly serene, staring off at the treetops.

"You know, a dragonfly is a harmless and beautiful thing. Blue-green and delicate. But I'm afraid of it. I know better, but I'm afraid if it touches me, it might sting. Lovely and fragile and fearsome at once. You came out of that river a dragonfly to me, Frank Locke. There may not be much real harm in you, but I'll not take the chance. Not yet. This rifle will stay near me as long as you're around here, and we're going to help one another."

With that, and a bit more of my lost breath coming back, I reached into the pants pocket for the can of milk — which had felt like a cannonball in there on the jump — and the lump of now pulverized bread, resting both on the porch edge between us.

"I'd like to give you these back, ma'am, and just say if you have any work needs doin' around here, I'd like to do it. Best I could, to make up for how I've been. If not, I'd be obliged to say thank you and I'm sorry and get to walkin' — out on my way and outta yours."

She looked at the contents of the pocket, then up at me.

"You think it's that simple, letting you go, thief or not? Do you know how long it's been since a stranger walked this place? You're not telling me everything you know, so I'll speak what's on your mind — because neither of us has been honest with the other. You know of the Proctors. I know you do. You come from Marshal, so you know every brick of the mill, because you work there, and you've heard more than a little about this place and me and my place in it. And it's all lies. Or, only cuttings off the truth."

I stared at my boots and held my aching sides, wondering how I could have been hammerheaded enough to suppose her ignorant of anything. Her sculpted way of talking caused me nearly to believe she knew more about what I knew than I did.

"Reckon that's so, ma'am. Reckon I pert near recognized you just off that riverbank, and hadn't never seen you before. I sorta knew you from all I'd heard of you, ma'am."

"Stop calling me ma'am. I could be your sister — if we rolled you in molasses to brown you down some. Here's the situation, Dragonfly: I've been keeping the secrets of this house and this cabin and this family for too long. Holding up my end until I've worn out. You could leave here now and feed people a little grist to grind in their mouths about the rich and peculiar Proctors — thinking they know us so well out here. But you'll not do that. You'll stay right here." She raised the gun to her left hand, away from me. "And I'll risk another chance to trust in you, against every instinct I have but one. I will try to rise above my weakest parts, and I'll expect no less from you."

"I've got to go on, lessen you've got some job for me. Like I said, I'd be glad to work some chores to make up for what trouble I've been, then jostle myself on outta your way. I've got women to tend to."

"You will not go. Not yet. And by the way, women don't need a man's 'tending.' I'm going to do what my daddy always said: Let faith disobey fear. I presume you came in here on the Lord's providence and it's up to me to make the best of that for the both of us. I'm going to show you some things hard to believe, but they're as real as I am. If you answer the urge to steal something from here again, take it on. You'll know why I say that soon enough. But if you even whisper of doing harm to the woman of that house, I will shoot you myself. If I have to chase you to the poles of this earth to do it. God forgive me for thinking about it."

She had risen to pace on the grass for that little sermon, wiping her eyes toward the end. She might have carried on, had I not thrown up.

"Ma'am, I know I ain't got much place to be askin' for nothin', but if I don't get to some resemblance of a thing to relieve myself, we'll have ourself a yard and a porch to clean."

I choked on the words and vomited again on the ground. The wrench of it seared a new agony through every injury of the last couple of days. My insides, to the marrow, felt lush with the very hottest soils of hell.

"Hold on. We have a bathroom. Come on."

With the rifle in one hand and the other arm around the crook of my waste, Sophia led me across the yard, where I threw up once more, nearly hitting the dog. I heard the horse follow us like a pet to the back door. We entered fast. The house smelled of fresh cooking, which fomented a searing rebellion in my depths.

"Right in here. Here you go."

She led me through a kitchen and down a hallway the sickness blinded me to see, before throwing open the bathroom door.

"I'm going upstairs for a moment. Can I leave you that long?" Her voice had turned soft.

I nodded and stepped into a roomful of sights that nearly shocked me well again. Under gleaming legs stood a bathtub, white as snow. Rounding it, a curtain, suspended from a ceiling finished in a blonde sheen of fine wood. Nearby, a pull chain and tank atop a bronze-color pipe, glowing down the wall, to a toilet bowl so smooth and clean I thought it better suited to carrying drinking water than the fruits of toiletry. The commode sat next to a white pedestal sink arrayed in cut glassware. Above that, a white-frame mirror hung on wallpaper full of blue and pink blossoms. Soaps and towels, perfumed waters and tooth compounds — all of it washed the entire room in the notion that rich people do not possess quite the same bodily urges as the rest of us. Or, if they do, the results must resemble the honeysuckle blooms that rise far above the cowpats. Thus went the first glance of my life at the finest in domestic interior plumbing. The mill had it crudely, but every home I had ever slept in required a path walk for outhouse relief.

Sophia had closed the door and I conducted the urgent business. The room was too warm but my nausea cooled and was soon gone, the worst left on the yard. Behind it my entire body felt like leaves after a dry spell. I pulled the chain and sat on the hard tile floor a moment, thirsting, but hypnotic with relief. Soon, I was inspecting the toilet as if it were some minor throne of heaven. It looked to me the way milk would if you could harden it. I had been near such an appliance on Pap's milk and egg-selling trips into Asheville, but had never experienced anything quite so gilded as this space where the Proctors relieved and bathed themselves. The dimensions outsized the room where I had slept most of my life. I remember thinking if a bed and some means of cooking were installed a man might do far worse than spend the better part of his days in such a room. A shuffle of feet came from the front of the house toward the door and I stood, rubbing hair down and gathering some wits. I had avoided a deep glance into the mirror, for what I saw resembled more a human cow cud than a teenage boy. I preened away the worst of it and stepped out just as Sophia reached me. A touch of gloom came with her — as if what she had seen had lain a veil of worry on her eyes. Yet she brightened deliberately, asking me if I found everything I needed in the bathroom.

"I'm right fine now, ma'am. And that's one fine commode you got yonder. They ought call *that* John the Baptist."

She snickered, yet the smile bending through this new aspect of her appeared an act of forced labor. Something in our short moments apart had drawn out a resignation. The iron in her voice thinned to vibrato.

"Still being yourself I see, Mr. Locke. Still a thief *and* a wit, I see."

She leaned against the wall and wiped at sudden tears with both palms. A glance at the ceiling, a clenching of her mouth — none of it would fully quiet the tempest that wet her to the chin. I hurt all over, but pain far deeper than mine lived somewhere in this house. I had seen such before.

"Your pursuit of death needs a rest, Mr. Locke. I'm about to give us both a respite we've waited for too long. Like it or not, you're soon to join this masquerade."

Sophia brushed my left cheek, as if trying to take some bewilderment away. She led me to the kitchen, enormous and modern beyond my imagination for that day, where I was given an overly large glass of the "Grove's Chill Tonic." The dizzying effect rose faster than any steam, welcome as a hot coffee in snow. "Follow me," were her only words as we left the house quietly through the back door.

The tonic had its strong way. I hurt a bit less through the backyard, plodding like some sycophant child behind her to the southeast. The dog had disappeared. Charlotte — hay rake still attached — tried to trail us until Sophia fastened her to the cabin porch. We hiked rising ground, on a worn little course through a wall of old hardwood and into a patch of evergreens, lean and standing high above the soft floor. On the way, she talked with an air of confession of how her life had been. Raised with store-bought wagons and tea sets and imported dolls, abandoning those early for steel fly rods and fishing with both Proctors along the quiet pool where she had found me. She spoke of parties, ornate dances the Proctors had thrown on the lawn, just the three of them. A family of living joy in its seclusion, hanging trellises with flowers and candlelight and setting the air aglow with kinds of music I didn't understand. Sophia's love of the Proctors poured out, celebrating their lasting courtship — dance and laughter, all so sublime the words nearly held taste and perfume. I tagged along as her audience of one, fascinated that she and Mr. Proctor had gone wildcrafting over miles of woods, filling knapsacks and days full of Cherokee remedy, carrying books full of native lore. Yet very early, Mrs. Proctor had filled Sophia's mind with reading and music and a love of learning about the faraway. It all felt like taking in the air of some cool-slumber dream — family glory veiled against the worst of the world, spent in this reserve of verdant cover and excess money. I ached for more as we stepped into a tiny clearing in the cultivated pines. Sophia turned quiet. Toward the center stood a dark, oversize weight of polished granite above a time-settled grave. She stepped to it, kept a moment's silent vigil, then knelt, tracing fingers across the name.

"This is where he is. This is your John Proctor, Mr. Locke. The one of all the talk and contempt. None of it can reach him now." The vibrato returned with the tears. She apologized, saying she cried some on every trip to this place. She said it healed her, and that she indulged it with gratitude, not regret. The date on the stone read November 23, 1926. John Proctor had been dead nearly three years, and for all his deliberate seclusion, the entire mill and the town around it appeared to have no hunch he was permanently gone.

"My daddy has taken his place at the party of God now," she said, never looking away. I knelt with her, a few steps behind out of respect.

"How'd you get him and that rock up this hollow here? How come nobody knows?"

"There are people who know he's gone. Very few, and they vow to take his secrets and ours to their coffins. They're the same who know he turned his back on the world, and in some measure because of how it treated me. They know he came to consider the want of money a nearly cureless disease."

She bowed her head, silent, as if building up a courage, then turned that resigned look on me again.

"Frank, I don't know why you're here, or what's to come of it. But it's time you knew him. This man came to believe greed stills the soul. He called it the worst part of himself and any man. That's why he built that cabin out back the way he did, with the front door turned away from the house. He built it as a retreat from a poison that sickened this family. And he taught me a cure for it, which you'll know in time. But I wanted you to know this life has lost a sweet and beautiful man, no matter the flaws you ever hear. And to answer your question, we hauled him up here on a wagon. Charlotte pulled him. We borrowed help from the Vanderbilt place in Asheville to cut the trees and make the grave. We shipped the coffin and the tombstone from Raleigh, and gave him just the small funeral he would have wanted right here in this place he loved. And neither my mother nor I has been the same since."

She paused and swiped again at a show of hurt, still trying to keep me from seeing fully through.

"I am so tired," she said, looking at the stone again, and eventually deep into me. "I love him but I'm tired of keeping my promise and holding his secrets and doing this work. I'm worn out. You dropped in, such as you did, and I'm taking you as you are, Frank. Divine vessel, cracks of thievery and all. I don't know you, but I will trust you as my relief. I'm working on faith and need here. Now you know he's gone, and I don't much care who you go tell. But I *need* you to stay with me awhile."

Rather than wait for my answer she went into rhythmic work, pulling a few scarce weeds apart from the stone and dusting off the ledge of it. I wanted more of what my ears could not quite believe.

"How'd he die?" I asked, stepping around to squat at the stone's back side, joining in the weed chore.

"Damned if I know. We were roasting pumpkin seeds the day before Thanksgiving. He left Mother and me with a spread of them at the kitchen table a little after eight, claiming he had a headache."

She digressed into another moment about how fully the man had loved her — his doting and overflow pride — with me much too afraid to ask how a child of such color came to live there. She said his adoration of Julia Proctor reached to the stars and back. He had shone with a love of both, stepping from the kitchen that Thanksgiving eve, saying they belonged in a picture.

"The two of us, just as we were. We'd been laughing silly about how I had split my pants dancing in the yard that day. He said he regretted he didn't have a painting of us exactly as he saw us at that table, with candles all around. She and I didn't go up to bed until very late. Mother found him cold, still dressed, across their bed. She came screaming after me in my room. We just stood trembling on one another and looking at him. That same sweet little smile. She and I lay down with him and rubbed his head and couldn't turn from it. Not even death would steal that smile off him."

By then she sat, knees up, on the grave, her back to the stone as if the place made for a comfortable chair. She had taken a small journal from somewhere — she didn't seem to have a pocket large enough — and held it, doing nothing.

"I come here just to be. Most every day. Sometimes twice. Just to sit or lie here and hold myself steady in the quiet, and I write whatever my pencil feels like putting down. It's a good medicine, and you're welcome to a dose yourself. There's peace in a grave stone. It holds gratitude for being above ground."

The excess of medicine she had given from that tonic bottle held me numb nearly to my nails. I took the offer and lay down behind her — letting John Proctor's tombstone part us, as if it were a cold book between ends. A nap seemed inevitable. I was too bleary to think much about what she had told me, so in stretching out I resolved just to live a moment in the shock of it and find out more as it came.

The cultivated pines walled in the clearing and gave a feel of sanctuary. They felt sturdy against the meanness of the world. I scooted further down, borrowing the stone's ledge as a pillow, and caught sight of a quartered daylight moon, silvery against the morning blue, pretty as an heirloom pinned to fine cloth. Sophia still leaned against the opposite side, joking of how often she came to sit there and wondering aloud whether the soul of the man she adored as a father ever tired of having the face of his corpse topped by the divide of her buttocks. Even if death and clay did surely temper the effect. The word soul — the casually true way she had spoken it — woke something in me. I contemplated that moon, taking what felt like my first real rest in weeks, and further stirred the quiet.

"You suppose we got a soul, or is what we're buried with all there is?"

"I believe we amount to a good deal more than dust," she said. Her voice eased around the stone. The reverence of it, I suppose, helped loosen that deep muscle that strains back how we truly feel. What poured out of me tasted of satisfaction akin to a long cool drink.

"I reckon if we've got a soul, mine's about as lonesome as a man's can get. How come I can look at that moon yonder and feel like I'm right near as faraway as it is from all the good I ever did know? Reckon I've gone and run myself so faraway I'll never find a way back to the only fresh good in my life. I'm a right unforgivable soul is what I am."

"So, what's her name?" Sophia asked after some pause. "And what did you do to her, apart from taking leave and nearly breaking your neck in that river?" I could feel it, even from the other side of that rock: The female smirk that grows from instincts only women seem to possess.

"Mary Lizbeth," I said, my mind drifting off. The granite behind my head might as well have been a feather pillow.

"She's Mary L. to me, and I'm right sure I got me a soul down in me somewheres, 'cause I can feel it. Feels like it won't do a thing but pain me somethin' awful 'til I die. Be the most lonesome place I'll ever know. Some dark house cryin' for just a candle's worth of light. She is a light — to the very sills of my heart, ma'am. I been so cold inside and just a glance at her in my thinkin' colors my insides like a Christmas fire. Ain't a warmer light in this world. Nor a sweeter heat in any man. And I ain't fit for even thinkin' on her. Reckon she figures I lay a corpse in the woods by now, which is fine by me. Best to die in her heart and just live with it. Better that than break her heart with knowin' I'm alive and not man enough to come tell her she is my own heart's warm hearth. My Granny used to say you can get over a broke arm, but you get under a broke heart. You carry it a long spell. I just hope Mary L.'s ain't as heavy as mine. If it is, I wish I could carry it for her. I'd break myself down to lighten any trouble she ever feels."

I finished and stretched nearly at slumber under the clouds, where they passed across the hole of the pine clearing. One of them moved over the view that had been my rich setting for the moon. Another moment's quiet, then Sophia's face peered around the rock. She crawled around to me, stuffing the book into her pants, a shard of pencil balled in her hand.

"Well, God bless the cornpone poet in that wilderness head of yours, Mr. Frank Locke. That was some speech." Sophia stretched beside me, putting her head against the granite beside mine. "Perhaps you should give that talk to her one day. And by the way, I'm living proof there is no soul alive who has to carry a broken heart alone. Not even here."

We kept still a moment under the moving clouds and dark blue and the little ghost of a moon.

"I ain't been gone from home two full days yet and I'll wager you I matter about as much to Mary Lizbeth Hunter as two bygone wintertimes. I'll bet you that moon yonder feels closer than I do to her. And it don't hardly look real on that sky, does it? Looks like some little smudge of a breath on a cold window. That's all I'll be to my sweet Mary L. — a little fog on a window. Soon gone for good, whether I go back or not."

The mild intoxication off that tonic had risen fully through my head. I'm a little surprised I recall the moment as I do. It was the first touch of drunkenness in my life, and the candor it washed out of me was surely amusing enough nearly to draw laughter from the grave itself. Sophia's voice smiled as she answered.

"You keep telling yourself that about her if it makes you feel better, but I'll take that wager of yours. I'll wager you a full U.S. dollar that girl will cry some kind of a tear at your standing before her again. Assuming you show up a little less than pie-eyed, jolly-juiced drunk, which is nearly how you lie here now. Sorry about that. But so far it has brought you out to me."

Sophia chirped a laugh. I prattled on another groggy moment about how high is the sky before my mind tottered backward. I began to cry that pitiable kind of cry that can link a man with his boyhood.

"I ain't no better than what my Granny called a she-rain. Just some little white scrap off a storm, driftin' around a ridge. Just a little fog scrap. Won't rise and won't fall. Good for nothin'. Nothin' to my ma. To my Mary L. I ain't no more than a thin spray of nothin'."

Sophia put her hand on my arm and gave the whimpering a moment to pass.

"Well, I suppose we'll see. We will find out if you're no better than a mist that's bound to dry right out of a girl's heart. You can trust me on this. I have ways to see these things. Ways you don't know about yet."

Her voice held that quiet tenor some people use to talk to themselves.

"And by the way, fog and that river that nearly whipped you to death yesterday are made of the same. Don't you go and short-weight what you mean to this world, boy. You can't always see it from where you are, you know. I know about that."

With that, Sophia rose and reached both hands to hoist me off the ground. No mule team could have dragged me fully from the stupor, but enough of it gave way to allow me to walk. Trailing her in staggers, I hiked in quiet back down to the yard, where she ordered me into the cabin, through the kitchen to the bedroom where I had passed the night. What we had talked about, what I had just seen and grappled to believe, amounted to treasure so great I didn't know where to begin. My mind seemed a house of rags, trying to hold everything in. I sat on the bed, fully drunk. So much so I stopped thinking and began talking again, carrying on with scant tearings off my past, recollections of Granny, then how soft it felt the first time I kissed Mary L. I started to say something about what I had seen Ma do to Ulysses, but a good sense stopped that and turned to some jabber — likely incoherent — about Eb's drowning, and how I reckoned at least one of heaven's angels was missing her shoes and corset by now, assuming Eb had talked his way onto the streets of gold. All the while, the long face of my female companion had nodded and smirked and "Hm-hmmed" at me as she scraped off my clothes — some of which were nearly crust — down to my underwear. I took scant notice.

"It'll get hot in here, but I doubt that'll perturb the sleep you're about to have," she said at the door. "A good bath wouldn't kill you, but we'll get to that in time."

She left, and the cool of the sheets had already pulled me into a doze when she returned, after what the daylight said was a very short time. She carried in a glass of shallow liquid, insisting I drink it. It was the color of a dark pine knot and flowed hot as any sapwood fire down my throat. I choked a moment. She stood above me, smirking again.

"I don't condone much in the way of whiskey. But I figure this and the tonic will finish off any latent foolishness you might have left in you for a good long while. I'll keep the gun handy just to satisfy myself."

And there my recollection of the day pales. I don't fully remember Sophia leaving the room. I do recall her saying something about the name Ebenezer — how in Hebrew it meant "stone of help," a notion that charged a little bolt of humor through me. After that I drifted off amid scatterings of Mary L.'s little grin and the feel of her neck against my cheek, and I grew blissfully aware of silence. The voices of inner sadness finally stilled, and I believe they muted less from alcohol and more by the care of this mysterious place of my landing. Even with the August heat leaning heavily against everything, Mr. Proctor's cabin bed and I bonded into a welcome darkness of rest.

The sun would not appear again to my fully open eyes until the following day. I became sick a few more times in the night, running out into the yard to vomit, then collapsing back into sleep each time. The morning brought the first rousing noise — the fizzle and bump of a bumblebee lost about the room — and I woke with little sense of time passage, other than my limbs felt rigid as rail ties from a sleep nearly absent movement. My head ached as if it held moving hot rocks, and every laceration and abrasion of the trip that brought me here combined into one abraded nerve. Yet I creaked out of the bed full of wonder. The obsession to sneak off this place and run for it had dimmed into a determination to explore the house, if for nothing else than something to eat and the longest drink of water my throat could draw. It felt like I had swallowed flour.

I rummaged the cabin's drawers for some clothes — a pair of heavy cotton pants the color of cornmeal and a black shirt — both too large but they would do, even though the thought of wearing dead Mr. Proctor's pants crept around my insides a bit too long. My footwear was gone so I went without, across the dry quiet yard toward the house, hearing the piano music before I reached the back door.

What I knew of music ranged from a cappella shapenote hymns at church to some Saturday night mountain string, played for dances and as front porch celebration of what work-worn fingers can shake loose from a fiddle or clawhammer banjo. Somewhere in there were Pap's improvised work tunes. All sung with a grin about such romantics as a woman called Sally who could pee a quarter mile flow and other topics that would bring chortling scold from Granny. The music of my world seemed to grow gnarled out of hard ground compared to what filled the warm late morning of the house. The piano notes tendered themselves to its air, yet surely reached the attic three stories above. They felt to me like chippings that had rained off the stars. Finely cut, falling together, like some delicate light only the ear can capture.

I followed it through the back door, my bare feet sticky on the wood floor but quiet as breakage of dawn, past the kitchen and onto the soft carpet of the great hall. I finally stopped before reaching the entries to two rooms flanking a front door that looked too heavy for ten men to carry. From its window, the foyer flooded with a mingling of stained glass color — a strong sweep of green and blue. The pianist played invisibly around the corner in the room to the right, and I squatted against the wall, so moved by the music I no longer cared whether any soul, living or dead, might think me out of place in this house.

My legs ached by the time the noise broke in. The rumble of a car, followed soon by heavy feet across the porch, approaching the door, reducing all need for a knock. Before I could fully rouse myself, the music had dissolved. Sophia breezed out of the piano room, fast to the doorknob. At the noise, I had hurried back from the light of the front of the house and held myself still in the shadows of the hall, waiting to be found and vilified.

The voice at the door, deep and lush as bottom-land cornfield, was instantly as familiar as every signpost and doorway of the town I had fled. It was The Reverend Lewis Sharpe — Rev. Lew to most people — the only full-time minister in Marshal, given that Rev. Pyles also worked at the mill. Lew pastored the Presbyterians, the richest among us, and answered his ministerial call with such language that folks held one of two opinions: He was either a great man of letters who seemed to have shaken the very hand of the human Jesus, or the most foul-mouthed of brimstone-dusted hell-mongers, sliding with all his followers straight backward toward the devil's torment. A few who held the latter judgment also deemed it adultery for a courting couple to kiss on Sunday, and I had heard one say sodomy and virginity were the same thing.

In my stillness against the hallway wall, I caught just a glance at him on the porch — the peppery beard flanking a mane of white hair, which draped heavily off the sides of his enormous head, freckled bald on top. He was a pale tower of a man, always crisp and dark of dress. I saw him stoop to meet Sophia's embrace and it came with an apology for interrupting the recital. She said something I couldn't hear into his coat then pulled away, and I heard her call him Uncle Lew. He was a common sight in a town that hadn't seen her in years, yet it seemed they had spent little time apart.

Sophia pushed him back, stepped out onto the wide covered porch and closed the door. I heard them talking — opening with his asking, "How is she today?" There was no resisting. I crawled down the hall, turned into the parlor with the piano, slipped under a table to the drapes, and balled myself under the half-open window to pick up the conversation. Under that eave their words fell, clear as the water I craved, into my ears. Their subject was the only other surviving member of the household. I felt camouflaged enough by the drapes to raise a peering eye to see the two of them leaning together against the porch rail.

"I can't do much with her, Sophie. All we can do is pray the good Lord rings some holy sense into her head. I've told you, I despise watchin' a soul crawl around lost in her own religion. Changin' her mind's about like tellin' my feet not to hurt."

This provoked a gentle anger. She swiped him away and stepped back from the banister.

"I will not hear such. I won't give her over without doing some battle to keep her alive. I will not."

Where tears had seeped onto her cheeks a livid weeping soon flowed.

"When she's gone, I have nobody. I feel it already. Lonesome's not just coming, Uncle Lew, it's here. I feel it all over me. Daddy, gone. And the only mother I've known hell-bent on leaving me absolutely alone. So help me, I'll turn my meanest parts on the Almighty when He takes her. I'll do it just to find out if He listens to that."

The preacher had come to her side. He held her face under his chin with one hand and the remainder of her seemed to absorb into the white of his shirt. His whiskers rested on the dark, tight pull of her hair, and I recall thinking I had never seen a white person touch one of color so. Her crying soon plowed into his chest, where he welcomed her in a whisper and the gentle brawn of age. He said nothing for a time. Only as her sobs began to run quiet and dry, did I hear him again.

"Girl, don't haul off and rouse up the hell asleep in both of us. I've tried a long while to break that same fever. Been so infernal riled up I couldn't find enough cuss to shake at God to get myself satisfied. Lord knows we're weak. He'd rather have us madder than all damnation at Him than to pay Him no mind at all."

He pulled her face up to his. I could feel a smile on his words.

"That's some love now, is it not? Any God that'd give the preacher's callin' to a riled up old puke like me. The Lord doesn't just put up with us. He loves the hell right out of us, honeypot. And you'll not raise your hackles high enough to stop Him. Anybody says otherwise, he, she, or it can escort my white ass to a barn dance to kiss it."

A spurt of laughter nearly betrayed my position in the window. I clapped both hands over my mouth, unable to tell whether she giggled or cried or both into the old man's chest by now. Her mood lightened a bit as she stepped away from him. I could hear her wandering the porch out of my sight, out loud in her own thoughts, soon watery again. I ducked down, still hearing every syllable.

"Why is it every bit of love in this world finally lands you in some sad place? Every dime's worth of it. Do you know how I would miss every breath you take in my company if something happened to you? I think about that. Can't help it. Can't help but think how it would be, saying goodbye to you. Never feeling you kiss my hand the way you do. Love's always fooled me into thinking it's my friend. Specious bastard. Love always just dies right out from under me. Treason's all it is."

This livened the old preacher. I peeked again to see his silhouette move fast to hers, the morning sun full behind them on the trees beyond the front yard. He grabbed one of her hands, then the other, and spun her to him. When he spoke, even in anger, the air just seemed to welcome his thoughts, as if they fell on a feather bed. What I heard next amounted to the finest sermon I had yet heard in my life.

"Dammit now, that's a lie, that treason business. You don't remember the first time they carried your bobbin' little head down that church aisle. You just about the prettiest little chip of a girl I'd ever seen in a white Sunday gown. You don't remember the day, but I surely do. I remember it like I'm still in that pulpit, seein' every glare cut your way, every spiteful soul who stood up and left. And after I preached, that howlin' pack of Philistines ran me down in the yard. Every single one sneered up and raisin' hell at me for lettin' a child of your color with her fine new white family through God's own door. You'd think I'd shoveled the pews full of chicken drop. And all we had that mornin' was a baby hauled in by the very arms of love itself. And you know from my tellin' it — the hellcats that morning were the minority. Most folks did not cut a shine and show dirty tailfeathers over you that Sunday, even if they didn't like it. I never understood why your mother wouldn't bring you back to that church. Meanness won a part of that day, girl, but love reared up to beat it down. That lady of this house raised up as fine a young lady as these mountains will ever see. It is a damned shame watching her run aground on religion, lookin' for faith. Saddens me deep, sweetness, it does. But she adores you. If such a love can thrive in the wicked sage of this world, then we're in fine hands. And don't you forget how you and the rest of this house have helped folks, even after they let fly a powerful load of malice on all of us. Some of 'em spit nails at one another, then howl and carry on about defendin' the faith. Damned nonsense. God's no kind of divine if He needs defendin' by the likes of us — and He does not. What He wants from us is that treason of yours. Love's all He wants. There is no making more sense of it than that, girl."

The smooth iron of his voice melted some toward the end. The two of them, in embrace by then, formed a darkened body of one against the backlight. He drew some long breaths, then let a final affirmation take a gentle place between them.

"How many times do I have to tell you? Preach this to you? Love's the only thing that quells some of the hatefulness in this old preacher. It's the very strap I take to my deepest-down devil. The only thing that strangles the hell right out of me. Apart from a little bit of that love we're all helpless, honeypot. Helpless as plowed ground in a rainstorm. I preach because our Christ plodded the mud of this same life — with a pack of damn fools around a whole lot of the time, by the way. He was a helpless man and the love of God on the same two feet. I've got to get across to your mother that he takes her as she is. Jesus knows what it's like, being like you and me — God help him. Though I'll take your bet I could out cuss him any day."

They laughed together and he rocked her by now, as a father would ease a teary child fresh from a fall. The damp early August breeze swelled the thin curtains around my now-aching crouch at the window, but I dared not move, fearing any motion might inform them of me in this newfound quiet. Both legs were solid with cramps, but the silence gave me pause enough to take in the richness of the room. Walls and even the ceiling papered in more flourish than I had imagination — every space filled with design fine enough to wear the words, "legal tender." The furnishings all buttoned and soft and plump with a celery color soothing to the eyes. The rug wore a much deeper green, almost black. It felt softer than the bed I had left at home. And all around were portrait paintings, containers of shined brass, three clocks ticking in odd concert, two on tables of dark red, the other on a heavy blonde mantle. I could touch the piano from my crouch. Doing so made me wonder how so heavy and hard a thing could feel as creamy as human flesh under fingertips. At my position, the sheers began to stick where the late-summer heat had soaked my face. I remember thinking Mr. Proctor surely never expected anyone who broke a sweat in his mill would do likewise in his fanciful sitting room.

Voices came through the window again. Sophia had composed herself, and I looked just in time to see her step back and glance at him, her body tightening, almost as if she were winding up to throw a rock. In my squatting place, I had braced for it. A chill surged through me when it finally came. Sophia told her Uncle Lew about me. How she'd yanked a hungry, chewed-up boy headlong from the river and why she couldn't care less anymore that anyone found out the secrets of the Proctor life and death and her place in it. She had just begun to ask the old preacher if he knew of any ill fortune that might have brought me her way when he stopped her and scuffed off the porch. I heard the door of his notorious Packard, and soon he came gravely back with an overly folded copy of the *Marshal Times* newspaper. He pointed to where she should read, asking what she had done with me. She never answered, but instead absorbed the page, whose words seemed to land against her like hot coals.

"Lord God, Uncle, Lord God. Oh, Lord no."

Sophia dropped the paper to the floor and wilted against him again, shaking her head. He embraced her in quiet, she let out some sniffling tears, and the effect flowed through the open window into me. Fear of what some words printed on a page had to do with my life's last two days was stronger than the floor under my feet.

Rev. Lew, ever the wag, soon spoke, clearly being himself, as if it might cheer and comfort her at the same time.

"That nosy gadfly swarm who run that paper have their sharp little peckers poked in most everybody's business, but I'll reckon they've nosed around and done us some service here, Soph. Where is he? Do you want me to tell him?"

"Not yet. I'm not speaking a word of this to him yet. We need to be easy with him."

A hail of possibilities stormed over me about what the news might hold. Yet they concluded it was word of Ulysses Tickman's death, leaving a widow and houseful of children. Sophia straightened up, wiping her face and picking up the paper.

"I have too much to think about now. I can't coax her to eat a thing at night. Midday is the only time she'll take even a morsel, so I'll try to feed her again. Let me get you the bag."

She handed the preacher the paper and burst in the front door. I held my position, hearing her spring up the stairs, soon back down with a leather case. She and the preacher exchanged the case for the paper and she walked him to the car. The only other words I understood between them were something about tomorrow night, just after dark.

Thoughts of retreating to the cabin, in the fear and wonder of all I had taken in, occurred to me, but I stayed. When Sophia came back through the heavy front door I was upright in front of the piano.

"What's that paper say about me? Or about my kin?" The questions came with a coarseness I didn't intend. Sophia startled.

"Sweet Moses in the water, good God, how long have you been there?"

"Long enough. What's it say? Whatever it is, I can account for it."

"I might find my obituary in it by now, the way you scared me. Don't you know it's rude to eavesdrop and snoop around?"

"I woke up and tried to find you, is all. Shouldn't oughtta done it, but never meant harm. Can't I get a look at that paper now?"

"This paper is mine, and I'll make it your concern in due time. Trust me."

With eyes refusing to meet mine, she unbuttoned her shirt. Not knowing where to look I stared precisely where no gentleman should. She stuffed the folded paper into her pants inside the shirt and rebuttoned, never revealing a truly private part. She turned from me.

"You and I will talk about many things in awhile, but I have things to do and you have other things to learn, so follow me."

My further protests to see or hear the news of that paper were ignored as we went to the kitchen, the noise of Rev. Lew's Packard dissolving behind us. Curiosity about where she would take me next had the effect of easing my mind, which had spent a young boy's lifetime getting used to carrying around fears of the worst. I was outwardly just fine. Sophia was far less so.

She popped a wall switch and the kitchen awoke in light. Even with the mill electrifying a good part of Marshal, most of us who lived in the higher places found our way by kerosene lamp. I had witnessed household electricity on my trips with Pap, mostly in homes of doctors and judges and the others of high estate, but here the effect came with grander scale. The kitchen lay long and nearly large as a factory across the back of the house, the light caught by glass-front cabinets and hanging copper cookware. A heavy table in a cream-colored cloth formed an enormous island in the room. Straight-back chairs for six flanked it. The iron stove stood so clean it looked seldom used, and near it one of the early electric refrigerators: A "Kelvinator," which filled the room with a low hum that seemed to sing out that I, at least temporarily, lived in the real world.

"She will engage you in conversation and she may challenge you some. Be polite. It's just her nurturing way."

Sophia said that while busying herself, almost in a frenzy of breaking eggs and gathering other food about the room. I sat quietly, trying several approaches to ask for that paper, but talk of how I had slept, how hungry I must be, displaced the topic. Sophia's kind effort to distract both of us soon turned to the enigma upstairs.

"Don't tell her everything about you yet. It's too much, and I don't want her fatigued before she eats."

"I don't mean to sound plumb ignorant, but who exactly are we talkin' about here? And shouldn't I shine up a bit before I go to meetin' anybody in this house?" I licked two fingers and raked at my hair, which still felt like river sand.

"She won't care. I've told her we have a guest who showed up distraught in the river, looking like he'd crossed the Styx (I took that as a reference to the woods). She doesn't expect you to shine. In fact, let me take you on up before I get further into this. You two can get acquainted."

With that I followed her up the wide stairs, protesting about my bare feet, then down a hallway to a nearly closed door. Sophia gave a delicate knock and opened it.

"Coming in, Mother. Coming in with the company. The young man. Something we haven't seen in awhile. This is our Moses-Odysseus I was telling you about."

Sophia went for the feathery body on the bed, bending to leave a lingering kiss I heard but couldn't see. I stepped just inside the door and hid to one side beside a high reddish chifforobe, out of the best of the light, avoiding the woman's face. Sophia spoke to her in the airy way of someone trying to lift a downcast child. There was the dog again — his face streaked gray with years. Without raising himself from a nestled spot on the foot of the bed, he thumped a few wags at the sight of visitors and then didn't move. A pair of hands, sugar-white, reached up to greet Sophia. The women bantered a quiet greeting with their fingers woven into an embrace. The elderly lady, what I could see, lay straight and small, barely showing under the drape of a sheet that hid her in its color of faded roses. The arms were thin as strips of river cane, but they had risen in eager welcome. In a moment's lunacy, I wondered if white bodies ever randomly gave birth to children of color. My head began a tally of every dark-skinned person I had ever deliberately touched and soon concluded they totaled far fewer than the number of my relations Mattie and Ulysses gave to the world.

"Come fully into the room, Frank. Emerge and say hello to the only mother I have ever known. The finest of all humankind."

The trouble cast onto Sophia by that paper turned more leaden after those words. As if they were in some way inappropriate to be spoken in front of me. I could feel her fight to raise some cheer for the three of us.

"Frank Locke, Junior, meet Julia Sophia Proctor, the pretty woman you saw in that photograph. Looking every strand as lovely today, may I add. I told her she had a gentleman admirer who had fallen for her picture like Narcissus for the pool."

I stepped out a ways. Sophia sat on the edge of the bed.

"You are as kind as you are disingenuous, love." The elder Mrs. Proctor started with a gurgle but her words soon climbed to a warm, womanly power. One more step and my eyes met those of the picture, completely alive but set in a face life seemed to have forgotten — the lines of it not so much aged but frighteningly thin. She struggled onto elbows, then soon lifted herself to a sitting position against the enormous oak headboard.

"Come closer, son. I'm heartened to hear you've looked upon me in my better days. I haven't seen a handsome man in far too long to think about. So long I didn't know the yen would feel this good to satisfy." The older woman tried to evoke a shared laugh but the younger turned somber, as if the weight on her mind grew at the sight of the dissipating woman before us. For a moment I kept myself in the private world of surveying the room — its light colors and frills — until the hand reached my way.

"You can speak, or shall I continue to charm us all?"

I stepped over and she took my hand with a squeeze so hard I thought my fingers might come back blue. I made another snatching contact with her eyes. In my memory to this day, they remain deep springs of learning, not absent suffering but not sad either. Their shades of blue-green had yellowed some, but they held a light clear as a child's.

"Surely you're not too frazzled to entertain a sinful old lady of music. Sit."

I took a place on the bedside while Sophia stepped back toward the wall. Mrs. Proctor soon held my face in fingers chill as a hailstorm, even on the warm day.

"What a handsome boy to have tangled with the wilds. Handsome and so very alive."

"I'm mighty pleased to meet you, ma'am." I looked away but she jostled my head until I came back to her.

"We are the pleasured, child. We have much love in this house. It keeps the loneliness dusted off. I understand Sophia told you of my husband's demise. She's held that news to her vest against my better advice. I have long believed everyone should know about this little world of ours here." I ventured some bland thanks for the meal Sophia had given only to be cut off. Her strength began dissolving into whisper.

"Handsome boy. Sophia told me of your dalliance with that river. Aren't you glad? Glad you're alive and young on such a day? Aren't we all so very thankful and glad. So fine a boy, straying in here. The Lord has a place for each one of us. I am so glad yours is here today."

By then she had settled into a distance, carried off to that place the aged mind can know better than the present time. She released my face, turning hers to the open window. I held her hand, feeling no grip in it at all. I had heard the discrete opening and closing of the door behind me. Each in her own way, both women had slipped from the room, the elder one still staring far beyond the window.

"My husband brought me up here twenty-seven years ago, and I fell so deeply for these mountains. They frighten a city girl, you understand. I feared at first I might fall right off the earth. But then I fell in love. I have been in such love with so much of this place. Living apart from what is hateful. Living so has brought such joy. And much loss."

She turned back, the sudden tide of strength draining further away.

"You are a kind boy, I can tell. I never want my Sophia in the company of a cad. She feels too much rancor from the world, even from here. And she's trusting. Like both of her fathers, God nestle them. You are a good boy? I can see my answer. I can see."

"I try to do right, ma'am."

Hearing this livened her a bit.

"I'm sure. Too quiet, though. Your reticence worries me. I don't mean to be impertinent, but tell me of your travels. You're terribly young to be out alone, such a rustic gentleman of a child."

The touch of her vigor had swiftly risen and waned again, as if speaking a few words amounted to a dawn-to-dark labor. She closed her eyes and whispered a wish that I would just sit with her awhile, which I did until the dog roused from its nest on the bed. Sophia soon came through the door carrying a bright silver tray.

"Terribly sorry to intrude, but ladies who entertain gentlemen must pause for lunch."

I stood and stepped back, noticing the graceful way the daughter presented a meal of homemade applesauce in a clear bowl. Beside it, a small blue plate held a single piece of ham, barely a shaving, and a dry scrambled egg — so scant a meal it barely hid the gilding of the dishes. Beside it, a large glass of water and a steaming cup of tea. Both women shooed the curious dog, who retreated but stayed on the bed.

"Mother, I want you to take your time with it. That last egg made you sick because you ate it too fast. 'Food is a blessing not to waste with haste.' Your words, back at you. The boy will wait."

The patient strained to raise herself, smiling, praising the tray, then scolding.

"Worry, worry, worry. Child, stop your sweet worry. I am an old woman who has reconciled herself to what it means to be so. I am in very good hands, and so are you."

Her head reclined its silken white to the pillow. She drew a long breath that seemed to stoke and freshen her mind, and began to recite — with a refinement that made my every syllable feel like a dropped mud clod. Her eyes kept to the beaded ceiling as if she saw far beyond.

"'The meek also shall increase their joy in the Lord, and the poor among men shall rejoice in the Holy One of Israel.' Isaiah 29:19. Blessed be the God who keeps us all." It was as though she lay in the room alone. A few shallow breaths and she continued.

"Strengthen me, Lord, Thou who art my strength and my redeemer. Take me to your bosom — the place of beggar's solace and truest goodness and the graceful order of things." Her eyes clenched on two "amens," then a smile shone back at us. "Now, give me leave, you sweet young creatures. The lady wants her way."

The pillow seemed to hold the face of a corpse suddenly wakened by the disquiet of so many frightened eyes looking down on it. Sophia kissed her mother's lips, they muttered some loving things and I heard something about the piano. "Play for me again, love. Chopin again. Ease me through the heat of the day." When Sophia stepped away her mother seemed nearly asleep with the tray perilous on her lap. We eased into the hall and the door barely latched, Sophia whispering, "She'll wake to eat. Always dozes a second before. Wait here while I step in this room for some clothes that may actually fit you." She disappeared through a door down the hall, leaving me to believe I had seen the last of the elderly woman.

A moment's silence, then came noise from the room. A soft smacking sound, punctuated with motherly encouragements and coo. I had to look. The doorknob sat above a skeleton keyhole, where my eye pressed to find the lazy dog standing astride the emaciated form under the sheet. He lapped directly from the crystal bowl, which was held cupped in the ashen hands of a woman smiling as her applesauce went the way the egg and ham would soon go in seconds. "Hurry now. Don't slobber and drip all over. Be done." I could barely hear the woman urging the dog. Then, with a pat of its head, she put the spoon into the bowl, set the tray aside on the bed and clasped her hands under her chin, seeming to pray again.

Watching this meditation seemed vulgar so I rose, eager not to let Sophia catch me spying. My head ached again so I stood against the wall, inspecting the heft of the rug with my naked toes and pondering the mystery I had just witnessed. Sophia emerged with a weight of cloth in her arms. I could feel her fighting the air of gravity that had settled from the news brought by Lew.

"Take these downstairs to the bathtub by the kitchen. Fresh clothes and linens." Her face was no more than an inch from mine. "I'll be along. We're going to give you a soak and scrub fit for a show horse. These clothes won't entirely fit either, but they'll get you three-quarters along the way. I'm trusting you, now. Be there when I arrive."

Words of praise and amazement at the elderly woman's eating sailed out the bedroom door as I went down the stairs — doting child to aged mother, the talk artificially light.

I walked directly to the bathroom I had already studied and sat on the cool of the tile floor wondering more about the paper in Sophia's pants, the way home, and everything else I had just seen and heard. The empty dishes finally clanked down the hall to the kitchen. Sophia soon came in, uncaring whether I was clothed, and dispatched me to the hall while she drew water warmed by a solar heater she said her father had ordered out of Florida. She had brought several products: A new cake of white soap, a paper-wrapped package of Dr. Lyons' skin ointment, a new bottle of tincture of arnica for swelling and bruising, and a used — but, I was assured, sterile — toothbrush with a half-bottle of tooth powder. From her pocket came a nearly dried up, but barely touched, jar of hair and mustache dressing and a straight-edge razor.

"Use what you need of all this, and from the looks of you all of it may be necessary. I'll find you a comb."

She scurried down the hall, with her usual speed of a racehorse with its tail afire.

Peeling off even those clean clothes I had borrowed that morning cut loose the stench of my time without a bath and left a spread of dirt on the floor. I closed the door and stepped into the water. Even in the rising hot day, the warmth of it massaged to the bone. The tub's enamel felt slick as channel catfish skin and clean as the meat. I pulled the curtain to hold the heat around too many aches to number, pondering this first bath I had ever taken in water not carried to an old tin plunge tub. I wanted to linger, soaking awhile, but didn't dare. The scrubbing went fast. I feared being burst in upon naked, and soon was.

"Making any way in the dirt?"

The knock served more to barge her through the door. Even behind the bath curtain, my legs scrolled up hard, as if my most guarded private part had just raised its flag before every giggling school girl in the world.

"Don't jump out of your skin. That's what the curtain is for. How's the bath?"

"Powerful nice, ma'am. But I ain't quite done." I worried now about her seeing my clothes on the floor.

"I know. I brought you underwear. Sweet Moses, it's hot in here. I need an ice bath myself."

The movement of Sophia's voice told me she had taken a seat on the floor. "Cooler down here," she said, leaning back against the tub, letting her head rest against the edge. I scrubbed off a bit more grime, asked about the paper again, then let the room fall utterly silent. A breeze finding its way through open windows of the great house gave the faintest movement to the fabric. The curtain parted us like two halves of the same, cutting us off from one another yet allowing inner places to be seen. I suppose the way it allowed us to hide made telling our remaining truth not only easier, but somehow purifying.

"Mother asked me more questions about you. Where you came from. Your parents."

"Ain't got a daddy, far as I been feelin' about him the better part of my days. He ain't fit for hog feed, so he ain't fit to think about."

"But he's alive," she said. "He is still alive?"

"If you call livin' liquored up on paregoric and every kind of needle dope a man can take livin', then I reckon he's livin'. Fightin' mad most of the time. Even when he ain't loaded up on that stuff he's madder than a mule with a mouthful of bees. Man's twice the devil for meanness, ma'am. That's all."

"Well, you don't seem so full of the devil, your proclivity to steal aside. I saw how tender you were with Mother. I'm sure you've been the same with your own. Would seem to me a father with a boy like you might rise far above hell."

I paused a moment and lay further down in the cooling water, letting every story ever told to me about my father distill into some clear way of giving Sophia what she asked. I figured to answer her would make her owe me what that newspaper in her pants had to say.

"Folks all the time wonder where Frank got it from. He wasn't always mean, they say, especially Ma. Ever since I was no bigger than a hen I've heard people talk of how he'd survived a meanness. Somethin' that happened a long time back when he was a boy. He never got it natural from his own daddy, is what they'd say."

"Your grandfather? You knew your father's father?"

"Never did, ma'am. Never did, but Ma told me what she knew about him. Said all she ever heard tell of him was about the sweetest man that ever was made. Gentle as a fresh-born calf. He was a little man. Little and couldn't hear thunder."

"Deaf? Completely deaf?" she asked, turning her profile to me. The bath curtain made known only the sharp lines of her neck and face in silhouette.

"Couldn't hear one thing, and never learned to talk plain. Just sorta grunted out a word or two since he had a fever as a boy. He raised Frank by himself. Frank's ma died of bleedin' the mornin' after she birthed him. They lived on Craggy Bald. Toughest country you'd ever see. That's where my granddaddy raised him, in a squatter clearin', real steep and high and tree-bound. Barely level enough to stand on, to hear Frank tell it. They lived in a little flap shack. Frank says it weren't a fit sheep shelter. Says if a woman down in Marshal hadn't heard and come up to take some care of him, he woulda never come through his first winter. But Frank sure enough lived. There ain't no killin' him. Folks say he'd never have known his own name if it hadn't been for that woman."

"Sweet Lord," Sophia said, barely audible, seeming to sense and brace herself for the worst of the tale to follow. "I've been near Craggy. How'd they survive up there?"

"Oh, they lived fine apart from that outhouse they lived in. This church woman from Marshal — a preacher's wife what helped bury my granny — come up regular and helped raise what you'd call my daddy out of a baby. They brought out a garden with a tomato patch. But they was in the sang business. Good at it, too."

"What business? What's 'sang'?"

"Diggin' sang. My granddaddy knew it from Indians. They called it little man root. From the time Frank could walk my granddaddy would hike him off in the woods and stay three and four days at a time, huntin' that little man root. They call it that 'cause it sorta looks like a long-legged feller standin' up. I've seen it. Comes outta the ground about May and blooms in the summertime. White blossoms on little green leaves down next to the ground. Gets little red seeds about October — look like blood. The roots is good for right near any ailment."

"You mean ginseng? I know what ginseng is."

"That's it. Then you know it makes a body healthy to take it, and people all over creation wants it for treatin' ailments and makin' babies. My granddaddy and Frank would tote it outta these hills on mule sleds to sell or trade it. Sometimes it'd fetch three dollars and a quarter a pound. Trouble was, too many people thought Frank's daddy was some sorta grunt fool 'cause he was deaf and couldn't talk much better than a baby. Frank helped do most of the bargainin' and tradin' — done it since he was no higher than a regular man's hip. He done it and never went to school as a little boy. Only learned to talk 'cause that church woman felt sorry and would come and play with him and read the Scriptures to the both of 'em. What readin' my daddy learned, he learned from her or learned himself. My ma taught him some, too. He can out-read most anybody, unless they're folk like your mother and you, I reckon. He never had much in the book way."

"Takes a fine mind to learn on its own," Sophia said. "I still don't see what made him as mean as you say."

"I ain't done. Could be how Frank had to take up for my granddaddy. I think that's what turned him on some parts of the world. Somebody was all the time makin' laughin' sport of the both of 'em when they travelled. And sometimes when they didn't."

"Who makes fun of a deaf, illiterate man? And his child? That's some wickedness, sure enough." Sophia had turned to face the curtain and me by now.

"Plenty makes fun. But far worse was done. Ma told me of this 'cause Frank never would. She told it this way. Said one day in high summer, he was no more than twelve or thirteen when one of these medicine show fellers showed up on that bald. Just come walkin' up the path with a big wood box rigged up to tote on his back. He came rattlin' off some tale of people in Marshal sayin' the two men might do some tradin' for roots. Cash money, but he had to see the product. All he wanted was to steal and maybe find where they done their best diggin'. My granddaddy knowed it even before the man turned a knife out of his shirt pocket and commenced askin' about money stash. Frank's daddy had already gone to cryin' and pointin' down the road and beggin' him off the place. Beggin' for him just to leave them be, best he could say it. Frank had stayed back 'til that man come at his daddy and knocked him backward to the ground, and that's when my own picked up a piece of a tobacco stob they had layin' around and rapped the bastard across the spine. The thief bowed and wheeled around, and as I heard it, that set off about the dirtiest fist-to-skull fight as there ever was. Frank was fightin' him hard, with my granddaddy cryin' and tryin' to stop it with that very same stick. He took to wailin' it at that feller, but the man musta been stout 'cause he got it away and whapped the little man back. Next thing you knew he had Frank knocked down with it, and that's when he raised both arms and drove the whittled-off sharp end of that wood stob into Frank's face. Right through his jaw. That stob tore all the way into his mouth. Tore him hard. Some people thinks he got the scar in the war. But that's how it come. The very one some folks still laugh at on him."

"Dear sweet God," Sophia interrupted, rising to her knees on the floor. "What happened then?"

"The man took off runnin' with his grabbed up medicine box jangling down the path. Frank's daddy — my little ol' granddaddy — picked the boy up, big as he was, and went off trailin' the feller. Blood flyin' by the milk bucketful, we reckon. Ma said my little granddaddy run all the way to the preacher's house with that good-size boy slung up like a bleedin' flour sack in his arms. Frank told Ma all he heard was his own daddy cryin' and pleadin' a deaf man's roar for help the whole way. An hour's walk, but they was there in no time. That medicine man couldn't have been more than a few steps in front. He might have run right past that circuit preacher's house. When they got there, nobody was home, so my granddaddy put the boy down on the front porch, took off his bloody shirt and stuffed the wound best he could to stop the blood. Frank had quit cryin' by then but my little granddaddy kept on, pacin' around and cryin' somethin' terrible and mumblin' and touchin' that bloody shirt. That's the last Frank remembers of him before he blacked out. When he come to, the preacher's wife was lookin' down on him on a couch in the house. His head — accordin' to what he told Ma — felt four sizes too big, and his weepin' little daddy was gone."

I saw it in the silhouette — Sophia swiping at her face, still looking my way at the curtain.

"Gone where?"

"Don't a soul know to this day. He just walked off into them root-digger woods and died, they reckon, but nobody found him. Folks did find the house all roused up on that bald. Somebody'd been in it. Folks suppose he starved or an animal got him or some combination. He musta thought his boy was dead, bled out dead, 'cause he'd dipped a finger in that blood and drew a cross on the porch wood where he left my daddy. Drew it straight as a saw line, and another one on Frank's shirt, where it wasn't soaked. Ma says that preacher and his wife finished raisin' him. Had him sewed up best they could, but Frank ain't trusted a solitary soul since. You see, diggin' sang will make you money, whether you live like you got money or not. Ma says Frank told her my granddaddy had pert near a thousand dollars hid in one of them old Sears and Roebuck crank washtubs under some burlap in that shack. When Frank got wits and strength enough to go back lookin' for it, it was gone. I kinda figure that medicine man curled back that day to ransack it out. Could be that preacher took it for his trouble of raisin' the boy. Or maybe my granddaddy got it, figurin' money's what drew the thief and it oughtta rot with him in the woods. Maybe he took it off somewheres and lived on. Regardless, Ma says when she met Frank not long after, with his head all gauzed up, he was embarrassed about havin' no money to court her the way he wanted. He hadn't been able to dig for sang since, best I know."

Sophia wiped at her face again, then broke a silence that came between us.

"I'm beginning to get a better view of your father *and* you. Why *do* you call him by the familiar?

"Because he ain't worth callin' nothin' else to me, most days. I don't want nothin' to do with any part of him and I'm proud of it. I'd rather have my little deaf granddaddy as my daddy than Frank Locke. I'd rather be a bastard than have such a bastard for a daddy."

She interrupted.

"Well, that's precisely the sort of thinking that makes a deaf man feel like he's not fit to live in the rest of the world. You understand that, don't you? Calling him and yourself bastard won't change a thing. "

"Frank's been called plenty worse and will be again. Hearin' about a man ain't the same as livin' with him. If you'd seen some of what he's done to my ma and me, you might say he weren't worth that long bloody run to save. I reckon every time it rains up on that little bald it's my poor little granddaddy weepin' out the shame of what he left to the world. Poor little man, to hear people tell it, wasn't born with a thing to be proud of, and Frank ain't give him a thing to be proud of since."

"I suppose that includes you, right? I suppose your granddaddy's ghost might never know a temptation to be proud of you?"

Sophia's questions struck me mute and suddenly aware the water's heat had long passed. The day had grown August hot, but I sat shivering, as if the tub were a smooth rock sprayed with January rain.

"Frank, you are about to become much more a man than a boy. I believe it's in you to make every soul of your life proud. I am going to help you. And I need you to help me. But there is business to conduct, right now."

Sophia had turned heavy again, yet not entirely somber. She slung back the bath curtain without so much a glance at my retreating nakedness, unbuttoned her shirt again and drew out the paper.

"I can not hold this another minute, Frank. Not one more minute will I wait until you are told."

Frank's second trip to the same Kentucky sanitarium, so long after the first one, happened with no family ceremony. Ma paid the money, saying she'd rather spend for the treatment than a coffin. I drove Frank to the depot in Pap's truck this time, watched Ma soak him with assurances of faith, kissing him at the train. After three weeks again he came back all crisp and polished, eager to work. Frank's second phase of paid-for sobriety lasted longer than the first, before opium befriended and betrayed him again. He wept nearly as much as he raged – often begged us to help him only minutes after raising the very cesspools of misery into the remains of our peace.

With Granny and Pap by then sharing that little patch of cemetery with Eb, Ma and I did well to see our way to the end of every workday, staving off exhaustion. Mattie, Useless, and their young were weight enough to carry. By the time Ma took that log splitter to my uncle's head, Frank had devolved into a figure akin to a loose floorboard – able to rear up and hurt us from time to time, but if avoided would merely lie there. Dead wood waiting for someone to get fed up and put a nail to it. I believe the afternoon Ma swiped iron against Ulysses' head, the eyes of her heart had actually long drawn careful aim on the devil side of the man she loved. I believe she had long hated herself for failing to kill the hurting and hateful parts of Frank Locke without burying that love of her life. The burden of it finally grew too heavy. Unlike Wordsworth's "Old Man Travelling," Ma had moved with pain, not with thought, when she attacked Useless. And I had failed to stop her.

"Frank, your mother is dead. She is dead and gone and I am about as sorry as a girl can be about that for you."

I lay shivering as Sophia threw a towel over my lower half in the tub and handed me the folded bi-weekly *Marshal Times*, warm from her body. What she had just said felt to me like a squall in words — slow to begin, but growing to a storm that covered everything. Its reality landed heavier still when I saw the printing above the fold. The event had called for a tiny special edition.

At approximately 7:30 the morning of August 4, Mrs. Dovie Evelyn Locke, 39, of Oconee Gap, was found by Sheriff Ernest Long hanging by the neck in her cell of the Mathison County Jail. The sheriff says she put an end to herself by use of a shredded bedsheet tied to the cell door bars. She was immediately dead and had been so several hours, according to the sheriff. Mrs. Locke was wife to Monroe Franklin Locke, Senior and mother to Franklin Locke, Junior. She is mourned by many friends in the Marshal Cotton Mill, where she worked, and the Panther Creek Baptist Church.

The sheriff says he installed Mrs. Locke in the jail cell shortly after noon of August 3, having discovered Ulysses Tickman, 34, also of Oconee Gap, severely wounded about the head outside the family home. He had nearly been put an end to, the sheriff believes, by the hand of Mrs. Locke, his sister-in-law, who confessed to assault by use of a splitting wedge found on the property. Mr. Tickman survives and is under the care of his family in the home.

Mrs. Locke's son, Frank Junior, went missing in the woods near the scene of the assault. An active search for the boy is under way as these words go to press.

I sat breathing in and out, feeling only cold. The kind that comes on a wind, so cold it burns. A numbing inner cold seemed to redden my insides with every draw of air. The paper fell to the floor. I shed the words of her hanging. They had already drawn too sharp a thought of Ma suspended dead by the neck.

Sophia broke first. I looked up to see the firm propriety — the resolute way she carried herself — dissolve into quiet grieving. Into one another we wept a hard, rattling, liberation of sorrows. I remember Sophia murmured something about tears healing well, especially when they've been stored and aged a long while from hurts that seem behind us. She cried harder after she said that. Other than to wipe my face and her own with her shirttail, her arms never gave way. Not even as my weeping rage came to full stride.

"Never should. Never should have fought him. It's my fault. It was me. Ma never stood one chance. Never hurt a soul. Never would have if it hadn't been for me rilin' up the way I did. Ain't no wonder she did it. A body can't take but so much. Can't take it. It's Frank's fault, too. Damned devil. He's the one oughtta be killed. And I should have put an axe to him, far back of this. Far back."

I began to pull away but Sophia held.

"Dwell on your mother, Frank. Just be. Just be."

Some shackles of loathing tightened around the man I wanted to blame, yet caught me in a frenzy. What seemed an internal madness dragged me from the tub. I wrapped in the sopping towel, not caring who saw what. Water flew all over Sophia and the room.

"Die, Frank. You die, Frank Locke. You die, die, die. You killed her. You sure enough killed Ma like you threatened."

I paced, and the words quickened. A maddened smile came over the barrage near its end.

"You filthy, blood-wallerin' pig. I should kill you myself. Ma's beat you, though. She beat you and got herself to a place you can't get her no more. No more hurtin' over your filthy self. She beat you. She beat you good...."

My knees finally hit the floor. Sophia was on me in an instant, having urged me to quiet on whispers, the way one tries to ease a spooked horse.

"Stop. Stop, Frank." Her hands finally squeezed my face to hers. "Stop thinking your mother did a right thing. I won't hear it. Your dead mother, God receive her, had her reasons for what she did. And they are wrong. Wrong, Frank. Do you understand? The wrong reasons. Understand me? That is wrong, wrong, wrong."

The words caught her up. She nearly screamed the latter part, a raving glare in her eyes, as if what had been done was done only to her. I pulled away and stood near the door, feeling her stand behind me.

"Do you think God wants a single life sacrificed that way? I'm sorry for your mother — a fine woman, I'm sure. But she failed herself and you and every other soul around her. Not in my house. Not in my world. Not if I can help it."

Sophia wept openly again, but I turned on her, nearing a roar. We soon yelled over one another.

"I shouldn't oughtta run like I did. I run off and left her to think she didn't have nobody no more. I left her to die!"

"Her choice, Frank. *Her* wrong choice."

"I coulda helped it. I shoulda helped her."

"You tried, Frank. I'm sure you did. She might have been beyond your help. Did you consider that? A woman can walk around dead for years, Frank, never fully alive, dying more by the day. Your mama just decided to lay herself down is all. Wrong choice. Wrong choice the whole way."

"She never had a choice, with all she put up with. You monied-up rich folk got narry notion what it's like...."

This livened a force in Sophia that nearly made me fear her. The rifle would have offered no stouter menace.

"You don't know a thing about my suffering or the pain of this house or me. You wanted her free of your father? Free of her suffering? Well, that's hard. It's hard Frank, and it takes courage. Easier just to die. Die in the soul, where she should have lived, then finished her own story. And now she's gone and left both of you and every happy breath she might have drawn. She's left the day of your marriage. The grandchildren who'll not know her. She left every other breath somebody might take to tell her she was loved. Damn that, Frank. Damn every bit of fear that makes a woman die and not live. I'm living with it upstairs right now. And I'm living with it every time I look at myself. Every day of my life here, locked away from the world."

Sophia's long dark finger had come within a hair of my nose. She grabbed my cheeks again, wide-eyed, nearly breathless, yet with a strength fit for steel on every word.

"This is worm food, Frank. Clay for the ground soon enough. Take this flesh, when it's more than fit for living, and send it off to the ground before it's time, and you backhand the very soul it holds. Deny what it can become. This house, my piano, my father's cabin — all of it used to be alive, Frank. I've tried to tell my own mother — every stick of wood that built this place grew toward some beauty greater than itself. But it had to live. Even a tree has heart enough not to kill itself, Frank."

I drew back my right hand. It reached about halfway before the thought of seeing Frank slap my mother seized my arm and my deepest nerve. I had resolved as the smallest boy no woman would ever take a blow from me. I could differ myself from Frank Locke in that way. Sophia never flinched or bolstered herself. She seemed to know no fury could carry me that far against her. Rather than retreat she reached for the hand, a stream of apologies flying off her. I had begun my own when the windows nearly rattled. Someone banged all urgency against the front door.

"Lord God. What's Lew doing back here now?"

She wiped her eyes and leapt for the bathroom door, telling me to stay where I was. Soon down the hallway came Lew's voice, growing near, talking about how we'd better hurry but could make it — rattling on about something that must be done for the boy. I had wrapped myself in another towel, desperate for some clothes, by the time they reached the door. Sophia, not that we had stood on any high modesty until then, knocked only after she opened it.

"You're a Marshal boy, so I'm sure you're acquainted with Lew. Everybody knows he carries the mill's purse, so you know him. I'll spare the formality. He had a thought, which I think is a good one if we hurry."

Sophia waved the man in. I asked for some pants and some time and privacy to put them on. He stepped toward me claiming his announcement had "no business waitin' for britches." I had known of him for years, yet only enough to nod and nearly bow when I caught sight of him in town. His face held a glory fit for the Exodus Moses, yet evoked the same awe that comes from surprising the nude — the urge to stare equally as strong as the obligation to glance and look away. He was a force of size and bravado, which I felt from both hands, clamping my bare shoulders. Little eyes the color of blue jay feathers glowed through his glasses.

"Frank, it is a powerful shame about your mother, boy. I am so sorrowful. Awful shame, and you'll not wade the sadness of it alone, son. Not with me in knowledge of it. I was nearly to town when I got to thinkin' they must be about the business of buryin' her right soon. Not long from about now. So I hauled myself back up here to take you. You can fight me on it, son, but I'll have to warn: You can run from her grave, but that hurt you feel will chase you until you get up nigh to a cuss fit in its face. Feel its breath and turn it back. Best if you go right after it. Get the battle started to get that grievin' whipped. So let's get you on some clothes and go. Come on. I'm fit for some grief-whippin' today. Let's get after it."

I looked away. Tried to pull away. "I can't go back to town, Reverend. I done too much harm."

"Son, what's done is not a thing that stayin' here right now can fix. I don't exactly know why you took off like you did, but there's not a soul down there who'll spit shame at you without answerin' to me, and they know what smoke I can raise. What say, boy? Let's get out of this gilded-up hinterland and go. We'll praise some Jesus and give 'em some hell. Now get ready. I'll be back."

He gave my frame a shake and left, slamming the door and yelling after Sophia, who was long gone. His feet soon thundered down the hallway and disappeared. I sat a moment on the edge of the tub, numb, feeling addled as a bird that's smacked a windowpane, when from the hall the argument grew my way.

"I've told him everything, so I might as well stop hiding. I'm tired of it and I'm going."

Sophia very nearly yelled it just before she burst through the door. She wore only some undergarments, including a long white slip, whose drape sharpened the edges of her womanhood. She thrust out a dark gray suit, still on its hanger, a slight musty funk oozing off the fabric. A white shirt with dusty shoulders and a heavy blue tie came from her other hand. She said something about it belonging to another man of the house, but I didn't ask. Lew paced outside the door, railing for me to talk some sense to her. I kept quiet. She ignored him.

"Don't worry about underwear. Lew says we'll be late as it is. Just put everything on and hurry. I'll meet you on the porch with socks and shoes. Leave the gentleman in the hall to me."

"What if I see Frank? Or some of the rest of my people? I can't. I ain't ready for such. And I surely ain't ready to get seen by Mary Lizbeth if she's anywhere around. I can't go. I won't go."

"Yes...you can, and you must. Don't argue. I've heard you talk enough to know you're sufficiently smart not to be a fool about this. You'll not go alone. You'll go with Lew and me at your back, and soon. Don't let me catch you three-quarters naked in here in ten minutes. I'll be ready in two yanks of an old man's whiskers." I could feel her trying to will some cheer into the moment. Lew had already helped knock the angst off both of us.

She left, meeting outside the door with Lew, who invited her to, "Go to yankin', but you're not goin'." He crowed on about how we didn't have time for a woman to primp up to go, and that she would be a distraction. He claimed she needed to stay home with her mother. The debate trailed away, Lew finally cut off by, "I'm a grown woman whose mind is made up. That's why."

I began to dress. The mystery terrified me, but the thought of turning on my mother's burial brought on a load of shame and dishonor I had no choice but to shed. Thinking about returning with Rev. Lew — with the vigor of his name and title in the town — gave the feeling folks would see me in higher regard, re-emerging as some secreted and grieving hero so brave he broke away from a life fit for nothing. Then came a glitter of thought that a few might see only a scoundrel fool, harebrained and yellow enough to run off into the woods. Lew burst in, finding me in a near mortal wrestling match with the necktie and collar.

"Let's get on, boy. She's gettin' her clothes on, bluster and all. I put the shoes on the porch, though I'll wager they're too big for you. No matter. Come on. We'll fix your tie in the car. Let's go before that bull-headed girl decides her mama, the dog, two horses and the kitchen oughtta go with us."

The old preacher was as tall and stout as he could be impious. He gave me a looking over, then raked his own comb so deep into my hair the teeth felt like they chewed brain. Following that came the inspection of my borrowed wardrobe, which he narrated with the most graceful cussing. Not the little rough pieces of cuss most of us used. Lew wrapped his with a silk baritone — into a smooth and near-reverential attack. Nearly prayerful. Blending "hells" and "damns" into every part of speech, yet somehow never quite harsh or bitter with it. Lew's swearing felt sanctified and good — like some hot and curative tea Saint Peter himself might sip as a purgative.

First he cussed the tie, the very moroseness of its color — nearly strangling me with the tiny knot, which he had cussed while tying it. He shook the jacket, cussed it, then cussed the dust and mold stench that came off it. Cussed the heat, cussed some water on the floor, then laughed, saying, "A touch of smokehouse talk always chokes the wind out of the blues." I confess it worked some, though fear had nearly replaced my sadness. Approaching the front door, his arm heavy on my shoulders, I let off another quarrel of "What-ifs" — all met with: "Let it all be, boy. We're in God's hands and with God's love to your mother's service we go. No more squabblin'. I am satisfied I am right, about this and the fact not even God's holy angels can do anything with that stubborn mule of a gal who runs this damned infernal oversized hell's-kitchen of a house. Any more bicker and there's bound to be a row. Let's go, so she can remind me how much I love her."

We had emerged through the front door by then. He spoke the latter part directly to Sophia, who stood waiting against the railing of the front porch, fanning herself with a hat that looked as big as the sky. Rather than some funereal gloom, she wore a dress the gentle white color of dogwood petals. The lightness of it fell long and full over white stockings. The hat matched the shoes, which matched the not-quite-dark and glowing blue that had always been the color of the ocean in my dreams.

For someone who had dressed in a strangling rush, she was winsome as art. In her other hand she held the journal she had written in at Mr. Proctor's grave, some pages folded, sticking out the top.

"Why thank you, Uncle. I am going, and I refuse to be grim. I'll trust we're sending off a lady of faith to her maker in a town that hasn't seen me in years, so right off to hell with the somber. Frank, we can all wail tomorrow, but we've done enough for today. God help us, we'll make one another strong. Now, put your shoes on and let's go, before my kind and beautiful uncle remakes an ass of himself."

The minister huffed a short laugh. She grinned, full of vaunt and glory, shaking her head, while I sweated in a woven chair, pulling on the dark socks and shoes that were just slightly too big. Lew said one of them would hold a winter's worth of cord wood. Anyone could tell he was trying to keep my heart light enough to carry.

The car soon rolled the three of us down the Proctor's canopied driveway into the soft summer afternoon — me in the back, the wind warm, and a scent of shady, damp ground all over us through the open windows. Lew groused about the heat as we wound along the main road, and I wondered why he wore a dark suit coat every day of the year. We were soon paralleling a strait of river where the pulp of my remains might have washed by now, trapped and rotting in some silted pool. I watched it through the trees, wondering why survival of the train and the water had happened. Why living through it had placed me on this road back to town to the cruelty of a mother newly dead.

Sophia had plunged head-down into the journal as soon as we left. No more than three miles of road lay behind us when she turned to me on her knees, wearing the satisfaction of a task completed. The Packard wound along the desolate string of road, threaded between the river and a high wall of rock. I kept a numbing stare toward the blur out the window while she talked.

"Frank, now our deal is strong. I'll help you more than your imagination can hold, as long as you keep true to me. It'll be hard when we get there. Don't know who we might see, and what folks might say or do, and I'm as anxious as you about it. After we talked at Daddy's grave, a little something began to come to me. A little love letter for that girl of yours, and I wrote it down here directly from what you said. Your thoughts, in my words, just in case you ever wanted to send them on to her. I thought we might see her today, so I have it here. It's the longest shot, maybe, but if you want her to see what you feel, here it is. I'll take down anything else you want to say — to anybody — and keep you out of any face-to-face you don't feel up to at the church. I'll write it right now. Just tell me."

I kept quiet. Lew urged her, "Enough talk, just give it on to him, girl." Sophia finished stuffing some pages into an envelope. Her gloved hand passed it to me, then came an impish turn of a smile. "It's all yours, Frank. *Almost* all yours."

"I thank you. Much obliged," is all I could raise. She squeezed my hand, nearly grinned, spun from her knees to retake the seat, and we jostled on in quiet. I slid the envelope into my jacket pocket without reading a word.

The town emerged hot and teeming with the afternoon's business. Every sight of it on this re-entry felt foreign and small — like I would never fit myself into the place again. We flew past Lew's river stone and mortar Presbyterian Church. In the shady yard of it some young boys and a lone girl busied themselves at marbles or other summery oblivion on the ground. We slowed for traffic just past the sag of the old livery, doubtless still holding the tombstone I'd bought for Frank. The thought of it drew a pang of guilt. Soon the cotton mill's red bulk glowered down our way from the end of the street. I slumped in the seat, guarded against the peppering of faces I recognized, some turning more than a casual look at Lew's car. Mackey's stood open and bright with porch conversation, so much so it seemed no sadness lay anywhere near the county. I took some quiet offense on my dead mother's behalf.

Across from the depot we turned for the bridge to the upward stretch, slowing nearly to a stop at the funeral home, a fairly new business, officious lettering of "Bookman Brothers" stark on the glass. The two-floor building also held the office of ancient and sour Dr. Lawrence Waters, known by many as Doc Vinegar and suspected of giving hypodermic shots of water to those who chronically annoyed him. He made himself an easy source of laudanum for Frank and those who bootlegged it, and I hated him for it. Every brick of the place had always held, for me, the sheen of death and all that can foul a life. A mere glance at what some called the "Bookman death house" made my mother's dying as real and strong as the odor of carnations at a wake. I had never quite believed Mary Lizbeth didn't mind the work she did for the place.

The entire trip had fallen into some quiet as we entered town, but became more so on the winding drive up the mountain. Passing the fork that led to Mary L.'s wakened me from the lull of passing trees. Nerves and thought warmed back to life. As Lew turned off the narrow road onto the weed-center trail toward the church, I broke the hush.

"Take me past the church, on to my house. I'd like to get me some of my stuff."

Lew fidgeted as he interrupted. "We're late as it is, son. We'll retrieve whatever after what's left of the service."

"Lew, just stop at the church," Sophia said. "You go on in and we'll wait for your report. Tell us what we should do." It was the only splinter of fear I had detected in her. She had ridden curiously through the town, turning her head as if to soak in the light off every old brick, board and nail of it. For someone who claimed such isolation, the town seemed to her a favorite story, often read. The whole place familiar to this woman I had never seen there once in my life.

The cars soon appeared slouching off both sides of the road, which likely still wore my footprints. The crowd was larger than even I expected. The curious will flock around the sort of death a place talks about for years, long after grass takes to the grave. The little church hadn't seen such even during revivals. Lew's tires ground to a stillness in the middle of the way, directly at the church's open front door. Singing emerged — "Leaning on the Everlasting Arms." Without a word, I turned to a quiet storm, quaking against a boy's shame of tears. Lew got out of the car and came to my open window.

"Son, it'll be fine. I'll go in to see what part of this you oughtta take. Find out where we might fit in without raisin' too much dust. It'll hurt hard for a spell, but it'll ease, we'll see to that. Soph, take this car on up the road and turn around. You two wait for me. I'll be back."

Sophia whispered something I couldn't hear, then slid under the wheel, closed the door, and eased the Packard on. I calmed a bit, looking back as Lew pattered up the wood steps and through the door.

"Sophia, please don't make me go in there. Please just take me on up over that hill to my house. I just live over the hill yonder. I ain't got this in me."

She turned the car around without looking at me.

"Shush, now. Lew's well-schooled in this kind of ceremony. I trust him that you won't regret a thing. Come on now. Let's move a little closer."

We got out, clicked the doors closed, and walked, eventually past Bookman's hearse, weighty and new, the wood wheel spokes deep in some flowery weeds near the front door. She had to park a good forty yards up the road, nearly topping the knoll that would reveal our house. I argued more to go on, but she took me by the hand and nearly plowed my oversize shoes through the grass. Lew had barely disappeared into the front door when he came out again, making way toward us.

"We'd best not intrude on in now, children." He spoke loudly enough nearly to reach through the church's open windows. He reached out for me, an arm around my shoulder as he turned toward the building. "They'll soon bring your mother's coffin out, son. Looks like a fine service was had. All full of people who knew the best of your mama. As I eased out ol' Rev. Pyles was carried off with some long benediction, raisin' unholy amens about how he can't remember the last time he broke one of the Ten Commandments. God help us all. But it's a fine, full church. There's been some good church had right in there today, even with ol' Pyles carryin' on. Your mama's soul would feel mighty proud, son. She is real glad and proud."

Sophia started to speak when I interrupted, looking at the dust on the dragged hems of my borrowed pants.

"How about my daddy, Frank? Or the Tickmans? You see them in yonder? I don't want to catch a sight of narry one."

"Never looked for 'em, Frankie, and don't you worry about that. You just grieve your mama, son, and let the pew wood worry about who makes the biggest ass."

With that, Lew turned us toward the car. By the time we reached it, amid more of my fear and protest to drive on across the ridge to the house, the funeral began its emergence through the front door and onto the lawn, always mowed before a burial. We stood watching in the full sun, Lew and Sophia flanking me with arms twined at my back, while my mother's little coffin led its congregation of mill folks and farmers, simple dresses and overalls and polished work shoes. Friends I knew well helped carry the flowers alongside some of the curious I hardly recognized. The funeral directors and Rev. Pyles were the only ones fully suited. All of it surfaced as the very picture of orthodox Mathison County, North Carolina — apart from the pallbearers.

Flanking the little box were four of Ma's co-workers, men stooped and worn from the spinning room, and behind them was the sight I could never have imagined. On one side, bearing the rear of the coffin, in the fullest plumage of her Alabama glory, walked school mistress Miss Evans. Across from her, helping with the carry, was her prodigy, Mary Lizbeth. She had doubtless not only served Bookman Funeral Home to dress my mother's corpse, but was among the first two females I had ever seen carry the dead. The women held the handles with both hands, as if to emphasize they held at least their share of the weight.

My eyes fell onto Mary L. and held there as the procession aimed for the little tan grave tent. Her head finally turned to catch a notice. She nearly stumbled, lifting a hand to cover her mouth and joining others in the crowd who blazed a stare at us. I wondered if they might not recognize me in the sheen of that borrowed suit. Mary Lizbeth unmistakably did.

We kept our position at thirty yards away, yet easy to see. A trend of whispers broke out, and a few of the congregation pointed. My overly conscious self took it all as an assault on my running away and my absence in the church at my own mother's funeral. Sophia soon reminded me I may be wrong.

"If they're staring at me, Lew, maybe I should go no closer. You take him on over."

"You're the one who wanted this comin' out for yourself, honeypot. It'll be fine, sweet. Come on. The both of you."

I protested that I was fine where I was. That met with Lew nearly dragging both of us into the cemetery, heads still turning as the crowd rimmed the grave. Sophia seemed suddenly emboldened. She swaggered beside me, tall and straight, the dress and hat in full flounce. We stopped just outside range of the voices. Mary L. had disappeared into the press, which I scanned for any sign of Frank. None. He was not there, and I soon concluded my mother's own sister had not troubled herself with this funeral when, across the yard rose the commotion. Borne on either side by a couple of adolescent farm boys taking orders from the corpulent Mr. Bookman himself, came a wailing and tottering swoon of womanhood. Mattie, in a deluge of tears, was surrounded by Marie Kate and the young Tickman herd. I suppose she had collapsed into a loud, conspicuous and not uncommon fit inside the church. Useless, reportedly bruised but alive somewhere, was absent, much to my gratitude. Marie Kate's eyes briefly met mine and swelled with surprise. We swapped silent humiliations and each looked away.

The graveside service took a brief form I could not hear, apart from a few traces of the 23rd. Psalm. It concluded with a rapid breakup of the morose crowd toward their transportation. Mattie, still bawling like a hungry calf, somehow took no apparent notice or recognition of me as the Tickmans were ushered away first. I never saw Marie Kate look back.

Nor did I cry. I would have thought the weeping around the grave contagious, but I couldn't catch it. Not where I was. The three of us had not spoken or moved, until Lew ordered us to stay as he stepped in, toward the human flow, to run a blockade against those who might intrude toward Sophia and me. He spoke to a few in words I couldn't hear, and Sophia backed me out toward the road.

"It'll serve us well to let the curiosity scatter a bit. Then you can go to the grave."

Her tone held a slight unease, almost a fear, in the face of more gawk and twisted neck. I watched the sheriff and two deputies take note of us, but Lew intercepted them as well. Among the last to leave the coffin was Big Miss Ed. She had most surely stood for the entire service in the rear of the church, hardly inside the door. She gave the box a pat of her hand and walked away with a shaking head, an enormous Bible hugged to near- disappearance in her bosom. Mary Lizbeth stood close to the gravesite in conversation with Mr. Bookman's son, Marcus, Miss Evans, and two of the teachers who served under her. The others had almost finished scattering to cars, wagons, or foot travel when I turned. On the heels of Sophia's prodding me to approach the grave, I had to find a place to sit down before a rising sickness did my sitting for me. It started deep in my belly — a swirl of guilt and remorse, unrequited grief, and more things I couldn't quite understand, all swilled in a broth of fear, I suppose. The day's heat helped brew it up into nausea. I remember staggering. Sophia caught me and we wavered to the car. She sat me in the back with orders to loosen the tie and breathe. She yelled something at Lew, then took her seat in the front, fanning me with her hat against the most humiliating sweat of my life. I recall a dimming sound of tailpipes and tires crunching the mourners away and remember hearing Lew ask, "What the hell happened?" Sophia urged him on and I felt him get hurriedly into the car as I slumped over in the backseat. Doors slammed and he soon cranked and pulled the Packard out of the grass, in a high-flung and quaint argument with Sophia about whether we should try to travel or just pause and swelter to death ourselves. He had just wound the engine high when the brakes slammed us into a rutting dirt-road skid that slung me nearly to the floor. I didn't see it, but Lew protested that he had almost hit her. Mary Lizbeth had stepped into our way.

"I need him for just a quick spell. Just a minute or two Frankie, that's all, if you feel up to it." Mary L. spoke with a calm, never minding the mother-of-God-laced scolding from the driver.

She had come fast to Sophia's window, then to mine, nearly out of breath. I had dreaded the first closeness to those eyes — expecting they might sling disappointment or a load of mad-as-hell against me. They instead held only a worry and sadness, all out-thrived by the gentle way of her.

"Frankie, just come with me a minute. That's all."

Sophia turned, back up on her knees, toward me. Lew interrupted, scolding kindly across the seat at Mary L.

"Girl, you wadded my drawers. What if I'd run over you here? Like we don't have enough gloom."

Sophia shushed him and came straight at me from the front, pointing a finger, as if Mary L. weren't there.

"Frank, we have a promise, I believe, whether you've fully made it or not. I trust you'll honor it. Now, go on. Go on with her whether you feel like it or not, or you'll kick your soul over it. We'll wait. If you're of a mind to be sick, this car's no place anyway. Take him on now, girl. He got weak and sick on me. Maybe a minute or two with you can juice some life back into him. Help him say his goodbyes. Like I said, we'll wait."

Mary L. had stepped back. Even when Sophia addressed her she never stopped looking at me. Lew and I opened our doors at the same time and I heard the sopping heft of him peel off the seat.

"Well hell, boy, she's right. And I'll do my waitin' in the shade, children."

He went off toward the ridge of woods across from the cemetery, muttering, never a look back.

"Hotter than hell's burnt biscuits in that car. Come on, Sophie. Leave them be. Get your fanny over here."

He continued on, waving both hands like a happy widower at a revival meeting, never breaking stride until he lobbed his posterior against the roots of an oak — knees erect, like a grasshopper's in reverse. A few swipes of the necktie against the bald of his head came before he swatted both hands at us and yelled.

"Take your time, boy. Might as well suffer the hell of this infernal August here as anywhere else. Lord, Jack Frost, get your britches on. Come chap ol' summertime's ass. God bless us all."

Sophia had followed with a girlish bound, barefoot, abandoning the hat, hushing at him with her arms, the white dresstail in a hurried sway. When she reached him, Lew caught a half-jesting smack across the head. He swatted at her backside and missed, with a playful vow of, "Dammit, girl, I'll tan you better than God already has." She threw a wry kick at him. He seized and wiped his face sweat on the fine dress, and she nearly fell yanking it away. Then she sat with him, and they fell into the gentle laughter of one another's company, shaking off some gravity of the day. Having gotten out of the car, I watched them across the top. The sight led me to believe there are few things so holy in the world as that laughter that grows out of souls freshly torn at the heart.

I turned, in a confluence of dread and fear, to find a vague smile across Mary L.'s face as she watched them. Lew's carrying on had made off with more than the awkward sadness.

"Don't say anything, Frankie. Don't say a word. Just come on with me. I told 'em not to bury her yet."

Seeing her braced me to the bone, yet moved a sweet pain through to the marrow — as if we had been apart years instead of days. The dark curls in a tide around her face, skin colored in shades of creek sand, deep with summer and the force of a seventeen-year-old heart. Her eyes shone wet and bright as a long mountain view after rain — at once delicate and strong, refusing to grant sorrow or malice a bed of its own. Even in that cemetery, in the hardness of the time, every line that formed her, everything she was, begged for a fingertip. She was, to me, perfect satisfaction. A near-holy place of rest.

"Mary L., I'm powerful sorry. I never meant a bit of harm, runnin' off the way I did. You been more sweet to me than ever I'll know, and if I could I woulda...."

"Hush now. Don't sass me with your sorries. That's a waste of good breath. You come with me, that's all."

She turned across the cemetery, fast toward my mother's coffin. The gravediggers hired by the funeral home — a quartet of farm boys, one of whose common name was Tunk Holliford — had retired to some shade behind the church, swapping whispers, kicking at the ground like four old hens, and conspicuously not staring. I lagged. Mary Lizbeth reached the grave before I did and placed both hands on the box. From ten feet, the little coffin's gray felt covering and the smell of the clay pile gave off a lonesome feel, made heavier by the grave's tent cover. My mother's open grave seemed a sacred place I was not fit to see.

"Whatever part of this you think is your doin', you best get out from under it right here. Whatever piece of your dead mother you find your own fault in — Frankie, lay it down. Cause your mind to lay it in this very hole in the ground and cover it over."

Mary L. spoke as if I weren't there, with her head bowed toward the lid. Some tears tried to come up and strangle her but failed.

"You know what I'm livin' with, Frankie. Haulin' fault around makes as much sense as heftin' up this casket and luggin' around your poor mama's bones your whole life. Fault and blame will wear you out and down. Don't you take your part of it."

"Can you please let me see her?" I asked, stepping close, in a rattle of nerves. "I want to open her box — just a minute." That turned Mary Lizbeth. She set a kind gaze onto me.

"No, Frankie. It's been too long in this weather. You don't want to look now. And not at the way she died. We wanted to wait an extra day to bury her to see if you'd come, but we couldn't. I made her real pretty for you. Put her in the sweetest little dress I could pay for — white dots on blue — and I did up her hair real pretty. Made her as cheerful as I could. And it made me plumb mad to see her that way. But it's none of your doin', honey. None of your doin'."

Toward the end she turned to me, the feel of the words melting across her face. She stepped close, lowered her head, and reached for my hands, squeezing them in a way that felt like rescue. As though to save me from falling into sobs. The truth is, the sick and weak part of me suddenly felt vacant as death. I felt I had grieved my way into a darkness all my life, yet the strength of the woman at my hand dawned somehow into me. And with it, came the first light of knowing I had done the very worst thing I could to her. In fleeing, I had lived down to the very depths of her father.

"Mary L., you've got more sense than any ten men I'll ever know. Enough to know I never left Ma or you outta malice. I left this infernal damned place. I let it run me off and I never should...."

"Stop it. Stop it now," she very nearly shouted, without looking up, grabbing me around the neck. So strong her hair flew full into my face. What followed came out in throbs.

"Frankie, I thought you'd gone off and died in the woods. I never cared a bit for the reason you took off. I know you, Frankie. I was just sure you'd left this world for good. I was grievin' you, Frankie. Been grievin' you ever since I heard. I wanted to run across this graveyard when I saw you."

I soothed and hushed her the gentlest ways I knew, catching sight of the gravediggers, all standing now, slinging glares hot enough to start a barn fire.

"I'm right here, Mary L. Right here."

"And so am I, Frankie." She pulled back and looked at me. "But for how long, I don't know."

I ignored that and dug into my jacket pocket for the letter, which I had yet to read. I figured it held the only decent and safe thing left to say, so it went into her hand.

"Somebody else put the words to it, but the thoughts is mine. They're every bit mine, and they come from a deep place."

She looked down in a moment's calm, then came at me in some stout force.

"Frankie, I don't know what this is, but I'm not done hollerin' at you yet. Did you know they've been plannin' you a funeral? They would have treated you as dead, not on the run. Do you know that? The thought of it almost cracked me in two, Frankie. It just about broke my heart. Can you see that? You're wrong. You think I'm mad, but I've just been empty and lonesome and scared as a bird in a hailstorm. But I will not break down."

I tried to ease her but she kept on, all teary and red-faced. She moved nearer, taking my face in her hands. I felt the letter come against my ear where she held it. Her words turned firm again.

"Not over you or anybody else will I let my heart break so it won't hold love. Frankie, your mama's like mine. Thought she couldn't steady herself without holdin' onto somebody — cleavin' to somebody who was gone, years back. But she could, Frankie. She coulda done it. She coulda done more than fine without your daddy or you or anybody else around her. She just wouldn't let herself. She didn't know how. My mama's heart broke so bad it broke her mind after my daddy took off from us, and I reckon your sweet mother chose the same, in her own way. I will not be that woman, Frankie. Not for you or anybody, no matter the hurt. And no matter the love that cuts a hurt into me."

About this time came the error of so many men. We who find ourselves in close witness to a woman stripping to the very nakedness of her spirit. In the midst of her fit of revelation, I tried to match her wisdom by opening my mouth.

"I reckon I'll spend the rest of my days tellin' you I'm sorry. I reckon if you can forgive me for bein' a hog-wallow fool, like your daddy and mine has been, you surely are the angel I've long suspected. Won't you read my letter, please?"

She had never let go of my face.

"You are such a mule, boy. Listen to me! I am not angry. There is no forgivin' to be done. It hurt me to my quick when I found you gone, but I have to trust. I have to believe in things better than either one of us. If I let my heart get all broke, it won't hold one bit of love. The break lets the love go. A broke heart that won't get busy healin' won't hold you, Frankie. And I will hold you in mine, no matter where you are."

She hugged me a long while, then stepped away.

"Mary L., I can't come back here right now. I've done gone and made a promise to that Sophia back yonder that I'll help her. I ain't got idea one what that means, but I told her I would, but I'll be back...."

"And when, Frankie? When might that be? We don't know."

She turned to the coffin again, gliding a hand across the top.

"This is no fit place for such talk, Frankie. This is your time to hold your heart full of your mama, not worry over me. I can't do this now. Not now."

I reached out to take hold of her, only to meet with her putting the unopened envelope back into my hand. She gave my fingers a long squeeze and pulled away mouthing the words, "I love you, boy, deep and wide." Sweat soaked the cream colored dress and fastened it against every motion of her running away from me. I shouted for her to stop, that we'd take her on up the mountain to her house, then I begged her to come back. She turned, ten yards away, swabbing at her face.

"Frankie, I reckon you got your own places to go and I got my livin' to do, too. Just you never forget, I have down in me a soft room for you. It's right here, deep down, and God help me I will keep it up. Keep it nailed up strong, Frank Locke, and you will have a home in me always. There's no runnin' from that, sweet boy. It's enough. It has to be."

She laid her hand against the place where her neck met her chest and began the hardest weeping I had seen from her that day.

"Take care of your home, boy. Mourn good for your mama there. She loved you somethin' good and fierce, and so do I, Frankie Locke. I will take care of my home, down deep. Take care of your own. Make it a good soft place. Don't you come after me now. Don't you do it. Just take me on with you. Just like I'm takin' you. I will never do without you, Frankie. No matter where. You will live in me."

She turned into a fast stride across the little graveyard. She paused at her mother's well-tended monument-free grave, and through the soak of my eyes I saw her place a kiss to it with her hand. By then, Sophia had sprinted to reach arms around her. They kept walking, to the road, around the corner of the church. Out of sight.

It was not only the seeing, but the feel of it all that broke me down. Standing witness to Mary Lizbeth's revelation of herself — the honest and trusting way tears and words came as if from a single well, and my wonder at what she had meant by it all — the whole of it filled me with what the day so loudly called for. I tried to muscle it down out of embarrassment, seeing Lew bouncing around the tombstones toward me. By the time he arrived I was head-down across my mother's coffin, crying, not wanting to stop.

"Let it fly, boy. Let the water fly for the angels to catch, and they'll come find you. Our Lord knows right where you are. He has *been* right where you are down here."

Lew placed his hands on my shoulders and said nothing more. He stayed through my wailing, waiting until every muscle grew too tired for any more. When I could barely stand, he seized me under my arms and eased me to the ground.

I turned and knelt at the casket, feeling the cloth cover's soft formality against my hands.

"Son, Sophie and me talked about it yonder. She's right. Your mother hauled off and did a wrong thing you have to live with. Damnedest thing, a body takin' the life from itself, but we'll help you past it. God help us, we'll gimp on from this little patch of ground."

I finally turned around, and Lew sat with me against the dirt pile while I caught some breath and calmed. I noticed he held the envelope Mary L. had given back, which I knew I had dropped but didn't know where. The gravediggers, hopeless of salvaging much decent daylight beyond the work to be done, now lay in the shade, taking no interest in my fit. Lew was quiet, fanning himself and patting my knee. No sign of Sophia until we heard the car.

I'm quite sure Lew didn't notice her approach it. She had raised the engine to life, gave three honks of the horn, then stood out of it, waving us to come.

"Son, it's time. Time to let this box go. Let the earth have what it craves. We'll carry the good parts on. We'll take your mama's memory on with us from here. We will. Come on now. Hug my neck and come on."

The preacher embraced me and I returned it. He felt like Pap resurrected, and I suddenly knew how much I had hungered for love, starved for the bearing of a man willing to show me how to become one. We came to our feet. He clutched a palm of dirt, laid it on the casket and said, with the other hand on my shoulder: "Lord Almighty, make a corner of Your kingdom sweet and soft and good for Your servant girl here. Make hers a world of sweet peace. And like salt to the sea, let us hide ourselves in Thee. Lord Jesus Christ, hold and forgive us, always, amen."

Without touching the coffin again I led us toward the car, pausing to skim fingers across the neighboring tomb rocks of Granny and Pap and Eb. I took with me some comfort Ma was not alone. The last few steps, I scanned the churchyard for Mary L. She, with the rest of the funeral congregation, had taken leave.

Not much was said when we made it to the car, apart from an argument about who would drive. Sophia won — resolutely — and I thought the day's sun had parched Lew's brains into mad dust when he said, "Hell, go on. This is your daylight comin' out, girl. Might as well take full control." Feeling the wheels follow the road told of a girl no stranger to the job. She moved Lew's Packard through the curves off the mountain with the same poise of her every step. Each turn toward town seemed a shove to my back, pushing me further out of the world I had known.

Ma's face seemed already faint in my mind — like the last sun of a winter dusk — and I couldn't stand the hurt of dwelling on it then. So from the backseat I scanned the woods, the deepness of them still and glowing in the cooling summer light, and hoped for a glimpse of Mary L. — wanting to jump out and fill her full of boyish love talk and regret. It was not to be. The downward ride was scattered with my private wondering about Frank, the absence of him, why he was to blame for every awful thing. Then came a spasm of guilt about my abandoned mother — what she might say about my leaving a job and tobacco fields and another chance at schooling. Then there was nothing. No nerve left to feel. Nothing but a numb and shabby boy, the engine sound on the window's breeze, and the kind distraction made by my company — improvising an effort to lighten the mood.

"Sarah's goin' to think I've stepped in some hole and gone down it for good. Been gone all day. She's all the time warnin' that one of these days the devil's bound to catch me, and I reckon she'll think he has. I can hear her now: 'Where in the cornbread purgatory have you been?' Sweet woman. Sweet woman. Mighty nice to be expected home."

"Well, Uncle, you married above your place in this life, that's for sure," Sophia said, nearing the mountain bottom and the bridge toward town. The steering wheel looked five feet wide between her hands. "So, gentlemen, my driving is quite divine, don't you think?"

"If you mean we're not all screamin' and rollin' off into one of these hollows, why I'd say it's Godly-fine, girl. Right damned good."

She whacked at him, vowing never to make his special chocolate cake again. He rejoined with a story of the last piece she had given him. How he had crumbed it all over the floor, and so delicious it was he'd decided to pick up and eat the crumbs, floor and all. One of those crumbs turned out to be a "dangleberry, fresh off the tailside" of Blossom, his wife's notorious little yapping mixed-breed dog. He had retched and cussed, and had run for the single bottle of whiskey in the house to wash the offal from his mouth. The tale drew the car full of strangled laughter so intense Sophia had to stop under some trees just shy of the river and the town bridge. Then the laughter erupted, and touched us all. When Lew, nearly choking, said, "Blossom's little hiney had not blossomed at all well that day," I said my first earnest prayer in a long while — thanking any God who would hear that He had, on this worst day of my life, at least placed me in the vicinity of a rare and good insanity.

We soon passed Big Ed just on the town side of the bridge. Lew's offer to give her a ride met with a, "No, thank you kindly, Rev. I do some of my best prayin' on my feets, and they prayin' me right on home. Day's coolin' off fine. Terrible sad day it is. Lord, bless that boy." Lew left her with a, "Jesus'll help us," and Sophia drove on, saying nothing. None of them seemed to notice I had ducked down in the back. I'm sure Ed never saw me, though I don't know why I thought it necessary to hide at that stage. I laid my face against the seat, expecting we wouldn't stop again until Sophia's front door. But we did — hard.

"What in the red devil are you doin' now?" Lew fired off, just as the car came to a grinding rest. I popped up just in time to see Sophia jump out in front of Mackey's store.

"I am going into this store for a moment, and I will not be discouraged." She rounded the enormous hood, straightening the dress and waving the hat in full fan.

Lew got out and they argued as she approached my window, both of them drawing passerby looks from a main street that bustled like a hen yard. "Holy foot fire, girl, are you tryin' to run me crazier than I already am?"

"Stop your worry."

"Well, somebody needs to fret. Your mother will think some varmint carried you off. This is no time to stir this town's pot some more. Not with a boy mourning his mama."

Sophia ignored him as she came to me.

"Give me the letter."

"I ain't got it."

"Well, I checked, and that fine girl of yours — as you say — 'ain't got it' either. She doesn't expect a lot from you on such a day, but she's gone home with a pain or two you can help ease. Now, you can tell me this is none of my business, but no matter. You'll thank me one day. Now, hand it over."

"He's got it." I pointed to Lew, and slackened into surrender.

Sophia sighed, satisfied, then reached a hand around my face. She pressed her lips onto my stubbly jaw, nearly at the corner of my mouth, and held a long moment there. The touch of it set my mind awhirl. The soft feel of her mingled with worry about the propriety of taking a kiss from a girl of deeper color than my own. Such intimacy — cutting through the onion-skin wall of our differing shades — was seldom talked about during my boyhood, apart from whisper. There was also the occasional blown-hard rant about race mingling violating the Bible. My first acquaintance with such talk came as a young child. One of the larger churches two counties away ousted its pastor on mere rumor his son had planted his seed with a sharecropper's deep-skinned daughter. People debated and friendships soured over it. Pap said nothing about the accusation but deplored the high-minded yammer: "Tongue-lashin' that man from the pulpit amounts to beatin' the mule 'cause the cow got outta the barn." Around that same time I had overheard a lawyer on the street speak of it. Some evil "mess in the nation" is what I thought he had said. "Miscegenation" was still a word too heavy for my ignorance when Sophia put the gentle beauty of her mouth to my face that afternoon. By the time she lifted it away, all I felt was a sweetness of care — along with what comes from an exquisitely drawn young woman trailing her fingertips across the face of an eighteen-year-old boy. Though when I glanced up to find Lew watching through the car window, my head reacted and jerked away from her. I sank into the seat again. A sorrow came instantly, with a gratitude Sophia seemed to give little notice.

She lobbied — nearly had to wrestle — the envelope out of Lew's pocket while he tipped an appeasing hat to the passing glares. If anyone took notice of me, which I doubt, it likely died on swords of the curiosity cut toward Sophia. She ignored the town's rush, soon back for a moment at my window.

"What do you think of this? Satisfied?" She held the unsealed envelope where I could snatch it away if I chose.

"Ain't read it yet. Not been of a mind, I reckon."

"Well, I'm going into that store, where I am quite certain I can make sure she receives it. Shall I take it on? How much do you trust me? *Do* you trust me?" Her voice was light, playful, yet strong-minded at once.

The wonder of what that envelope held strained me nearly to grab it. Yet I sat slumped and quiet, afraid I might not understand what Sophia had put down of my feelings.

"Take it on, then. I ain't got to see what it says. And I reckon I ain't fit for much but makin' the poor girl cry. What you say's bound to be right smart. Smarter than me. So take it on. If there's some good in it, I want Mary Lizbeth to read it first, not me."

"Suit yourself. I've composed well. You'll not be sorry." Sophia smiled the same familiar satisfaction, then she saw Lew — objections and all — into the driver's seat, as if she might need a fast getaway. She sailed across the busy street — the dress and hat in breezy flow — and disappeared through Mackey's screen door. The store's usual front porch flock had twisted its collective neck to stare at her, every eye as big as an owl's.

"Well, let's pray she comes out as well as she went in. Dammit, if I have to go in there...." Lew muttered, then we sat still a few minutes in the clatter of passing cars. Into our waiting soon came a wind that spoke of a distant thundershower. I remember taking it in. The freshness of it reminded me of Mackey's ice-barrel drink bottles. From my peering shelter in the back I saw a few people throw up a wave of recognition toward the car. Lew gave each one a swipe in return, jabbered a bit about Sophia worrying off "what few chicken hairs" he had left on his head, then he turned. I never saw coming what he had to say.

"Son, sit up here a minute. Sit on up. Don't fret about somebody seein' you. Nobody's lookin' who you ought worry about. Let word spread you're alive. Long as you're with me they likely won't approach. They'll figure you don't have much sense to start with."

He chortled a bit on the last part — clearly the laugh of a man dulling the edge off his own nerves and the news he has to give. I raised myself, watching the glow dim in his eyes. Across the seatback Lew's face took on that paternal aspect a man gets when what he's about to say will become an heirloom — words as a fixture of the heart.

"Frank, you never raised it, so I haven't said anything 'til now. I was intended on tellin' both of you this when we got back to the house, but since the girl's bent on spendin' next Christmas in this oven of a town and that store, I might as well go ahead now."

He paused in a deep breath, the richness of old pipe smoke all over the stillness of the car. Something about his manner, the feeling off him, thrives in my memory — most vividly the way the eyes took hold of me. I put myself down into the kindness of them, rested in the peace they held. Were the voice not a note or two lower, I would have believed the man had given harbor to my Pap's resurrected soul.

"Frank, I figure you're wonderin' where your father was today. I know you're lookin' for him. Well, he went off with people who scoured the woods after you, and now he's the one lost. They knew where you went in. When the sheriff brought him word of your mother's row up at your grandfolks' place, and how you took to the trees, well, your daddy had one high-hackle fit."

"A fit's about all he's good for," I interrupted, glancing off at nothing through the window. My throat began to swell as he went on.

"Look here, son. Look at me. Your daddy was in a fit about you. It was the very day you left. They let him see your mama a minute in the jail. Sheriff says she was squallin' herself to pieces. Your father came out of there and gathered the remains of his wits into the search. I actually saw him, son. Caught sight of him in a truckload of men with lanterns, just yonder in front of the courthouse. He was gray as cinders. Had some wicked case of the shakes. Looked near-drowned in his own wallow, in a fit of worry, and on he went with 'em. He carried on with some high hollerin' after you. Desperate man, son. When the dark chased the men out of the woods, they had to rassle your daddy into comin' out, too. Everybody was just torn deep with upset."

About this time, Lew's palm took rest against my knee.

"Son, two men kept vigil around a fire in your grandfolks' backyard. Right there where the whole damn business happened. One was Dewey Hammond. You might know he's in my congregation. He came all upset, tellin' me they wanted to watch through the night. See if you might give a yell or find your own way down out of that mountain. Some figured you already had. That you slipped off to hide somewhere out of shame. The sheriff had hauled your daddy on home, scared he was worn plumb to death. But the man would not rest. Son, he walked back up to that fire in the night, borrowed a lantern and went back in. Both of those fellows went arguin' with him a few hundred yards up the path, tryin' to talk sense the whole way. But there's no makin' sense with a man's grief. Your daddy just kept walkin', best he could, hollerin' for you and sayin' nothin' else. Can't much blame the men for turnin' back in the night woods. Dewey says the last they saw, your daddy was swingin' a lantern up that mountainside. When they got back to their fire they could still hear him yellin' off after you in the night, where a dozen men had tried and given up. They said he was so mournful, it was like he was beggin' back his own soul from the dark. They thought he'd come on back in an hour or so. But Frank, best we know, that's the last anybody's seen of your father. Dewey said he had looked so sick, like he might be slow as a terrapin, but he'd almost outrun the lamplight itself up that mountain after you. He said he and that other fella I don't know were heartbroken they couldn't stop him. Ashamed, too. Dewey claims not many know of it but the sheriff and me, so far. So God help us, I suppose we'll all have to guess what's happened to the man, son. But we surely know this. Folks underestimated your daddy. We all surely did."

The cooler breeze died for a moment, leaving wet heat growing to a stultifying mass around us. Lew finished telling me how relieved the sheriff had looked to see me at the cemetery. Rather than landing hard, the news had merely lapped against my mind, eased by the deep and soft bearing of the source. He told me all would be well, regardless, and he spoke it with that restful and believable sadness of ministers who truly wish the worst of life were but lies we could choose not to tell.

Silence came, and Lew gave it place. I sat there, straying off into what he had said, watching parts of a cloud drop onto the high ridge beyond Mackey's and the rail tracks. Each a piece of lost and delicate she-rain. "Look at the she-rain, Frankie. Wanderin' off from a storm, like some pretty little soul, lookin' for home." The words of Granny's voice were as clear in my head as the cooling air. The sky above the cloud shreds turned quickly leaden, and off it came bursts of wind again, with the smell of a rain I could see crossing the mountaintop.

That moment, watching the mist adrift along the blue mountain wall, I understood for the first time: Lonesome is often not a feeling at all, but the longing for one. In that quiet with Lew, a full, human feeling seemed as lost and far off as Granny's beloved she-rain. Not one inner part of me would fall fully into the wilderness of hate or sadness, nor could I quite rise away from them. Adrift is all I was, not fully alive, and it occurred to me (my mind of the time straining to grasp it) that I had let myself amount to no more than a human tearing — an aimless scrap, thrown to the wind. I was caught between sorrows below and joys far above — just a blowing fragment. Even in the cemetery that very day it had been so: The graces of Mary L. seemed so high and apart from me, and the flowers and ground of Ma's grave a reality I couldn't fully believe. There I had stood, just a piece of a boy, flimsy and ragged, torn off from both worlds. And now in the car, my mind drifted in tatters, caught between the news of Frank's loss — what it said about the caring he had left in him — and the wretchedness of the man I had long known. I thought then my life might always be, as I recalled the Bible saying, only a vapor, wafting between goodness and sorrows, never fully touching either. Rather than waste time trying to feel or understand it more, I opted for more things I could know.

"Did my mama know what he'd done, that he went off after me? When'd she die?" The words came out more chilled than I intended. Lew was about to break his own neck looking for Sophia at Mackey's front door. But I never felt abandoned. He turned to me again.

"Son, I just don't know. They found your mother after breakfast time. I don't know if she knew about your daddy goin' off missin' or not. I doubt it. She surely knew you were gone, though."

I could tell he regretted raising that last part. He continued, but on a detour.

"Now listen, Sophie doesn't know about your father bein' gone. That fine girl of yours likely won't know it yet either, unless the word's gettin' out. Dewey says ol' Sheriff Long admitted he's tryin' to keep it quiet about the man runnin' off lost that way after you. He and Dewey looked some, but didn't find a thread of him. Sheriff doesn't want to lose another man in the lookin'. So they quit lookin' for either of you."

He patted my knee from the front seat, then shot a look back to the store, deliberately changing the topic. "Forgive my talk, son, but I'd soon bet every cotton-pickin' gambler in heaven and half the ones in hell that girl's found trouble in that very store. I don't care what I've promised her mother and daddy, I swear I'm too old for all this cover-up business." He looked at his watch. "What in the devil is she doin' in there? God A'mighty. God A'mighty, help us, I never thought she'd hightail off and do such as this."

"So they quit lookin' for him? For both of us?" I interrupted, looking off again at the mist, seeing it dissipate now on the mountain as rain and thunder came further over the ridge. Lew looked mortified to answer.

"Yes, son. I suppose word will get out, and it'll look different in the next paper about your daddy gettin' himself lost after you. Dewey told me that the sheriff supposes a hopeless grown man who takes off in the dark woods — fightin' those tryin' to stop him — well, that man does not figure on survivin' to come back. I believe he thought much the same about you both. But listen, that does not mean your daddy is lost for good in the godforsaken sticks. Nor does it mean some good-hearted people won't care...."

Shouting broke Lew off. It cut in hard from across the street — that sort of loud prelude you get seconds before insults turn to knuckles and blood. A wood box of goods lay dropped and spilled on the street, cars stopping and swerving before it, and there was Sophia on Mackey's porch, bent over Reba Mae Smythe, both women swapping unintelligible, but no less boiling, slanders.

"Oh holy God, no. Hold on, boy." Lew fired the car to life and lurched it into a U-turn toward the melee. "Oh holy sweet Jesus, Mary and Moses, Lord God..." and more, poured out of him.

The Packard groaned across that street nearly as fast as the porch's fixture known as Old Pop Ledford scrambled up from where the row apparently startled him off his chair. A crowd had drawn like fizzling barn flies to the yelling women by the time Lew stopped the car only feet away. "Stay here," he snapped, fighting with the door handle. He got out roaring.

"Sophia. Sophia, hush your mouth. Quiet. Both of you. Quiet your hellion mouths...."

The crowd parted with wonder to let the preacher through. I sank down into the back, hearing the argument pull Lew fully into its womb.

"You better get her on outta here, preacher. Best take her on, if you know where she belongs."

Reba Mae's voice quivered along that divide between a mouthy conniption and burning hysteria.

"Ain't never seen such. I'll not take sass off no big, brown leather strop of a gal, I don't care how fancied up she thinks she is, all dressed up or not. Sass me? We'll not have such from your kind, girl. Now you listen to me...."

Sophia replied, each word long and low and sharp. I peaked up to see Lew had taken a hold, urging her to the car, but he shushed and begged in vain.

"You listen to me, and make certain you hear." Sophia pitched closer, with a finger up in Reba Mae's face. "I stepped across this porch minding my business, having had courtesy enough to smile hello at you on the way in, and that's all I did, Miss. And you fire off the kind of filth you spat at me? God forgive me, lady, but I'll swear the heart that beats in you is blacker and blinder than the bats hanging in the sags of your bosom if you meant what you said to me. Damn what you said to me. Damn you for what you said."

By now Mackey and two more men had holds on Reba Mae, trying to hush her as well, which of course emboldened the woman's stance for a fight.

"Preacher, I don't know how you know this streak of dolled up molasses, but you'd best shut her up and take her on, afore she riles me to where I dirty my hands, bloodyin' her colored self."

With that, the two women shot toward each other, nearly breaking free of the men who held them. Lew quickly took on the mien of a man twenty years younger, grabbing up Sophia, who kicked and huffed at her opponent, "God save me. God save me from this place and time and what I want to do to you. God save you, too." I could tell the urge to cry had joined the fight, and she was about to lose that battle. Lew's comforts held like iron as he eased her into the Packard's front seat. But I saw the tears roll loose as he slammed the door. A few in the crowd, some shaking heads and trading looks of disgrace, had picked up the groceries she had dropped to the street. Lew took the box and was practically to the driver's seat when Reba Mae yelled a final round, never minding the chastising she was taking from Mackey. It was something about how she reckoned Lew's wife didn't know he was "all hugged up with a little coffee-ground concubine...." With that, the preacher led his tongue straight into temptation.

"Reba Mae, I'll ask you one more time to fill that cornbread hole of yours with some sense and quiet or I'll take off my very own drawers to gag you with. God'll not hold malice for me sayin' you are an ignorant coward of a woman, and you have shamed yourself and this town today. God help me. If despisin' the hateful filth you've spread out here on this street was enough to send a man to torment, then hell's best hands might just as well cobble me up a bed — and I'll pray not to find you in it one day. You test my faith, woman. But you know what? You know what this mess you made proves? Just that a God good enough to forgive such as you, is a damn long-reach better than this preacher even thought his God could be. Thank you for that, Reba Mae. God bless you for that. God bless and forgive me. And God bless this town and these hills that have to put up with the both of us."

With that Lew thrust himself, winded, into the car, where Sophia cried just above silence. A crowd of better than forty people, I suppose, had heard the latter parts. They scattered as he rammed the car in gear to spin it, aiming fast for out of town. But before he did, a sticky little stand of freckles, Maggie Potter, no more than seven — always in unmatched boots and some faded color of soup-stained dress — approached the Packard. She reached through the window and dropped Sophia's lost hat into her lap. "You near-forgot your lid, ma'am. Here it is. Mighty purdy," she said, then scampered into the melee's afterlife.

The smell of rain poured through the car windows. A few drops fell into little explosions of dust, but it never came to full downpour. Lew pulled Sophia to his shoulder, and she fell against it, as if a brokenhearted daughter to a father. Not a word was said until we were well past his church, out into the curves along the river, making way toward the house.

"Uncle Lew, she fired up with me. Do you know what she whispered, there in my hearing, as I came out of that store? There in front of me, so no one could fail to hear. She asked which I had stolen, the dress or my old black daddy's liquor money to buy it. 'Gal's been sleepin' in the coffee grounds. All fancied up in her daddy's hooch money. Wallerin' in the coffee grounds.'" Sophia mocked her some more, finally sobbing all over the words. "Why would she talk that way to me? Why would you soil another soul that way?"

Lew hushed her, calling Reba Mae just a lonesome old catty fool, too ignorant to know she's a fool, but smart enough to know better. I expected he'd lecture Sophia on why she should have minded him and stayed out of Mackey's, but it never came. He drove on, holding her to himself.

I'd heard stories of lynching and some nasty ruckus happening elsewhere, but had never seen such. The truth was, the blacks and whites of Marshal and the mountains around it lived and worked in close peace, but in parallel castes — the lighter always implicitly deeming itself above the darker. The latter dared not rise "out of their place," as many of the even well-respected people saw it. This was the world in which we all survived: White in the mill spinning room, black offloading cotton outside — farming and worshipping and schooling near to one another, yet apart. The foul words too often used within that co-existence somehow found a place alongside kindness between the races. Hateful names took on a normalcy often excused with, "Bless-his-heart." They never fully broke the peace, and had never seemed to me as foul as they truly were — until what I had just witnessed. Reba Mae was pitied as a sallow old maid, but widely hailed a fine Christian woman — one who cared for the sick and cooked for families of the ill and dead. The fight she started with Sophia amounted to slicing into the heart of my place and times, showing a gore I had lived with all my life but never fully seen. What I witnessed at Mackey's, especially in the grief and death overflowing the day, began re-creating me into a man who could finally appreciate the mess even a sapless, seemingly innocent human life can make. Hearing the hurt pour from the front seat of that Packard sparked me full of want to better the world, even as it made me detest some portions of it all the more.

Sophia calmed, then spoke as if she had read a piece of my mind.

"Have you ever been thankful you're alive and tired of living at the same time? That's how I am tired. I am so tired that way. "

She addressed it to Lew in that near-whisper that can come from a soul trying to cast away from the world, to be alone with her thoughts. He responded only by cradling her further into his right arm and driving on. It was as if I were not in the car.

The road veered from the river before the almost-hidden right turn, directly into the high trees. The car rumbled across what seemed a finely built bridge to nowhere. A rush off the fast creek below announced the start of the long Proctor driveway, which soon climbed through shade so thick it could make noon feel like dusk. That little bridge might as well have formed a viaduct to the heavens. The town and the day felt more than a million miles behind as the Packard wound and climbed toward the house. I cast my aching mind into the passing woods, letting the motion numb the day's sting, and that's when I caught it. A glance of Frank. Just a blink's worth. A daydream flash — as if he stood expecting us at the edge of the heavy woods. The image was not what the town had murmured years about with shame, but an upright man, hands confidently pocketed in a dark suit, the face fully dressed in his potential, an easy and warm sense of all-is-well in his eyes. For that snatch of time, he became my father — scar and all — and not merely because of that moment's look at him. A newness of the man emerged on what I thought I heard breeze through the window.

"You belong, son."

He said it. It made no sense to believe, but I knew I heard it, as clearly as I saw his eyes beam the spectral moment into mine. The voice lingered, so strong it slung the feel of ice into my blood. The sight of him felt like a spray of summer rain on the sweltering ride — clear and real, yet so quickly gone it's easy to believe it never was. Leaving a yearning for more. My head craned out the open window for a look back. Nothing. No man at all. Only the waving of tree limbs and smoke of dust in the car's wake. That and the words, "You belong," drumming against my disbelief.

I drooped against the seat back, remembering how he had said the same words years ago. Eb and I were sparkling mad, throwing rocks in the creek behind the church. Some older boys had run us off, saying we were too spindly and stupid to join their game of cow pasture baseball. Eb had given them some red-hot snuff-spit and hell-fire lip, and they vowed they would have whipped him if his head hadn't stunk so much. That day he'd used a homemade lard-and-axle-grease pomade, and one boy said it might make them all sterile, or at least run girls off for weeks. We had skulked away to our cover to get them thoroughly cussed in absentia when Frank suddenly emerged down the path. "You got to show them fellers you belong, boys," he had said, shaking his head and drawing on a cigarette. "Does no good to cuss 'em. No sense lettin' them shame you. Lay in there and show 'em you can play. You belong. Make 'em know you belong." He turned back up the path toward the church and left us to wonder where he had come from. I supposed he had followed, in hiding, just to watch us play. The eyes had been sober, clear and strong as corn liquor — the very same eyes that had impossibly met mine just now on the edge of those woods.

With the Proctor driveway feeling like eternity, I figured the strain of the day had brought on the vision of a man who was not there. It was no haint, as Granny would call it. Frank was lost, but still alive to me. Alive, and doubtless more than ever the town's talk of shame.

"Shame he can't straighten up....Shame what happened to him, all scarred up like he is....What a shame, man as smart as he is....What a waste he is....I'd be ashamed if I was him, treatin' hisself and his people so."

I had listened to such lament all my life. So much so, the words, "You belong," would not quite fit Frank's voice, though I was still sure they had. What I thought I had seen and heard from the backseat of that Packard soon faded into hatefulness. The shame-talk of neighbors can swell like a lasting bruise into those they pity. A.C. — his burned drifter bones dry now somewhere in the wild — had thrived on the shame of others. But I suffocated under it, and knew the man who fathered me felt the same. I wondered if the people of Marshal cared enough to say even a tiny prayer for my father, much less consider why he'd long needed one. I thought how far shame lives from real care.

By the time the house came into view, my father was merely Frank to me again. I hated him for making my mother and me the hitching posts for the town's pity and our own disgrace. I blamed him for her dying, then despised him for making me care that he'd run into those hoosegow woods after me. I hated myself. My family's life, piteous as it was, had never quite gotten thrown into so awful a fire as the one Sophia walked through on that store porch. I hated Frank for deserving to burn with humiliation more than she did. I loathed that place in all of us that pays a breath's worth of attention to the meanness of: "At least I'm not like that dirty rag." Even some contempt for Ma slipped in. A detesting of how she had lived with such a man but refused living with herself. I hated myself all the more then. Truth is, from its dark place my heart cried for both of them, and longed for them so hard it felt like strangulation. As Lew slowed the car, the house rising to full view, I remembered something Pap once told me, years back. He said love and hate are like fresh-drawn milk — two parts of one in the same vessel. "Let love rise, boy. Rise like sweet cream. Let it rise right out, and you thrive on the taste of it. Don't fret about the rest, or you might just as well milk the mule."

We coasted into the shadow of the Proctor place, its white bulk a solid mass of clapboards and balustrades and wide porch wrapping around. Pap's wisdom touched some vigor to my mind, stirring a wonder of what I should do next. Seeing that house, its size and design as alien as the ocean to my naive mind, at least gave me comfort that I would not go hungry for a time.

"I made such a wreckage of things. Such ruin for you, and for all of us." Sophia rose from the quiet of Lew's arm, crying more of the same until he stopped her.

"Hold on now. Just hold yourself a spell." The old preacher wiped at her face as though the tears were dirt. The usual thunder of him hushed into a comfort, whose serenity spread through the whole car. "My grandmama used to say, 'God don't cotton to ugly.' So make that ugly cry quit wipin' its feet all over your fine face."

"I ruined everything," she argued, looking away from him, sobbing all the more. "And now you'll have to live with it in that town. God, the temerity of that woman...."

"Oh, hell if you messed up a thing, girl. Bound to happen is what it was. Bound to happen one day, and today might as well have been it, unless you plan on spending the rest of your breathin' days locked away up here. And listen, I am not afraid of a single soul in that town, least of all poor old Reba Mae. There is not a soul in this world I'm afraid of, except for Sarah, who likely thinks I'm dead by now. Sarah, and Blossom. Now that little dog scares the hell out of me. Especially lately. She's been squattin' to pee on my side of the bed just before I get up in the mornin'."

Lew's levity was as deliberate as it was useful. He looked back and winked at me. A slim wire of a smile bent through Sophia's crying after what he said next.

"And, speakin' of a pee, I've got to get myself to one. If I don't borrow a commode, girl, next thing I know I'll be out of this car and into your woods, rainin' out a toad-choker. Help her out, Frankie. I'll be back."

He left the car door open and sprang up the steps, waving one hand, holding his groin with the other, and clowning back at us. Sophia shouted behind him, "Check on Mother. Tell her I'll be right there."

She said something about being gone far too long, then climbed from the car. "Come here, Frankie. Please come here."

As soon as I climbed from the car, Sophia nearly fell onto me — the warmth of her breath soon flowing about my neck. My arms hung dumb, in a moment's disbelief that she actually desired a return of the embrace. I finally returned the hug, noting with my hands the small of her back's fall and rise under the damp gloss of the dress. The feel of brushing against too intimate a place came over me as my hands fell to let her go.

"Frankie, I am sorry. This should have been a day raining graces on you, and I had to go and draw a wickedness out of its ground. Do you forgive me? Please say you do."

I said there was no forgiving to be done, followed with, "Forget Reba Mae. She ain't got sense enough to get in outta the rain." Sophia then pulled me by the hand up the stairs to some heavy woven chairs on the porch, leaving the car wide open. She turned and drew something from her dress pocket. I soon recognized it as the envelope that held our joint letter to Mary Lizbeth. She kicked off her shoes and squatted to hand it to me.

"I have more of an acquaintance with that whole town than even Lew knows. I could have had Mackey get this to that girl of yours, but I stopped. It's not right. They're your thoughts, but they're my words. So here. Open it. Read it. If it's right, you'll know. Then, if it's what you want, she'll have it. I'll make sure."

I fastened my eyes on that envelope.

"Do you want me to read it to you?"

The offer raised a touch of anger. I write this convinced she did not presume me semiliterate, but the notion of it skewered me at the time. Having watched Frank's near-obsession with a newspaper, I had read them dutifully just to beat back the thought he might know something I didn't.

"I am not entirely ignorant. I can read it just fine. I reckon this day's worry plumb wore me out. But I ain't too far spent to see the words."

Sophia deflated a bit on the heels of that. She began to pace the porch. I tore the fine paper, pulled out the folded page and set my mind into it. Soon the only hints of life about the house came from the creak of boards under her feet and the imagination of how my voice might sound if it could carry the refinement of her longhand. Each phrase seemed a fine thing I could never earn or afford.

Dearest Mary L.,

What is put down here is not entirely mine. The words belong to someone else, a near-stranger, but they form the makings of my heart. I have shown its softest place to her, and there she has seen the impress of you. She has felt where you have lain inside me.

Mary Lizbeth, I wronged you and have done so with a sorrow that will see me to my heart's final motion. I am so very sorry for leaving as I did. Though I pray you will understand how doing so made me less a blind man. For now I see how far you shine through the lonesome dark. How you have shone to the very sills of this man's soul. I am unfit to think of you, to let myself become dwelling for such a woman as you, but you grace me nonetheless — with every tender remembering, warm in my innermost places like Christmas fire. You will warm the last breath I draw, and I will be glad. Because of you, the dark is no place I will fully know.

Granny — Lord kiss her soul — used to warn me I could get over a broken limb, but I must get under a broken heart. Mary L., mine breaks now for my mother. So heavy and broken it is. Yet all the good will not flow out. Some goodness and beauty will stay. A thought of her and a remembrance of you will help make it so. You help me to lift and shed the ruins of myself. I am so thankful to you.

I told the friend who put down these words for me that I surely am no more to you than a breath of fog on a winter window. Though she will remind me again how such a vapor, no matter how small, arises from the warmth of living. The thought of your breath, no matter how faraway, blesses as it reminds me to live well until I may feel it again.

Regardless of what is to be, I do adore you, Mary Lizbeth. And I will keep the light and warmth of you deep in me, no matter what comes, even through my stormiest day.

Truly, always, your love,

Frank

P.S. Mary Lizbeth, Sophia Proctor here, the writer of this letter, just to assure these are his thoughts. This boy carries in himself gnarls and tangles but something far greater underneath them. I believe you will never dwell fully behind him, and that his heart will make a fine place to dwell.

When I finished reading it the third time, I looked up to find Sophia turning a smile onto me, arms crossed, leaning again on the porch banister, as though nothing coarse had come anywhere near her that day. She appeared satisfied with what she saw — as a child fresh to a big Christmas morning.

"Judging by your eyes, boy, maybe I should have forced it on her in that cemetery. It makes a pretty nice drawing of what you told me yesterday, if I do say so myself. Even if I did compose it in that sultry car on the road today."

She came and sat above me on the chair arm so that the bend of her hip touched my arm. A clot swelled in my throat and refused swallow. After a cough and a sleeve swipe at my face, I handed her the paper without a look. She wiped my cheek with it.

"I'll copy it over if that's what you want. Let me know what else to say. We'll make sure it finds its place with her."

I sat looking at the floor, finally letting a thought of Mary L. catch up with me. The day had held too much to miss her the way I wanted, or appreciate fully what she had said in the cemetery. The echo of her words in what Sophia had written made me nearly believe water could become wine.

"Like I said, I took it from what you told me at Daddy's grave, not that you likely recall much of that." Her arm slipped around my shoulders. "You have to remember I've been witness to the smitten kind of love. I've lived with it most of my life in the two people who raised me. I've lived with the longing for it, too. It did me good to write that for you."

I had just begun calling up the courage to turn and thank her when Lew's feet rumbled their noise through the open windows, announcing that he would soon blast through the front door.

"All right, children, I'm all flushed out and takin' my leave. Frankie, go get that food box outta the car, but wait for me there. Sophie, come here."

He led her away from me by the arm, but gently so. I heard him ease her again. He said something about wanting to tell the whole town the truth about everything and that it would happen in the Almighty's circumspect timing. Just before I left range of their talk, Sophia asked the name of the little girl who had handed her the hat in town. By the time I got to the car he held her wrapped in his arms, patting her head as a father takes a child just fallen from a swing.

They soon said goodbyes, and bounding down the steps he shouted back that her mother looked fine but was asking for water, which sent Sophia flying through the door. I became his next mark, and the aim was sure as he stopped me at the car door — my hands full of groceries, Sophia's hat, and the suit coat I had shed miles ago.

"Rev., I'm powerful thankful to you for all you done for me today." I stood holding the food box, watching him move so close I thought he was going to climb into it. His face became all I could see, the little eyes pushing their forceful and caring way into mine.

"God's joy and my pleasure, son, but I wish it hadn't ended so. Frankie, I don't know what that girl's told you, but you've got the good sense to see this. She has lived a far piece from the world most folks know. What I mean is the hatefulness of it makes about as much sense to her as Greek does to a woodpecker. The Proctors made good and sure of that, God bless 'em, and God forgive 'em. They raised a beautiful stranger to the world, kept her apart from the worst of it, best they could. She knows a lot of the music of this life, but very little of its noise, son. And you're one of the first around here to see her grown. Not even my Sarah knows about the whole ruse. I reckon it's no accident you fell into it. She tell you about her daddy up here?"

"Yessir, she did. Showed me where he's buried."

"Well, I reckon you know she's been the one runnin' that cotton mill in her daddy's name since he died. I was her daddy's go-between, and I've been hers, and it's a miracle we've carried it off. He and the mother of this house in that bed up yonder believe they had good reason to turn on the town and the whole be-damned world. I figure the whole county's worth of people are on the verge of findin' out they've been the fools in this crazy masquerade, and I'm part of it. I suspect the good Lord put you here to hold my girl up through the hard course to come. I love her, boy, like she was my own. You take God's care of her. You'll see some of me, but you're God's man for the day up here. Don't forget it. There's plenty more for you to find out about this place and the whole business. I'll leave her to tell you in good time. I reckon time'll show you. Now come here, put that infernal damn box down and hug my neck."

I complied. Locking into Rev. Lew's embrace almost made me, again, believe my Pap walked earth anew. He patted my shoulders and left an arm around one.

"Now listen, boy. You need to be careful. Sophie's a girl same as any other, only she's been put away. She's lonesome, and more woman than girl now. Twenty-years-old. And I know she's cravin' a man's attentions worse than a flower strainin' for springtime. Now I suppose you'll live up here a spell. Make sure you behave like a gentleman if any confounded coquetry gets to happenin'. Understand me?"

"Yessir," I mumbled, glancing down at our feet. "Ain't never heard it put that way, but I ain't much of a mind to go ko-kettin' on nobody. Don't much have it in me."

Lew shook me full of fatherly reassurance as he laughed. He was kind — guarding my ignorance against a full assault of embarrassment.

"Atta boy. Don't fret. There's plenty 'round this place that's hard to understand."

He raised my face to his eyes, which suddenly seemed to hold a force of the sun.

"Now, listen well to me one more time, then I've got to go. This has been a hell day for you, Frank. You know more than ever now — death knows right where to find us. Bastard'll follow you every step of your days if you're not careful. Fill you full of blame. Make you nothin' better than hateful and afraid. Don't let the shadow of death stay on you, son. Livin' a good life will never disrespect your fine mama. I've buried a lotta people. And I've seen the livin' make death and its guilt their bedfellows. Don't you wallow with 'em."

"Yessir. I'll remember that. I'll remember everthing you done for me today." My words softened, but I straightened before him, as if at locked attention to make him proud. He smiled and slapped a hand to his chest.

"One of my old seminary perfessors used to say, 'Pray like a coward and God'll make you brave.' Tellin' God He's all you got is some fine prayer, boy — especially if you're mad as all hell. The Bible's full of such. Let God take a hold, son. Let Jesus help get your tail-kickin' boots on. We'll give death and ever' kinda hurt in this world the ass-kick that only love can. We'll make that ol' death within us rattle and shiver right down to his water-wand. You hear?"

I laughed with him, and he made his way to the driver's door. He bellowed toward the house, "Sophie, keep the bees outta your britches. I'll be back in a little while," which the mountaintop hawks surely heard. He turned back to me once more.

"A hard old sadness has visited this house before, son. It knows the way here, and judgin' from what I see it'll soon be back. We'll pray and be ready. And we'll both laugh and give it hell."

The Packard soon roared, turning around. I returned a big wave Rev. Lew thrust out the window, watched the blackness of the car meld into the thicket down the drive, and missed him already. Wishing I had known him this well all my life.

I put on the stuffy suit coat, then Sophia's box of food, her hat, and I marched through the front door as though we all had a place waiting in the house. Soft female voices, unintelligible, descended the stairs from what seemed the matriarch's room. I eased the cargo to the kitchen, awing still at the size and gilding of everything in the place, then searched and found a broom for the porch. Back out there, surely for the better part of half an hour, I swept, having cast off everything but the borrowed pants and shirt. I covered the entirety of that porch, its furniture and the great front steps, so assiduously a passing stranger would have thought the place my own. I did it because Ma would have thought it right, earning my keep. But also, the more dust I moved the less I thought about the worst of the day. The more I seemed to belong where I was.

I was pulling weeds along the driveway when Sophia interrupted, back in the sand-color pants and white shirt, one-handing a tray of ham sandwiches with fresh cucumber and warm Dr. Pepper. We took them slowly together on the front porch steps, gathering in the quiet and late-day yawning of woods deep in summer, and chatting sporadically about the lightest things we could find on such a day: Wonderings why a salty tongue craves sweet, which led to her telling of Dr. Pepper's invention a long time back in a Texas drug store, an odd fact I was ill-equipped to doubt. In the growing shadows prematurely darkening the house, we lulled our worries into a light slumber, not quite long enough, each of us reclined on a wicker chaise far more comfortable than any bed I had known. Sophia rose first.

"Frank, I'm going to check on Mother, and she wants a visit with you. I've told her about your loss and your day, and she wants to say a condolence before she rests. So straighten yourself as you wish. But I plead, do not speak of what you saw me do today. Lie if you must, but I don't want her to know I've been gone. And certainly not what came of my time at that store."

I agreed. After a visit to the palace john down the hall and some crams at shirttail, I set my bare feet to the stairs, sweating with worry. A rap of the elder woman's bedroom door drew a quick bark from the other side. The first thing I noticed after she murmured me in was the old rust dog, wagging and satisfied, stretched beside her on the bed. She introduced him as Byron.

"Please, child. Please come to me. Come to see us."

A white gown draped on her as if hung to dry. Her arms seemed thinner than I remembered. Yet they raised an invitation of embrace. I accepted by taking her hands and a seat on the bed.

"Hope you're feelin' some better, ma'am."

The coming dusk had put some breathable air back in the room. Her hands came cold to my face.

"Son, my mind is on you. Sophia told me of your mother. Peace to you, child. The peace of Christ to you, if it dare come near this place."

She pulled up, pressing a cheek to mine, the feel of it fragile as a spent tea bag. Her features held the truest sadness of old disappointment I had ever seen, even on my own mother. She wilted to the pillow and merely looked on me for awhile, as though she could see under every door a boy's soul will try to keep locked shut. I tried filling the quiet with some bravado about how I had been around a lot of dying in my time and would be okay. She squeezed my hands, never looking away.

"Dear, I understand you've received such advice, but I must offer it again: Don't you carry this. It is her act, not yours. And you come this way by no chance. I am sure of that. And grateful."

Each phrase had seemed to need a deep breath. I thanked her, saying she and Sophia and Rev. Lew had been fine family to me in a short time, and that there was nothing to be done. This met with a rising vigor. The feathery voice hardened.

"Son, there is much to be done. The longing is yet to be done. The want of what's been taken from you. That longing will make a Sisyphus of you. Even when you think you've ground the rock of it to dust, long behind, the longing will roll back on you. The Lutheran school girl is long gone out of me. And I intend no disrespect when I say this — but damn every bit of hurt in this world. Damn it for both of us."

She turned away from me, to the still sheers of the open window.

"Lord curse that wicked empty place that is missing someone you love. Send it to the hell that is its home. Lord, God, don't let this boy live with it so long."

Her eyes had turned empty, her mind casting far beyond that room.

"Lord God, forgive an old lady and love this boy with her. Love this boy, Lord God, and the souls of the dead. Love him and my sweet Sophie. Lord God, what I have done. I mean no blasphemy. Oh, Lord, I mean no harm. I have never meant harm...to her or to any...."

The weeping piety carried on awhile, as though she drew it through the window. Holding her hands and answering, "Yessum. It'll be fine, ma'am," eased her some. Her mind finally landed on a clearer place. She raised herself, fully with me again, back with a look of defiance.

"You beautiful boy, I read a goodness in you. You surely have eyes that see down into my girl. If not, you would have absconded with the meal she gave you, and the pride of knowing you came into this world a few shades lighter than she did. I suppose the fact you came as Sophie told me you did, suffering as you have, makes you some parcel of God's own breath in this place. Lew believes so, as well. You are, most assuredly, one afflicted, lonely miracle of a boy. God knows I have pined for one."

"Ma'am, I reckon if I'm the best breath God has goin' on earth, then the whole business is pert near goin' to choke toward doom."

She gave me a sharp pat on the leg, then raised a finger to my nose.

"No. No. I'll not hear you speak of yourself that way. You are a blessing — to me and to my sweet Sophie. She is a moth trapped in a lamp globe, son. A beautiful prisoner to the fading light of this place. I have made myself too much the light of her world, and the world apart is not fit for her. You must see to her. See she finds her way, as best she can. I am a vulgar, Philistine of a woman, but I see God's hand in you. This is between us. If she tries to prevail on you to interfere with me, put it from your thinking. I have become a religion to myself. God and I have a quarrel to settle, and you surely are part of it now. Just let me be. Let me be with God and the work of my faith. Dear sweet boy, such a memory you place in me. Such a want and memory of one I have lost. God be with you...with you in the want of your mother. Peace. Only peace to you...."

She weakened again to the bed, eyes closed, praying, "Strengthen me. Make me Your holy sacrifice, Lord, thank You. Hold my people as Your own, Lord God, as in ages past. Guard the one I have lost. Forgive my failure of him. Forgive my cruelty toward You, Lord of ages past. Hear me...hear me, Lord...accept the sacrament of me, Lord."

I slipped from the room with a pat of the dog — dazed, but with little of my former desire to set feet to the road. Until now my belief in matters divine had formed mostly in a furnace of hot malice about prayers unheard and long forgotten. If Granny's work-coat God had a mind, He had something mighty peculiar on it around this place, I thought. I had just enough curiosity — confusion and all — to stay and find it out.

Down in the kitchen, Sophia asked little of the encounter, seeming determined to avoid it. She instead busied herself over part of a meal. In my time upstairs, Lew had come back to the house with Sarah, dropping off the best funeral day pounding they could muster from their own kitchen. Part of it was half a leftover chicken potpie with two fried hen legs sticking from the crust — as though the bird had crash-landed herself into the pan.

"Lew said he stuck those in for Sarah — a reminder that God wanted her to use her legs more than her mouth and hurry along when they got here," Sophia told me. I must have looked grave, for she said, "He just wants to make people smile, especially on a hard day."

"You reckon he's plumb lost his mind, or just a far piece on the way?" I asked. We smiled, pulled out the legs and devoured them standing. She told me the letter had gone with Lew to its destination. I thanked her for it again, trying to hide how the mere thought of it set me off somewhere between thrill and terror.

Sophia put the rest of the meal away, apart from a small bit she prepared on a tray for her mother. I offered to take it up, insisting on taking my bed out back, but Sophia was adamant I had a place in the house. She showed me the bedroom whose door I had passed upstairs. It was large, dense with rock maple furniture and the feel of abandonment. The chifforobe hung full of clothing, most of it the size I had borrowed and all a touch moldered from hanging idle. Sophia gestured as though I were welcome to everything, then leaned against the high bed and crossed her arms.

"You have behaved in a way that deserves an explanation, Frank. From me. And you will have it. The whole of it. I'm going to feed Mother, and play something for her. I always read to her a bit before I work out back a little."

"I'm right thankful, ma'am. You've been mighty kind to me."

"Stop calling me ma'am. I'm scarcely older than you." A lightness had come over her. "Give yourself awhile. Rest here, explore the room, and meet me later — out on the cabin porch. Never mind the dark. I'll be there."

She wandered out, patting the door as she closed it.

Rather than explore the room as tempted, I opened the enormous windows and reclined on the bed — restless, aching and spent — struggling to quiet the day. The time alone brought gloom. The throb of not being expected home anymore. Of having no one to expect. Fear that all good was gone. I thought again of Eb, wondering how his dying felt. If he had a soul, did it step apart from the drowning cold? That brought the inevitable and grotesque curiosity of my mother's hanging. How much hurt there had been. Had it turned her warm and calm, set her into good company, far above funeral talk? The mere wonder felt like capture between the worst parts of drowning and hanging. Strangling on grief and smothered in the thought of death. Yet forced to live — as near to hopeless as I thought I had ever been. The thought of Mary L.'s cemetery tears and her odd goodbye deepened the feel of it. A hard sleep had begun trying to force through when the sound of the piano came.

The notes sailed from the parlor. Muted, but no less fine and alive by the time they eased under the door and through the windows, to fill the mountain twilight of the room. The same music I had crept in on earlier that day. Graceful, again, as strands of light — raising my wits out of the black. It drew them as if they were cold water from the ground, up into a quiet place of mind, a changing of view. The faces mended, happy and good. On the music, I steadied, and found a way to some long-craved peace.

I woke to calm — crickets and frogs and a cooling breeze in the near-dark — knowing I had slept too long. The time in the woods had rendered me stiff as the bed slats. The only light came from some moon through the drapes. As fast as the dark allowed, I snatched on some shoes I rummaged to find and made off for the cabin. I creaked down the stairs in thoughts of what Mr. Proctor's ghost might look like. Some electric light from the large dining hall sprayed its glow through the front of the house and down the lower hall. The place utterly quiet but for the outdoors and the off-synch tick of clocks. I moved out the back door of the great house to find a glow, telling me Sophia was exactly where she promised, on the cabin's front porch. "Reckon I'm a snatch bit late" is all I could think to say, rounding the corner. Two oil lanterns hung burning on the eave. Sophia reclined in a rocking chair.

"Don't sit. We're not staying here. This night's too pretty not to see what's in it." There was not quite a smile. Her face held a warm little arrogance, so delicate it appeared unreal in the tawny glow.

"Follow me. I have something to show you and even more to tell." She handed me one of the lanterns. "Feel up to a little hike?" The smile finally came.

"Reckon you know where we're goin'. I'll keep up." I was as curious as I was troubled and afraid — trying to hide all three.

She hoisted a heavy folded quilt off the other chair and headed toward the path that led to Mr. Proctor's grave. I followed closely in the lamplight, finding it impossible not to notice the form she gave the cotton pants through the simple act of taking a step. Though I hadn't understood the word he used, instinct said my eyes were defying Lew's departing advice about lonesome young girls and the ways of young men.

"You fear the dark, Frank?" She asked, never turning around, about the time the light hit Mr. Proctor's headstone. The clearing allowed in a hint of the moon.

"Not much sense bein' scared of it, I reckon. Mary Lizbeth says the dark's like a pillow for your mind. Just a place to rest is all. I remember her sayin' folks scared of the dark don't ever see the stars."

This stopped Sophia so suddenly I bumped her, having walked with my eyes fixed on the path and her backside. She turned, held up her light. It uncovered what I thought a strange little tangle of feelings on her face, unutterable, and no more than three inches from mine.

"You do love that girl, don't you, Frank Locke? She has a pretty way with you. Pretty as what you just said."

"I'll reckon she does, Sophia. She surely does. I surely do."

It was the first time I remembered comfortably using her name, the sound of it feeling not quite right, but good. I stood still, marveling again at the sound and look of her — each word as rich and fine as her face. Her breath smelled just faintly of some spirit I couldn't identify. The deep shade of her color, I noticed, far outshone the darkness around us.

"Your music. That there piano of yours. It all set me to thinkin' like I never quite had before. I was worried and saddened sick, but that music was tonic to me in that bed, Sophia. It put the very best of my ma and my Mary L. back in me. I reckon if there is a God I can believe in, He surely loves what you make grow outta that piano. I sure wish my mama coulda heard it."

The latter part came hard, like I was talking through honey. Sophia's other hand dropped the quilt, came to my neck and held. The slightest moan rose on her breath. She pulled from the hug and spoke to me in a quaint formality so delicate it became a music all its own.

"Chopin is an act of God. Just a little piece of the Holy in my hands — taught to them a long while ago. My mother gave it to me. I give Chopin back to her. And you."

I said nothing, trying to keep ignorance under cover. The night bugs had begun to whir and beat against the lamp my aching arm held to her face. When she pulled my cheek to her mouth and let it pause there — longer than on the street in town — I lowered the light, taking in the softness of the dark, having forgotten we stood in what otherwise might have seemed the outer wilderness of gloom. I brushed a kiss to her cheek in return. As she let go, a spasm of guilt came.

"We oughtta get on, I reckon," I said, raising the lamp again. By the time I bent to pick up the quilt, she had turned.

"Just a bit further. Come on. You'll see."

Out of John Proctor's clearing she stepped to the narrow hint of a path into the woods — not one to be found by any who didn't know it was there, especially in the night. I followed near, wishing for some boots instead of dress shoes. The soft floor was slick under a pine thicket, rising, and we climbed what seemed like a mile through it, some distant lightning flashing through the trees. I started twice to ask the destination and whether we would ever be seen again, but elected merely to huff and climb.

The grade eventually eased into another clear place, and were it not for the lanterns and the pewter-glow moon beyond, a body might have stepped clean off a ledge to his end. We stopped on a swell of rock that formed a high stage on the mountainside. Our tiny lights revealed a sheer drop. We surely looked like a couple of lightning bugs moored against an edge of the world.

"Over here, Frank. Watch where you step."

Into lantern range soon came a wall, too steep to climb. The mountain rose beyond it, and at its base, nestled into a little place not deep enough to call a hole, the light fell against the door of a safe. Old and small but stalwart, "Sears Roebuck and Company, Chicago" across the black door. Streams of rust ran from the hinges and little wounds made by the weather. The nesting place had done little to protect it.

Without a word Sophia pulled back the door, no need for the combination to throw the latch. The safe was wide open to the wilds. Inside it, stacked in rows up to its ceiling, banded as though fresh from a bank, lay far more money than I had ever dreamed of seeing in my life. We both squatted in front of it, in the fitting gold of the lanterns, Sophia allowing me a moment's look. I remember finally saying something akin to, "Holy sweet Saint Peter."

"It's nothing but money, Frank," she said, raising her light to my gawk and stare. "I have it counted and fixed in a ledger, and do you know why I'm showing it to you? Because I figure it's the best measure of trust, first of all. It wouldn't be hard for you to find a way back up here tomorrow, or even just shove me off this cliff this minute and fill your pockets. Now would it? But I believe in you. Notice I didn't bring the rifle. If you're the man I believe you to be, I can trust your knowing of this. There is plenty more around, stashed. Plenty more. Too much. And plenty more to know."

"Well, that's more than I ever seen." It was all I could think to say. I still hadn't looked away.

"Okay, you've had your look. Now come here."

She yanked the quilt from my arm and spread it closeby, taking a seat on it and shooting forward on her backside.

"Come on. And douse that light."

I did, wondering how we'd relight it to get back, and took a seat beside her on the quilt, spread against a sheet of rock. Our eyes soon tuned down to the dark, letting the moon and lightning reveal the view. Beyond the ledge at our heels, ridgelines lay drawn in dark indigo, fall and rise, dissolving into the sky's night blue. Stars scattered as though the heavens had a screen floor.

"You might as well know everything, Frank. Everything about my life." She spoke with relief, and sighed looking out. "I love this place so much. My father did as well."

"It is mighty fine," I said. "Awful fine."

Sophia scooted closer but never looked at me, letting her hand find mine where I leaned back.

"'I have kept many things in my hands and lost them all, but that which I have placed in God's hands, that I still possess.' You know who said that, Frank?"

"Got narry an idea. Been a long time since God and me saw much eye-to-eye."

"Martin Luther said it, a long time ago. And the man who raised me vowed he would live it."

Snatching the opportunity, my unknowing mind and my smart mouth joined hands, drew back my tongue, and fired off that I knew a couple of Martins but, "narry one Luther, livin' in these parts." It just cracked clean out of me — straight from the tar of grief and misery that had baptized the day. The laughter yanked both of us from the mire of where we had been.

"Boy, I am going to trim that tangle of weeds in your brain," she quipped, giving me the same whap Lew took at the cemetery. She was light with me, a comfort against my fear that even a smile amounted to frolicking too soon, trampling a disrespect on my mother's fresh grave. "I suppose I ain't got much decent business, crackin' off like a fool," is about how I put it. Sophia's hand left mine and drew both knees to her chin.

"Frank, a good mother wants a child to thrive, more than anything. It might scrape your hurt for me to say it, but I'll wager that you were your mother's dying thought. And not just a crying out for you. It was a want of beauty for you. Beauty and not sadness."

That set Sophia's mind away from where we sat, well beyond the mountain night and the long heaping view beyond.

"Frank, it's time you heard what I have never told anybody. I've never had somebody to tell. And I have so wanted to tell it."

Thus began a story of the Proctors on a train trip to North Carolina's coastal Wilmington, where John Proctor was born. Once there, he had secured them a little lacquered buggy, and the couple were coursing the early morning streets when a man stepped out of the shade. Just walked out in front of them. His Sunday clothes draped sodden on him, as though he had bathed in tears that had washed through the white oyster shell dust covering him from the road. Wrapped in a bloody green dress, clutched under his chin, the baby writhed — full of fuss. The man stuttered in pleas and cries nearly melting into the child's.

"Frank, I've spent my life trying to get his voice in my mind. Mother said he more than begged them to stop. He was a great graying steeple of a man my color, and just about torn in two."

"'Help me please. I pray you'll help a man near as helpless as this child. Been prayin' all night to find me some folk that looked fit for askin'.'"

"Mother's spoken of it so many times, and I've ached to hear his voice. Ached for it every day. A girl wants to know the sound of the man who put her in this world. And I never will. "

She told me even as the buggy slowed, the mother who raised her had practically broken both legs and her neck climbing down from the perch, giving Mr. Proctor a chewing out for getting in her way.

"Frank, he told them my natural mother had bled out her final strength during my birth. She had been in her grave two days, leaving behind the hungry squall of a baby. He'd been lost in worry of what to do. Claiming he had no people he thought fit to care for her."

"'What's a unholy man like me goin' to do with somethin' so fine by hisself? She's too fine a pretty little thing to take raisin' from an old widower like me.' Mother said it was the sweetest and saddest thing she had ever heard."

Sophia seemed to take a deep comfort in revealing this to me. She went on to say both the Proctors vowed they would find him some help. That surely some local midwife could help him keep the infant. The man stood weeping and just looked at them. Clutched the child closer than ever.

"Frank, I've decided he did some of the hardest and kindest and most reckless things a man or woman could ever do," Sophia said. She kept looking out from our perch, seeming lost in the dark of the valley below us. "He admitted he was a minister of God's holy word who had brought unholy shame to a nineteen-year-old girl of his church. She had protected him, hadn't told — at least not with her mouth — and he even preached the girl's funeral to a church full of dead glare. He claimed the only congregants willing to take the baby were old women, not far from their own graves. The dead girl's parents had walked away scandalized, saying nothing. So he promised God. Promised he'd give her to the first hands who would dare to take her, as long as the face held love. He claimed he'd sat in the shallow wash of ocean surf all night, its sound the only calming the baby would take. He said he had prayed himself into the idea to read folks' eyes for love, and not fail to let her go with the first real love he saw. In return, he'd trust in the God who'd taken the child's mother."

Sophia said it was either faith or folly, depending on how a person might view it, but to her what followed had been the clearest answer to a man's prayer she would ever know. There in the shade of that Wilmington street, the woman soon to become her mother had said, through her wonder, "'Well, she is a glory. God, what a glory she is. What is her name?'"

Sophia softened, turning away.

"Do you know what he said, Frankie? He said she hasn't a name. He said he couldn't give the child a name and let her leave his hands. He supposed such a child would take her name where she found a Godly home, and he would trust it would be right. Mother says he wept like a wounded little boy, taking me down from his chin, beginning to let me go, and carrying on about sins God would forgive when people would not. He declared he would spend the rest of his days and nights praying God would make certain giving such a child away was the best he could do. Praying how he wanted her loved."

Sophia went on, pining again to hear his voice in what her mother had told her.

"'Please, be God's people to care for her. Try to love her. The Lord loves the littlest sprig on this earth, ma'am. Try to love her that way. Please, folks, love her that way.'"

"Frank, I've listened to my mother live in that memory over and over. That — and how he touched a long kiss to me before he finally held me out. The sacred way she claimed he looked. He was present with them and far off at the same time. Deep in the loss already, Mother says. She feels he was letting the sorrow of it get acquainted with the faith needed to carry what was done. She knew he was far from sure about laying me into a stranger's life. Mother believes Almighty God surely wrote peace into her eyes to ease him."

By this time, I sat convinced the rock that held us in the dark also had me at the very verge of the most far-flung tale I had ever heard — truth or lie. It grew more so as Sophia told me it was John Proctor who took her. He had come near to tipping his wife into the horse to reach for the child. *His* were the first Proctor arms to flow under her. The man who had sired her turned fast, shambling away, in quakes of suffering. Mrs. Proctor — having already begged him to consider and be sure of things — chased him with her best solace. She promised love and care, made offers to flower the dead mother's grave and see that contact was kept. With the infant a yowling ball of fidget by then at his chest, John Proctor had called his wife back. Later telling her the man's choice had been made, and was best lived with in private. As Sophia had heard it, the giant man never looked back. With his head lobbing down, he had slipped between row houses, making himself gone.

By then, Sophia lay back, skyward on the rock, smoothing her hair as if to fix up for any eyes that might be in the stars.

"There is good reason my father, John Proctor, moved without waver to take me, Frank. Not that my mother wouldn't have, but he had his own reason to receive a child of my color into the bosom of white privilege. I believe it's because he had lived another way."

Sophia gave no opening for comment. I lay back with her on the rock, eased by the firmament — its vault of lights on blue dark — listening to what the town of Marshal had no chance to know about John Proctor. He was merely talk to most people — always an odd ghost, unseen in years. Sophia, though, knew him as the son of a whoring bootlegger, fathered by "God-only-knows." A Wilmington street boy who ran his mother's liquor and his imagination all over a city that held more people of color than whites in his day. His mother shunned daylight like a bat, eased by her own backyard brew which the boy helped to make, so he took regular company with an aging Catholic woman who lived in the neighboring house through a cane patch and trees. She was a great dark curtain of mixed weave — claiming African, Hungarian, Spaniard, and a lightening tinge of Irish. In the tavern she ran, she taught the boy to cook, to read, and the power of the meekest among us to weaken a strong man's hold on his money.

Sophia told it so clearly I could see his life: A boyhood industry from his early days — full of drunks, harlots, confidence men, street preachers, white sailors, stevedores, and the sundry living streaks of oddity who will color a coastal river town. From such frayed ends, the man who would become her father fashioned a mind and will strong enough to raise himself apart from what the rest of the world thought or felt or did. It helped him go from selling leftover soup along the Wilmington docks to owning sizeable portions of railroad stock by the time he was nineteen-years-old.

"John Proctor didn't even know where his own name came from, but he gave a good one to me," Sophia said. "It always felt like he took me and loved me without so much as a blink of worry. With so much confidence, that John Calvin and the earth's Presbyterian entirety might have thought the Proctors predestined to take a stranger's dark-colored baby into a big life built from nowhere. So Frank, it seems your life and mine have a few bits in common."

I outwardly agreed, though privately thought we had as much in common as the moon and a lightbulb. I lay there still trying to get my mind around what I had just heard. Sophia went on, her voice in a clearing, having escaped the heavy brush of grief.

"Frank, I came into this family for the same reasons I was given away, I believe. Don't get me wrong — there was love, no doubting that. But the man who did the giving and the people who did the taking — they all *feared* what had been, and what might be. I am a Proctor out of fear. And that's not entirely good."

Her hand came back to mine. A deep breath blew into the night before she went on.

"Frank, I am not the first child Jim and Julia Proctor had to raise." She looked away from the stars toward me. "The other one is a large reason I am damn glad you fell out of those woods at my feet, boy."

The moon cast just enough of itself to reveal a worry I had seen only in Mary Lizbeth's eyes — the night she told me her secret of A.C.'s burning in that rock cleft.

"They have a son. They had him late in life, by most measure. He was more than just a boy when they took me in. He was a tall fifteen, by the picture I've seen. Thrown out of three boarding schools, and nearly cast out of his grandfather's house in Rhode Island by the time he set his first glare onto me. Frank, I know you think it odd, how I've managed to stay hidden and survive up here."

I avoided a clear answer, though did confess to what I had taken from the eavesdrop of that morning — Lew's recalling the scandal in the church when she was a baby. I said, "A few folks think the Proctors had done some crazy mean thing to get rid of you 'cause they was ashamed of takin' you to start with. Then you got a whole lotta folks that just don't care."

"Well, they didn't just hide me from the town of Marshal. My parents hid me from what they considered the worst of the entire world. Protected me, they thought. They feared they had failed to guard their boy, so they cloistered me. Alexander is his name. They couldn't protect him from his own family, or even himself. They failed to stop him from feeling ashamed of where he came from. Of his own father. And of me. His grandfather made him even worse."

"I'm not any stranger to feelin' ashamed," I said. Sophia ignored me and went on.

"Our father rarely spoke of him when I was little. Though I know he wanted to give Alex a great leg up in the world. He built an enormous business — four textile mills in two states — and not one with a wall strong enough to keep out the facts of where he came from. He couldn't block the truth that he never really went to formal school his entire life. John Proctor had no finery in his name. He lived well with it, but some people would not — even his own blood."

Sophia rolled to her side, facing me with recollections of the woman who became her mother — someone I scarcely believed I had actually touched: A girl born to the brightest shores that run along that sea of what seems ancient and boundless American money. Great tides of it that can drown what a child might become in the merits of where she comes from. Money just about as abundant and pedigreed as her maiden name, Julia Sophia Hampton, of New York, Newport, and tragic old foyers — high and hollow with expectations. She was the only child of a mother who had soon died of influenza. This made her the Hampton banking family's greatest hope and prize — raised by multiple housemaids, polished by tutors, shipped up to Matthew Vassar's college for a final sheen on her mind and tongue. Her father, Robert Hampton, daydreamed out loud of a grandson's potential, even before his little Julia had abandoned dolls, and he worried about her restless ways. When she met John Proctor in a train station in New York, she was twenty-two, adventuring through the city to escape the dearth that overwhelmed her oversize life. He twenty-five, traveling on his own, in town merely curious to see what the town was about. The fact he had already raised himself into the start of a well-invested fortune, growing high into land and textiles, did not matter. He was rooted in what Robert Hampton considered a bordello upbringing and street-urchin liquor-running. Even his thriving cotton mills, in that man's eyes, were no better than a stockyard of penny-labor lintheads. The Hampton lineage amounted to a great old forest, and John Proctor the common soil beneath it. From the high boughs of her name, the graceful blonde seed fell so hard and deep into him, the couple had to escape. They set the hell-raising blather of her father's disapproval behind them and ran down to Charleston to marry, barely two weeks after their lives had filled up with one another.

"Frank, some of what my mother gave to me she had already given the sweet man who became my father. She adored him. Lived to imagine new ways to love him. Taught him the things she knew of books. And there was no counting the everyday whispers of how he loved her in return. He said he loved how she could make the smallest things matter. And her father still saw him as a little piece of living grime, scrabbling away with what he didn't deserve. My mother's father didn't speak to her for years. Nothing — until Alex came. That announcement reconciled them all a bit. But Mother says the first summer the boy spent at her family place in Rhode Island began to carry him away. Her father actually told the boy — just a child — he was better than John Proctor and he ought to act like it. Can you imagine? Telling a child his mother's name by itself makes him better than the whole of his father's life?"

I didn't speak of it, but lay beside her remembering how Pap had told me a similar thing about my own father, only with a kind sadness in his voice. A regret that Frank Locke couldn't seem to "get any better for my mother and me than he was."

There on that little cliff of the night woods, Sophia had helped me see for the first time how closely pride resembles dynamite, useful and dangerous at the same time.

A malice stretched into her voice as she told me of the Proctors losing the boy. They lost him to the feel of his grandfather's life, which plied their child off into the acreage and acquaintances and vanity of living as if money is a life, rather than a mere part of one. And yes, the Proctors themselves had felt some of that same conceit. Having moved their wealth into the North Carolina mountains for the same beauty the Vanderbilts found there, they deemed the place benighted — worthy of industry and some assistance, but failing to measure up to their son. So, in rational tears that fall from assuming it was surely for the best, they let the boy go. Set him loose into the preparatory schooling their money could buy a seven-year-old. Sophia said as she hears it, he soon turned off into a high-minded, foul-tongued, blustering conflict of a soul who never wanted to come home. Alex fought the idea of home — and more than a few of his classmates — which made his grandfather more determined than ever to save him. No matter the school, or the family money and clout, nothing did.

"And I became the black powder, Frank. The little charge who blew things up. To hear Mother tell it, when Alex arrived here on the train for Thanksgiving, he found her on the porch with me bundled up in her arms to greet him. I had been here more than four months. A dark little secret, except to the people who'd seen me that one, and only, day in the church. Alex took one look at me, and the cracks in this family broke wide open into war."

Sophia told it as her mother had: Introduced to his new little sister on that porch, the teenage Alex Proctor pronounced, with some glib laughter, that, "Grandfather will surely approve the business of raising your own housemaid." The remark came with the suitcase still in his hand. Sophia said her father's face, rather than flaming into rage, had just seemed to die. He was standing next to the boy, fresh from the train station. Her mother had told her, "Every shimmer of life in your father's eyes went dead, as if Alex had pushed the man's last measure of hope to its end." Mrs. Proctor handed her husband the baby, and with the calm of someone getting the mail, stepped to her son and slapped his face. A reddening swipe, hard as the floor wood — so hard it addled him backward and knocked the suitcase to the floor. In words cold as that late November, her mother spoke over him, "You have dishonored your father and this family the last time, and I will fight you myself if you dishonor this child!" This met with his screaming how dare she, and that he hated her and that Grandfather would ask what cotton field she had been sleeping in now. More would have flown out of him, had John Proctor not stopped it with his right fist, swung against the temple of his only son. It came with the force not just of street fights as a boy, but — Sophia's mother believed — the muscle that builds from lugging too much disappointment around. As Alex fell against the railing and down the stairs, Julia went frantically and maternally after him — baby Sophia kicking in a calm and happy oblivion on a porch chair, where her father had put her down.

"Mother says she had never thought Alex held the sort of venom he revealed that day. When she reached him at the stair bottom, he fumed off some swearing. Then he kicked her. He kicked his own mother — so hard in the chest her wind must have gone one way as she went the other. My father told me he had tried to forget seeing her scrape across the bricks on the walk and roll into the yard. All Mother remembers is trying to breathe and hearing my father pounding down the stairs. He sounded as she had never heard him. The noise of a soul torn wide open. To her, there's no forgetting how he screamed at the boy, 'Get up, get up!' He yanked him up by the hair. Wrestled him toward the driveway. 'Foul your mother's love for you. You are not fit for hell. You look...look what you've done to where you come from.' Mother says the boy had no room for a word. My father just kept shattering the air around him. He finally slammed Alex against the fender of their little demi-tonneau Cadillac. He composed himself some, then said, 'I've let you turn on me, but you'll not get another chance to wound your mother. Or dirty the child of this house with your mouth. Off to hell with you, boy. You take your fool learned self to hell, and take your granddaddy with you.' Mother has remembered it to me many times. Too many."

Sophia raised herself from looking into the sky to take in the view off the rock again. A mist had begun to gather far down below us, brightening everything with its echo of the moon.

"My father tore his own boy out of his life," Sophia said, very much lost in the thought of it, the story seeming to have taken her away from me. "He gave him the car and said he didn't care how he went. As long as he did. And to come back only when he'd made himself fit for his mother. Otherwise, stay away. Alex left his suitcase, took the car and abandoned it at the train station. And he never said a word to Mother. She had gotten up and gone after me on that porch. And the whole broken mess of it became a sickness without cure. After that, letters went unanswered, and a part of the Proctors just ceased to be. They expected more from this life than it would give, Frank, so they turned away from it. Just turned on what the world had shown them it was. But they loved the living hell out of me. They filled the places where Alex could have been with love for me."

Sophia let some quiet linger and I stepped into it.

"I reckon a man like your daddy, where he come from, probably saw men hurt women aplenty," I said. "Can't much say as I blame him on that boy. I mighta done worse. Sure have wanted to."

She kept quiet, got up and stepped to the ledge, too near for comfort — a silhouette of long thin lines looking out, as if awaiting advice that might come from the broad hum of the woods beneath us. She kept a long silence before turning to sit in front of me, and what she said felt like a dream. Had she not shown me the stash of money in that rusty little safe, I might have thought it all just a fanciful lie.

She spoke of a John Proctor trying to forgive himself for things, and not just his row with Alex. Shortly after it, he sold the mills he built in South Carolina. He never could stop talking about the trip he'd taken down there — stumbling onto a little scrap of a boy, all squatted down on a courthouse step. The child was showing his hand to three or four more, who swarmed its deformity like bees who couldn't quite decide if the honey before them were sweet or rancid. He told of getting the hand caught in a weaving machine — not a scarce occurrence in a business thriving on fingers tiny and delicate enough to thread them. They worked in clamorous rooms kept hot and humid so the threads wouldn't break. Proctor had stepped close enough to hear, and to see where three fingers and most of the boy's right thumb had been sliced and ground to stubs.

The sight led him to go looking for a fine educator who would draw other fine educators. He eventually found Miss Evans and brought her in from Alabama on a shared idealism to create the finest mill school in the South. The two of them presumed mill and farm life would run all children into learning, which had not come to pass — for mill salaries had become just about an unbreakable habit. That defeat, so close to the loss of Alex and the church's one-time scorn of his new infant daughter, sent the man retreating even further into his wife, and the baby each of them vowed to guard.

"He turned hard," Sophia said, her chin still at her knees and my tailbone aching by now against the rock. "He built that three-room cabin down there himself, deliberately turned it away from the house, made an office in it, and as I grew up that's where he taught me the business. He trusted the Marshal Cotton Mill to people he paid from afar, and then made me run the books and know every thread of how it worked. He'd take me down there on holidays when no one was around. Otherwise I was to stay protected by home."

She leaned back away from me, toward the ledge, drawn off again, as if the night itself could listen.

"God, I miss my father. What I wouldn't give for just a whisper of him. Saying I'm a Proctor no matter what people say, and that he's proud of me and that the world will know why one day. He always said so, and Lew says the same, and I have to believe the only two men I've ever known in my life. Until you, Lew's the only other one allowed on this property. He's carried the money — the cash payroll — and still does. My father didn't even like to touch it. He fell into hate with money and everything about it except for what it could do to raise people up. He turned on how he made it, but he still wanted my mother and me to flourish in it. They both decided that was best done by making their own little utopia up here with me and trying never to leave it. This was world enough for them."

Utopia sounded to me like Cherokee for stepping outdoors to make water, but I kept that to myself. The thrall of the telegram held it back. Sophia went on, marveling at the uproar it had caused, arriving six years after the Thanksgiving row with Alex, amid a scatter of unanswered letters in between. Robert Hampton had telegrammed to summon his only daughter to Rhode Island, alone, which was not to be.

"Frank, I know you'll not believe it, but Mother took me with her." Sophia leaned in, as if a child with a secret bursting to get itself told. "I was six-years-old, and this place was all I knew. My father fought it, didn't even want *her* to go, but Mother would not give in. She shopped in Asheville for just the right black dress, stockings, little black gloves, and fabric to fashion two layers of black veil to finish how I was to hide. My father said I looked like a little walking lament — 'sorrow on legs' — Mother telling us it had to be so and I would understand why one day. I could speak in curtsies and thank yous, but was not to laugh when people stared. As I remember, they stared more at the beauty of her. Onto that train we went. Both in black, from the Asheville depot all the way to Rhode Island that fall. And I surely looked like some vision of Poe's darkest dreams. Just barely remember a few asking about the veils — Mother telling them only that we were traveling to mourn. She claims every soul seemed to assume I was white as the small of her back under all that dark cloth."

Sophia was right. My scant mind grappled with doubt, trying to believe her, just as it craved to hear her tell the rest. Her words, especially in the dark, forming finely drawn pictures of memory. The rock and cry of the train across what seemed infinite land, the colors and sweep of it unreal to so isolated a child. Then the ocean, boundless to the eye. She remembered lifting the veils to take it in, thinking so much water looked like where blue mountains had melted. Newport itself — a wonder, she said. Among the mansions, Hampton House stood so large she feared seeing giants around the corners. There was the way a voice rang off the high ocean-color walls, and the marble, cold as the hand Robert Hampton had placed on her arm from his bed. A remnant of a man — an old and dying one — lay among the chateau's gilding and servants, his life as small as a blade of grass in the great lawn.

"He scared me. *People* scared me, because I had been around so few, but he was a terror. I remember his face looking like the place where all that's hard and sad in the world made their beds. I remember being afraid the way he looked might leap off him and make a home on me. Mother made me stand there, though, beside that enormous bed. She wanted him to look at me and be sure of what he said he wanted to do. She needed no force to make him look. And I remember him saying, 'Well, so be it. I'm too old and tired and disappointed to make quarrels and take a child's name in vain. Take it. Take it all, and let me be.' It was years before I understood what it was."

Sophia turned, then, and told me the thing that can still run the adrenaline of disbelief through my smallest vein. Robert Hampton had resolved, for a final time, to change his will.

She spoke of it without awe, as one might talk of how dry the weather has been. He had willed nearly the entire fortune — houses, land in four states, his interests in banks, shipping, automobile-making — all of it to the former Julia Hampton. Julia *Proctor* — still much to his regret — but the daughter he saw as the purest reflection of himself and her mother, Victoria, whose portraits shone with light off the chateau walls, burning with joy and sadness at once. The old man claimed Alex had proven unfit (the boy had been kicked out of Brown for drunkenness just shy of graduation), though he would continue with a generous allowance for a time, as long as the lawyer found he made no more trouble. Hampton still held John Proctor accountable for the boy's flaws — which further chilled the reunion — but the dying man's daughter had clutched her father's withering frame against herself for a long time, warming the goodbye into something more easily lived with. The vastness of the room soon filled with final parting. She thanked him, not for money, but for her own learning, which she promised would pass to his adoptive granddaughter, Sophia. The child had sat quietly close by, changed into a new red silk dress, kicking her feet against a velveteen chair.

Sophia's last memories of those two days in Rhode Island poured into the warm dark. She had walked with her mother and the doting and longtime servants to Victoria Hampton's little fenced grave by the sea behind the house. Goodbyes spoken there had felt holy, even to a young child whose fingers later wandered and played along the great home's piano while waiting for the car to the train. For a little girl isolated in her learning, there was no forgetting the adventure of Newport, or her mother's crying again at her own piano back home in North Carolina. Barely two weeks had passed before word came of the Hampton patriarch's death. He had been buried, as he wished, privately at sea.

"That lady you met in the bedroom down there, Frank — she has money enough to live a thousand beautiful lives, end to end. But she's lost herself. She's falling, Frank. As if life just shattered beneath her."

Sophia was up walking again, pacing too close to that ledge, the moon surrounding us in what seemed a muted daylight. Watching her form move against the mountain sweep beyond, I stood with a thought of moving toward her. She stopped and turned to me.

"That shattering of her world has thrown her down. Broken her in two, and still she tries to protect me. What her father gave her, she has given to me. I'm the only love who hasn't left her now, and that stands to make me a very rich woman. I'm already living up here in a throng of money, and all I want in this world right now is not to be left by her. I get everything when she dies. And that's when I'll have nothing."

The revelation summoned only a stillness. As if what she told me rested a moment in the night air. I needed that moment to take it all in.

"Why hasn't that boy of hers tried comin' in here to get his part?" I finally asked, moving a little nearer to where Sophia paced again, head down. "It's narry wonder he ain't tried to kill you."

The natural steadiness of her voice began to quake. Some inner part of Sophia felt pulled away.

"If he interferes, Mother can cut the allowance from under him. Change whatever life he makes for himself in New York. There's that, and the fact that Father cut him off at the heart. Sawed him off is more like it. He's well-warned never to come here again. Alex is a coward, Frank. He's a coward, yellow as his mother's hair used to be, and that's about their nearest resemblance. I've strained to believe any portion of him came from her."

"Reckon you're right about that business, him bein' yeller," I said, moving closer still, trying to ease her some. "And if you ain't seen hide or hair of him by now, maybe you won't. Don't seem all that confounded complicated to me."

"Well it is. He doesn't even know his own father is dead, and he's just about killed his own mother with menace. Alex has his revenge with a pen. He's written terrible letters to this place, full of poison and threats toward me — both of us, really. Lately, Mother's written threats of her own in return, and she's signed my father's name to help keep the boy away. And doing that has nearly finished her. She's too fine a woman even for a protective lie. That's part of what's broken her down. The boy was furious about his grandfather's will, and my father knew it. It's why he and I horse-dragged that safe up here, Frank. There's plenty more money than that. Lew keeps some of it, and my father and I have cash money scattered all over this farm. He told Mother if something happened to him and Alex came after the Hampton fortune we were to give it to him. Save ourselves and sign it over, then gather up the brush money — make our lives with that. That's what he called it, 'our brush money.' He taught me how to run the business of money, the mill and all. It's as if he knew I would have to one day. And so I have. I have done it with Lew's help, in this protectorate up here — forging names, helping my mother lie to Alex and duping the whole world into thinking John Proctor is alive. And Lord God, how I wish he were. I am tired, Frank. I am worn and I am afraid." With that, her inner foundation gave way. She broke down, away from the ledge, homing toward me — the sound of her breakage filling the ridge behind us, surely reaching the fog below and every roosting treetop bird. The hold she took around my shoulders felt the strongest of my young days, and I returned it.

"I'm such a fool, Frank. On this hard day for you, I've weighted you further with all this. I am so sorry." Her crying deepened. "I am not afraid of Alex, damn him. If he were to kill me, I'd die unafraid, of death or of him. But I am scared of living and dying alone. I need you to help me. I need you to help me be something other than alone."

The raw hurt rained out of her into my shirt collar with sound beyond words. We stood in its storm like a pair of blown-over trees, one holding up the other. Sophia cried out a fear that felt alive with pain. She had caused me to *see* the notion of alone — *feel* its breath and the beat of its heart. The idea of alone, even in my learning of it from Mary Lizbeth, had never before felt like it came with a name to be given. That it had bent its name into a branding iron to scar everyone it decided to claim as its own. Trying to stand strong for Sophia, I pressed down my own grief, the pain of the day and the last few. At least ten minutes passed before she restored herself to order.

"Ever feel like God despises you?" she finally muffled into my shirt. "Sometimes I believe Mother's been right. God must surely punish us for the joy we've known in this place. And one another. It has been our Eden on the one hand, and a circle of Dante on the other. I do wonder what we might have done to earn what curses this family."

I lingered a moment, catching her meaning though not the name, then pulled away, sifting my words through a weave of sympathy and resentment.

"Well, if there is a God that goes hatin' on people, spewin' down curses and such, I'll reckon He hates poor workin' people a whole lot more than He despises the sweet fancy rich. I can't quite understand everthing about you. How you've lived up here and all. But I've seen what it does to a young'un's eyes when she goes without somethin' to eat for too long. I've seen my own mama beat down black and blue when I was too little to do anything about it. And I reckon I'll spend more of my life watchin' the stoutest men get broke down under work and livin' that's both too hard. So any God that would hate you so — well, let's just figure He looks at me and mine and sees not much more than fleas flyin' off some dead three-legged dog. I'll not believe in any such God as that."

By the end I had turned away toward the trees, regretful of how it came out. Sophia came pulling at my shoulder.

"Are you quite sure you're no relation to Lew Sharpe? Because you sound just like him sometimes."

Her composure had found its legs again. She turned me around and took my hand. I remember thinking hers felt soft as flower petals, especially for a woman who did some minor farm work.

"By the way, I get carried away with myself at times. I agree with you. Come here."

She pulled me across the quilt to the ledge. For a heartbeat or two, I thought she intended us to jump.

"Here, sit with me. You should know why I said that. Why my mother is not the woman she used to be. I intended to wait to tell you, but I believe you're up to it."

Sophia dropped her haunches to that high ledge as if they and the rock were old friends, dangling her feet over what felt like the very chin of Mother Earth, a fall into what looked like the swallow of blackest eternity waiting below. I eased down, grousing about having time to eat a whole chicken before we might hit bottom. A touch of levity can make a fine mask for a boy's terror, at least until the girl he's hiding it from sobers the very air itself with the Holy Bible.

"She's tangled up in Matthew. Matthew 6."

Sophia tightened the clasp of our hands and bounced them a few times on my leg.

"Mother is ill from starvation. She's starving herself, Frank. She's breaking her body with her mind."

Heavy silence. I almost spoke of seeing the lady feeding her food to the dog from her bed, but kept that quiet.

"Look down there. What do you see?" Sophia pointed down into the rock rim's shadow under us. I leaned over, timid as a shy child.

"Narry thing but the dark."

"Well, that's nearly all my mother can see of her faith. The dark is about all she's known since my father died. Something about losing him sent her into the Bible, and one quarrel with the Almighty after another. She's blamed God for taking so many loves of her life, and for the awful ways of people, and God knows she is furious about a world that wouldn't have much to do with me. Not long after we buried my father in secret, she began almost cursing God, daring Him to change the awful way of things — with me begging her to stop. Then she'd drop into a terrible grief, calling herself a sacrilege, not fit to live, apologizing to the heavens. Lew spent hours trying to get her mind rested back into some lighter place. I remember he told her hating herself for being mad at God was like chasing the hem of her own ball gown. He said she could chase it for all eternity, stagger and fall around, and be loved no more and no less. It did little good. She wouldn't go to the horses or hike with me anymore. Lew and I tried every face of God we could find: The never-leave-nor-forsake, the holy-washer-of-feet, the Jesus who loved the most whoring of women. Lew even gave her the view of a God who'd rather we be mad at Him than ignore Him. He told her being mad is only love turned inside out, and that the Lord knew how that felt. But my mother possesses the will of rock and a mind of fire. When Lew showed her the forgiving Jesus in the book of Matthew, she pointed a few lines down, where it talks of cheerful fasting for open reward. She asked what's wrong with holding God to His letter. Then began giving me her food at the dinner table. Stopping our studies at odd times to pray. When Lew told her Jesus never called for starvation — nor did he want folks lopping their own hands off as the Bible says— she'd just tell him God and she were in a loving and wholesome dispute and not to worry."

"I knew a boy like that," I interrupted. "Cecil Harwood. Went to school with him, long as I went. He used to think every single revival preacher was hollerin' right at him, and got to believin' that near all he did was a sin. He just went plumb crazy, prayin' all the time. Would pray forgiveness for the nakedness of takin' a pee. You'd catch him walkin' with his eyes shut, mutterin' to God. There come a day in town when he prayed himself straight into big Betty Martin. He staggered right into her armload of shucked corn and Mason jars, and they fell all over one another. That bit of prayin' got the Lord's name took in vain."

Silence again. A humbling kind. Sophia felt as far from me as the blotches on the moon, and I wished I had been sitting on one of them with my mouth shut. I listened, then, in a feeling of eavesdropping.

"There's no thinking ill of her. She feels she failed God and the world around her and can't find the proper apology. I know that. And God knows I hate watching her waste away. God knows I've tried to cheer and care for her, clean her up when she's sick all over. I wish I could know why there is so much sorrow visited on such a grand lady. So much she would try to fast it away. Why God lets a soul believe He's sent every foul thing that's come into her life. She's taught me from many books, but I just don't understand that. But God knows she's a woman devoted to love. Just trying to fast more God into the world, I suppose. Maybe get Him to shoo away enough of its dark that times would grow better for me. I've asked her how much faith she thinks one woman can have. How many mountains she's seen prayed into the sea. And she just eases me away. Lew still brings us communion up here. But that fasting is still the only sacrament she seems to see anymore."

Sophia had spoken in that low strum of thinking out loud. It began to tighten, as if holding back another rupture of the heart.

"So you see why I said that about being alone? My mother and I have been up here too long, living in books and ourselves. We've crept away some — I've even run away a couple of times. But it only reminded us that lonesome is a stubborn follower. Once you've known it, no matter how much good comes, you're afraid it knows the way to you. My mother knew the wicked devil of it from her beginning. Lonesome came to her when her own mother died. I feel like I've been acquainted with the bastard most of my life, too."

She turned back to me.

"So I guess you're some part of a miracle up here Frank, whether you want to be or not."

I deliberately looked away before asking my next question.

"So, you suppose your mama's tryin' to do what mine did?"

"No. Not as she sees it. I've asked her if it's slow suicide. Begged her not to leave me, and she's vowed she wants nothing more in this world than to be my mother. She claims what she's doing is more for the next world than this one."

Sophia squeezed my hand, then pulled my head to hers.

"Frank, I am, again, so sorry. I never should have spoken of this. Not on this day. I was wrong."

"Don't matter none. Don't matter."

We sat for awhile and let the woods have their say, taking in the late hour. I had always loved the boundless look of night — how it could draw shades against the glare of here and now, leaving only room for a restful memory or dream. Our quiet there in the dark, for reasons I can't define, siphoned me full of thoughts about Granny, so stout and clear they quelled the worst of the day. I soon began to tell Sophia how much Granny loved the fog, of her wishing she could hold and carry the she-rain home in a box, loving it all the more because she could not. No one could possess it. "The she-rain minds only God," she would say. "It goes only where the good wind takes it. Never fights the wind or minds the night." Sophia listened, sighing some agreement, exhausted from the pouring out of herself. Granny's thoughts soon became a soft bed to both of us against the rock.

I woke stiff — feeling a little like wet clothes frozen on a line — yet flush with rest. Sophia had lain back first, and I had drowsed off with her for what must have been an hour. I longed to read Pap's watch, but it lay in the cabin, destroyed by my time in the river. I was used to hard work and little sleep, so I could scarcely believe I could nap there with both feet still hanging over that cliff's edge. The night had gone deep and full, carrying the moon to a high small hanging place, and it saw us wake to a newness of mind. We had swapped one another's worries, which meant we got up off our resting place intimates for good. Groping around for the matches to light the lanterns, there was some laughter. The dark of our times proved no match for the strengths of being young.

"Reckon you and me can make ourselves a deal?" I asked as we stepped away from the safe's little clearing.

"Name my end of it and we'll see," was Sophia's response, homing toward the trail and our descent into woods. I followed so close my nose could nearly peck at her hair.

"Here's how I see things goin'. I can do any work I see needs doin' around your place, plus pert near anything else you find for me to work at. And you can get the dumb outta my way. I quit school for tobaccer fields and that mill. You got books and learnin' I ain't never dreamed about, and I figure you and them might get me a good far piece away from mule pats and cotton dust. If you teach me just a little of your way of talkin', maybe I can shed the lint outta my eyes and see myself about halfway up toward bein' fit for Mary Lizbeth one day. I'd like that, if it ain't no trouble, and I'd never forget it. Never let a letter of your learnin' fall outta my head."

Sophia stopped so hard I rammed her a little. She paused and gave a half-turn of her head to my lantern.

"Boy, you have no idea what you mean to me, do you? What it means having you here. I want not much more in this world right now than to help you — just to keep you around — but I'll do it only if you expect too much. As I said, we'll untangle some of that wilderness mind of yours. But if I catch you expecting too little of yourself, I'll kick you between your biscuits so hard you'll sneeze my toes. Does that sound like a deal you can make?"

"Yessum, it does."

"Fine. And did you hear what just happened again? I *can* speak a taste of *your* diction. We're not so far apart, you and I, thanks plenty to Lew and my father's ways. Now, come on."

Never having turned fully toward me, she carried on down the path, almost in a trot.

"What is it about time with you that swells my urge to send rivers through the woods? If I don't hit a bathroom soon we'll both need a canoe to get home. Come on, before I drop these pants and trust the dark."

A July shower dripped fresh on the leaves when they brought it home from a graveyard shift. I was still a schoolboy – no more than seven or eight – in the hiding of the tree house for some morning peace and pipe tobacco. My folks had fought as reliably as sunrise that week. The din of it still flowed under my mind's door when the noise of the truck that gave them a work ride rousted me to climb down. I glanced around the corner to the front porch, where my mother preceded him into the house, saying something about getting a box. Frank paused in his porch chair, an old straight-back, where he liked to muse aloud about the reasons he and the world weren't fit for one another. He was different that morning. Made so by what he pulled from his pocket, as gently as a man might handle a raw beating heart.

"Come here now, darlin'. I don't mean no harm." The doting came out raspy, but nearly childlike. "That's a darlin', now. Sweet darlin'."

I climbed to the porch, so guarded I might as well have been sneaking up on him.

"Whatcha got?" I asked, against instinct.

He never looked up to answer. Kept his eyes fixed down between his knees. That's where he held it, cupped in the same palms used to raise an axe handle toward Ma three days before.

"Just a lil' ol' bird. Lil' mess of a bird. That's a darlin'. It's awright. Awright now, baby."

A wren, so small it could roost in a tablespoon, had flown into the mill the day before and finally thrown itself against a windowpane. The smack reduced it to a gray lump of smoky feathers, trembling and almost gone. Frank's thumb caressed its head and down its back – its frame still so dazed and hurt the beak gaped for wind that wouldn't quite come. He said Ma reached it first, handling it with the hem of her dress, fearing lice. She installed it, with little hope, in some scrap cloth to see if it would survive the shift, but my father soon took it to his heart.

255

"Ain't right, just lettin' the mill cats get at it. Just a baby of a thing. Can't just let you die. Not like some floor lint, stepped all over."

I left them both without a word that morning. Walking off down the mountain to school I remember thinking I might come home to find it asleep in the scar of his face. It was just about the exact size. A helpless bird seemed to fit him better than I did. Perfect fit for him, I thought. Just right.

The rest of that day brought thoughts of where I would bury it. By the time I walked home, after some wandering mischief with Eb, the bird was gone. My father had petted it hours on that porch without a move, seeing its breath and wits come back enough that it flew off.

"Reckon some angel had its eye on that lil' ol' bird. Sure 'nough did." He talked about it that way for a week. Closer than I had ever come, the bird tended to sober him.

T he days that followed my mother's funeral brought little change in the news of him. Frank Locke, Senior never emerged from the woods. Lew's regular visits kept us versed in how a few men revived the volunteer search. He finally had to tell us of a town caring little to traipse a mountain in search of a walking dead man tongues had long ago tossed as living trash. Lew shook his head, claiming he couldn't shake thoughts of the man's broken soul, rattling the trees after a son lost only to him. I confessed some satisfaction in it — Frank's spirit wailing off alone. Just him, the woods and some cinders of lasting mourning. I admitted it soothed me, though never quite enough to numb the fact his apparent death in the woods had spared him news of my mother's hanging. His ignorance of that — the mercy in it for him — kept a little part of me longing out loud to find and kill him again myself. Lew returned only a calm look and said, "Sip that tonic 'til the jug gets heavy. Then I'll help you set it down." I failed to get the meaning.

Sophia's kind devotion to quiet eased like a medicine of its own. She allowed me time and space to work the great home's garden, orchard, hayfield, and barns in reticence. I had declared not feeling up to talking much more about my family because I was ashamed. This met with, "I don't see a solitary cause for disgrace. What shames you, from now on, will be up to you."

The days spent in her way of life soon evoked some new thinking — clarified that vision of my father I thought I had caught from the back of Lew's car on the driveway. The death of Frank — something prayed for through my boyhood — began to raise a desire for the father I knew he might have been. I deemed it a gentleman's honor to keep that to myself as well, groping in silence for a feeling about him that would fully satisfy. The hateful thought of his carcass, animal-torn and maggoty in some loamy thicket, dueled with another force: The undeniable love that had drawn him to look for me and die in the wild. The more lost each day made him, the more Frank *became* my father — despised, rancid, and wanted at once. The hating of him and yearning

257

for him turning fusty and hot, as if my soul were swallowing oil and water brought to a boil. The feel of it lined nearly every moment I spent on the Proctor farm for days, cooled only by the notion my mother saw into every thought. To mourn her became a satisfying ache, a drive not to disappoint her. A grief practiced in quiet.

Some good fortune came in the near-absence of time for dwelling on sorrows. As Lew himself put it one day, Sophia worked me "harder than a cat covering its own mess on a mirror." I never knew quite what that meant, but I learned plenty more at the Proctors, led by almost muscular force to the vigor of books. My lessons began with Miss Charlotte Brontë's heroine girl. Sophia managed to make Jane live in a boy who feared he might enjoy fine books about as much as he liked rope burn. When ordered to pick a book for study, I chose *Jane Eyre* from the table in John Proctor's backyard cabin, figuring a story fit for the man's hideaway would at least chase away a trace of my dull human donkeyness — and maybe not bludgeon me to death with boredom. Plus, as I figured it, what better than a girl's story to train a boy to write to the girl he adored. Jane and I, it seemed, were destined for one another.

Sophia and I read aloud from the book every night, and we grew a routine of study, work, and each other's quiet company. She made me write down thirty words and their definitions every day from an enormous dictionary on a pedestal in the parlor. Thoughts of them began to act as an elixir to the mind as I explored the farm for brush to clear, wood and hay to cut, anything in need of some care. The garden of corn, cucumber and tomatoes Sophia tried to grow through weeds rose to new life under some watering and a hoe. I tended also to the grandeur of four horses, including the one who had nearly killed me. I nailed at fences and barns, taking what rest a seething boy can find in the cushions of perfunctory labor. This work kept me far afield of the lessons Sophia and Mrs. Proctor held together for hours in that upper room. My help around the place — long needed — seemed to give them more time together. Sophia shared some of the chores — a bit of mowing and care of the house — but I tried to take on as much as I could find. All the while sweetened by knowing I would receive a reward simply from sitting in the vicinity of an open window at Sophia's piano time.

She played reliably in late afternoons or early night, pouring the house and yard full of a music I didn't think possible on this side of whatever eternity held. I reclined to a porch chair or even the cool of the lawn to take it in, feeling each note rise into my mind — seemingly drawn there with the strength of water flowing toward the sun. So much so that one day, early in my time at the Proctor's, I dared step into the parlor to join her on the stool, hardly acknowledged by eyes wired to the music page. Atop the music for "Concerto for Piano No. 1 Op. 11," I noticed what appeared to be the name Fred atop the inscrutable writing, and soon deciphered

Chopin. When she finished — lamenting she, her mother and the heavens heard every flaw — I clapped nonetheless and pointed.

"Well, that's not how I'd spell choppin'," I said. "But if you'll play off some more of that, I'd chop you fireplace wood for a year. Can't quite figure that Fred feller writin' such a fine delicate song for splittin' and choppin' logs."

Sophia's laugh spilled before she could catch it. I joined, assuring her I could exaggerate my own ignorance a bit in the name of fun. That evening, with me reclined on a thick rug of the parlor and her on a divan, she taught me the difference between axe work and Frédéric Chopin. Then she read to me for an extra hour from that book about Jane Eyre.

Miss Brontë's book slowly became a music of its own. Sophia compelled me to read again before sleep what we had read aloud that night, just to gain sight of words and diction I hadn't known. Even the most terrible places of young Jane's days — loveless family, orphanage, and the breaking of hearts — they all had the effect of a healthy intoxication. Reading about her, as best I could read at the time, stretched out my mind. Ventured me to relax and find passage far beyond the self I had known.

"There are no lovely writers who do not read," Sophia would say. "In keeping our bargain, you'll prove that to yourself. Taking in this book will help you compose a letter to that girl of yours. There are billets-doux inside you, Frank, and we'll see them out. Jane and I most assuredly will usher one from you yet." When, confused again, I said I'd never heard of any Billy named for dew, a roar of hilarity virtually tumbled her from the sofa. That one wounded a little. It caused me to turn a bit quiet for a day. Her apology left me fitful to learn a third of what she already knew.

I saw very little of Julia Proctor those days, staying dutiful to work, Miss Eyre and the dictionary. Lew came for mill business with Sophia, which I avoided for fear of hearing more talk I wouldn't understand. While they met at the desk in the cabin, I spent some kitchen time with his wife, Sarah Rose, who came with baskets of meals that would last for days. She was a drawling vessel of mild vinegar and sweetness at once, gently plump all over, with a throaty giggle that trailed close to every move. She made no secret of an opinion Sophia cooked worse than a bony child bride. "I'll not give up," she said, lighting the stove one day. "We'll keep you all baptized in my red-eye gravy. You watch it raise that lady upstairs like Jesus liftin' Lazarus. You wait. God'll save that lady yet, or some prize pigs and I will die in the tryin'."

Sarah Rose and I spoke little of the lady's fasting, nor did we surmise out loud any reasons for it. But a change came. My days there saw growing amounts of food going up the stairs, and a lighter aspect to Sophia's face coming down. Julia Proctor had begun to take a few bites, amounting some days almost to a meal. Sophia felt my merely being there on the farm may have encouraged her. Lew thought it the fruits of saving his breath and letting God have His way with the lady. Sarah Rose claimed it was the divine force of the proper hands folded in prayer over a frying pan.

I kept my peace and began to behave as a near phantom around the place much of the time, staying to my room in Mr. Proctor's cabin, where I had secreted another dictionary and some paper under the bed. I had found that garnering a new word into my head — or even a wider view at one already there — tended to shatter the walls of what I had been. Sometimes a feeling of the hopeless, high and grim, would rim me without warning, even after some good talk and study with Sophia. It came as a sense of no horizons: No reachable aspiration, no hope of retreat. A stubby pencil ambling around a page, in search of letters that fit the feelings I possessed, became my finest tool of self-repair.

About a month after my mother's funeral, in a morning grayed with late summer rain, I sat rocking on the cabin porch — that pencil stumbling over another unreachable letter to Mary Lizbeth — when Lew rounded the corner. He gave the day and its mud some heavy stomp and blasphemy and handed me the envelope.

"Mackey reached this to me before I preached two Sundays ago, and damned if I didn't stuff it in a pocket and not think a spade's worth about it 'til Sarah found it this mornin'. She wagged me good and full of hell about it's late delivery. But I told her the ink's stouter than my memory, and so's the spark betwixt young folks. So here you go."

With a slap against my shoulder and an, "All will be more than fine, righter than this confounded rain," he turned away, around the corner into the hard drizzle, amusing himself by wondering out loud "where Noah left that cotton-pickin' boat."

The damp envelope held my name in Mary L.'s familiar hand, small and confident. I tore in to find a single page swept with the same.

Dearhearted Frank,

I have cried about the way I left you at your sweet mother's grave. I left too much of a proper thing inside me that day, not said. Please forgive that. I pray you'll not turn away from good thoughts of me.

I figure by now you know about your daddy, and with you already strangled on hurts more than old men ought know. Miss Evans says it'll not do, telling a boy what to do with his heart, but I'll not hold my tongue with you. Not one time again. I am right sure you sleep with ache stout enough to crack a boy open. I pray you let it fly. I have hurt a lot the same. If I could I would take hold of what hurts you, haul off and give it a sling. It'd be gone from your heart if I could make it so.

That I can not is no matter. Your sweet, fine letter speaks what I get to be. Miss Evans says I read your letter about as much as I breathe. But I make a part of my home in it. Like I've told you, the two of us, we know how to make a good place for one another, no matter the where or the time. Might as well say a soft quilt spreads out in this here girl. A mighty fine part of you rests on it in me.

Nobody but you and Miss Evans knows what all I live with, so you can rightly figure I learned what I'm about to say on my own. Frank, when your worries go to bothering you, turn on them. Don't you give them a look. Don't you sleep with your troubles, give them time of the day or place to sit down in you. Settle your mind on how good you are yet to be. And make just a bit more room for this girl, no matter what comes. Spread you a quilt in your mind. You sew it up the right way your granny did. You make it of our time together and you never mind the hurt of your day. This girl will do the same, best she's learned how.

I beg and pray this adds a bit of sweetening to your dreams. You sure sweeten mine. Our place in this world will not change that.

I love you, Frank Locke. Your Mary L. will store up a love for you, always.

I read it over five or more times, each time raising more of her from the page. The note cast off some worry that our talk in the cemetery had added up to some permanent goodbye. That paper placed her with me, as if she'd run drenched onto the porch with a laugh out-sounding the rain. I sat a long while in the swelling feel of that, the letter folded into the pocket of the shirt I borrowed from the house. Looking up through the rise of pasture and trees brought a sense of her that could nearly level the ground.

The letter found its way into every pocket I wore, kept to myself for days. Sophia had given me the clothes from the suitcase Alex had left on his last day there. They made a slightly better fit, but with no work clothes among them, I kept to Mr. Proctor's pants. Pruning and mowing the neglected orchard took two weeks of saw and sling blade work, taking breaks with *Jane Eyre* and a tablet for some scratch and dabble on a return note to Mary L. The solitude of the trees gave me rest enough for thinking, but the "can't-nevers" and the "never-heard-tell-ofs" — still wired into my head — were too much in the way. The determination to write Mary Lizbeth with my very own words, chosen and polished by some improved state of myself, had evolved into the hardest work I had ever done. No satisfactory letter would come.

In that very frustration one day, I had gone back to Mr. Proctor's gloves and his saw when Sophia came dodging limbs up the hill to my orchard work. She carried a basket of biscuit-and-apple-butter glory from Sarah Rose. We ate to the crumbs, swatting bees and taking in the shade of a weeping old tree and the sweet trace of apple decay. Its aroma risen from years worth of discarded harvest bettering the surrounding ground.

"What would you say to a dinner — the three of us?" She spoke lying against her elbows, looking down at the house, whose great green roof looked big as a cornfield.

"Mother had the idea. We'll fill the dining room with candles and talk and you'll learn. Frank, I am thrilled and must celebrate. She feels up to being downstairs for the first time in a very long while. It'll become your first night with both the Proctor ladies at once, if you're up to it, and I believe you are. Just knowing you're here as a gentleman improves her."

She looked at me, livened with gratitude at the last of that. I muttered some warmish agreement, and Sophia went on to apologize for how in just those few days she had drifted away. Since she had given me *Jane Eyre*, even with our nightly tutoring carrying on, the slow recovery of her mother had consumed her. I had been left to myself — and gratefully so. I had agreed again to the dinner and even to the wearing of another suit from Alex's abandoned wardrobe, when Sophia got up and paced around, trying to ask for something else. With hands in the back pockets of her pants she kicked at the ground like a schoolboy waiting for an admired girl to pass by.

"I haven't had a fishing partner since my father died, and you've worked this place too hard. I had no intent to make you an employee. What would you say to our taking a little walk back to where I found you? It's a sacred place to me. Truly holy. I want to go back before any chill sets in."

The next hour found me rummaging with her about the cabin, and soon in full kit of her father's best fly vest, field pants, and the sort of gear most boys hold in their dreams. I had agreed the summer was taking its last warm breaths, and that the day was ripe for such a trip. While I went turning over rocks for crickets and grubs to place in Mr. Proctor's bait screen, Sophia checked on and settled her mother upstairs. My awe at Mrs. Proctor had turned more to wonder. Our few brief talks held lasting effect. As if the noble way of her had knocked at my innermost doors to be let in for good. Few people have that way of living in every soul they meet, even when the meeting is but a few words or merely a glance.

Sophia soon came to the cabin porch as one long motion of khaki and dark green, a canteen strapped over her chest and a light pack slung across one shoulder.

The big field hat she wore the day of my rescue dangled from her left hand. We studied one another in silence a moment. I recognize it now as one of the first times my eyes stepped fully through the skin of a person not my color. Even in that outfit, she was in the deepest sense to me a young woman — risen to the first steps of willowy adulthood, graceful and strong. I remember the strike of this thought: She was the only woman I had ever seen who could stand anywhere near the beauty of Mary L.

"Ever use a fly rod?" she asked, inviting me to follow her up the pasture toward the trees.

"Never even seen me one 'til I fetched myself here. Been a cane pole man my whole life. Suppose a stick's a stick to a fish."

A smile made itself heard. "Trenchant thought," she said, not turning around. "I suppose it's a good thing boys don't take that same view of girls. Or so I'm warned."

The path that had brought me to the Proctors looked familiar only in scatters on the trip back. In its first few hours on the property, my mind had cobbled at dull-witted plans to get back across the river to catch the next train — impossible without a commotion of broken limbs or dying. Each idea arrived more asinine than the last. Following Sophia's flouncing hat through the high trees now brought a whispering thanks to God for bringing me her way for this long.

The clearing emerged in a soft gold, the afternoon almost ripe for fish to rise, and I saw why Sophia's heart elevated this place so. More than an eddy, the water formed a long and gentle bend — a river of its own, fed by the main stream but held peaceably away. The island that divided them rose as a great wall of thickest trees, the whole protectorate drawn in shades of green. The water came in little swirls of calm — easy wading from the soft beach of worn little gravel. Even the river's rage I had fallen into from the train became a serenity, the noise of it cut by the island woods into reverent peace. If I had drowned in this place, the flotsam left of me would have found no richer Eden for burial in this world.

"My father said God was extravagant here. Left more pretty in this place than most any other. Daddy used to daydream out loud to me about coming here one day and catching the Holy Father Almighty cooling His toes and taking in the quiet. I've had too much quiet in my day, but I never grow tired of it here."

Sophia thought out loud as she reached for the old leather rod case given to me to carry, watching the water all the while. The air held Cadis flies, bits of flight tender as the cotton mill lint angels of my mother's lore. In the deeper shade of a rhododendron overhang, fish rose to peck them, nipping down any bug daring to light on the resting flow. A rod soon stood assembled in the same long, dark hands that had yanked me from the water fewer than five weeks before.

"I usually fish one of Daddy's hand-tied flies, but let's not waste your cricket-gathering time. Hand me one. We'll soak him and see what happens."

The first jumped free, but the second one she hooked, blowing on it for luck. I held the rod while she stripped off her boots, drew up the pant legs to the knees, and waded in with hardly a ripple midway to her calves. I began trying to build and thread the other rod but couldn't take my eyes off the cast she made. Having clicked off some line, Sophia sailed the cricket across the channel, laying him to a delicate water landing. She made the line relax so well he might have landed asleep on the current. He drifted, untouched.

"Not quite the spot," she muttered to herself. "Come now, Soph. Bend this river into what you want it to be."

She coaxed herself aloud into a second cast. The cricket took longer flight, the landing soft as before, and he floated in kicks into some overhang shade. I saw the fish rush. Water broke as if it were glass, her rod bent into a beautifully unsettled nerve, and soon a fat bream fussed and churned the shallows at her feet. She drew him in, unhooked and bid him a grateful goodbye — smiling all the while, nearly as if I weren't there.

"I made him mad, but we made up. Your turn now. Leave the rod and come here with those crickets and some of that quiet of yours."

Her glance alone, the rascal glow of it, had me shoeless and out to wade before that bream could recatch his breath. Her voice lightened as I eased close by. As though intended to remind me I fished with a girl.

"Let your arm turn into mine, cane pole. We'll make a fly caster of you, and the fish will be charmed. This is my daddy's rod. Chaperone enough, don't you think?"

After I led another furious cricket to the hook, she wrapped my fingers just below hers on the cork rod handle, and we cast. The bug snapped off into the limbs behind us.

"Our endeavor is to catch a fish, not beat the hell out of bugs and the wind, you know." Her face had taken on a polish, a catching of light.

"It's more about gentility than strength, sir. That's what this demands. Just hold, barely a touch."

She drew down some line. Soon my hand and arm felt the rod tip throw back to a pause, into which Sophia whispered out loud, "God help us." In just the time taken to say it, the line looped full behind us and she brought the cast forward, giving the cricket another delicate landing on the water's lull.

"Daddy taught me that, 'God help us.' He claimed saying it gave just enough time to let the cast mature and the rod do its fine bidding. Now, you try."

Through a dozen or more tries with Sophia at my shoulder, God seemed to show a fondness for Sophia and the fish more than me. When I finally landed a cast that satisfied the teacher, she broke into a girlish applause — so full of her own triumph it staggered her tail-first into the two feet of water that held us by the legs. I caught her around the middle before the plunge fully swallowed her, and on the way up she fell into a contagious fit of laughing around my shoulders. I helped her ashore, all fish now terrified, safe and well behind us.

"It's a justice, I suppose. We've each pulled the other out of this little pond now," she said, sopping from the belt down. "You were a load deeper, so I'll take more credit. Turn around. Face the river and take off that shirt."

I protested that my shirt was dry but complied, hearing her sodden trousers strip to the ground. She took the shirt from my outstretched hand. "Okay, turn around now." I did — finding the shirt wrapped loosely around her lower hemisphere, her own shirt tied up where the tail was wet. This revealed the narrow lines of her torso.

A mossy old tree, fallen for years, soon turned into a lounge. Sophia draped her pants across a sunny span of it to dry, spread an old woolen blanket from the pack, and we sat against the log, taking in the heat of the afternoon on the sand. There followed some talk about the place — its peace so near the foaming river two hundred yards through the island trees, and my good fortune to have passed this way. That set Sophia's narrow bare foot tapping mine against the cooling ground. She kept her face to the treetops, never once turning to me.

"Frank, would you please hold my hand? I would like it if you would take my hand and hold it for awhile. There's no harm. You won't betray a soul."

My left hand reached up to be claimed by her right. She squeezed it and went on.

"Frank, I know you think I've taken leave of sanity on this land. With all I've told you, there would be no surprise. In some ways you're right if you do think this. I have grown a touch mad. My entire life's been this farm and the goodness of two fine people who dared take in this tossed-off little disgrace and raise her. They did their best, giving me parties, filling me with what they knew. But I still want things. A little fullness of this life, more than living in the newspaper or magazines. To dance with a boy and feel him against me. I've romped this place with only imagination to share myself with. Do you know the only child laughter I've ever heard is my own? And I've all but forgotten the sound of that."

"I don't much think about such. Except plenty of folks I know would ruther swap places with you than ever grin again."

It came in so coarse a way I squeezed her hand and nudged closer, annoyed with myself and sorry. She shook her head as if to agree with my temper, seeming grateful I didn't vilify her any further.

"Frank, I know I've possessed more books and toys and things than a nation of children and a world of girls deserve. Since I was just a kitten of a girl. But all that having of things never shook a playmate out of those trees for me, now did it? It never would draw a warm sweet boy out of the woods. No matter how hard I imagined more than one around me. You came out of that river groping for some breath — not for money. I've just longed for another set of breaths up here. God knows it never struck me to pray a boy would wash up here — nearly like Arthur's sword. If I hadn't caught your eyes more than once trailing down into my shirt to 'peel my apples,' as Sarah Rose would put it, I would think you a myth or dream. Not quite a real boy."

Her words had fallen into a sultry ease, slow as steam-rise off a teacup. Fingers loosened, seeming to invite the tightening of mine. I feigned a nonchalance — quietly and fully embarrassed — hoping she hadn't caught my stares cast at her other places. She livened, sat up looking at me. My try at small talk about wanting to torture another cricket with the fly rod failed. I lay under the force of a woman determined to strip her lonesomeness down to its Skivvies, too long covered in her mind.

"Frank, do you think I'm a pretty woman? Do you find me pretty?"

I answered I did, as if speaking to the strands of light through the river birch trees twenty yards behind her left ear. She forced me, by my chin, to her eyes.

"I mean it, now. You've seen many more girls than I have. How do I compare?"

Finally reclaiming enough of my nervous system to utter a sound, I said, "Bein' right honest with you, I'd reckon there's not a gal any twenty boys could stitch together in their best dreams, would quite compare to you."

It was a wadded-up compliment fit only for the worst embarrassment, I thought. Worthy of fixing a stare to the sand, cleaving to the hope that disgrace is almost never fatal.

"There is a sweetness in you, somewhere." She spoke from her knees with a pat to my chest. "One of these days that girl of yours will take her full drink of it, Mr. Frank Locke. One day you will let the best of it pour."

She lay back down beside me, and we lulled in the weakening heat a short while, until she showed me the remainder of a thought she had kept mostly clothed.

"You've been a solace to me, Frank. More than you can tell. I've been too many hours at that piano with an audience of the walls. Too long by myself."

She took my hand again. I shut my eyes, thinking my mouth should stay likewise, and gave her fingers a squeeze to assure the best part of me was still listening. She storied away.

"Here's something you don't know. I hadn't done a reckless thing in my life until just about a year before Daddy died. I got myself dressed up before dawn one morning, wrote a note that I'd be right back, took some money and eased the car out for Asheville. Just wanted a day out on my own, but I grew no closer than a gas stop just north of the city's edge. A grinning fellow there asked what white man I'd killed for such a fine piece of automobile. I guzzled some rage and asked if he'd ever eaten off the plates of somebody not his own color. He growled off a vow that he had not, and never would. So I warned him he never should. I cautioned him to look what it had done to me. Then I handed him far more money than I owed — just for the wicked hell of it. The look on his face said the fool actually believed I was a rich white woman poisoned dark by eating off the dishes of what he called, 'colored folks.' I drove straight back, crying about worrying my own folks to death, but still dying to go. Just dying to go to that town. I knew both of them would lecture me at least ten more times about a world not fit for me. But I still want a place in it, Frank. I want at least a little more of this world to know I am some portion of it. To take what I've been given here to it. If that makes me ungrateful, then so be it."

I reaffirmed my hand in her grip, taking note that her foot and lower leg rested now on mine.

"I reckon there's no harm or blame, wantin' things," I said, raising myself some against the log and watching where the little pool bent itself out of sight into the trees. "Can't much blame you. It'd be like holdin' somebody guilty for bein' alive."

Through the trees of the island, almost as if it rose off the river's heart, a mild breeze came — cooled, I thought, by some nearby rain.

"Frank, do you think your Mary Lizbeth would hold a malice if you danced with me?"

The question took away any breath that might carry an answer.

"Just once, right here? We can with no betrayal, don't you think? I'll make any amends by having you tell me things about her. You and her. Will that be all right?"

I stood and invited her without a word. Sophia tightened the shirt around her waist, where she soon placed my hand, and we swayed around the river-sand floor. Her face came across my shoulder as she began to hum — a feathery music, unfamiliar. We held each other in it until her mouth brushed my cheek. A trace of her scented the air and stayed as she moved away for her still-damp pants, then a cover of trees for pulling them on.

"You've surely had some fine people in your life, Frank Locke. I don't know who they are, or were, but they're helping you live up to something. Mother always warns about living down to the worst of this world. But there's no worry about you. You are a gentleman. Don't you ever forget that."

I gathered the blanket and rods, feeling obliged to receive my part of the swap for that dance: To speak of Mary Lizbeth out loud.

"Mary L. and me, we never did much fishin'. Mostly just walkin'. She's fairly in love with findin' her way through a thicket."

We fished and talked a little more, and I finally made a cast that pulled another fat sunfish from the dark green pool. On the walk back to the house, the sun reclining behind us through the trunks, Sophia asked what made me care so for Mary L. I groped for words to fit how such a girl can lift a boy with one piece of her hair straying home on his coat. I spoke of the dullest chores done with joy in a talk with her, or with the help of her hands as we tended her goats. Of just being close to her as we cut wood, killed and dressed hens, canned beans and hunted for patches of creasy greens together. Work with her never felt like strain or boredom to me. The nearness of her always distilled to a remedy beyond words.

The talk had moved to Mary L. and me walking the hills to find a bit of Cherokee medicine Granny had taught me. Toward the middle of this, I realized I was walking and talking almost to myself. Sophia had stepped out far ahead on the trail. It became my first acquaintance with the effect of one girl's heart feeling wounded by hearing too much about another, especially from a boy. I realized her heart was no different from my own.

By the time I caught up we descended through the upper clearing, out into the high view of the house. Her talkative way came fully back later in the kitchen through a supper made of pork biscuits, late corn rescued from the weeds of that garden, and some Sarah Rose mulberry pie. We studied some *Jane Eyre* — near Rochester's attempted bigamy with Jane and the insanity of the attic — and the time between us was lively. As she prepared her mother a tray, a near-elation had taken its place in Sophia. We later talked expectantly into the night of how the world ought to be, then Sophia turned some ragtime out of the piano — songs she'd heard only a few times through the radio. When she bid me goodnight, she told me again I was a gentleman, and she thanked me. I praised her, seizing the moment to bow my thanks in return. She said her mother claimed divine renewal had come their way. A mortal sign of a redemption, for which the lady — who had lost a son to the world — had so long fasted and prayed. At the back door another kiss came to my face. I pledged to help Mrs. Proctor down into the dining room for the dinner I silently feared the next night, then set off into the dark to my cabin bed. The faces and voices and the other pieces of life behind me took their usual place in it with me. Yet grief and I had begun to live in some silent peace. Sophia and her mother had helped clear my mind's way to a landscape not so fitful with old qualms and new worries. Thoughts of my mother and — on some mildly deepening levels — my father, became a pulse that helped lay me into some true rest. The comfort of knowing their lives would not become mine. I believed that made them glad.

Something in the darkest hours of the morning stirred me to sit up with some springwater and the quiet for a quarter hour or so, and that's when I saw her again. In the few weeks I had spent on the Proctor farm, I had noticed a dark figure slipping around the back — leading Charlotte, saddled in full tack kit, around the house. I would have thought it the sight of a horse thief the first time had the moon not revealed Sophia's long womanhood, easing by with a sizeable box tucked under her arm. It was the third sighting since I had been there. On that morning I waited up for her, sipping some cold coffee, staying tucked deep out of sight in a chair on the cabin porch. She rode the horse back close to two hours later, swinging the box, now unloaded, toward the barn. By the time she slipped through the back door of the great house, it was almost dawn. I returned to bed full of wonder, resolving to let her reveal the meaning of this to me in her own time.

The sun was three hours up and had already seen me to some feeding, muck, and hammer work around that horse barn, lost in some wonder of what I had witnessed. The day shone with the texture of late summer — of a season aged and comfortably worn — settling warm and cloudless light over work to be done. I had just set a saw to some new fence slats Lew had brought in days before, when the first of the screaming tore up the hill. It blew through every crevice of the barn and soared into the rafters. Sophia — calling down God's mercy and yelling my name for help. A spewing cry, of the kind that speaks of streaming blood.

I rounded the corner to find her sprinting across the backyard in a terror that scalded my ears from forty yards. As I bounded down toward her, the throes of it were bending her at the waist.

"Frank, get help. Get her some help. Oh Lord God, get help. A doctor. Find Lew. God, oh sweet God, she's gone, I know it."

"What's the matter? What's happened?"

"I don't know, Frank. Just go. Go now. Take the car, fast as you can make it."

She ran in near-convulsion back into the house. I gave a glance at Mrs. Proctor's open bedroom window. I remember the drapes drifting inward, silent.

That car will not crank. Too long idle under its cover. It most surely won't crank. Those became my thoughts, panting fast up the hill to the other barn that held the Cadillac — all the while counting the cost in time of saddling and bridling a horse. I was wrong. The car rattled to life as if it had heard Sophia itself.

A slam of its bumper against the swing of a double door is the only sound I remember hearing between that barn and where the road stretches along the river before descending into town. I pushed it into a skid a time or two in curves along the river road, my mind running far out ahead of it into the possibilities of what had occurred and what I might do about it. The long black hood soon nosed onto the main street, with me in a sweat. At least one woman scampered out of our way as I steered for Doc Waters' place. I ground to a stop and made for his door. Locked. Stillness. In a fit of profanities I set the car into a squalling U-turn toward Mackey's. By the time I pulled up he was out, wide-eyed in front of a crowd, all struck slack-jaw by the sight and noise. The car, as I had set it into a rage, must have sounded like a raising of Gomorrah.

"Sweet God, boy, what the devil?"

Sophia's influence, already beginning to cleave to my tongue, fell away in the dire time. I couldn't help but sound fully like my old self.

"Gotta get help up the Proctors' way. Somethin's bad wrong. It's Mrs. Proctor, dying I think, and Doc ain't nowheres down yonder. I was told to get Rev. Lew but don't know where to fetch him."

Mackey was soon in the car with me, barking stop and start orders down the street, and running into every place he thought the doctor might be. When the café, the depot stand, and two fairly random-feeling houses yielded no sight, he flew into a rare fit of railing.

"Infernal bald-headed sawbone, there's no tellin' where he is. Whole town could catch the hydrophobee before we find him. Get me back to the store and leave her idlin'. I won't be but a minute."

He threw open the door and was out before the car fully stopped, flying around the hood, yelling for people to stand aside and calling a name I knew. Valeria Cochran soon emerged, so fast her red hair and blue dress looked like risen sails. Mackey dragged her by the arm and she cried for him to slow down unless he wanted her yanked from her shoes. She was a youngish widow of a railroad man, and was known to midwife and care for children amid her job as a spinner in the cotton mill.

In that time of our mysterious need, Valeria became the closest thing to medical care at hand. Mackey fell with her onto the front seat and said, "Mash your foot plumb to the gearbox." The store and town soon behind us, the car came to a nearly wide-open roar.

We seemed to outrun any complaints Valeria may have had about her kidnapping. She sat stunned, likely by fear of imminent death by a high-speed crash into the river. By the time I fishtailed the Cadillac onto the Proctor driveway, she had gathered enough of herself to school us in what she did not know about first aid. She told us her own mother was sickly, and ornery to go with it, and would throw fits for a month if she didn't get a lumbago rub at lunchtime. Mackey patted her leg and said we'd let God and the needs of the day make her into what she needed to be.

The car slid practically onto the steps, and Mackey bounded out.

"I'll assume the trouble's in the house, upstairs, son."

"Upstairs and right — at least I reckoned so when I left."

Before I could round the first fender, Valeria was staggering behind the old man where he dragged her onto the porch toward the door.

"There better be a baby that needs some birthin' here. Or I'll matter as much as Fannie peein' in the ocean."

Mackey slammed through the door as if he owned the place. Valeria paused, clearly in some awe, vowing to take off her shoes before stepping into such a house. But she found herself yanked in. Their noise trailed away up the staircase bend.

I had taken the porch steps two at a time, but the sound struck me even before I made the top. Of the kind that will seep from a young child, weakened by a burst of sorrowing. By the time I reached the door, I could hear Sophia from upstairs. As I recall it now, it was purely the sound of a heart throwing itself softly against unbelief.

"Frank, son, we'll need some help here." Mackey soon came down the stairs wiping his forehead and eyes with the apron. I had been pacing at the bottom, afraid to follow any further, feeling it not quite yet my place. From above, out of sight, Sophia wept, and it showered through the quiet of the house.

"She's gone, son. Been gone, and in one terrible mess."

Mackey looked off into the parlor, seeming ages beyond it for a moment. His face flushed to the red a man can turn in the work of stifling how he feels.

"Believe she's choked on her own sickness. Can't say for certain, but it surely seems so."

His confirmation of what I suspected jarred us both into a moment's stillness.

"What do you reckon I oughtta do?" My question tried not to intrude on the place his thoughts had gone, even as he stood three feet away on the steps. He answered from a still wandered-off mind.

"You stay right here and keep the door for now. Valeree's up makin' the best she can out of it. She can't get the poor girl to let go. Terrible thing to look on, Frankie. Never seen quite so bad a thing. Poor woman. Poor torn down thing."

He finally turned and moved down to me, near enough to whisper as if the wallpaper had ears. A hint of the death room came off him. That lasting indignity of vomit so stout it catches in fabrics and stains through to the mind. The odor can rise through me to this day.

"Son, I suspect you've been up here long enough to tell. It looks like that woman went to her corpse just about starved. Never looked on such. You have any notion what ailed her?"

I glanced off through the same parlor windows into the trees from which Mackey's mind had just returned.

"Ain't never seen or heard tell of half what I've seen around here, Mr. Mack. Reckon some of it won't ever be enough of my business to figure out. Both women's been powerful kind to me, though. Powerful kind. I reckon that's all the sense it's supposed to make to me right now."

Mackey seemed to feel the angst swelling in my throat. He sensed it enough to brace a hand to the back of my neck.

"It'll all be fine, son. We'll see to it. I suppose I'll need to get a loan of that car now. Don't suppose anybody'll mind. You stay right here and wait. She'll have her hands occupied, but if Valeree's tongue raises dust, don't give it a thought. Tell her I'll be right back. She's not nearly the mad heifer she seems, and thank the Lord A'mighty we had her handy. You're a good boy, Frankie. You've done some mighty fine good today. Mighty fine. Your mama'd be awful proud. Awful proud."

With that Mackey stepped out the door and off the porch, swiping a backhand at his face. The Cadillac soon disappeared down the drive. A brief thought to go inspect the scene upstairs dissolved in a fear of imagining how it might look. A near-calm had replaced Sophia's crying. It seemed to speak of a peace not meant for me to disturb so I paced and waited, pondering the tick of the clocks and the plates and silver not to be set for that night's dinner that had so excited the gracious women of the house. Not more than twenty minutes passed before I heard the familiarity of Lew's Packard, slow in its approach — telling me he didn't know of any trouble. I braced to bear the news of Julia Proctor's death.

My meeting him on the porch said almost all that needed saying. His asking what's the matter led to, "You ought get upstairs right quick," which filled his little eyes with fright. He bounded up with a, "Holy Christ, help us," and I stayed, minding the door.

The next four hours saw the place covered in that seamless way of life only a death can bring. Lew came gravely down the stairs and went without a word for Sarah Rose, who returned with him, carrying two boxes of food and a mouthful of orders — effusing, "Sweet, sweet holy Jesus, it was bound to happen," on her way up to the room. Mackey had already come with the sheriff, who soon left and returned with the hearse, evoking more of my expectation Mary Lizbeth would follow. Her part-time vocation of dressing Mr. Bookman's female dead for pay would draw her to the scene. I was sure of it there at my post beside the door, where I had been satisfactorily ignored. And I soon learned I was wrong. Lew came out and held court with the sheriff and the men of the funeral wagon, which left and came back two hours later with a glossed maple casket I was summoned to help tote. We carried it in thumps and staggers, as reverently as we could manage, up the stairs. Reaching Mrs. Proctor's room brought a scent akin to turpentine and, on the heavy bed, what appeared hardly a gesture of where a woman had been — the body gowned in a dress of light rose, her limbs so small they scarcely raised an imprint. Nestled close by, Byron lay panting as a quiet sentry, throwing a wag or two as we entered. He refused to shoo, so I eased him off to give the casket room on the bed. Sarah Rose and Valeria had cleaned and arrayed Mrs. Proctor into a repose of the dignity I had felt streaming off her every word. Sarah ordered the men out, saying the ladies would handle her into the box as if she were the "Mother of our Lord," and before turning away, I managed a good look at a face that told me there had been no bickering with death in that room. Mrs. Proctor wore a satisfied, impish little smile, as if to tell a secret on dying — that it held no menace, and that we all should know so. She was a teacher to the very last of herself.

I waited in the hall to take my place carrying the box — which felt little heavier — down to a pedestal that had been placed by the great windows of the parlor. Sarah Rose ushered us all back so she and Valeria could set the lady's hair and face into a final arrangement they saw fit. The men took themselves to the kitchen and the boxed food. I went for Sophia, where Lew had removed her from any funereal chore. Byron saw me out of the parlor from his new post on the floor at the head of the casket.

Upstairs her door stood locked, with some faint talk coming through. I took it as a sign to carry myself back down, away from any prying, to venture a try at quieting my mind. On the porch I shifted a wicker chair to the dining side of the home, away from the casketed window, to sit with a heavy Holy Bible from the parlor's library. It seemed a proper reverence, reading a phrase or two from the Psalms, plus I thought it made me appear less an oddity in the way.

That post saw me through more of the day and the business of the house. I watched Lew see the sheriff out to the car, where they talked a long while. It turned nearly to a squabble from where I sat — the old preacher taut, shaking his head and pointing toward town with the fortitude of a man spinning off unimpeachable orders. I had never seen Sheriff Long defer so to anyone. He left all straight-backed and full of nods and duty, as if Lew's commands added up to the very tablets of Sinai. Climbing back to the house he turned his attentions to me, pausing where I now stood on the top step.

"How you doin', son? Sophie's askin' about you. Tell me how you are."

"Reckon I'm fine for a boy made sad. What am I to do, Rev.? Reckon I'm not much good up here now and ought go on home, finally."

"Well, that's some fresh steamin' cow pie if I ever heard it," he said, gripping me around the shoulders. I could feel him honing his talk into a language he thought I could grasp, trying to cheer both of us at once. "Boy, we're bound to make the good Lord's best outta this. There's no runnin' from what's to be done here. There's a hurt girl who needs her heart tended, and that's part your job, and it won't be quit. Now, I was just comin' to tell you about tomorrow. It's a day the whole town and three damned counties will talk about after we're *both* hoary in heaven. So you best set your feet under Sarah's table and stout yourself up. She and I'll take spells sittin' up with the body, and we have that gal, Vanillia, or whatever the hell her name is, to help. I offered her five dollars for her time. She said she would tend to the dead in a mansion like this for free. Do it 'til the moon fell. But her little fingers sure swarmed my five simoleons like flies on a pie scrap. Took that money and sent the sheriff to tell her mama not to fret. That she'd come home soon enough with the saddest tale ever told. Said it would knot the neighbors' drawers. Very words she said. God bless her, that girl's mama hatched herself a hellion. Nice one, though. Right nice hind end."

He winked, and the touch of levity gave my feelings an upward bend. Then came that kind of one-arm embrace a man uses to remind a boy not to coat his mind in the worst of what might come.

"Now, I've got myself a sermon to write. Got to get it to full bloom on a page and in my head. Don't you fret. This is your time, son. Don't fail it. Be what you're put here for. Your time's nearly come, and mine's nearly been here and gone. You'll see. You'll see aplenty tomorrow, just fine. God'll help us. Good Lord will sail our fannies through. We'll be mighty fine."

With that he turned into the house and left me flummoxed. I could more easily divine meaning from the stars than some of Lew's mind. But he had a way of soothing me enough this time to bring on a scant hunger and a need to make myself of some use. I slipped around the house through the back door to avoid any contact with the casket or its sentry and found Sarah Rose in the kitchen, in hushed soliloquy about Sophia, almost praying it out over a plate of white beans and cornbread.

"Lord, put a hand to that poor sweet girl's back. Jesus Lord and Ruth of the Holy Bible, what *will* she do now? Frank? Oh, thank the Lord, come on in here and get you some nourishment with me. I've the whole long night ahead to hear my own self talk."

She drawled on with some wishes she'd brought the dog — her "sweet, stinky little Blossom." I stepped into the bathroom to wash, then ate with her at the big kitchen table, taking a sip or two off a jar of her home-brewed fruit wine she claimed would see us both through "this pure awful time."

"Lewis has some big doin's in store for tomorrow, young man, and we'll need your hands to see our Sophie through. Fine, busy old preacher man of mine, won't show his own heartbreak 'til I nearly whip it out of him."

When I asked for particulars about my place in all of it, she chattered on without answering, as if I weren't there, rattling the kitchen full of out-loud thoughts and chores.

"Lord, sweet Jesus, Mary and Lazarus, I hope the man knows what he's up to, raisin' this into a fuss fit for buryin' the whole state of North Carolina. But it's high time for the preachin' I've nagged him to do for nigh twenty years. Dear old preacher man. Lord, he won't listen to a thing I say. Not one thing. I've warned him. I've said if the Lord turns out to be a woman, he's in for one mother of a hell-fire broom-whippin' before Saint Peter sees him to glory. Oh, now, listen to me, Frank. Sweet Lord, listen to this old woman make light of a terrible time. Lord, my tongue — God bless it. File the barbs off my wire."

She talked and scraped a pot and scattered more such prayer around as if the Omnipotent stood there with a dishtowel, then wept against the reality of a lost friend and a girl's lost mother. I helped as I could, then excused myself out back to the humid first light of dusk to tend the horses and close up the barns, busying my hands to quash the feel of what had been that day.

In what I deemed a miracle, the horses had stayed in the fence, whose gate I had left blasted wide open on my run to town. By the time I finished, the smell of the wind carried warning of a rainstorm blowing near — the gusts already high in the trees and sounding through the loft where I stowed some new hay. I remember thinking Sophia would store no less grief for a mother whose blood she didn't share.

It was close to dark with clouds when I came back to the kitchen. Lew stood in rolled sleeves at the stove, boiling coffee. Valeria walked around the hall with a plate in her hand, picking at some supper and gazing about the house with the wonder of a blind woman whose eyes had just wakened to a palace of Solomon. The room held an air of sobriety Lew usually tried not to allow.

"Frankie, Sophie's askin' for you. Poor thing's sick of Sarah and me. She needs a friend besides some old Methuselah. She's in her room, where she's been. Go on up now." Lew said it without so much as a glance at me. "Yessir, I will," was my reply, sweeping at the wrinkles of my clothes and restoring my shirttail on the way. The thought of passing the parlor chafed a nerve. As I did, I drew notice.

Sarah Rose had lit at least three candelabras, whose light fluttered and shared the room with the open-window breeze. Turning at the stairs I found her reclined and knitting on a sofa pulled up next to the open casket. She hummed out the softest patter of "What Wondrous Love is This?" — singing it to herself and Byron, who lay not quite asleep at the sofa's other end, his head propped on an arm, in sight of Mrs. Proctor's cold face. Sarah glanced up and gave me a smiling nod, without missing a note or word of the music. The look that came off her seemed to well up the whole house in calm. Something about the manner of that woman held a little girl's joy no bleakness would put down. I smiled in return and took the stairs with the will of a man who'd been born in that place.

"I wondered if you'd left me. Come in," answered my tap and whisper of her name at the door. She sounded weak as the lamplight inside. I stepped in to find the corner room utterly open to the coming rain, a billow of drapes rising under the wind's cooling entry through the long windows. In my time there I had never entered Sophia's room, and I found it as expected: Furnishings weighty as the rest of the home, the bed a high throne with steps, a dressing table and body-length mirror, a desk, a wall of shelves, and books on tables, whose delicate coverings pooled on the plush floor. I moved toward where she lay on the bed with her back to me, long and unmoving, fully dressed in the usual cotton pants and a white shirt, her feet bare atop the spread.

I had nearly reached her when the feel of eyes came. That sense of being taken in by the gaze of someone. From the bedside they came into view. Propped against the wall was the enormous portrait I instantly recognized from Sophia's story of the grand Rhode Island world. Mrs. Proctor's mother, Victoria, in what the dim room showed as a blue gown. She stood as a woman in her twenties, in a willowy little bend at the waist, the painting framed in dense, deep carving — the whole of it much too large for even the Proctor house. The artist had long ago found and kept a gentle sass in her face and safeguarded the life in her eyes.

"I'm scared, Frank. Stay with me, please, just awhile." Sophia spoke against a cloth she cradled, never turning to me. I climbed gently beside her, unsure what to do until her arm raised an invitation.

"Please don't leave me to myself."

My forearm slipped around her waist, though I declined to mold myself fully to her form atop the high bed. The lady of the portrait chaperoned our intimate place, and I soon could see Sophia held a dress to her face, letting it flow between her knees. I presumed it a favorite of her mother's better days and still fresh with the lady's essence. The sight pulled me down into the thought of my own mother's clothes, untouched in folds of our house, still abandoned.

"Just be here with me. I need a miracle, Frank. I just need you to become it."

Sophia broke, and wept into the dress for awhile. I held her and stroked the gloss of her hair, trying to ease her only with whispered promises that I would stay, until she fell off to a slumber. I don't know when the oil lamp went out, but I woke in the dark to rain, the shower of it more a draping than a fall against the roof, as if the clouds knew the place was one of mourning and needful of rest. I got up to close all the windows, expecting she may rouse to talk. But she lay still.

I reclaimed a place on the bed beside her, stretched and let the rain lull away fear of Ma's suffering and any thought she may have sent her soul to hell by the taking of her own life. There came a thought of Frank, a pity, wondering where the remains of him lay in the storm. For all the sadness, though, the room held a solace about itself. The peace of it brought on a dreamless sleep that lasted beyond dawn. I woke from it alone, but for the gaze of the painting. The room lay utterly still, full of early light and the call of some morning birds. Taking Sophia's place, a change of clothes spread beside me on the bed, topped with a note written in her sweeping hand.

A gift I sent Lew to pick out for you last week, not expecting what has come upon this house. Please put the suit on, never minding where I have gone. I must take myself away from here for a bit of time. Tell Lew not to worry. I know his plans and will not let him down.

Sophia

The suit lay as if a valet placed it on the bed — the color a marriage of gray and blue, the shade of a low sky just before lightning comes. With it, a white shirt of dense cotton, and on the foot of the bed a pair of leather shoes, thick with newness and hand labor. I complied at the long mirror, shedding the work clothes of yesterday and pulling on the pants, which felt skinny as a water glass. Then the coolness of the shirt and the long double-breasted coat, drawn to taper close about the waist. With the outfit there was a folded narrow tie the color of coal dust with white flecks. I stood ignorant of tying it so I stuffed it into a pants pocket, where I found the other note. It, too, in Sophia's hand, clearly written days earlier and forgotten.

Mother and I want to thank you for being a gentleman, a discreet one at that, and perhaps these will serve as a beginning of our gratitude. Lew selected them at our behest, and we look forward to toasting their meaning. Wear these clothes in goodness of health, wellness in learning, and the best of times to come. Cheers, with gratitude from your new friends —

Julia and Sophia of the Proctor House

I folded the note back into the pocket, pressing it deep, as though that would ease down the knot that rose and swelled in my throat. A clock on the night table read a quarter to seven, so I eased out of the room with the jacket across my arm and carrying the shoes, as if fearing to wake the house itself. Before closing the door I gave a glance to the portrait. The eyes looked back with approval enough to send me out into the hall determined to make use of my mind as much as my hands across the hard day to come. The sight of Mrs. Proctor's closed door across the way became that day's first blow.

The home smelled of bacon and strong coffee but kept silent. I creaked a time or two down the stairs to peer into the parlor. Lew sat in the same dark pants and white shirt of the day before, dozing on the couch with a Bible and some notes on his lap. Byron kept vigil at the casket head, where some morning sun came through, a part of it touching the streaked gray of Mrs. Proctor's hair on the pillow. The dog stirred a bit at the sight of me, which woke Lew.

"Lord, good morning, boy. Was I off asleep?" He wiped at his eyes and found his glasses.

"Reckon so, Rev. Where's everybody else?" I did not enter the room.

"Sarah Rose took the car and lit out for a home bath and an errand or two. She took that gal, Wisteria or Vaneria or whatever her name is, with her. I suppose we have that woman-child hostage. But I don't want her scatterin' around blabbin' down into town and spoilin' things."

"Sophia left in the night I reckon. Left me these clothes and a note that said she'd be back."

"Oh, I saw her slip down and out the back before daylight. She thought I was asleep." Lew spoke in a yawn, rising and straightening himself. "Mighty fine suit, don't you think?" He eyed me up and down. "Sophie sent me for it, though for a better day than this. Told me to guess on the pants since I'm a man. They're a bit long but they'll do. You've got room, at least, to relieve yourself. Where's your socks?"

It hadn't completely worried me that my feet were bare. He said we'd borrow some. I thanked him and he vowed to help me get fully dressed, tie up the tie and all, saying, "If it's one thing a preacher knows it's how to wring his own neck." With hardly a wane of the smile that crossed him, he then stepped to the casket and let his hand gently tap Mrs. Proctor's before brushing the backs of his fingers to her cheek. "Poor sweet old girl, why'd you do this to your fine self, I will never know. Lord, help us. Help that Sophie to see this fine woman off."

His eyes saddened some, turning to the floor.

"I suppose I know where Sophie's gone, son. We'll leave her be. She'll be back in fine time. You know much about dogs? 'Cause now the dog won't eat. Poor old thing won't leave this room. He's already wet the floor for me to clean up. Just lays at this box. Thought maybe you might husband him into takin' some breakfast after we take it ourselves."

Lew gave the dog a few pats and led me to the kitchen, where we fired the stove, scrambled eggs and ate Sarah Rose's biscuits during some small talk. He asked how I was doing in the losses of my own, and I told him, "Fine enough." He soon launched into telling me exactly how they had buried Mr. Proctor in secret, paying extra to a funeral director in Asheville to make certain the work stayed private. They hired the casket bearers off a jail highway crew down in Polk County, where any interest taken in the house or deceased would stay in the distance and locked away awhile. He said today's ceremony would be about as different from that one as dark is from daylight.

He started to tell me more about the plan for the day when a truck rattled to a stop out front. "Gravediggers, must be," Lew said. "Rained like hell last night, so the boys will work some wet clay. Let me go see about 'em. Make sure they don't dig the whole confounded place up."

I had assumed Mrs. Proctor would lie next to her husband on the property but had given little thought to the grave work to be done. Lew stepped into the hall and turned back to me.

"We'll leave here no later than a quarter to four, son. You just make sure you're in here and ready in time. Ready to do what I've asked of you. It'll be hard takin' that lady outta here, you understand. Mighty hard. You'll be God's man today. You'll rise to it. I'll be back in awhile."

With that he disappeared, leaving the house — so far as I could tell — to a dead lady, a grieving dog and me.

I sat wondering why I had put on the suit so early, and without a bath. So I slipped out back to the cabin to change into the set of Mr. Proctor's oversize work clothes I had used. Sophia's absence tempted me to search, but I agreed with Lew she would get herself found when she wanted. So I set myself to some useful passing of the day until whatever the funeral would hold. First, to the Cushman "Bob-a-Lawn" grass mower Mr. Proctor had left. I had enjoyed getting used to the mechanics of it, and deemed it fitting to see his wife out of this world with a clean-shaven lawn. Cushman called the engine a "Husky," and it sounded of the name as I pushed and sweated through its velvet noise and the damp grass smell for three hours. My last water break reminded me of another job at hand. I pulled the Cadillac up to a well pump near the barns and gave it the best "Octagon" soap scrub I could, restoring the gleam to its black. Lew's Packard and then the sheriff's car returned to the house during the work, but no one appeared in the backyard. I watered the horses as if they belonged to me, retrieved the suit from the cabin and slipped, filthy and stinking, back into the house to find it full of voices to the front. I was almost finished with a cold bath when Sophia's voice appeared at the other side of the bathroom door I had made sure to lock.

"Who's in there?" she asked with some life restored.

"I'll be out in a minute."

"Well, it better become a quick one. I need a bath as much as you."

"Where'd you run off to?"

"Never mind. I've been where I wanted. Where's the car?"

"Up at the barn where I washed it. You're not drivin' off somewheres are you? Lew's calm, but he'll have me in a box if I lose you again."

I instantly regretted the latter choice of wording, even as she sounded unaffected by it.

"I just need to get into the car."

"It's all open. Send Lew back here before you go, would you? How you feelin' now?"

Nothing. The sound of her feet disappeared behind the door, and Lew soon came banging it and railing about time getting away from us. I stood nearly dressed, opened the door and handed him the tie, which he knotted around his own neck, then looped it out to cinch around mine. He handed me his comb and some black socks of unknown origin and said if I didn't want to field a dozen questions about where I had been for more than a month, I should wait upstairs in a bedroom until he called me. As I passed the parlor, he joined Sarah Rose and a crowd of Sunday-suited men fanning themselves on the porch. Byron lay glum beside the casket, appearing not to have moved. Some eggs I had tried to feed him had gone untouched.

I chose Sophia's room to wait, instantly checking the window just in time to see her rounding the barn corner in her khaki day clothes, a large trunk dragging weighty from both hands. She went out of sight. For the next half-hour I studied the room — taking in its mix of books and leather fishing rod casings and some girlish frill — trying to look beyond the rest of the day. A glance or two more out that window revealed the yard in dog day stillness. I remember hoping Sophia had come out of that steaming barn by then. There was no stopping to wonder what business she had there in such a time. The portrait and I were getting better acquainted when Sarah Rose stepped in without a knock.

"Better wait downstairs, Frankie. She's about to get out of that bathtub. I need to get her up in here and dressed."

On the main level, I decided finally to put on the shoes and wait, staying, as best I could, out of sight. I helped myself to some cold chicken and a dining room chair, cloistering to a corner. Their voices had climbed the stairs out of my sight, and Sophia and Sarah Rose came down sooner than I expected. Sarah's call to Lew out the door might as well have sounded a bell. The first of the ceremony's time had come.

Stepping into the foyer revealed to me Sophia, standing on the bottom stair, a straight and living tower of black. A high-neck dress of bloused pleats draped long to black stockings. In one hand she held a wide black hat rimmed with matching veils, appearing so thick they would nearly blind her. The other hand held a pair of lace gloves, white as high summer clouds. The hair kept its usual sleek style, pulled back from her face. We stood staring, as though one hardly recognized the other, until Lew came in, asking the minions milling about the porch and front door to give the girl some space with her mother. From outside I heard Valeria grouse that she wanted another look at the burial dress she and "Mrs. Rev." had driven forty-five minutes, one-way, in the heat to buy.

"I'm fine, Uncle Lew. Just a few minutes, and I'm ready to go."

Sophia stopped me as I turned toward the porch.

"Frank, I'd like you to stay. I need you to stay with me."

Sarah Rose nudged her husband out, urging him to let the children be, and before leaving he handed me a clean handkerchief. Sophia put the gloves into the hat and took me by the hand to the casket, where I stood hearing her soft talk of dreading this time. She told me of long denying a feeling it had been closing near, and of how there's no getting fully ready for such an ending. Stepping to the room's library alcove, she took a volume containing Alfred Lord Tennyson and turned the book knowingly to "Crossing the Bar." At the casket she read it aloud, and the clean force of her voice broke toward the end. As she bent to kiss Mrs. Proctor's forehead, I counted the fall of three tears against the pallor. Had I not known better, I would have sworn the faint smile the lady wore to her grave warmed at the landing of them. Sophia stooped, letting her cheek caress the cool vacancy of what had been. Touching a final time the face of the mother who had brought her into some of the best of this world.

"Rest well. I'll not squander what we made together. The vulgar will run at the sight of what we made. You watch from where you are. I will make you and Daddy so proud. So very proud you gave this girl a name."

She broke fully down for a short time. I held her and wiped her face with Lew's handkerchief until she composed enough to meet my eyes and softly mouth the words, "Thank you. Thank you, Frank."

She turned away for a moment, then knelt to Byron, who gave some wag at the proximity of her. I watched her ease a motherly care into him, then she rose, straightening into a resolve fit for battle, and calling to Lew through the open window.

"I'm ready now. It's past time."

When he came in she gave a final order, on the verge of more tears that never quite flowed over.

"I want to stay at the piano as you take her. I will not watch her go into that death wagon. If she were here she would chide me for need of practice. And so, I will practice."

Lew agreed, and brought in Mr. Bookman and his son to close the lid. Though not before Sarah Rose came bending over, holding the corpse by the face for a goodbye, overflowing with assurance all would be right.

The casket bearers consisted of some people deemed the region's finest, which made them men I hardly knew. One I recognized as a circuit judge, another a Methodist minister, the sheriff, and two reticent strangers — all in suits, all recruited to sweat through calm orders, most of which breezed off Lew. He nudged me to the handles and we lifted the box as Sophia drifted to her place at the keys.

"It's the first piece she taught me on this piano. Uncle Lew, she said she played this when you baptized her baby girl in this room. The girl's going to see her off with it."

Lew nodded and raised his hand to bow the room in prayer. I believe I have remembered it well here.

"Lord, lover of lepers, heal the hearts of this house. See us through the hurt of this day. Show our broken hearts to the shores of Your spirit and a soft place to rest. Make us nearer to what our dear Julia has become: One of the family of heaven, at the banquet table of Your graces, fitted for the garments of love. And, while You're at it, help this old preacher call down some of that heaven and hold it forth. Keep me from haulin' off and raisin' hell today, Lord. I know You are close by. You know us all and You love us anyhow. In the name of our Christ, we ask You to bless us as we go. Amen."

We had just moved the casket to follow Lew out when Sophia set the room aglow. I expected some of her high piano finery, but she played "Jesus Loves Me." The simple confidence of it reached through the windows all the way to our loading the box into the coach. Lew sent me back to bring her, stating I would drive Sophia and Sarah Rose in the Cadillac, trailing the Packard and the hearse. Sophia was out and latching the door by the time I reached the porch. Her hand came to mine without a word, and the air around her seemed to silken in the motion of the dress. We had just stepped into the sun of the top step when the first of the tittering came.

Older boys, giggling with the verve of little girls, swarmed at the edge of the woods, taking cover. They were the gravediggers, all in their early twenties and caked to their uppermost crevices in red clay. They looked like four sag-hatted human freckles, dotting the verge of the Proctor lawn. I supposed they had come down to gawk at the house and cars — each up to his cranium in the foolishness of grown men still mired in the ground of unshaken adolescence. In their retreat to the trees, two of them let fly scraps of conversation, loud enough to reach the porch.

"That's the same big colored gal we seen up yonder in them woods. Tell me you wouldn't ride up on that, too, if she weren't black as the ace of spades...." That and more trailed off into some snickers as they ran.

Sophia hardened. Pulled back against me. She could not escape hearing it. I stiffened to soar across the yard after them. The noise of their thick-wits smacked me harder than any strop. But down at the car, it seemed to hit Sarah Rose with the force of a thrown rock. She had just installed Valeria and the pallbearers into the Packard. Before I could move she slammed the big door in red-hot pursuit.

"Hey! Stop your clod-buster fannies right where you are. All of you. Right now. Or I'll put a mule bit in your yappers right here. Sharp-mouthed little sumbitches. You'll find some respect to put in that mouth or I'll shut it my unholy self."

Lew sprang from the driver's door out after her.

"Sarah, Sarah leave it be...."

"Woods won't hide you from me. I'll leave a hickory-switch welt on every tongue in there before I'm done. Come down here slingin' sass all over God's creation. I will whoop on you 'til the first frost freezes sweat on my hiney. You hear me?"

She never looked back, uncoiling into a dress-swinging run, calling the gravediggers out of the shade. They obeyed, covered in droop — two removing their hats and bowing heads while she filled them full of hip-handed rebuke that bounced to the highest treetops. She next turned to Lew, who stood taking it in, hushing at her, close enough to stop her from drawing back a haymaker.

"I'm takin' this pack with us, and I won't be stopped. Such as this will not stay up here at this house while we're gone. They'll hear your preachin' instead. Maybe it'll reach through the mud *and* the stupid."

She turned back and shooed them around the house, ordering they get their truck from up near the open grave. The older Bookman barked from the hearse for them to hurry, wiping sweat and taking some of Sarah's chide. She blamed him for hiring such boys for a man's work. By the time the Ford flatbed, full of their newfound humility, groaned around the house, I had seen Sophia to the front seat of the Cadillac — having rumbled off a few of my own threats against them. I thought it might comfort her to hear I was acquainted with three of the boys — knew they possessed the pooled smarts of the bag of rocks I wished I had possessed when their mouths shot off. The levity had no apparent effect on the wound. Her face stayed fixed as iron, as did the gloved hand fastened to mine. When she let go for me to close the door, an imprint of the lace remained. Rounding the Caddy's long nose — flush with a pride the diggers had seen me in the suit with the car — I noticed Sarah

Rose hiking her dress and climbing in to drive the truckload of her prisoners. She cracked off a comment about serving as their kind warden, a fate each man might have traded his own mother to escape.

With that the doors closed and the hearse led — easing Mrs. Proctor down the shade-tunnel drive, toward the town that had not seen her in just about twenty years. Sophia sat, erect and quiet with the hat in her lap, and without call to look behind the car for who came with us. I knew he slipped out to the porch behind the casket. I had nearly tripped over him. His trot behind us now might have eluded me had I not glanced to check the rear view for Sarah and her leg-swinging freight. Just as we turned onto the highway, Byron, in full arthritic gallop, rounded the old flatbed Ford, aiming for the hearse. He was pure old dog — heavy, ancient, close to blind — but full of the will to join the entire procession all the way to town if it meant finding the now-dead woman who had become his life. When I stopped the Cadillac to retrieve him, I became fairly sure he would not have climbed whining into the back had Sophia not risen to her knees and called out to coax him. Sarah Rose had skidded the truck to a stop behind us and thrust out her head for a shout of, "Thank you, sweet Jesus," as I helped the old boy onto the car's backseat.

Mr. Bookman and Lew never paused to miss us. I had to push the Caddy hard to catch up, setting Sarah Rose and the boys in our dust, out of sight. Sophia kept to her remote self, apart from soothing the dog. We had reached the river before she spoke a word.

"Frank, you recalled my mother to life. I believe you gave me more time with her, and I thank you for that."

"She was a fine woman, your mother was," I said, watching the Packard and hearse lean and rock through the curves.

"You don't have to go back, you know." By now Sophia's gloved hand cradled the dog's panting head that rested between us atop the seat back.

"Which way you mean? I suppose I've shacked up on your hospitality so long now that I don't hardly know my frontside from my backside. Can't loaf off you forever, I reckon."

"I mean the mill. You don't have to go back to it. Or to any of what you came from. You don't have to go back. And you shouldn't go back."

I knew of nothing to say, so I said nothing. Sophia's tone — and sight of the casket through the swaying curtains of the hearse — held strong against any venture to argue. I followed on.

Nearly a mile before Lew's church the parked traffic began to appear, leaning off into ditches and weeds. Cars and farm trucks, mule wagons, even tractors — all powdery with grime — scattered along the roadsides to announce the crowd, soon in view. The blocked street in front of the courthouse swelled with what looked like acres of standing humanity — more people in one place than I had ever seen. The sheriff and two deputies had gone ahead to make us a way. The hearse and Packard slowed to walking pace, excusing their way through the parting flock of thin bones and wide stares, ogling children and men matching a child's wonder at who the funeral coach contained.

At the first brink of the closing crowd I had felt Sophia tighten on the seat. She let out a sigh, something akin to, "God, help us," then put on the hat and disappeared under its veils — becoming even more the dark mystery to the throng just outside the glass. Byron began to pace in the backseat, anxious and hot. Easing him became her diversion while I scanned faces, feeling some recognize me at the wheel. The rest fixed a glare to my passenger. Where that crowd belonged at such a time of day witnessed to the fact Lew had closed the mill for the event before us. I later learned he had gathered the crowd through Mackey and the sheriff — helped by the fast reach of every gadabout gossip around — putting out a word beyond the county line that an unforgettable history would get made this day in Marshal. It worked nearly too well. The overflow of that square held the size and feel of an imminent hanging. Granny had witnessed one as a girl and talked often of the eager human swarm it drew.

The procession crept to its end on the courthouse green, near the very center of a multitude that spilled onto the road and against the buildings beyond. A stream of ropes and pegs and lawmen tried to cordon them apart from us. Anyplace someone could catch a view stood occupied. Children, and a few women, sat on the shoulders of men. Sunday hats came off on sight of the hearse.

"I'll wait for Lew," Sophia said, fixing her sight on the men forming lines to bring out the casket. I got out to help but Lew and the hushed rumble of the crowd turned me back.

"You stay with the girl, son. I'll need you to help me see her up that way in a minute." He gestured to the courthouse steps, which wore the stage nailed up for every Fourth of July. The town's old Western Electric loudspeaker system stood waiting.

"Act a day over your last whippin'," soared from behind us. Sarah Rose had come in faster than I expected. She already had the gravediggers up, standing stiff in their dirt crust and blushing — all on high display across the truck bed. "This'll be a holy place, time we're finished. If I catch another saw-briar growin' outta any mouth on this truck, I'll give you the strappin' I stored up for the children I never had. Then I'll fetch your own mamas to do worse. You understand me?"

The human cargo nodded, "Yes, ma'ams," and faced the podium, humble as cows. She slapped the leg of one until he removed his hat, then gave each a pat of affection on his boot tops, in full stride toward us.

"Now I do this outta love for you boys. Don't make me sorry I haven't whipped a one of you yet. You'll stand here like you've seen the very Holy Ghost or I'll come back, turnin' on you. I am a God-lovin' woman but your vulgar mouths turn me hot. Any one of you makes an ass of himself, he'll think he's walkin' hell barefoot in summertime. You hear me?"

She came, almost running, to Sophia's other arm and whispered some inaudible comfort while the casket went by at Rev. Lew's lead. He held up his Bible, and it might as well have been the staff of Moses. The humanity parted to make us way. I suppose any boy such as myself — even braced as I was by the suit — would stand a little overly conscious of himself, centered in such a time and crowd, and I did so. But the feel of my invisibility soon came on. Before we could take our first steps fully into the crowd, I found the collective eye of the people swapping only between the casket and the dark anonymity on my arm. The dueling enigmas — of death, and a tall woman blackened in veils — gave me cover. Had the crowd been deer, I could have led each to slaughter by hand.

The yelping whine turned Sophia back toward the car. Without a word she pulled from between us, running back to let Byron free. He ambled down from the Cadillac's backseat and took his place with us, unmolested up the courthouse steps, deliberate as a judge behind the casket. The grieving sag of him finally filled Sarah Rose to her brim. She snuffled and wept aloud as we walked, and the feel of it went through the three of us. Out ahead, about the time Rev. Lew reached what amounted to the crowd's front row, the music began.

The song flew from shadows under the courthouse pediment. Lew later told me he had ordered they take hiding there, cuing on sight of the coffin. The choir of the Little Mount Zion Baptist Church came singing across the stage, in sways of glory, onto the steps. They formed a two-line a cappella of "When the Saints Go Marching In," raising the hymn out over the crowd, loud as the courthouse clock dong. Each voice welling up as fresh and strong as the faces were shades of deep brown. Mathison County white people, many of *them* hued nearly sorghum-dark by working in the sun, called Little Mount Zion the "colored church" — deeming the label as polite as holding a door for a lady. The tiny sanctuary held itself on a balding cliff of red clay and jack pines, six miles or so out west of the town. Pap used to say the scarp was so steep, it made him half-sure the mill's dock men who built the sanctuary "had to shotgun the nails into it from the road." The church had no piano, but the choir was known to draw some of the region's milk-skinned people out to take summer rides, slipping through woods and pausing to listen. Mount Zion's hymns and circuit preaching flew out the windows like blown feathers, bound to make a Holy Spirit bed for the hardest of hearts coming near. This late summer day on the courthouse square, with Mrs. Proctor's casket carried up between them, that same choir in full song hushed the crowd. Lew had the Mount Zion songsters dressed in not quite new cream and green robes, borrowed from the floury-faced choir of his own Presbyterian Church up the street.

Sophia had my handkerchief by the time we touched the first step. Climbing between the nearness of a few faces I recognized, it occurred to me the crowd mostly amounted to people looked at but not fully seen. Until I heard the yawp. A familiar bawl from behind. Something about "that little Locke boy all prissed up," and it ran heat through to my spine. A glance back down into the throng brought Leo's steer-size head into view, just as he took a shushing mouth slap from his mother. The very sound brought instant fear that I might find Mary L. somewhere close to him. Thankfully, no. The rest of the parted multitude stood still as trees in the sound of the choir. Through the swarm I had heard some other chatter of my name, most of it stoked full of surprise I had survived. None of them a voice I trolled with my eyes to find. I worried Mary L. — likely somewhere on that square — might note my intimacy with Sophia. Yet worry paled against the thought of my mother's final breath, drawn alone in the courthouse jail before us all.

At the top step of the stage Big Miss Ed knocked that out of me. A pounding slap to my shoulder, her smile leaning in with a, "There's my boy, and don't he shine up good." She led the choir, but missed hardly a lyric's worth of the hymn to comfort us. Sophia stopped at the brush and pat of the lady's stout hand to her cheek. A moment held still between them, a joining of minds, an unspoken, "All's going to be right." Ed's eyes filled with the longing to draw every agony of the day into her enormous self and carry it off for good. She became the only part of the crowd Sophia seemed to take in.

The wood of that makeshift stage answered our steps. The thud of it felt to me like a thunder, a reminder every eye had likely turned up for a look at us. I gathered nerve enough to look back at the crowd and caught sight of an upstaging: Leon Luther Spivey, sitting in the glow of getting noticed. Unaffected by any chill of death, paying no mind to the bearers placing the casket on a pedestal out in front of the podium, Leon and his overalls had climbed to dangle bare feet off the platform's center edge. He was a boy of nine or ten, known even to his father as "Little Double L." — since his little sister had outgrown him. I could see him mock some fellow scamps below who lacked his nerve, both legs swinging full of satisfaction with himself. Folks many rows back could see his jowls work a man-size mass of tobacco bigger than his mother's fist.

Feeling a duty to shoo him off, I urged Sophia on toward the half-moon of stout church chairs on the stage. As I drew near the boy, Lew rounded the heavy podium and beat me to him, firing off a kneeling sermon the first three rows were bound to hear over the music.

"Son, this is not quite your place, and I'm about sure that tobacco's bound for heaven's gate, 'cause it looks like you've chewed the torment out of it. Now I'm about to hold some church here and would approve of your either swallowin' that gob to the glory of God or respectin' the dead enough not to spit it all over creation. Don't just let fly of it. Wad it up in your pocket. Lookin' at a mess of that dog squat on the ground here'll just make me mad. All right? Be a good boy now. Get on down and peck around for you a place. Find your mama or the first dresstail you come to and hang on."

Leon complied, spitting the tobacco into both hands — which cradled it as if the chew would return, precious, to his jaw at the final "Amen." He hopped down and melted into the crowd.

I aimed for the red-cushioned oak chairs, which Lew had also borrowed from the Presbyterians for the occasion. Sophia had chosen the center one behind the pulpit. Byron had waddled over to flop, groaning, restless and panting at her feet. I stepped over him and took a seat beside the stillness of her, the dress and the veils draping around like theater curtains, dark and grand — more expectant than mournful or sad. She moved only to take my hand.

Big Miss Ed had led the choir back into the shadows to stand in front of the courthouse door. They hummed another chorus of the hymn until the preacher made himself fully ready at the microphone.

He turned, and gave a nodding smile to Sarah Rose, who blew back kisses with both hands. Sophia gave him the same through the veil, gripping the lace glove deep into my hand again. One of the funeral men had stepped to raise the casket lid, which gave Lew pause. The crowd herded toward the stage in curiosity, straining for any glimpse of whose funeral merited such ceremony. I made my first real study of them: Backs bent by work or age, legs by rickets, and certain souls by the weight of too little hope. A fast scan of the faces brought my eyes to Mattie, far toward the back — her chin raised above a new-looking white dress, and my Uncle Ulysses beside her in a jacket I knew had been Pap's. Gauze wrapped his head, so fully it covered one eye from my view. He stood frail in the orbit of their younger children, Marie Kate visibly absent. Mackey stood toward the crowd's middle, beside him his little green-stick of a wife, Maude Ada, barely visible in the shade cast by the undeniable hair tower that crowned Miss Evans. And to her right, in a dress the color of blue around a new moon, Mary Lizbeth appeared reverential, the dark curls falling so long and full I don't know how my eyes failed to magnetize first to her. From my seat, her sense of marvel about what the hour might reveal appeared not quite so strong as the town's. Even on the distant glance, she wired a peace into me, as though she lived detached from the worst of the world and our place in it. In that one look, there appeared a knowingness and allowance in her about Sophia's life twining with mine. Though even from twenty yards, I felt the patina of a heartbreak on her, and rummaged my place in its cause. Only Lew's call to order, sounding nearly drawn from thunder, threw a breach between us.

"I was glad when they said unto me, let us go into the house of the Lord."

The words clapped off the public address system, then rose and fell like a charge over the crowd. He raised both arms in towers of suited black. This drew silence, as if his hands called up a salute from every mind.

"This square will become the holy house of God on this day. Let us keep it so. I ask in the name of God that every soul of this place hold itself reverent." The white mane that rimmed his bald head flew back onto his shoulders. "Lord, may the words of this old mouth and the meditations of every heart in its hearing be acceptable — or near as can be — in Your sight, our strength and redeemer, amen."

Silence again. From our seats his back was to us, but I believe he glared over the crush below.

"This will likely prove the final sermon you will hear from this old filthy-mouth preacher. Thus, I will endeavor to make it one for the ages. I will try here to preach what your grandchildren will discuss long after my sinkin' grave raises its first wild daisy weeds. When I am done, it is my prayer our hearts and way of life right down to our drawers will be changed. The threads of old secrets will unravel, and fits will get thrown. But this old preacher will speak truth. I should have let it fly long ago."

"Bring it, preacher," flew on a male voice from the crowd. Lew turned once more to Sarah Rose, then to Sophia. His eyes sparked with that rareness of a mind cut free to run. He turned back, and gave himself a two-handed bracing against the podium. Within a few seconds, I believe more than a few forgot that a woman's corpse and a funeral lay at hand.

"Ladies and gentlemen of this square, some women will hike their dresses and yank down their drawers for just about anybody. From the very lore of our faith, right up to this town, we know some will actually do it for money."

A rumble. The laughter might have grown, were it not for the fervor in his question that followed.

"Are there any whores among this congregation today?"

Silence again — of the kind that comes when no one can quite breathe. He gave any dissenters little room to cry heresy.

"Not one honest whore on this town square today? Narry a Jezebel in the bunch? How about a hopper of whores? Not a single tart-lovin'-cat-house strollop among us? Gentlemen? Ladies?"

A wave of groans joined the snickers of a few to break the quiet. Sophia tensed in a whisper of, "Sweet heaven, save us." I glanced down to find on Sarah Rose a face that spoke of sucking lemons and smelling flowers at once. She was stifling a grin.

"Not one honest whore in town this day. Well, that's too bad. For our Lord Jesus had a special way with whores. A warm, gentle way and love for harlots, according to this new covenant, which is our comfort on this tearful day."

Lew thrust his Bible heavenward. The cover flapped, lively and big as a blackbird in his left hand. A single female "Amen" flew up and off the courthouse wall, heaved from the choir behind us. A bearded judge and two old lawyers down front muttered to each other.

"From Luke's Gospel, chapter 7, beginning verse 37: Listen, people of God, for the word of God."

He brought down the book and read of the woman Luke called a sinner: Her intrusion on a meal in a Pharisee's house, washing the feet of Jesus with her tears, drying him with the very hair of her head. The reading grew louder through her kissing and anointing the Christ with an alabaster flask of perfume. Lew called it the precious sweetening of a whore's trade — a symbol of the way her life had been. Her sacrifice, not needed to acquire the love bound to come from the anointed. He filled the square with the Pharisee's objection and the so-called greatness of the woman's sins. The preacher concluded with the grace given by a Jesus who sent her away in peace. The great book thumped closed and a quiet held. My eyes met Mary L.'s again, found her shrouding her mouth with both hands. Lew's voice raised again.

"People of God, the word of the Lord, held forth to us. A story of one sinner of a woman our Christ so loved. Her sin no greater than any of our own."

Two more female "Amens" soared — one from the choir behind us, the other from the crowd. Lew threw open his arms, held them wide.

"A whore of her day broke the box that was her life on the feet of our Christ. She loved and kissed him, with all the finest people lookin' on — safe in their rage and contempt, their secrets and their shames. And if some poor harlot came and offered her very way of life at our feet today, what dirty words would we call her? What hell would we raise?"

Silence took its place again. A few more walked away, shuddering with disgust and dragging their children through the crowd. Yet it remained so dense we couldn't see the ground, all the way to the buildings at the other side of the closed road. The people stood rapt, I'm sure as much by the funeral's peculiarity as any single word. Lew quickened the pace.

"I ask again, if a harlot, poor of heart, came here naked in her pleas for mercy, what would we say of her? If she wore the scandal of whore on this very stage, jay-bird naked, cryin' out for God's perfect law of love we make it our business to break and mangle all to hell, what would we do with her? Forgive my language, children. This is hard medicine for our hearts this day. I fear too many of this square would gang up and spew her with damnation. I'm afraid we might take our own hot little stones up against her. Believin' we don't deserve the scald. Or might we stone her in a prayer? Some might say, 'God bless that nasty little hustler's slattern of a heart.'"

"Ladies and gentlemen of this square: If you despise the filth of our humanity, and if the wicked and their wicked ways of this world light unholy fires in you all, this old preacher knows what you feel. I have felt it, too. I have lived hard with it — my poor wife knows."

A deeper quiet came over the people, so as not to miss a breath. Sophia did not move against the stares. The veils seemed to cast a touch of menace back at more than a few.

"People, the woman who lies in this box before us, years ago, dared carry a dark-skin child down the aisle of God's own house. When she did it, the day made me ashamed to call myself a Christian man."

This set off a murmuring. He let it loiter and die.

"I was ashamed. Shamed right down. For some people of my own church tried to make that woman, that child, and the fine man with 'em feel like chicken-house filth. Worse than any in this corn-fed county. All stripes of hell got raised over a sweet child, whose flaw in folks' minds was findin' herself born unwanted and the color of soup beans. Or maybe it was her bein' loved by a finer house than their own. No matter. The child never knew a bit of it that day, thank Christ. But the whole family never came back. And I never blamed 'em for never wantin' to darken the door of our Lord's house again."

Lew reached into his pocket, pulled out and gestured the fisted contents back toward Sarah Rose, who squinted and smiled at him through swipes at tears. The one look at her filled him with brawn.

"Folks, not long after the fits of that awful Lord's day, I was hell-bound to quit. Quit preachin' altogether. And Lord knows how I cussed some of you and the children you sired and bore. Never wanted to preach, here or anywhere, ever again. But my fine Sarah Rose handed this to me."

He held it out high over the casket. Some people toward the front winced and ducked. As though he meant to heave the contents of his hand against the nearest reachable head.

"It's just a little ol' rock. Just about black as coal, most ways you look at it. Sarah said it's just a rock, fit to throw at a stray cat. Just a devil of a rock 'til you hold it out in the light. That's the very thing she told me. Damned if she wasn't right as any rain again."

The stone rested on his open palm. I could see it catch the late afternoon sun on the makeshift altar, but the crowd would have to take his word.

"People, there's more little mica crumbs in this rock than there ever was hair on my head. A little lump full of stars, is what I have here. I've carried this little old rock with me ever since. Carried it to remind me our God sees light in the darkest swale of our souls. It has kept me from raisin' hell-fire whippin' welts on more than a few standin' about this very square today. Might've even spared me a seat-of-my-pants-whippin' or two. Children of this mournful day, God has been in this rock for me. Cuttin' the shine that holds back my tongue *and* my hand. Your old preacher here's a lot like this very courthouse. We've both seen a few whores and liars, thieves, and proud little pissant gossips in our day. Killers of a body *and* the church-goin' tongues who murder souls with a whisper. And me, plenty times, the worst of all. Folks, the Lord knows what parts of you I have despised. I've chapped my heart's hind parts hatin' on what I've seen. And more than once, the pin-dot shine off a dark little rock blinded some of the hate right outta me. Reminded me of our God, lover of whores and fightin' old preacher men. A God who needs no stone slung in His defense."

He looked up again, turned a glance back at Sophia, then went into full rail. Both arms splayed as if to catch what he called down. Lew had kept most of his tears and malice dammed up until then, but I could feel them begin to rise and soak the words. He bawled toward the sky.

"And yet I am mad as hell today. A mad, brokenhearted old man shares this stage with other broken hearts. The lady we'll bury today lost her way, and I'll be damned,

Lord, if I know why You let it be so. I want to bow up, cock and throw this rock, but don't have a blasted angel to aim it at."

He calmed, pulled a handkerchief from his pants pocket and wiped his head. The left hand still had the rock, rolling and tossing it around, and it might as well have held the congregation. The people stood wide of eye and utterly still.

"But I look at this rock and know the good Lord cuts me a forgivin' shine. How I wish my dear friend in this box could have seen the same."

Lew looked again at Sophia, seeming to feel her staccato breath that I could hear, and the shake of her against the chair and my hand. He winked, smiled, and turned again to the crowd.

"The fine woman of this box before us today looked in the mirrors of her life and saw failure. Filth. Imagine that. She held a gift of music, the finest learning, love of children, and love for all of you — though you didn't know. She possessed more sense and learnin' than any five of us, and lost herself tryin' to earn the love of our God. The very same love He surely gives for free to whores and every little sawed-off swindler bastard Jesus can find. The nastiest stink-mouth beggar gets that same love. There's no earnin' it. But ladies and gentlemen, she tried. Fasted down, tryin' to redeem herself of a sin I never fully understood. Just fasted and prayed away. Me beggin' her not to. People, her faith floundered on the rocks of religion, and that knocks a sharp break in this old man's heart. But that's not the whole of it. The whore of our Bible story today broke that perfume jar to say she'd change her ways. I believe this great fallen lady we'll take to the cemetery today broke herself tryin' to pray up and change some parts of a world she could not abide. I believe she starved herself tryin' to fix a mess of humanity that would not change. She was too fine a woman for such humankind. What she saw of this world suited her about like my drawers would fit Sarah Rose."

The whole square, timid about it, tumbled out a laugh at the latter, joined by Sophia and Sarah. Lew grinned back at all of us. Joy and sorrow seemed to stand together in the look of him, up off the bed they had long shared in a back room of his heart. As the chuckle waned, he changed tempers. A breath or two more of his anger settled over them like ashes in the summer calm.

"Brothers and sisters, this lady, my dear friend, died worn down. Broken. Hidden away. And here we all are to learn of it. Saint Augustine said God made us for Himself and we're restless 'til we find Him. But friends, I have lived as a restless old servant of that God. Restless with secrets I have long wanted all of you to learn. On this sad day, when I will bury a dear friend, I will speak that news held too long. We got you all here with the promise of a funeral *and* of a revelation. So it will be."

"Tell it, preacher. Aaamen, tell it on, amen," came from the nearly hidden choir.

"Folks, some of you surely figured it out by now, if you're old enough. The woman we will bury today is Mrs. Julia Sophia Proctor. A good woman of a mighty fine house. I'm here to tell you John Proctor, the founder of that mill yonder and plenty more, adored that woman. And as you wonder where in creation he is on such a day, well, I'm finally here to say — *he* is dead."

This drew a wave of groans. The shock sent the tight human pack into fidgets.

"John Proctor fell dead just about three years back. He's *been* dead. Been dead and buried with the same heartache that sent him and his family away from this town. And ladies and gentlemen, I'd lie if I said it didn't give me some joy to share with you the reason that man and lady so held themselves away from here. It was not of pride in their money or learnin' or shame of a solitary thing they'd done. I am most honored. Fact is, it beats some of the gloom off this day for me to introduce their child. Grown to be the woman who's made one fine liar out of me. For I've been part of the kindly little con the Proctors pulled over most all of you. Their girl put on the mask of her father to run the main business of this town, and hardly one of you knew it. *She* has kept the books. *She* managed the customers and the payroll as if she were him. It was *she* who fed your children's mouths. And with me *her* emissary. Even you mill foremen thought my friend, John Proctor, just some odd hermit too good to live with the rest of us. Well, not so. This girl back here sopped up the smarts of *two* people who took to love and raise her away from what's hateful. They brought her up into one of the great lights of this preacher's life. Guarded her against the serpent venom they found in the *very church I love*. People, she and the Proctors have occupied too many of your tongues and too few of your hearts her whole life. There was a row at the store a few weeks back on account of she just showed up. I hear folks still raisin' Cain over that. But people of God, today she has brought to you her sadness. The wounds of her heart and her secrets. And God is watchin' what we will do. Sophie, come on. It's time. Come on up here now."

He stretched an arm back her way. I could nearly feel the crowd move as she freed my hand and rose, silent but for the silken whisper of the dress, and the shoes, mildly thunderous across the plywood. She stepped to Lew's embrace, which drew her waist to his. The hat and veils held their place, but Byron did not. He raised and shuffled to her, with sagging tail, and collapsed at her feet. Lew held her and carried on.

"Ladies and gentlemen of Marshal, ours is a God greater than any times are hard. No matter the meanness or the messes of our hearts, we are loved with a love outlasting sorrows. There is a light within us. Stronger than our lonesome, hateful dark. Stouter than the undertow of this world. And some proof of that stands right here." He turned to Sophia, who hugged him in a slight wilt. I could tell the preacher felt it. He ratcheted down into a mellowness, letting it breeze onto the crowd.

"Honey, I want you to take that truth away from here. Our greater Maker loves you and you'll not flee it, no matter what people say. It's past time this world saw the beauty your mother raised. Take off that hat. High time you raised the curtains and let shine your day."

Quiet hung again. I had been watching Mary L., who had stayed caught in the thrall of Lew. Her eyes had brushed against mine only when he touched the sin of murder, and the look between us had held, trustful and kind. The mildest curve of a smile bent onto Mary L.'s face as Sophia's white gloves raised the hat of unlifted veils and held it all down, surrendered, by her side. Across the square that should have held little surprise, a murmuring wave came up. A mingling of shocks and outrages and a few, "They Lord have mercies." Some male I could not see to my right shouted up a lone jagged word that brought Lew's free hand up hard and high.

"Hell no, now. Off to hell with that chicken-yard talk. I'll hear no foul mess. This is a holy place and time, even with me up here. Let this square keep silent."

It did, as though Lew's very word might have calmed the Sea of Galilee. The sun was setting hot by then. Gnat clouds roiled in the steamy glow that covered a herd of people craving shade. Children squalled and faces glistened, but I saw no one leave. Sophia was unmoving except to wipe at her eyes. Lew raised his voice.

"Look at her, people. I'm proud to say I baptized her. Long ago rinsed this child in the same holy sacrament that washed me. But what's God want us to call such a girl? You can call her rich, for that she is. Lonesome and hurt, she is as well. Though there is but one true thing we are called upon to call her. Same thing God wants me to call any who ever slung a vulgar notion at her. We are to call this beautiful orphan child what *we* are. The very same title given that Jesus-kissin' whore and *all of us*. Especially on this day, when we'll bury the only mother this fine young lady's known, we are to call her — *loved*. That is what she is. Thank God Almighty, loved is what we *all* are."

He turned once more to Sophia and paused. Pulled her hanging head to his.

"Honeypot, grief is the bill we get for lovin' somebody else. Hurtin' the way you do is the cost of love, and it's a mighty fine bargain. You are loved in return, girl. Loved up mighty well and good."

The motions of trying not to weep ran in little waves over the crowd as he pulled her into an embrace that held every set of eyes I could see. Lew kissed and wiped her face as if no one were there to see, then turned back to the podium. I hoped for some glancing contact with Mary L., but she stayed fixed to what might as well have been the twining of a father and his wounded only child in that makeshift pulpit. The look of her cast back an almost wry feel of hope. A ripe sense that all was more than well.

"Marshal, I do not know what will become of the mill — other than to say, as far as I know, it will stay working in trustworthy hands. We'll just have to trust God, is all I can say. And we're in good hands. You are looking at the owner. That mill is entirely hers now. There will be work, and there will be pay, thanks to this fine young lady right here. Makes me proud. Makes me stand here proud and thinkin' — if our God turns out to be a *coal-dark woman*, anywise akin to this glory standing with me here, I'll liquor myself up on worshippin' that Lord 'til they freeze Judas outta hell. Assumin' that's where he is."

He let that idea float out and take its place. Allowed it to raise a calm chatter. Toward the back I saw a few slip away, among them the whole Tickman family — likely resigned to the fact there would be no flinging out of free hams at a public funeral after all. I suppose when Lew's talk turned to the topic of work, it felled the attention of my gauzed-up uncle faster than Booth's lead to Lincoln's head.

"Now, people, we will go from here to bury this fine woman of God next to the man she loved, and we'll do so in private. We will leave this girl be with her grief, but would welcome any who want to wish her well as we go. If you bring some good love, you're welcome. Anything else, just take it on, and God help you."

Lew threw a look back at me. What poured through the lens of it warmed my blood.

"Let us not forget, too, there is one of our neighbor boys back here. He's lost both his folks in a short time, and narry a hand has reached to him today, best I could see. Might be time, people. One thing's sure. That boy and this very girl have held up one another by the hand of our Almighty. May this town take some learnin' from them."

That brought back Mary L., who strewed a silent peace to me across that twenty yards. A renewal, lasting to this very moment.

"Before we go, Sophia has a word."

The idea of hearing her brought the congregation to a calm fit for infant sleep. She lowered her face to the big round spring microphone, let Lew thumb-wipe both her cheeks, and lifted out her voice. Dauntless and clear, it spread into a gracing fall over the square. Grief found little room to break it down.

"No matter what has been, I have sat too long here among you without showing my gratitude. Thank you all for your kind patience. For your care of today."

She paused for a moment's looking down, as if to order some old thoughts for their debut, then looked up with a confidence fit for Cicero.

"This is too long in coming as well. Years ago my father and mother came to loathe the thought of children at work in a cotton mill but did too little to stop it. When word came to us of hunger or other privation, we sought in secret to ease it. My parents made way for a finer school, but still did too little for the poverty of minds. So let it be known, here over my mother's dead body, I hear the calling that the young must go far longer into school before they're headlong into permanent work of any kind. My own father in his day was wrong not to raise more fight against hard hours and mill-working children. Even after law intervened, we've let too many lie their way to steady pay when learning should be their reward. The pictures of Lewis Hine teach us what is right. I know just my saying so makes my mother's soul glad. You have it on my word, no family here will live in a poverty of schooling the young. Not if I can help it. And I *will* help."

She raised her hands to the podium. Drew deeper breath. Looked up and out as if to cast her body over the crowd. What followed flew strong as every church bell clang in the whole of North Carolina.

"But lest any here mistake it, *my* name is *Sophia Proctor. This* mother, the only I'll know, gave that name to me, with the riches of her mind, as my father did likewise. They took me from nowhere and loved me as their very own bone and blood. I will adore them to my own death. If any objects — to our family, or such love, or to my being here today — I welcome your reasoning. Shout it now. My dear mother said foolishness is seldom wise enough to hide. If any wishes to prove her wrong, I'll grant you this breach to speak your mind."

The challenge soared with an echo off the primitive sound system, and it drew back only murmuring stares. Some in the crowd bowed their heads, as if some suitable retort might reveal itself on their shoe-tops or the ground. Lew returned his hand to her back, and I saw Sophia tauten to receive any vitriol that might sail toward the stage. My nerves wound where I sat. But a peace held. The audience struck itself mute for her final say.

"Let this place then witness a bit of solace, given to myself. When my father died, Mother used these words at the edge of his grave. They had long dwelled as favorites of both. Today, *I* will become *her* voice. We will hear some of the Lord Tennyson she adored."

"Sunset and evening star,
And one clear call for me!
And may there be no moaning of the bar,
When I put out to sea,

But such a tide as moving seems asleep,
Too full for sound and foam,
When that which drew from out the boundless deep
Turns again home.

Twilight and evening bell,
And after that the dark!
And may there be no sadness of farewell,
When I embark;

For tho' from out our bourne of Time and Place
The flood may bear me far,
I hope to see my Pilot face to face
When I have crossed the bar."

With that, Sophia stepped away, fighting back what was clearly the fullest cry that I had felt stir in her for the recent days between us. She stood still, between the reclining dog and Lew, who raised a hand in a call to reverence.

"People, we have heard a beauty here, and you have listened even to me. May I say I'm mighty proud of most of you. Let every head bow and eye close for our benediction."

Hats surrendered. The standing of the choir, with Sarah Rose and me, became the only rousing. Lew raised both hands.

"Lord God, forgive this broken-down old hatchet-handle of a preacher. Forgive his grimy talk and wash down his heart. But mostly — ease the fire of hurt in this our dear girl. Give her peace, as You hide us all in folds of the garment of Christ, who knows how it feels to walk around hurt. Lord Christ, we break your heart givin' hell to one another, and this oughtta make you madder than a smacked hive of bees. On this sad day, Lord, help us love you by lovin' all the whores, drunkards, and hell-wiped human maggots we can find. Even as you love this foul old preacher you let get called a man of God. Christ, you knew Peter was a weak little cuss when you wiped his feet at the final supper. Lord God, You made Saint Paul say love beats everything — religion and all. Lord, help us know there's not one soul here You love a solitary gnat's hiney less than all the rest. I pray in the holy name of our Christ who knows us and loves us anyway. Now I am done. Amen. And all God's people said — amen."

A spoken chorus of that final "Amen" went high from the choir, springing up in places throughout the crowd. Lew wasn't done.

"Folks, we're blessed to see the Mt. Zion choir up here. And I am not through callin' on all of y'all to keep your tongues as sweet as this choir is fine on the ear. They will send us off now."

He stooped back to tell me he would see to Sophia, motioning that I was to get Sarah Rose off the stage through the crowd. Dark suits rimmed the casket to lead, and Byron took the cue to rise, ancient and struggling, to follow, with Lew behind, Sophia on his arm. I offered likewise and Sarah Rose took my arm with both hands. As we waited, with the choir humming toward the stairs to sing, she said, "He did mighty fine, didn't he?" Steamy-eyed and smiling, she patted my forearm. "That's one fine bald-headed old preacher man. I do love me some of that old man."

The choir lifted up a loud take on, "Swing Low, Sweet Chariot," mostly female except for the two baritones — one I knew from the cotton bay at the mill, the other a sharecrop farmer. As the procession passed down the stairs, Miss Ed gave the casket a brush of her palm, petted at the dog, hugged Sophia's neck, then nudged me with a singing smile that spoke of a soul untouched by any fear of her own demise.

The deputies, helped by ropes held between them, formed us into a narrow chute through the dissolving crowd. The people separated virtually without chatter except for mothers chasing their offspring. Many of the smallest children in the crowd strung themselves along our way, straining eyes and arms toward Sophia — reaching for even a touch of the long and sighing darkness of her dress or the white of a glove. She slowed, extended her laced fingers to touch theirs — stick-candy drool, dirt and all. The line of children included Leon Spivey, his chaw back in place, and tiny freckled Maggie Potter, who grinned as if handing Sophia her hat that awful day at the store had bound them for life. It was as though Sophia gave off a beacon only the very young could see, her skin shade holding no barrier to them. If I could have seen Sophia's eyes that moment, I am sure I would have found the look of a stunted childhood nearer to blooming. It occurred to me Sophia's hands, fresh from their teenage years, were knowing their very first touch of another child.

Toward the line's middle, in a blend of staring adults watching us pass, I caught sight of Reba Mae Smythe — whose assault on Sophia at Mackey's had stung me with the venom of my own sins. Reba Mae in her faded Sunday dress, lost in a bottomless gawk at her victim, became a portrait of who I had been. The sight of her disclosed how my intimacy with the Proctor house had drawn change to my mind. How even a short stint in a radically different life can sew a new cloak for a soul to wear. In Reba's wonderment, I saw the newness of myself for the first time. I felt the change Sophia had fixed onto me.

Without jutting any long gaze into the throng, I tried to look for Mary Lizbeth. Leaving the stage had cost me sight of her, and keeping up with Sarah Rose took away a chance to look and, nearly, my arm. The gravediggers on the truck stood erect, still at the full attention she had demanded. She let off a cheering tongue whistle loud as any catcall, then molded her diction to fit their ears.

"Well, I'll be. You fellers minded me just fine. Y'all stood right there and proved the Lord can work through the mud. Now, sit your filthy fannies down."

From the Packard Lew yelled for her to come ride with him. She shook him off.

"I hauled these dirt-diggers down here and I'll see 'em back. You just keep up with me is all."

She dress-hiked herself back into the old Ford, cranked it, squinted, ground the first gear hard, then launched the flatbed full of men into a breakneck U-turn. The boys cleaved for life, one grabbing at the other to stay on. No one who saw her swap hands on the wheel to steer out of town could have suppressed at least a grin.

I turned back, figuring to drive Sophia, and still craning looks for Mary L. into the heavy scatter. Lew summoned me with a whistle not quite as loud as his wife's had been. As I approached the Packard he gestured toward the front door saying, "Make her be quick about it, son. It's time we got her on outta here. What she has in her head now is not my idea, by the way, so don't blame me."

Sophia was still drawing furtive looks off some loiterers as I bent through the window. Her eyes were swollen but resolute and clear. When I started to speak her hand touched my mouth to stall me.

"Frank, you've done enough for me today. You proved yourself the gentleman, and it's time I let you be. I'll bury my mother just as I've lived with her. It'll be between her and me and the quiet. Now, this is what I want you to do, and I'll hear no argument. I know you have business down here. I've seen her. I know who she is, better than you think. You have a home to tend a bit, and that must be done. You take the Cadillac and get about that business. Go home. Do what you need. But I'll need one more thing from you tomorrow. You'll know what it is when you prove I can trust you to come back with my car and what I've put into it. But even if you don't, everything will be more than fine. Do you hear me? All will be right."

She pulled me down into a holding kiss against my face, and for the first time I kissed hers in return. The casket bearers, wiping sweat in the backseat, said nothing, and I cared not to hear from them. My asking for explanation met with her raising the Packard window toward my neck. Lew had the engine already cranked and nearly took off my head revving away, vowing to see me later.

Through stretching shadows and the swarm of pedestrians, the hearse joined the recession, its front passenger window full of panting dog. Byron had invited himself to join the mistress he adored on her final ride.

I stood feeling suddenly less a part of the Proctors and more a full member of the town again. I detested this. The choir was done and the square lay broken into scatterings of conversation. A few lingering gazers rimmed the Cadillac but it was safe, so I turned from it to find Mary L. People stood anxious and flummoxed — at a loss for how to pass the remainder of this holiday, and trying to divine its meaning for themselves and their neighbors. Running through them, in neck-straining surveillance, I could hear them struggling to believe what they had just seen and heard. A few tried to stop me, but I would not. At the far edge of the square's northernmost edge, rather than doing the finding, I was found.

"Franklin, wait. Wait right here, sugar. Hold that stampede of your horses a moment."

Miss Evans, more chic than somber in a dress the color of ripe plums, had caught me around my waist. Her arm felt as hard as her Alabama vowels stretched long. The sweep of streaked hair, creaseless face and kind gray eyes might have stalled ten men. She stood beside the car bought with her family's old Alabama money — the same family money that helped endow her mission to educate the benighted mountain coves of North Carolina. It was a little wood-spoke Buick roadster, young and lively, the color of sage under a black soft top. The tiny rear window revealed Mary Lizbeth's head, turned slightly to the mahogany wheel. I stood valuing the missing of her. One turn of her head would have sprung the lock — forcing the teacher into a wrestle to hold me back. But Mary L. held the pose, unmoving. In a blinking, Miss Evans spun and faced me away from the car without letting go.

"I vowed I would dally here and wait for you if she kept her promise to me, Franklin."

"Just let me thank her, ma'am. Thank her for writin' me like she did." My pulling away met with a hard clench and a look of equal force.

"Lord, you overgrown honeysuckle boy. It's no wonder about you two."

She cupped my face in her hands, pulling it away from straining toward the car.

"No. No, now. Listen to me, sugar. I finally talked her into moving away from that detestable cabin — that bonfire in want of a match. She's in my house now and away from the goat pen she was living in. I have made fine way with her feelings. I shouldn't tell you this, but wanting word about you just about wept that girl dry."

"Ma'am, please just allow me a minute. It's all I need. I was plannin' to write her another letter. Please just lemme talk to her...."

"No. Son, you do not get to worsen her right now. That girl's worried herself half-mad since you left. Even after she knew you were alive. Do you understand me? The young lady's heart nearly had to bury you and endure all the talk around. She and many more thought you dead as Caesar."

I moved again for the roadster, but the woman's hold was sure. People passed with eyes gorging on us. I cared little who saw or heard.

"I love her, ma'am. Reckon I've knowed it most of my days, but I never rightly told her so. Not in the proper way, and it's time I did." I pulled away but she stepped to bar me again, then spun me around, facing my back to the roadster.

"I love her too, sugar. I know how your insides feel. Do you think I'm some cobwebbed old-maid fit for the crypt? Do you believe I can't carry another soul in mine? Back outside Montgomery a boy fell hard for *me*, then went off and married where he *didn't* land. Don't think my doilies don't have a tearing or two. And don't think your girl there wrote you entirely by herself, either."

Her eyes, inches away, never veered. They kept pulling mine away from the car and its passenger.

"I just want her to know I never meant harm — takin' off and all. It's way passed time she knew I'll walk hell's worst to make the finest I can for her."

"Lord, son, do you think her a fool? I've heard more stories about you than I've heard birds sing. All about the food you put in her half-starved mouth. It runs my soul straight through — knowing you were children when you did that. I know all about the two of you taking your raising in the woods together. I know how you lived on one another's company. She told me about the scraps of her own dress hem she tied on trees so you could find your way up that ridge to meet her. Just to take the warmth off one another. Lord, Franklin, I know how you staved off your own sleep to care for her on her sick bed. And I know how she gave herself to you, too. Women and girls are no good at such secrets. She *adores* you, boy. But I won't let you love one another into a bigger poorhouse. Not with what that girl has for a mind. It's way too soon for love letter babies."

The street had all but emptied. Lew had ordered the mill closed for all shifts of the day, so the clatter of farm trucks and mumbling mouths gave way to a hush. Into it, the teacher placed what she had waited to give me. Her hands steadied my face to receive it.

"Franklin, your girl there is going away. She's mined for the courage and words to tell you, and I've tried to help her, but she kept the secret even before you ran off to the woods. She is more woman than girl, son. More suited to a college lady's way than milking goats and dressing the dead in this nearly God-forsaken town... bless its heart. Now, I've helped make her a way to the Queens College down toward Charlotte. She'll begin the winter term, just after Christmas. I've dogged and marshaled some people to help me put her through. And she's saved some money of her own."

The news of it smothered, heavy as all the sun ever on the world. At the few yards between us on that little main street, Mary L. felt suddenly as far from me as the stars. I tried to speak, but nothing came. Only a heaving breath, then a lowering of my face to hide. Miss Evans lifted it with a drawling velvet force.

"Sugar, sweep that end-of-the-world look from your eyes now. This is not it. None of us gets to choose whom we love. But some of us can pick a finer way to live. And the two don't fit all the time. Now, we both know that part of this town poured out a river of hurt onto that girl. Many a time you've been the best port she's had. A girl won't forget how to find such. You'll just have to trust that — if you love her enough to want the best she'll be."

About then my temptation found its second wind. The teacher's eyes had been darting over my shoulder, and there was finally no resisting the yearn. I turned backward to see the roadster window full of the late-summer skin and dark curls. Every bend of Mary L.'s face in that moment seemed to compose a silent oath to me — the same one that had shone toward the stage during the funeral. A covenant, with only a touch of sadness, calling for some help and promise from me in return. That look, even in memory, still feels like a lasting kiss to fingertips. That perfect grazing of nerves. A move closer by either might have turned it vulgar. The look became enough. Gracefully enough.

Miss Evans yanked me back once more by the arms.

"Franklin, there is time for making yourselves ready for goodbyes. But she's been too drawn to the missing of you. And too full of dread to tell you all this. No matter how she seems, it hasn't helped seeing you again. Wondering about you and that house where you've taken up. Folks talk, you know. You've lost your mother and your father, I know, boy. And you've missed that girl like I'd miss my hand. That, and what I've told you, and all she's known — it's all too much for both of you right now. And don't think I haven't nearly had to tie her tail to that car seat to keep her arms from around your neck here. Leave her be awhile. I have her. And I believe in the both of you. You're not so gone that I can't school *your* mind back from tobacco rows and that cursed cotton mill. I will not easily tolerate watching *you* go to waste either. I've read what you feel. Do you hear me? You'll not live and die below the means of your mind either, if I can help it!"

She shouted the latter part. Had to, for I had nodded and pulled away, setting off in a jacket-shedding run toward the Cadillac. No glance back. Only retreat. Some escape. Answering a stout yen to see what remained. Thoughts of my old house bordered on a sudden madness, driving me almost full-throttle out of town. Though, as the enormous car ground onto the bridge toward what had been the home of my raising, there was no resisting a look at where Miss Evans and I had stood. The little sage roadster was gone. I steered through the leafy rise of switchbacks in a rolling sweat, past the turn to Granny and Pap's, then the fork leading to where Mary L. unfailingly used to be. A thought came of her ever-neatened shack, vacant but for the hush of what it — and she — had seen. Every yard under the tires seemed to lessen my fury. The look that had joined us those moments before had lasted no longer than a breath, but the car brimmed with what Mary Lizbeth's eyes had said. They felt to me like a dew that falls after the hottest day of the year. That single look from her gave promise to what might lay beyond the windshield.

The car and I made our way around a few of our walking neighbors, and I hardly noticed the stares. Passing the old church and the cemetery, I honored both with a glance but no stopping. Across the hill the cabin appeared, familiar as the feel of a risen boil, but made different by the ground covered to reach it again. As I eased into a stop and got out of the car, there came a cannon-fired regret I couldn't take Sophia's hand as the funeral boys lowered her mother to the grave. I hoped she was as well as the day would allow.

Instead of the knee-high overgrowth I expected of the yard, it surprised me with a spread of weeds freshly cut — all lain over by a sling blade way too dull. Their smell held a tang similar to a bitten apple. A single rocker stood still on the porch where three had been, and the walls met me with a dreary mottle that fouls my mind to this day. I clicked shut the car door as if the little farm were sleeping, then stood taking in the chat of crows and the wonder of who had been there. The thought soon dawned that the last time that house and I lived together, both my parents were at least alive, if not well. It held now only an air of starved dreams. I stepped onto the porch, gave a look through the front window. That air then turned as real and undeniable as an empty room.

If a house could be stripped beyond its patina, plundered down past the splinters, what I first found that day in ours would have come near the result. Every stick of

furniture, the tiniest thread of drapes and throws, the fireplace andirons — and even
the nail that held the picture made of me at my baptism — all of it was gone. I stepped
in a little surprised some glass remained in the windows.

The floor creaked its usual way, but echoed what I had feared, suspected, and
soon had confirmed. I eased out through the kitchen without even a check of the
other rooms, figuring my Tickman relations had looted them every bit as well. I had
just backed out of the barren smokehouse when her voice came, sharp at first. It fell
from up close to the spring and the first barn my Pap had built long before.

"Say yonder! Say, you? They law...Frankie? That's sure 'nough you, ain't it?"

I nodded a heart-stopped hello to Marie Kate, who scuffed her bare feet down
the path through a scatter of spindly chickens. She held three spongy tomatoes in
one hand, apparently harvested from my mother's overgrown garden up the way.
The other hand dangled Pap's familiar twenty-gauge shotgun. She approached, not
quite so hollow-eyed and sallow as I had seen her at our Granny's rock before my run.
Though what should have been a girl's frame stood hardened and drawn beyond her
late teenage years. Her pants I instantly recognized as my own, rolled at the bottom,
cinched up with my belt nearly to her ribs. She wore an old mystery of a shirt the
color of overwashed denim, and the red-hair skin matched a voice almost barren of
young woman joy. Everything about her stood determinedly flat, except that look in
her eyes. They cast an ease I had never seen in them.

"Boy, I first had you figured for plumb dead, and then long gone. It's a wonder
you ain't dead now. I might have hauled off and shot, thinkin' you's somebody else."

"I figured to be dead a time or two," I responded. She had startled me so, my
heart felt like a bird trying to flee the cage of my ribs.

"Well, you might as well be dead if you're lookin' to fetch much fit for a nickel
around here."

She raked me over with a look.

"Them is some fine clothes you've fell into somewheres, feller. Would've
sweetened your ma, seein' you in them. I sure miss that woman. And some small
parts of your pa, too. I reckon you know what all's happened."

I said I did, and when I stepped toward her to finish asking how she was, she
raised the gun barrel a nudge my way — suddenly fearful, hardening her mouth
down to a little cleft. Every aspect of her turned to steel. She began to pace, studying
the ground, as if an explanation might resurrect from it. I stood still and let her
confession run.

"Frankie, I don't know where all you been, or what you got in your head, but they come and took pert near ever'thing outta that house. And I had narry a thing to do with it. My ma hatched the doin' of it, draggin' along my dizzy, filthy pappy — who ought to be in the ground instead of your ma. Now, I admit it. With you and your folks gone I'd done took up livin' over here to get away from him. I was sleepin' on my own quilts on the floor in yonder. They was my own, outta respect. One mornin' right after your pa went off carryin' on in them woods after you, they come in and commenced haulin' out things. Hauled a good day's worth with Pap's very truck you left. When I come walkin' in from work and caught 'em, I pitched me one hell-cat fit, Frankie. I said Aunt Dovie was barely cold, Uncle Frank just a spit's worth of gone, and they knowed you'd come with them folks to your ma's buryin'. So there weren't no doubt you was alive and might be back. They just went on stealin'. Said it was what's proper, and that it was time I come home to help care for my family. That's when I lit out walkin' that path you beat between here and Granny and Pap's. I was madder by the step. I went to that house and done what I'd dreamed. I took this here cannon right from under the bed where I knew it was. Fetched it and the box of rounds. When I come jostlin' back here, the first thing I did was throw me some of this shotgun fire into them trees yonder. Blowed it right over my pappy's bound-up noggin, close enough that he fell screamin' hard like he was hit. I stepped up and straddled him. Told him if he ever so much as thought to get on me or this place again, what was left of him and the birdshot I put in him would get carried off to *three* boneyards. With nobody bawlin' after him. Ma come out the house, hollerin' I was crazy, and they both staggered off runnin'. Time they cranked the motor, I'd loaded again. Fired off a peck of holes in the tail of Pap's truck you left. I felt right bad, hurtin' the truck that way. But they ain't been back, and I ain't seen hide or crack of 'em since. I scared 'em right good, I reckon. Been left alone since. Done my work without a day's missin' at the mill and minded my business is all. Ain't had to splay my legs and service that sweaty old pile of lazy bed slats since, neither."

By the end she had seated herself, Indian-style, on a rock outside the smokehouse door, apologizing for how she looked. Hearing of the assault on her own Tickman blood placed my mind far afield of what lay behind me that day. I reached to help her up, careful not to startle her into another raising of that shotgun. She only sagged, half-dragging the weapon with me to the porch, saying she was sorry for everything. I tried to solace her with the notion that it was bound to happen. When she questioned where I had been, why the mill closed for the day, and what had come of that mysterious and much-talked-about jamboree she deliberately missed in town, I told her every truth I could think to tell — of the Proctors, Sophia, Lew, Mary L. and all. She inquired whether I had come back for good. The first sight of the house, the savagery of it, had helped me decide.

"I'm back to dig up what money I've hid, then lay this place behind me. Leave it in the dust of my shoes."

I left silent my intention to spend the night in the car and make my way back to Sophia's the next day, bereft of a plan beyond there. Toward the empty animal barn, Kate quietly followed me, the gun still fixed like a spooning bedfellow across her arm. I found a mattock and shovel — with little marvel that Mattie and Useless left behind all instruments of labor — and climbed through the crackling leaves of the woods to count off trees. On a dense and steep wall of the cove above the house, we reached the one whose trunk held a paling white paint mark. Under it, between two roots, I swept back the cover and dug out a little wood case Pap had given me. I had wrapped it against rot and dirt in a torn quilt soaked in vinegar. Opening it revealed the exact one hundred eighty-four dollars saved from yearly tobacco farming — with a little generosity in there from Pap. Only Mary L. and I knew of that money's place in the world.

Kate said nothing, barely ogling the cash. She followed my carrying of it through the softening dusk back down into the house to find even the kitchen had taken some pillage. The emptiness, the absence of my mother's hand or voice about the place, knotted my throat. But a chore at hand can loosen the grip a sadness will take on the heart. I walked to my room which — as Kate explained — had been partially spared looting by the good timing of her madness with the gun. My small clothing chest stood under a litter of her lint-covered dresses. My bed remained, and under it, with the help of a claw hammer still nestled under the sagging mattress, three floorboards came up to reveal a pair of coffee cans covered with cloth tops. They held a combined ninety-six dollars squirreled away from my own years of work. Since I was ten I had lied about my age to gain jobs in the cotton mill.

"Some fine money, all that," Kate said, helping me move the bed back against the wall. "Got me a bit stuffed back. Goin' to buy me my own place one a these days, finer than this, with narry a bit of help from any man."

Stepping out into the barren center of the house I noticed the closed door to my parents' room. Intending to check it later for any lingering strand of my mother not thieved, I followed Kate back to the remains of the kitchen, in which Ma had taken mansion-worthy pride. I fired the stove and helped scramble some barn-nest eggs Kate gathered to go with tomato sandwiches, listening to my cousin glow about living and making her own way.

We passed what remained of the strongest daylight on the back porch, relieving some of her lonesomeness for an ear. She talked of her mill overseer calling her a "cracker-jack spinner." She said she would have had money to leave home much sooner had the law not interfered, running those younger than fourteen out of cotton mill work years back. I warned her that tobacco farming since childhood and doffing in that mill had bought me little of the freedom we both craved. That livened Kate to tell me, with some lilting revenge, about her parents.

Losing her mill income and the charity of my mother had left Mattie and Useless little choice. My uncle — vowing he and the Lord finally found one another when that log splitter spanked his head — had turned to some backwater street preaching for handout money. His sideline of bootleg liquoring only had to be foisted a little deeper underground. My Aunt Mattie now regularly boarded the train for Asheville to sell eggs to doctors, as Pap had done, and to scrub commodes after the fine guests of the Grove Park Inn. As Kate told it, my mother's assault on Ulysses drew so much sorrowing whisper from church women that her younger brothers and sisters lived now twenty miles away at the Emanuel Home for Children. An arrangement their mother called temporary, though the children likely wished it permanent. Kate's voice held a longing to see them. I listened without another mention of the lavish place I had made my home for weeks, wondering what place preening Eb might have taken in all this, had he lived to see it.

After Kate told of staying married to the gun because her folks over the ridge lived too near for trusting, I took my money out front to the car. The conversation had grown as tired as her eyes, which wakened some on sight of the Cadillac. I eased it to some hiding behind the house, intending to take my sleep on the rear seat — too worn, I suppose, by the day's adrenaline to hold more than a breath's thought for the next day. The boxy trunk rack seemed the safest hold for the cash. By the time I opened it, Kate stood at the other end, giving the hood some wide eyeballing. Just as well, for it spared me the shame a boy takes when any girl sees gaping shock come up in his own eyes. Opening that trunk nearly melted my legs in dumbfounded wonder. Staring up at me were the faces of more money than I thought any three hundred men had ever seen.

"They sweet mercy law, Frankie." Kate had wandered back, likely to check what had stung me silent. "They's more dollar bills in that than leaves on every tree in this world. Sweet holy Moses law, I never reckoned Moses, Mary and Joseph had such money as that."

The bills, multiple large values of them, lay stacked in two big travel trunks, telling of where Sophia had gone before the funeral. She had emptied the safe at the ledge, and by the looks of things had garnered other stores of cash never shown to me. She had stuffed the trunk full. In the shock and the gathering dusk, I just about missed the note in an envelope stashed between the front rows of bills.

Kate leaned in to catch the waning sun's glow on the page. Given she had permanently left school years before even I had, I doubted much of Sophia's hand would find route into my first cousin's mind.

Dear Frank,

By the time you finish a read of this, you will know, in a small way, how grateful I am for the care you have shown me. This money is yours, for you have been extravagant in your kindness. I grant it to you on the condition you make our Jane Eyre *the first of many more of my favorite books absorbed by the sun of your eyes. I have made those eyes a warm and happy dwelling place in my memory. I will live to my grave with remembered looks of them. They will watch over the finery our time together has draped about my heart. I doubt it possible to live quite such elation again. Even in this cold well of my sorrow, you are a miracle light to me, which will remain. No matter our place in the world, our days lived here will outshine all the sadness of my life. I wanted you to know.*

I pray the Lord who gave us our weeks together will fit me into your eyes once more before I send them off to see where they belong. I have need of a favor from you and am most grateful in advance if you are able to return to grant it to me without further commitment. If not, I will understand. I will trust that parting our ways forever is meant to be. If it is to be thus, please accept my thanks here for becoming God's gentleman for my needful day.

If you can return to me, please come with urgency – of hours, not days. If you do not, I bid you peace – for you and the home you make in this world. No matter the path to reach it, you will take it no less loved.

Always,

Sophia

I held it, breathless, reading both the pages again, assuring myself I had all the words. Kate nudged and demanded a read of it out loud, which rapped me with a thought of, "You're-as-nosy-as-your-mama," but I complied. Hearing Sophia's words aloud — even through my stammer of that time — lifted them out to live, as if companions able to place their hands on me.

"That gal's sparkin' for you like axe on a rock, Frankie." Kate spoke, pulling back and straightening her red hair, as though the writer might see her through the page. "I thought you was all swimmy-headed stuck on that Hunter gal you carried on with so much. You was lovesick for her worse than havin' the chokin' hydrophobee."

I folded and pocketed the note, walked without comment off toward the house, and stood facing the gray warp of its wood — wondering a moment what had held the entire farm together for so long. When I turned back toward the car, Kate stood eyeing the money trunk, as if it held a glory from which she could not look away — fit for the awe of watching a child born.

"Never thought I'd see such in my days, boy," she said as I walked up. "Some gal's hauled off and give you that money, car and all?"

"Not really. And listen, I got to go now, Kate. I'm obliged for all of what you've done...."

"Well, not quite yet you don't." She interrupted, nearly having to chop her eyes off that trunk. She gave a scant glance at me and walked off as if I were to follow. "Seein' that money reminds me I got me somethin' to show you. Best go and show you now. That old stick bone man said you paid for it. So he brung it on. Fetched it up here in his truck, back about a week ago. Said you'd bought it for your pa."

We walked through the damp and breezeless sundown to the rear of the smokehouse, for the thing had been too heavy to drag far. She had helped the ancient blacksmith rope and heave it out of her view, away from the garden and yard. She hadn't wanted to live in sight of the cold, speckled stone, or what it said. Between the wall and little red-mud cliff, the chiseling, in its well-ordered revenge, lay at my feet.

Nobody

Born: Somebody   *Died*: Manure

After some voiceless standing over it, Kate lifted the burden of silence with hardly a glance from the tombstone.

"Frankie, I ain't said narry a bit of this to nobody, but I seen your pa. Right up yonder not far off that rock where you talked to me that day you took to runnin'. I helped the sheriff and them men what looked for you. I told them where you went in, and told your pa the same. I'd built me my own little fire on that ledge to wait, hopin' you might see it and come on back out. The rest had quit, and it was about pitch dark when the poor man come hollerin' up that trail after you. I was about to go back down to the house when he come talkin' to hisself, shakin' and cryin'. I was the last to lay eyes on him, I reckon. Tried to tell him you's going to come on home. But he went on. Not a spit I could take to stop him. And narry bit of a doubt he wouldn't come out, neither. My pappy's the goodest for nothin' man ever borned,

I reckon. And that night, yours was about the most tore up. Just tore up and down, Frankie. Then your good ma went and done what she did to herself in that jail. Lord, Frankie, I had to dig myself out. You's done gone, and me wantin' to be as gone as you was. This is far as I could get, I reckon. Far as I need — for a little spell, anyhow."

By the time she finished the sun had dropped us into longer shadows, which cooled the back of that little smokehouse for what amounted to a communion of goodbye. Mostly silent. Her story and the words of the tombstone finally settled it into my mind.

"Keep yourself right here, Kate. Far as it is for me to say, this place is yours for the keepin' — long as you want it. This and the tobacco patches Pap give me — yours for the livin'. I'm right sure I'm done with the whole business. You can be, too, when it finally wears you out. Not a soul we buried is bound to rise up and say where we've rooted is where we have to grow."

On the way down the path to the house, she asked me again where the trunk money came from and my intentions for it. I said the money was no matter, for it was not mine, which she claimed not to understand. Having turned away without another look at the grave marker, my thoughts aimed for my parents' room — what remained of it. Kate followed me to it, full of warnings unheeded. I found it as vacant as most of the remaining house. Scavenged by the Tickmans — of all furnishings, hairbrushes, combs, shoes and clothes. All that remained, near the center of the floor, was a pillow, still in the case. It carried the mildest scent and watery stain of my mother. I held it to my nose, and Kate left me with it for a brief spell in the room's late-day glow.

On the way out I thanked Marie Kate again for the meal and the keeping of what remained of the place. She said she was to work a graveyard shift and needed to sleep a short while before it. I nodded, and as I hugged her my hands read the bones across her back. They defied her resolve. She felt as frail and aged as the county's oldest woman. Vowing to be right back, I left her the pillow, which she took in the hand not still full of a shotgun, then she jaunted to the back door. On a fading, "All right then," she latched the door behind me.

The walk alone up the familiar path seemed to loosen some of the knots tightened into my nerves for years. Worry of what had been and what would come — for the first time in my memory — possessed no hold. A peace, soothing as rain sound, became my only companion toward what had to be done. It gave off a feel of the rightness of present things, of dark as the mere catch basin for a coming light. By the time my shoeless stride reached the barn, the calm felt like a wakening from sweet-dream sleep, bracing body and mind for the chore that was calling.

I had found what I needed at the wood chop by the chicken house. The stout weight of the maul — blunt at one end, sharp at the other, the handle smooth with wear — filled my hands for work too long undone. Behind the smokehouse I slipped to lather myself in the sweat of a frenzied labor, shared with a bit of good healing rant and tears. I crushed the grave marker into unreadable gravel, small and jagged, cutting deep into the oldest thoughts of my father's worst times and ways. The labor felt like balm to a wound. It powdered the ground in breakage of stone, the sparks and crackling noise all curative — a commencement of finally feeling well. More than rock, it was breakage of a long and hardened ill, finished in a relief better than any broken fever. The work had turned into a medicine for which I had no name at the time. A tonic I would need to take, in doses to the heart, for the remainder of my life. The name of it would come — soon enough.

Against the swing of the maul, the stone soon resembled the very opiate Frank Locke, Senior had commonly crushed to take in hiding behind that same smokehouse. On a pause to take in the satisfaction of the sight, I caught some breath, finished the ruination of my new shirt in a good wiping down of my head, and turned out for the remaining day that stretched ahead. Replacing the maul where Marie Kate would split logs with it again, I doused face and thirst at the spring and carried her a spare bucket of water as gratitude. Walking down the path gave me a view of my old tree house — its solace of a few boards nailed up out of reach. But for the inescapable memories in this story, that was the last time I would see that backyard.

As I reached the back porch the light came only in shards of gold on the car windows, dimmed by the sun's recline across the ridge and through the cove's trees. The place lay quiet but for birds and a few mosquitoes in full whine. I found the back door locked and jammed from within, and beside it a cloth-covered plate atop a note, barely legible on a piece of Sears catalog, written by what looked like poke berries between Kate's fingers.

Here's some biskits I made. They's right fresh. I'm asleep so I can get gone to make me a dollar. You get gone and make me proud. M.K.

Even knowing the car noise would likely wake her, I crept from the porch to the trunk and back. From the plate I took the stale, ugly biscuits to remain polite, then under the cloth I left every musty saved dollar I had dug from the farm's ground, plus a few stacks more — figuring Sophia would make no protest against such a gift. Imagining the surprise bound to assemble on Kate's face when she found the money, I cranked the Cadillac and backed to turn around on the front yard. I gave one glance back, no longer than the glow off a firefly. The house seemed to return it, with a look of dead but not quite gone. The windows made me think of Eb's old marbles Granny had given me the week after he drowned — all chinked and drab but not easily thrown away.

At the hill's crest the old church and cemetery came back into view — the first of two stops I had in mind. I killed the engine and walked barefoot, taking care not to step on Mary L.'s mother's grave. On it's tended grass lay a wilted bundle of wild daisies, their stems wrapped in wet cloth. From there I could see another bunch, wrapped the same, sagging across the unmarked clay that was Ma's piece of ground. I soon knelt above them, throwing my shadow across the heap where some grass had just begun to grow, certain the flowers came from Mary Lizbeth's hand.

I had heard of people talking to graves, but felt this time called for surrender to what the place itself had to say. In that early dusk, it spoke a serenity, not at all lonesome. The language formed on a quilt of remembered good. Rare as it had been, my mother's laughter came up in my ears, so true it withered the awe of her dying. Nearly real enough to crackle the air. I remembered her with Granny and Pap, and me as a boy — the ring of fun we formed around Eb's venture at taming a calf to ride so he wouldn't have to walk everyplace he went. The little heifer had thrown him mildly into Pap's barbed wire fence, but with enough force to split his pants through to his pride. Ma was the first one to reach him, laughing, managing with both hands to curtain off the worst of his disgrace until Granny got an apron around his southern hemisphere. The rise of that memory — and why that one, I still don't know — came with a truth about dying: That it can never raid the finest storehouse of our remembering, nor wound the love of what we keep there. When I stood to leave, the graves themselves had their say. I noticed Ma lay buried between Granny and Eb. Her remains guarded well. No room for Frank, or for me. It was as though someone had known not to hold any ground there for us. I stepped away tearless, figuring to carry on the best of what I knew of them all. Letting them live in me. Leaving that ground to its silent work.

As the car eased beyond the aged complexion of the church, a touch of Rev. Pyles and his angry-God sermonizing stirred to mind. It quieted as I recalled something I had witnessed not a week before. Nosing around the elder Mrs. Proctor's door one afternoon, I had heard Rev. Lew tell her that believing we can *earn* the favor of some furious Almighty made as much sense as thinking a dog can raise the dead because dog is God spelled backward. I dwelled on what he had told her about living up to boundless love all the way down the mountain. The thought helped carry me across the bridge and through my temptation to turn toward Mary L.'s new life with Miss Evans in town.

I steered past the square and the men disassembling the day's stage, speeding beyond the stares drawn to the enormous car from Mackey's porch. Two men restoring the borrowed funeral wares to Lew's church gave the same wordless look, and the road soon steamed in the smell of rain. A little storm had visited the rising way out of town without so much as knocking at where I had been. My wondering about Sophia held sure, but there was just enough light left for that second stop, rolling into the weedy pull-off I had in mind.

Some crooked posts stood guard against a drop to a deep part of river and the rail trestle at least a hundred feet below the edge of the road. I shut down the engine and climbed down into dripping trees, where they perched on an earthen wall. After a few yards, the ground leveled slightly, granting a view. Instinct had long told me that a glance off this place, just under that curve in the road, would reveal the piece of the French Broad river that had pulled Eb down to his end.

I stood awhile and remembered the look of his death: The finality that whitened his eyes, chilled his face and slackened his limbs. The thought raised questions of his soul. Had this been part of his last view? If the boyhood baptism by Rev. Pyles had washed enough soot off our souls, had Eb caught this vision of the river canyon on his spirit's rise to the next world? My mind found rest in the marvel of it, cushioned by the fact that Eb had become the first person of my age to take leave of his life before living could fray him. He had leapt alone off the high part of the trestle that day because the rest of us feared the fall. Over his coffin some folks had muttered about a foolish boy, but I had longed for a breath of his courage. I had envied how it must feel to soar from that place I feared to climb.

From my roost on that ridge there was also no escaping a truth that has embroidered my thoughts nearly every day since. The fact that Eb died far short of where his life might have taken him. He had been a boyhood stand of grins and home-rolled-cigarette satisfaction — outwardly fearless of all he could see and, as far as anyone could tell, dreamless of what lay much beyond his nose. He had finally allowed his own bluster and that river gorge to put a stop to what might become of him. A riverful of distant rain had stilled his life and kept its own. The river had helped our Eb die and had gone its pitiless way.

The thought always brings me back to Granny's little blessed she-rain. Traces of fog, on their noble way between heaven and hard ground, surrendered to the wind yet determined to rise. The mist speaks to me of lives fully mortal, yet answering high callings of a world beyond what we can see. Souls never fully lost to selfishness, recklessness or fear — strong and delicate at once in their rise and fall.

It felt good to stand and see the river. Looking down at where Eb had drowned I could almost hear Sophia speak of living beyond her present state. Mary L. had spoken of the same in her own way. I remember thinking both women called me toward a manhood I had once deemed impossible.

I stood at that view for at least a quarter hour, inching my toes to the cusp of leveler ground, taking in what a fearsomely pretty place the world is. Wondering how grand it must be beyond that gorge, and dwelling on how much it matters how we forge our way. The sultry dusk had begun its change into early-night blue by the time I climbed back through the cool of the trees.

As I started the Cadillac and pulled away, I held myself guilty in Eb's death. I had played a part in a mortal injustice. Once settled onto his forbidden place on that trestle, he surely feared what we other boys would say if he failed to leap. He had bragged down at us, declaring he could do what we would not, finally so wedded to the duty of it there was no turning away. No matter our warnings, we had led him to leap that day he died, for he knew the laughter and scold he would live with if his courage failed. Treading that greenish calm of water, we had become the wreckage of cruelty — the very hands that helped yank a boy down. I believed I needed to atone, in some way, for that.

My mother told of an ancient widower, Thad Weaver, a kind wisp of a man. Having outlived his farming legs and been taken in by a daughter, he haunted the courthouse steps most days, trolling for conversation – his heart surely lonesome as an abandoned bird's nest at home. Ma said she always heard his great-grandchildren treated him as they might an old yard tree – fit for a climb when they took the notion, but mostly ignored, its joy too long taken for granted.

Always strewn under him, without need of leashing, lay a mongrel she-dog, all wags and wallow, gray-streaked black. She became a catch rug for smiles from passing children on the courthouse square. The old man said he called the dog Abe "'cause she's spindly as Lincoln and a pert near identical likeness of him in her face." You might figure, a sweet bitch dog with a man's name rendered Thad into even more the courthouse novelty. People adored laughing with him at the thought Abraham Lincoln had a namesake that squatted to pee and came into heat.

One little boy in particular, helping his father on trading trips to town, fell for Abe. He fell hard and deep into love with her. A mutual love – of play and roll and adoring one another on that square.

One of those times, without showing a hint of forethought, the old man, leaning off that bench, said, "Boy, this dog has more in front of her than I do. I want you to take her on. Take my Abe on with you and your daddy here, and be good to her. Take her on now. She's rightly yours."

As my mother had heard it, Thad creaked himself down, kissed the animal on the head, and she returned the act with one of those looks only a dog can translate into love. The man wiped at his face, gestured through a long argument full of wig-wag with the father, then told the boy they should wait there until he walked off to make the parting easier on Abe. The boy knelt petting the dog, who watched her former master gimp up the street. Thinking out loud as boys will do, the child had taken note of the single walking shadow in the morning's sun, where for years there had been the strolling shade of two.

317

*Thad Weaver stopped coming to the square, and in less than a month he died in his bed —
nearly one-hundred-years-old, full of memories that stretched far before the Civil War.*

*Abe and the boy passed better than five years together in their isolation, far up into the
scarps outside Marshal. The aged girl saw him to the edge of adolescence. He finally carried
her — in the burlap wrapping of cut sackcloth he had washed — to her grave he dug at a gravelly
creek side. He wanted his Abe to lie near the clear water's music until the end of the world.*

*The first time she told me of this, my mother said, "Your daddy would have lived as a far
more lonesome boy without that dog. His sweet old Abe. I'm right sure I'm the only one he
ever talked to about her. One thing's for sure: She showed him love's a thing you earn by the
givin' of it away. That old dog helped draw his soul out to live. His deaf daddy and that old
girl first taught your daddy how to love. It's a wicked shame, what he snatched up from livin'
in the rest of the world."*

Pap used to tell me a little fear will save a man's hide, but too much will kill his soul — assuming he knows what to fear to start with. Such a balancing of fears occupied the ride as the big car and I homed toward the turn and up the Proctor drive. I braced to find Lew and Sarah Rose, maybe the sheriff and Mr. Bookman, with the place lit full of that cold chicken afterglow that will loiter about a house where a death has come. Out of the woods the Cadillac lights rolled from the driveway's last bend to meet eyes with Lew's Packard, parked at the walk. In its stillness, every window of the great house was black as the old preacher's coat.

I had climbed out straightening myself before I noticed the first jumping pricks of candle glow through spindling on the porch. Sophia's voice soon followed it as I climbed the steps, wiping sweat and tucking in my shirt.

"Well, well. I give you opening to steal my car and you bring it nearly straight back. Poor old Diogenes should have lived to see the fine likes of you."

She sat reclined in a wicker chair in front of the piano room windows, the candle on the floor barely enough to reveal her change into the khaki pants and one of the loose white shirts I had come to know. The sound of her felt lighter than what seemed fitting for the end of such a day. The long, low dangle of her foot patted the floor to wave me over. Byron lay heaped in some heavy breath at her feet.

"Sorry I took a spell. Been seeing about some things."

I moved closer to the light and took a seat on the banister, in the faintest view of her face. She showed no curiosity about those things I had seen about or where I had been. And she seemed absent any surprise I had returned.

"I seen what you wrote, Sophia. And that mountain's haul of money in that car. Wouldn't be proper, me havin' it without earnin' it, but I'm mighty proud you think I'm fit for such. Fit for anything that has to do with you. I'm thankful for everything

319

you've been to me. And what I reckon I'm a trying to say is I'm back to work some for you. Back to earn a piece of my keep and get what fine learnin' I can. You've done some mighty fine good for me. I got good reason to keep at it, if you'll have me."

As if Sophia hadn't heard a word, she raised up and stepped over the candle toward me. I could faintly see the moist swelling lingered about her eyes, but they carried less of the sorrow found there when they left me in town.

"What do you think of a God who allows a boy and girl to lose their mothers as we've lost ours? So close in time. A wonder, is it not? That, and how you and I ended up together to live through it. If someone wrote it in a book or magazine, nobody would believe it. It could only be true. Who would dare imagine it?"

I said nothing as she took a seat beside me on the banister. Through the near dark she held a gripping look on me. The swing of her foot nudged at mine.

"I know I sent you away. But I wish you'd been at the grave, Frankie. I wish you'd heard what Lew said. He put a hand over Mother's casket and warned us he was about to flout the unholy father of all history. He said that Herodotus claimed the bitterest sorrow in life comes from wanting to do greatness but reaching none of it. You know Lew — he had to disagree. He said no — the bitterest sorrowing comes from achieving all you set out to do, only to find none of it was worth a damned bit of the doing. That's when he walked up and slung that arm around me and said my mother never had to worry about such. He said her greatest achievement still lived and breathed and walked about this world. He claimed she raised up and taught a fine girl. Set off that smile and hugged me to that scratchy jowl of his. He held me there a long while, and I've sat here wondering how I can live up to that."

By then the words had turned heavy. She took a tight clutch of my hand, aiming her eyes at the dark of the house. I could feel her inner push, down against a swollen heart about to spill.

"Frank, I *will try*. I *am* determined. Somehow I will live up to both those people who raised me. But I will not do it here. I will not live more of my time here. Not beyond this night. I begged you back because I need your help to leave here, Frank. Alex has been telegrammed. Lew went to town yesterday and sent it to the last address we had for him. A boy should know when he's finally alone in this world, so I told him so — all about his mother and his father — and I know he'll try to come back here. Come to claim what he believes he can, or just remake any trouble he can think to make. And I will not be here to catch it. I will not be his victim or watch him sully a thread of this place I love. I won't watch him grieve, either. I will not witness it."

"Where you plan on headin'? There's no other place you ever lived. What home you got now besides Lew and all this here?"

"I'm going to Rhode Island tomorrow, Frank. Mother's long told me her father's house is mine, empty but for a caretaker or two. She made it legal. It's the only other place I've ever spent a night with my mother, not that I remember a lot of it. But I do know the feel of it. It holds the feel of her — and her mother I've heard so much about. That big portrait upstairs and my clothes and a few other things will follow me to Newport."

I objected, wondering how she would live, only to learn of the fortune that came with the place she was going. She offered no number, but made clear it was so extravagant our minds together would strain to reach around it. She then gave me no more room to challenge her.

"You are my dear friend, so I know you will see me through this. You will help if you care for any little part of me. You will gather me up tomorrow morning, early, to the Asheville train station, then you'll come back here to stay as long as you need. You will do it with that money I gave you, which I will not allow you to refuse. And I pray you and I will share letters as long as our living allows. I *need* you to do this, Frankie. I need you to wait for Alex because I won't leave Lew unguarded against him. You wait for Alex and do what seems fit. I'll write down a little something for you to give him, then leave the rest to you."

"What *about* Lew? Lew *and* Sarah Rose? What've they said about this mess of chicks you're gonna try hatchin'?"

The mere sounding of their names nearly raised what she had pressed down. Thought of leaving the only grandparents she would ever know all but pricked her soul to bursting.

"Lord God knows, I kissed and hugged and thanked all over them before they left me here tonight. They surely don't suspect a thing of my plan. If I have to do more farewell than that with them, Frankie, I'll never make it off this place. I talked Lew into leaving the Packard and taking their ride home with the sheriff. I told him I'd get some comfort in having a car here with you gone. He argued they should spend the night but I said no, I needed some room."

I ventured another try at talking her out of the plan, but she cut me off.

"I'll venture Sarah finds a ride back up here with a meal before noon tomorrow. We have to be gone, Frankie. If you had waited until tomorrow to come back, that Packard and I would be down the road. You'd have found all this written on a piece of paper tacked to the door. I half-wanted it so, because it'll come to the verge of killing me to leave *you*. To say goodbye. But I will, God help me, after you help me tomorrow."

She hugged me, brought a hand to the back of my head, and spoke into my ear.

"We found one another in some hard need. But how you have blessed my need, sweet friend. I will thank *you* for the rest of my living life. Please, see me through this. See me through."

My arms had a strong hold on her by then, and for some moments we each decided just to be. Wordless in the living of the time. I finally breached it with some more argument that she should stay there with my help. But that met only with a wall of orders about what I was to pack and send later — for tomorrow she would travel lightly for speed and the mercy of slipping out through the briefest send-off. She begged me again to help with that, for she knew it would be hard. Money would amount to no problem for either of us, she said. She would take some cash, and Lew would know where to find the rest I was to send. Alex could claim no part of the enormity left to her in far-flung bank accounts. The stash in the Cadillac was mine to defend as I saw fit, but on an honor pledge: If I ceased to read and learn as she had taught me, I was either to find my way to Rhode Island to return it and take a whipping, or I was to give what remained to the poorest people I could find.

We moved then to pass some of the night in the numbing distraction of busy minds and hands. We ate some of Sarah Rose's funeral leftovers, swapping rational thoughts of how it was good Sophia had grown used to a big quiet house during her mother's fasting time. I brought a trunk from the attic and helped with some packing, determined not to allow my companion to be alone unless she asked. I listened as she wondered out loud how it must feel to buy a handful of store candy the first time as a child, or share a bottle of Dr. Pepper with a young friend on a porch. We soon acted out the latter in the dimly lit kitchen, taking from the wooden drink cartons Lew kept stocked. We never spoke of Mary Lizbeth or of any future things or how far Rhode Island lay away. When she asked me to lie with her on the bed and ease off the last of the day, we talked into the dark of strange and smile-worthy things our mothers used to say or do — marveling at how akin two very different women can become in the raising of another human life. Their glories over a lost front tooth were every ounce as strong as their fits about tracked mud and torn seams. It brought easy calm, and the measure of her breathing said Sophia slipped first toward sleep. I soon followed, drowsing in the hints of far-off lightning that cast around the room. The fall of her waist under my arm on the bed called to my new devotion as a gentleman as much as it incited a temptation. I remember a final waking thought of feeling watched, wondering if the soul of either mother could see or feel through that dark into the peace of our time together.

The dawn came in a humid sheen, hot long before the sun fully rose to stretch down into the cove. Sleeping in the suit pants and shirt wakened me to the feel of lying on a steam cloud. Sophia was stirring beyond the slackened drapes and the open window. When I said a good morning she came and kissed my forehead. Said she wanted some time at her mother's grave, and I was not to follow. She smelled of a bath and stated I was to eat and bathe and be ready by the time she returned. When she left with Byron, who had slept beside the bed, I began to comply, finding another new suit draping a nearby armchair. A whitish tan, fresh white shirt and gold tie — all ordered for me in those days before Mrs. Proctor had died. The generosity turned handy, even as the finery of the goods took on a somber daub. The beauty of the clothes felt smeared with hopes gone long ago. Though I fought to disobey this notion, knowing the women of this house deemed it poor manners not to celebrate unexpected beauty.

I filled the downstairs reservoir box for a cool-water shower, shaved, dressed — jacket included, for the day seemed to call for it, heat and all. Then I boiled some coffee, which tasted almost as strong as whiskey. Early light rose and moved about the house, resting on places and things I knew my friend would find nearly impossible to turn from at the door. Waiting in the parlor where the casket had been, I thought we should have left last night. The coming of day imparted too much. The light too honest on the piano, her books, her mother's volumes — the furnishings of the only life Sophia had known. The house stood dense with the safety of how things had been, and hollow with how they were changed.

I took the liberty of carrying her trunk down to the front door, then waited in some dread. My weeks there had nurtured a liking to read the first lines of many random books taken off the music room shelves, but that morning none of the books would hold my mind away from the worst of what I expected to come. From a table next to the piano I finally lit some attention to an old magazine and a story by a Scott Fitzgerald I had heard Sophia coo about, trying to get me to read it. "The Offshore Pirate" — full of a sea in blue silk stockings topped by a haughty young yacht (my ignorance divined it was a boat), its deck gilded with a lordly young woman of supple mouth, fitted perfectly to a man's mind. I would later in my life see many familiarities in that woman he described and deem her as fecund as the ocean itself. Even on a first read, I was sure Fitzgerald and I had admired the same girls. That day, and many since, the first few words of his story spoke to me of young lives as among the most sincere forces in the world — honest about how the world makes them feel. Rising through the hardest times to make those around them feel things in return.

"Frank. You ready? I've fed and spoken my peace to the horses and the rest of this place. Our time has come."

It all flew loudly up the hall from the back door, boarding up my time with the magazine story. "You'd better be ready, my dear boy. We have to go. You've hauled down the trunk? Where are you?"

A rustle of the pages drew her eyes to me in the room. She stood in shin-rolled pants, muddy at the knees, dangling boots in her left hand, the shirt tied above the hips. They were the expensive sporting clothes of her father's inspiration, perfectly belted by some naked dark narrows at her waist, and not at all masculine against the remainder of her form.

"That what you're wearin'?" I said it rising from her favorite reading chair. "If we don't go soon, the only thing wearin' this suit is bound to be a little pond of saltwater."

She looked at me long enough for a tiny smile to form where the morning's sorrows had been.

"Well, what a figure you strike, sir. That suit has found itself a fine way, I see. It has found a gentleman, has it not?"

The question met with the silent answer of a thankful look — then a moment's blossoming of sweetness beyond words between the sexes. It lifted some weight of what had to be done.

Sophia finally broke away, and swept up the steps with a promise to be quick, Byron jostling in pursuit. I wrestled the trunk out to the Cadillac's backseat, turned the car around, then hand-burnished some mud off my shoes on the front steps. By the time I came in Sophia was already dressed and down — walking the first floor in another long dress, black again, of a crepe that seemed too delicate to wear. I caught glance of her carrying the same hat, veil and gloves that had finished the funeral disguise, clearly waiting to help her take an unmolested train passage north. The other hand held a satchel, much larger than a purse.

I waited just behind the stained glass of the half-open front door, figuring she and the house needed some parting time. From the porch I soon welcomed the thought of how different we were. That our memories of a childhood home diverged like light and dark. My leaving Marie Kate and the cabin the day before would fail any comparing to this. The sound of her steps told of where Sophia paused in what had been her home. Hearing her walk spoke of a quiet recollecting, a recalling into herself the spent voices a house will give as a farewell. As she clipped to the front door I noticed she held firm, her outer feelings sturdy as the oak floor. I thought perhaps she had made it through the hardest parts of the morning: A last trip to the fresh grave, some final walking over sacred land, a passing of her father's cabin, her mother's room, the textures of what had been nearly her only place in the world. Sophia had but one fence to clear, and it was one I had feared for her. At the threshold of the house she kneeled to the wagging frailty of the dog. The sight of Byron tripped her poise. And the fall from it came hard.

"Okay, now, my sweet boy. You promise me you'll be good for this gentleman our God chose to care for you. You be sweet and remember me. Don't you forget me. Or that fine mother you loved so, and wouldn't leave. She loved you, and so do I, you dear boy. My dear old friend."

The dog whined almost to a howl, in a frantic move toward the door. She had to push him in, and toward the motion's end she floundered to her knees — a collapsing to hug the stretch of his neck. It lifted out a kind of shared sorrow I had never heard.

"Don't you grieve the way you mourned Daddy, now. Don't you lay up at those graves. Or in that garage next to that car because you smell him on it. You keep strong for me, you good, good boy. You sweet boy...good sweet boy. Sweet God, why are you doing this to me? Why do you make so fine a life, then make it hurt so?"

I reached to lift her where she had folded herself face-down onto the slats. Above the yelp of the dog, the weeping that tore out of her bloodied my mind. Clotted the air with grief already held too long.

"Lord God...Frank, take me from here. Take me because I can not go...I have to go. Why does it hurt so, Frank? Help me, God, help me, Frank. Help me to go."

I bent to ease her back and pull the door latched. Byron climbed and clawed and bawled like a child behind it, and the sound would thrash a county's worth of nerves. It was as though the house itself sobbed that morning for what had come its way and gone. The ancient dog held the home's final breath, the last of its family lore. Bending to part with him seemed to break Sophia into mourning both the Proctors again, sorrowing every lost thing adored about them. Slipping arms under the collapse, I carried her down the stairs — in highest care not to trip over where she draped — and the weeping covered the yard, surely beyond the treeline. At the car door her legs came back enough to get in while I sprang to retrieve all she had dropped on the porch. Even over the Cadillac's tailpipe, the dog howl trailed us well into the woods, the house out of sight before it fully waned. Sophia slumped against the door into my handkerchief. She never looked around.

Out onto the river road, moving eastward now, I husked off the jacket without stopping. The car's speed thundered hot through the open windows, enough to keep down talk. Sophia dabbed and straightened at herself as the worst of the leaving began to pass. Her voice stayed thin as lace for a time.

"Frank, I will never forget this. This hurts too much not to last me forever. And it will never cease to move me, what you did today. What you've done every day you've been with me."

"I'd say I'm the one who ought get busy with the thankful talk. I'm still not fit to carry the money in this trunk, much less take it from you. I'm obliged you'd have me in your house. Y'all have been way more than kind to me."

"Stop that. Stop it now, please. I need to muster some force before there's anymore goodbye work done today. And I'll not hear debate about that money. It's a tiny part of what this girl has and owes you. You know what I said. If you stop feeding that mind, you're to pay it back. Don't make me chase and check you for ignorance in ten years."

Sophia lightened a bit further, acting as if her bones had come back. The willow's grace had begun to rise again after hurt had cut her down.

The road curves finally ceased to trace the river. The surroundings spread and flattened from granite cliffs to some wider space. We came into a swath of high trees, fully cloaked in September kudzu. Hot as the day grew, I knew the green of that vine would soon surrender to frost. The first nip of winter would turn my beloved summer a dormant gray. Each of those passing trees might as well have been a talisman for my daring that morning.

Something about a warm season on the verge of long gone stirred the inner place I had always kept for Mary Lizbeth. Pap used to say, "One woman of the house will make it dandy, but take in two and it won't be fit to live in." He claimed my father did that very thing with paregoric and every other kind of opiate he could find. Frank made opium the worst kind of lady friend, and I understood what Pap meant from early boyhood. But regrets will cause a boy to set aside what he knows. Explore himself. Maybe find he has room for two women to dwell inside him, as he might have feared. I lived up — or down — to that, however you, reader, choose to see it. On the outer verge of that summertime, I took that honest inner look around at my newly emerging self, then hauled off and announced what I found. Did it right out in the open, there in the rise of morning daylight, without even slowing the Cadillac down.

"Sophia, you can take this the way you want, and I beg pardon for speakin' up so now, but I sure wish you wouldn't set a foot to that train. Or if you do, that you'd take leave of your good sense and take me on with you. That's a wish of mine. I figured you oughtta hear it. I figure there's not a cat hair's worth of shame in you knowin' I take some shine to you. You *and* Mary L., but she'll soon be gone from me, and damned if I know how I oughtta feel about that. With all we've been through —

and hell if I care who knows it or what they say — it had to be said. I had to speak it. So right there it is. Complete and done."

The rush of air through the windows took over, the sound helping smudge away the worst of the awkward moment. Even pretending the road needed my eyes I could see Sophia looking straight lines at me.

"Lord, Frank. What a time we're living here. What *about* your girl? Your Mary L.? Don't tell me you're all in a fit now to take leave of her, because I won't believe it."

"Like I said, she's takin' her own leave of me. Least I reckon so. Miss Evans wouldn't let me see her down in town. Said she's soon bound for some school close to Charlotte. She never got out of the woman's car, but I'm right sure I'll die lovin' on her. I don't care if she digs out to China, and I reckon she loves me in return. But I still don't know what there is to be. I'm sorry to come out with this on so sorrowful a day. But my insides feel like they're growin' a briar patch in a stout wind. I just thought you might be smart enough to help a boy figure out himself. His feel for things. And what he oughtta do with the whole business of livin' with this."

I said it with eyes fixed mostly to the windshield. Sophia reared toward me and threw the hat on the dash, wiping at her face as if to erase something there.

"Stop this car. Stop it right here."

I slowed to the first side-grass that would hold us. A clump of jack pines and a boggy place spread low and lush off toward the river, which was distant now, only a shimmer in the green. Some grasshoppers clacked in the high grass.

"Frank, I don't know. I don't know the whole of what you feel, what she feels, but I can say this for sure — there is little surety in such. I've been shut up in a cove most of my life. Fished. Studied. I've run a business as well as any man. Moliere or finance books or piano — they don't hold any secret cure for the lovesick. That I know. The *feeling* part is a mystery."

Her face moved closer, filled the view. A quiet sympathy came up in the way she looked into me.

"I've longed for a boy in my hand longer than I can remember, and I never had one before you washed up out of the trees. I'm as mystified as you, Frankie. There's no learning this answer apart from the living of one. The *choosing* to live it. That's all. That, and this: The feel of you on that farm has been holy cure to me. And unless you're a fool, this will not surprise you."

Both arms slipped across my shoulders. Her fingers felt like ribbons to my neck, and the kiss came lush and warm. The salt of the morning's tears became my first taste of her mouth. The long bow of her waist gave way under my left palm, and any passing driver might have noticed the sinking of heads. I followed her draw. Fell across her on the seat, and there was young disregard for the protocols of dress and tie and growing heat of the day. The kiss would surrender to none of it. No church talk, nor long Latin words for bigotry, no thinking at all would detach it. Sophia's very first long kiss of a boy, then second, turning to more, down the dark passage of her neck in answer to the heave of a young womanhood walled back and yearning to climb over. Had her feelings not paused our collapse into one another, that roadside, and any passing rattle of wheels or voyeur birds, might have witnessed the naked beginnings of a family. That much I did understand.

"Frank, Lord God. God, I'm sorry...."

Her palms came suddenly to my face. They stilled me across the dress buttons both our fingers had scattered open to her navel.

"Dear God, I'm a selfish girl trying not to get cheated out of her living, and here I go swindling a girl I scarcely know out of her boy."

"Sophia, I'm the one fit for shame. I'm the one with a girl he can't figure out, right here on top of another one he won't leave alone."

I said it into the skin of her torso, trying to raise myself some but she pressed my head into herself, so hard the thrust of her heartbeat seeped through. We caught some breath.

"This is enough, Frank. We'll have to settle up on this being enough for both of us."

She let me raise within sight of her eyes, the look of them so far off through the windshield I might as well have lain in the clouds.

"My mother used to say she didn't have to bear me through her womb to love me. She claimed to have a mansion inside herself for me. I suppose that means I don't have to see you to adore you. I know what another face of love feels like now, and that's enough. It's enough for now. You've taught me that, boy. You sweet unreachable boy."

"I'm not much on teachin'. I'm more about learnin'. I've done myself plenty of that around you."

A mild sadness tinged back onto her as I raised further, noticing my thighs between hers through the slightly risen dress. The heat strangled but there was little care. She pulled me back down into a clutch to her chest, absent the inner fire that had been. There was no missing the grief over her mother, where it retook its place from the moment's recline.

"That girl of yours has a good man in the making. You're a living faith to her, boy. God forgive me, but I don't believe that girl will suffer if I cleave you to me a second or two. I need to take the feel of you with me, Frank. It'll make me less alone and less afraid. I need to remember how you feel on me."

"It's not right fair," I said across her breast, "you havin' to go and me barely commenced to learnin' enough to get myself fit for a fine woman."

Her fingertips crossed my face and held to my mouth. A vehicle slowed but never stopped. The sound of it trailed into the insects still beating at the calm beyond the open windows.

"You don't see, do you? Listen, don't take offense, and don't carry it around, but you're a reason I have to go, Frank. Not the only, but a fine one of them. If I don't, we'll make trouble for one another. God knows how I'd love the making of it. But it can't be."

"I wish I knew what was bound to be," I answered against her. "What I oughtta do. Mary L.'s got Miss Evans. You're both up and goin' off, and I'll have pert near nobody. That makes me powerful sad, Sophia. Damned if I'm ashamed to say so."

"Hush now. That's not true, that business of the nobody, Franklin Locke, and you know it. Mother used to tell me of her commencement at Vassar. Of it's seeming more an end than a commencing, with all the farewells on every breath. But that's all she could see from there. This'll become our commencement, Frank. You don't have to see a soul to know a soul is there. You just have to be, I suppose. That's the best answer we'll find. We'll be, no matter the where, and see where it carries us. We'll see where being in this world takes all of us."

Having nothing for an answer to that, I pulled up and kissed her on the forehead, then gently to the mouth. I rose back to the wheel, sopping through my shirt, giving little thought to trains or their schedules. Sophia rebuttoned the dress, reached for the hat and lay back fanning at herself in the breezeless morning. Her face stayed skyward, eyes closed — as if to pull drapes on a dressing of her thoughts. Though I felt she would have spoken them aloud even if I hadn't been there.

"I used to hear him through the door, trying to reason with her. Trying to tell Mother there was no God she could comprehend. No Jesus so wicked he'd take her fasting as a bribe. Lew loved to quote a tiny piece of Job. There toward the end, wherein Job sets himself aright with the Almighty. When he admits he's uttered things he can't understand. Things too beautiful for him fully to know. I'll take comfort in that the rest of my life, Frank. My dear learned mother tried to understand too much, so she settled on living too little. We won't make that error, Frank. Some things are too beautiful to say. Too perfect to be lived out in our time. It'll have to be enough — just to know what we know. Just to be."

Following that, some unrevealed thoughts took their place between us — enough for an old cattle truck to rattle by, bound surely for the Asheville stockyard. From the bed the cheerless eyes of a steer reached back and caught mine, then looked away.

"Reckon you're more right than *I'll* ever understand, girl," I finally said on a look across the dark fabric of where she lay, her left leg straightened over my lap. "I'd break myself into sticks, livin' up to such as I've heard come off you."

"Don't make me 'Amen' now. But you cleave to that thought, my dear boy. Lord God knows, I could not do a piece of this without you here. Let's finish what we've started. We should go."

She shimmied onto her seat again, straightening more about the dress, vowing we'd best drive before we suffocated or she changed her mind. The big car soon came to speed and inhaled some fresher wind into the windows while Sophia, with my handkerchief, rubbed and composed her face and hair. Our conversation, as I will never forget it, turned to finer times with her mother. Then to some wondering about the odds that such a woman as Julia Proctor would find, and devote her life to, "just a little throwaway scrap of a girl," as Sophia put it. I chided her for saying it in such a way, forcing a promise she never would again. The thought that our mothers' souls might witness the remainder of our days — and maybe want to shush what came from our mouths — drew a hint of a smile that caused me some pride.

Our stop had come twenty minutes before the first Asheville traffic. The feel of its bustle — the fluster and clap of the streetcars and the other careless city voices — made things urgent and real. Sophia put on the hat, adjusted the layers of veil, pulled on the gloves and turned quiet. Her leaving had turned again into a fact neither of us wanted to face.

I had been by road to the Asheville depot only once (Pap had talked me into riding with him and Ma to fetch my father from the sanitarium). I aimed the Cadillac up and down the wrong streets twice, but only for a brief time until we came upon the butter-color stucco of the long train station overhang. I parked and pulled out the lighter luggage, taking mental notes of the crowd along the platform. How Sophia planned to stay hidden was a wonder. A Pullman car would gain her some privacy, but the veil would surely prove no match for the intimacy trains forced on everyone who bought a little piece of their small inner places. Sophia rose from the car into a regal stand and took her hand away slowly from the closing of its door. The lingering seemed a silent goodbye to her father, a sense of it trailing her as we stepped away up the stairs.

She had bags enough to kill two men, and I dragged them to the door of the waiting room marked, "Whites Only." Sophia's drape of mourning drew stares enough just about to convince me people could see through the dark, into the disguise, but no one showed anything beyond a look. The fact was Sophia carried herself across the platform with a bearing that spoke of owning the boards, the tracks, and every inch of grazing land between the depot platform and where any soul on it was bound to go.

The suit fetched a few looks at me as I went back to the car to wrestle out her trunk. Dragging it back, I noticed Sophia leaning outside that waiting room with the bottom of one foot against the wall, gloved hands folded on her thighs. A tiny boy was looking up at her, as if he had caught his first sight of the sun. He wore travel-wear fit for hearing preaching, and the sort of smile a child forms as he musters the nerve to touch the most delicate glassware in a stranger's house. He scampered into the waiting room as I approached. The turn of Sophia's head said they had marveled thoroughly at one another.

She drew me to her and whispered through the veils for me to buy more than just her passage. I was to pay fare enough for a full Pullman car or as close as I could get. She handed me the little satchel.

"There's more than enough in there, I believe. If you need anything more we'll open the big case, but I'd rather not."

I took it without a word and stepped toward the window with a single look back. The tapered sleeves of the dress, the dark stockings — every inch of her skin stood covered. I tried to imagine the swelter of it in the still-rising heat of that day. The depot smelled of coal smoke and tobacco and the sanitizing that comes when people try not to reek of themselves at their worst. It instantly struck me: I was watching an adult catch nearly her first whiff of the public world.

At the window the suit bought me some respect before the first money appeared. A face full of white beard and darting gray eyes hardly blinked at my request for a carload of passage almost a thousand miles long. He didn't have a full Pullman, but I managed to get most of one: Southern Railway from Asheville to Salisbury, North Carolina, then a Southern to Washington — where Sophia would take a Pennsylvania Line to New York, picking up a New York/New Haven/Hartford into Providence, Rhode Island, then on to Newport. A single coach fare would have been a little shy of thirteen dollars. The amount I passed under the grate that day would have bought a good portion of a large tobacco harvest. In return, Sophia received assurance of some separation from the masses — without having it forced on her by the glass partition between blacks and whites in the coach cars. As for eating, and other movements necessary to arrive at the mansion she had visited as a child, the veils would have to do in keeping her color to herself.

I stuffed the stack of train coupons into the satchel, making sure to segregate it as best I could from the remaining gobs of money.

Back at the waiting room the two of us took our places amid some gawks and whispers and said almost nothing for awhile. We had more than an hour to wait, which we passed virtually undisturbed. The long wood benches tended to washboard the human backside and make a body prone to wander. A few, mostly women, roamed our way, offering a condolence touch to Sophia's laced hand and a question of who we were to bury. "Her mama, and it's butchered the heart plumb outta her," became my stock answer, enough to win them away — most staring back at the curtains over Sophia's face. She thanked a few herself, even took a neck-hug from one emaciated man, with no sign anyone caught on to the ruse. I kept a right hand across the backs of hers on her lap, holding there until it was time.

The call of the Asheville to Salisbury sent up a congregation, which we followed to the platform. Hoisting her luggage to the porters held back feelings — as if the work were a fine valve — but soon the hustle toward boarding left us no choice but to face one another. The threat of a minor late-summer storm had formed, huffing and dreary. Her luggage load and Sophia's care taken not to lose the hat or veils in the wind were such that most people were on the train by the time she turned and placed both hands on my shoulders. A long breath from her billowed the dark fabric.

"Reckon I'll hear from you when you get up yonder?"

She stepped closer.

"You'll hear from me by the time you get to the house. I left an envelope on the piano seat. There are notes in there. One for Lew, and for Sarah Rose. I wrote you some instructions on your care of them, the house and property — and what's to be done when Alex shows himself. I know he will. And I wrote a different little something for you."

"Not quite sure what I got myself into here, Sophia. I'll do my finest best not to let you down 'til you get back."

Her head took a moment's bow into a sigh.

"Frank, coming back here is not in my plan. To earn that money I gave you, you'll take your own leave of this place. I know you that well, boy. I know you're in for a fine life. A fine life and then some."

Her hands had dropped to her sides in the clang and hiss of a steam train about to roll. I stepped to rest my cheek against hers through the thick lace divide.

"You'll write me now. And you make sure you write me right quick-like."

"Frank, I can't. I thought about it after I kissed you back there. This girl's not strong enough for letters between us. They'll just make for us a world neither can live in or get out of. I can't get lost in there."

"How am I to figure you're all right? How're you to keep up with my learnin' out of books if I can't show you?"

My face went fully wet, mostly at seeing water drop from under the veils into a roll down the black bosom of her dress. She caressed the side of my head, reaching with her other hand to still the hat against the warm wind. The tremor in her voice firmed.

"My mother used to say a sweet thing to me from the time I was a little girl. She said I was a star the Lord made in the dark, and that I fell just where He knew the world needed some light. I have to believe the same of you. Franklin Locke, you are my raw and fine stone. You fell on this part of the world for me to find. I must put you back. But the light of you will always warm me. Remember what your Mary Lizbeth told you, Frankie? Her vow to keep a place for you? I'll keep one of my own. You'll never go out of it. You keep some little place like that for me, and we'll be all right. We'll do the best we can and be more than all right."

A shaking guided its way through her. Both hands had come folded against my chest and she looked quickly around, then nudged me toward the side of the car, as if that put us out of sight. The power of Lew seized her tongue as she whispered, "Oh, off to hell with it." One hand pulled off the hat while fingers of the other brushed my lips. A soft touch of her mouth followed and held. I wrapped my arms about her waist, and to this moment my only regret is the missing of those eyes I had longed fully to see. The coveted kiss came so fast, I failed to get my look at them.

"Hey, now."

The voice shot up from behind me. I pulled away and turned to find a big stand of male overbite, vacant-eyed, in a worn suit far too small for his frame. The jut of his teeth had long ago secured for his lips a separation and divorce. So much so that even closed, his mouth seemed full of piano keys.

"That train ain't got time for no such business as that, boy. And you got no business mixin' with such as her. That ain't your place. You hear? Ain't you got good enough sense to see what color you are?"

He had most of it out and was nearly on us by the time I spun, searing, against him. What came across his face told me my right hand held his throat before either of us thought it probable. He had some age and size on me, but he fell into a stagger toward the depot wall. Expecting Sophia to intervene made me urgent to finish him. He grabbed and flailed at both my hands, but I held — one to his neck, the other up into the most treasured storehouse of his pants. "Quit...quit your fightin' me, now, I ain't done narry harm to you," strained and rattled out of him on a scraping fall to the floor.

"You'll shut that mouth. Or this whole deck is bound to see what color the devil made the inside of your head. Do you hear *me*? Good-for-nothin', suck off a hind tit...."

He surrendered, choking as I let him up, and ran for the small crowd drawn by the noise. A look back showed only the wall of the Pullman and its vacant open door. Sophia was boarded — already away.

A thought of pursuing her rose and fell fast. Then the run — around the depot corner to leaps off the front steps, my jacket almost a cape behind me through gusts of the little rising storm that never fully rained. The same bounding stride that sent me to the woods the day Ma crowned Ulysses saw me fast to the car. I would not watch that leaving train. I would not stand longing to be on it, or get back what it carried, or force any longer goodbye on her. I vowed to be finished living in between things, even as I pummeled the steering wheel in some private sorrow. There was, for the first time in my life, a work before me demanding courage and other parts of myself I could not see. The whole of the chore far greater than the labor or the laborer — stretching as might a fertile land, whose gateway was the old road the Cadillac and I soon put under ourselves.

At the Proctors later that day, Sarah Rose, Lew and I eased one another. I gave the preacher his note left by Sophia on the piano seat, never looking at it. After Sarah read the one I handed her, she roamed and filled the house with some soft crying while Lew sat on the porch looking off over the trees a long while. Sarah and I carried meals to him there twice and found him wanting to be left alone. Holding to the same little smile that spoke of a grief and pride no language will contain.

In the text of my letter, Sophia asked that I read it at that piano and not cleave to it, nor let any other do so. I was to destroy it, keeping the contents to myself, which I have done to this day. Though I feel it safe now to share that she gave me the reins of her work done regularly in the dark. Lew had long ago linked the Proctor house with Big Miss Ed, who kept both connected with every little outpost of privation she could hear of, or find, in the county and some parts around it. It was the work I had caught her riding off to do on my waking during a pre-dawn in the cabin. Sophia had been raised to feed the hungry in secret. So she did so in the deepest part of night — not merely with money, but actually slipping around with the help of Lew and Ed to make sure a hungry child or broken-down woman or man was less so. They left boxes of food and medicine and notes to tell no one — at times using the Cadillac as their mule to haul it, with Lew keeping it fueled. Sophia's hand on that page asked that I carry the work on, which I did. The note had finally revealed the deep well from which anonymous charity had flowed to the Tickman children, as well as Mary L. and her mother, over many years.

I will share also that I complied with her orders on Alex. Sophia's telegram of his mother's death drew a response weeks later. Shortly after Wall Street's 1929 October crash, Lew eased up the driveway with the Packard full of Alex and his stench. The only son of John and Julia Proctor spilled out — dark-suited and ragged from a night of wallowing in the Mathison County jail for getting off the train belligerently drunk — the entirety of him as insolent and demanding as the inside of a whiskey cask would allow. The two of us showed him around, gave him some wailing room at the graves he had yet to see, then shared with him the papers deeding the entire property and the cotton mill to Lew. Having explored the full vacancy of his homecoming, and demanding train fare to Asheville, Alex vowed there would come an apocalyptic fight to get back what was rightfully his. I handed over the fare, then invited him to stay to supper so we could feed him a proper final meal — before I killed and buried him myself. Seeing the threat about to come to pass, Lew pulled him away and drove off to put him back onto that train. The enormous sum of money Sophia had given to my trust stayed unmolested in the old safe up at the ledge, though I confess to sleeping with a rifle the remainder of my time on the Proctor farm. We never heard from Alex again. What became of him must remain as much a mystery to you as it has been to me.

He didn't seem to notice the third grave I had dug beside his mother's. Byron — Mrs. Proctor's doted-on companion, especially through her fasting and death — had kept to his own denial of food. Of the kind that will come from an old dog grieving the loss of past loves. He spent large parts of each day lying at her headstone, in her room, or in the barn with John Proctor's Cadillac — still looking for both and spending his nights longing for Sophia at her door. He welcomed my touch, let me see his gratitude, but kept mostly solitary until I found him limp and cold on Mrs. Proctor's deathbed. He had whined and begged for me to let him through her door again. I wrapped him in some clean sheets, built a box myself, and saw him to his grave — vowing never to enter that room another time.

Mary Lizbeth never came to that house, though she might as well have breathed in its every room and onto the pages of each book I read from its shelves. I carried my devotion to her around during my time there. When she left for that new life at

Queens College, some of my Proctor money went with her. It helped cut her a path toward learning through the same Depression that saw many a well-heeled young life off into waste. The letters we swapped spoke in smiles of the town's few wagging tongues who kept carrying on about both of us: The whore who had to run, and the Locke boy who would amount to a pile of nothing, no matter how Miss Evans tutored him with money he had surely stolen from a house full of scandal. To confess a bit more, it was another woman — Miss Brontë's Jane Eyre — who schooled me best in throwing off such talk.

So there remains only the end of this story. But it will not come from me. You will hear it from a girl I deeply love. She started me on the telling of it, knowing the end could come only over my dead body. So she will reveal it. I have ordered it so.

Though Sophia will surely forgive one final revelation from the note she left me on that piano. At the end of it, she quoted a bit of Oscar Wilde — whose name so well-suited me at first I doubted his existence, thinking she had made him up. She claimed he said every man wants to be a woman's first love, while every woman desires to be a man's last romance. She wished for me the good fortune of finding both in the same set of loving eyes. She closed by wishing me times that would allow for such good fortune, claiming she had faith her life would dwell in the same.

Which brings me to my last of this tale. Before you read those final words from that beloved girl, she needs to know one final thing I have kept to myself. Little more than a month before Lew found Sarah Rose smiling dead in their bed, Sophia — in defiance of her own vow — sent me the only letter I received from her during my remaining caretaking of the Proctor house. Something in the writings she and Sarah traded through the mail caused her to feel the lady's death coming. She wrote to me that Sarah despised the "funeral home death reek" of a carnation. Hated their very sight. Sophia ordered me to make certain only a single rose came near the casket, and that I was to hold Lew up through the trial of his life's hardest goodbye. I was to be strong enough for the two of us, and *I* was to read something at the graveside. She claimed to have drawn it from our quiet times of conversation, composing it from little shreds of things my Granny used to say. *I* was to read it, she ordered, and then dwell on it, in a deep part of myself.

So, with Lew seated at the service, smiling up at me through the cracking of his heart, I complied — leaving this as Sophia's way of attending his goodbye to a wife of nearly sixty years.

"People, do not ask, 'Where are the flowers for a fine woman?' for none will quite compare to her. Hers is a beauty risen above their blooming, dwelling as a fount of their sweetest rain, so lovely even as it falls. So fine a woman we must yield to the suns of the heavens. Even as we thrive on the bouquet of her that remains. Even as she perfumes our earthly garment of God."

Epilogue

December 13, 2005

Reader, I'll sift these final words through a mighty heartbreak. A fine one at that. It is my honor to set them down, given you've come this far at the hand of my father.

Though before I reveal more of him, a brief introduction. I am breathing proof the length of a girl's given name will not widen the aisles of her love life. Nor the minds of the boys she's fancied. Uncle Sam knows me as Julia Anne Elizabeth Locke. A little much, you surely think. A syllable for every teenage boy my father ran off with his speech on how I might change the world before any man or stretch marks lay hold on me. Though my mother always said it's not my name but what I'm called that helped keep me at times lonesome as a church on Christmas day at the beach.

I have remained chronically unmarried perhaps because boys will run like the tide from a girl whose nickname and job speak of one who needs a mustache trim rather than a wax and pluck. Folks have called me Hunter since my cotton diapers flapped the North Carolina summer of my second year. My father started it, never minding that people accused him of wishing I had been his third and final boy. They're wrong. I knew from girlhood he hung Hunter on me for my natural gift at jailbreaking any crib to crawl the weeds — bound green-kneed and half-naked for the nearest woods. That, and my early thatch of brush-crackling black hair known to curl in a revolution against anyone's will. He claimed if I were to wear the ways and the plume of my mother, I might as well carry a piece of the name he first found her

337

living down and up to at once — deep in the Tarheel mountain blue. Plus he claimed he just liked the sound of it on me.

So Hunter has followed me through grade schools, Duke Law and years of poor dating, even to now. Even Mother's resistance to the name finally broke down. She had to stalk me with the yelling of it so often she later admitted the mark of it fit down almost to my DNA. My brothers — the retired Marine and the obstetrician — may blush a moment's ignorance to this day if their own children were to ask, "What's Aunt Hunt's *real* name?"

My brothers know of it, but we rarely speak of the money. Nor has the name of the woman who gave that money often risen between us. My first acquaintance with her gift came on my tenth birthday. President Truman had just named my father, Frank Locke, Junior, one of the youngest U.S. Attorneys in the country. I celebrated by crying over a bicycle. The fine, new one given me for my special day had not quite the bell-shine and sparkle raying off the one I truly wanted at the Western Auto. Daddy told me money's made first for what a girl needs — and that the right amount of wanting a little more of anything is part of the fun in being alive. Then he said, "A girl who pouts so perhaps ought to drop her panties for a cheek-peek in a mirror." See if she thinks "her butt-biscuits care much what the bicycle looks like." That came with a warning, for he knew me well enough to fear I might actually check them in some crowded store window or car fender.

That birthday, on our way to take my mildly used tricycle and some new clothes to the Elijah Children's Home, he first spoke to me of someone he loved giving him a large load of money he had not earned. He said it was to be used for a fine thing he and Mother needed, and that one day I would understand. When he told me girls who cry over everything they want are bound to cry all the time, I took it as a holy commandment — believing that wanting a thing too much is the surest ticket to want it forever. When I asked my mother about that money from my bed that night, I first learned about the two tobacco crops my father raised on a big borrowed farm to keep from buying so much as a gum stick with that great gift he never thought he deserved. When he left that borrowed farm for the University of North Carolina on a provisional admission — helped by teachers he paid to tutor him — she believed he had spent scarcely a dollar of it on his own satisfaction. Asking about the giver of it netted me a sighing kiss and quiet tucking into the night.

Through my young life my parents scarcely spoke of that woman I never saw, though at rare times I heard a gesture to her noble sort of greed. Her avarice for fully living — leaving a pretty little tearing of herself on as many fences as she could clear. The extravagance of reaping family where only a lonesomeness was sewn. When I grew old enough to appreciate the latent scandal of it, my mother confessed that woman amounted to the other romantic love of my father's life. A love not outwardly indulged. She knew of it, even though he didn't speak of it. Mother claimed she gladly lived with it, for she said that other woman had given him to her — and in his finest form. She claimed he never would have followed her out of where they were born, had it not been for that woman. This Sophia had lit him a path to what he could become, and he had not wasted an ember's worth of her goodness to him. Mother believed them a divine nexus in their time — without which my father might have fallen to smother, as his grandmother might say, "in the coat pocket of God." Reaching for any device she could find to teach me a bit of Latin, she said the life she and my father came from had a way of making ignorance "caput orbis terrarum" — the capital of the world. Mother said my father — with Sophia's help — refused to make ignorance into his ancient Rome.

That we lived with, and were happy to allow, another woman in the house of his mind would come to strike me as the worst kind of greed in the father I loved. Much too much mercy from the mother I adored. So at fourteen or so I raised some fences of my own. No *man* would center himself in my world. This Hunter would stalk no such affairs of the heart. I would live in my own sanctuary. A barbed wire independence. Built stronger than my folks had made their own.

That turned to folly, strung out far too long.

Reader, two years ago we buried the pretty remainder of my mother, The Reverend Mary Lizbeth Locke. Nearly timeless she was, but for the silver clouding of her hair and the lines of selfless joy charted about her eyes. The divinity regents of Duke can take some rays of credit for making her into one of the Methodist Church's early female bishops — a finely rounded *woman* of God, fit for the near-dresses the clergymen for years have worn. Topping the dark robe with a blinding grin, my mother lived long and well enough to baptize the infant Guatemalan love of my life. My daughter, Elizabeth, who came without planning with me from the Christian mission trip my father harassed me to take. That the child might wither in the dark of an orphanage or the deeper black that is a slum would not do. She would not pine for love as long as I was alive. This lawyer daughter of the Lockes had to pick the fight that brought her home with me. She arrived barely in time to feel a sigh off the adoptive grandmother she will never know.

When Daddy found the two of them together the last time, they were taking in the morning air and light on a March day glowing oddly warm. They were in the pooling sun on the upper porch of my parents' home, just off the lapis-colored Atlantic where it meets Wrightsville Beach. Mother loved to babysit her there for hours. Daddy said the baby snored on her lap that morning, and that he instantly knew it to be the only breath drawn to the chaise where they lay. "I never knew being so satisfied with the outcome of things could wound a man so," is what he managed through the swallowing sobs of the call that pulled me from court that morning. "Your mother died a satisfied lady, love. Close as she could get to a child. It was a good, peaceable long way from where she began. Our good Lord is surely glad of that."

We buried my mother in the shade of an old cemetery where slaves lie. She loved its little church and the view off through the silhouetted cypress trees to the bright marsh green that rims the blues of water. She had ordered that my father never entertain thought of carrying her back to the mountains. They hung in her mind in shades of adoration and despising — I knew that well. They were part of a conflict kept mostly to herself. The afternoon of her funeral, on that porch where she died, my father told me privately the fullest reasons why, and of this very book he would write to reveal more than her secret. I knew some of her girlhood: A runaway father and the bloody insanity of a mother's dying. But nothing of the rapist A.C. had ever risen. Daddy claimed he told me of it first, saying my brothers would know later that day of their mother's burning a man alive. He told the minutiae of how it happened, showing me across its vulgarity to the safe and quiet place where they had lived together with the worst of the memory. Then, in the salty balm of that porch, he eased me down into a comfort, as only he could — looking out at the ocean as if he had found some fine remains of her there anew.

"Hunter, you know your mother used to raise hell with the dead old fathers of the church. That one in particular, I forget his name, who claimed a woman bled from her privates once a month to mourn the seed-wand of manhood she would never have. She worked at not despising that fool. Couldn't get over his thinking God might dare give a woman penile-envy. Your mother used to want to dig up the old sage. Resurrect and smack him one. Tell him if he wanted to poke around the curses of a woman, he ought to take a good look at where the vital water of a man's life comes from. That it takes some bloody hell to strain a newborn man out into this world. You've heard her preach it. You've heard your mother's Mary sermon. How a just girl bled a scandal boy into this life, and him a bastard child in the world's eyes. Then having to watch her Jesus sodden the ground with his own blood. Blood of Christ. Watercolor of love. Hunter, sweetheart, your mother cleaved to that in a way her congregations might never fully abide."

He pulled his eyes off the water to the baby, then to me. His palm, reaching high onto my back, felt like a piece of saddle left in a hot day's rain.

"Like I said, love. Your mother was a child when it happened. She killed that hellion man with her hands. Tortured him to death, and it brought her no relief. She still had to shed the hate — of him and herself. She used to tell me there's no stouter proof of a living God near us than the peace she found in forgiving that hateful beast of a man — and herself at the same time for killing him. Far as I know, what's left of him is a scatter of bones in the woods, but your mother carried a burden of him and what he did to your grandmother all her days. By grace she lived with it. Let herself take a free grace no soul could earn — every day. Preached love and tried to show it, married people, buried more than a few, baptized a legion, and thought herself the most forgiven girl ever to live this life. She used to say any God who'd grace and forgive her surely had to be love Himself. She always claimed we find the sweetest 'I love you' in this world in an, 'I forgive you.' She used to tell me that forgiving becomes an, 'I love you' colored in 'The best is yet to be.' The most real love there is. God knows I loved her. I loved your sweet mother for everything she was."

My father and I sat in the afterglow of that a long while, listening to my brothers' children laugh in their oblivion across the yard through the gold dusk of the beach. Elizabeth slept on my lap through the whole thing in the mellowing of the ocean, together with Daddy's quiet way.

We've had two more years with Daddy since. Two more years during which he began writing down and showing me the story you have just read on the pages behind these. Two years that have ended just now.

Reader, I write to you a near middle-aged attorney in a private practice, the mother of an adopted toddler as stout of will as she is near perfection, and now the recent fiancée of a beautifully long-suffering man — my George. A chef who curses only at inanimate things and who loves me up in his eyes. He is a promise of my father. The right gentleman Daddy knew I would finally fail to scare away. The one who stood with me this week. He held the baby while I mourned and eulogized my father, the Honorable Frank Locke, Junior, District Judge of the United States, beautifully retired. George has seen me through Daddy's pneumonia, to the final kiss of his cooling face. George held onto me as I met the woman who, at her safe distance, lived as the other love of my father's life.

Mother had actually sent for Sophia years ago in her will. If Mrs. Sophia Proctor-Thompson were living at the time my father died, the lawyer was to send notice to her home in Southampton, Long Island. If she were able, she was most encouraged to come. Come and mourn him and finally feel at home, without fear of intruding.

Mother and Sophia had swapped a lifetime of friendship, drawn in handwritten notes under our noses. Until these two weeks of the influenza-pneumonia that took his life, I didn't know of it — and I learned Daddy for years didn't know the full measure of those letters either. In his hospital suite he told me Mother had willed them to him. The will had come with a note and a key just for him, leading to a church gym locker where the enveloped pages were stowed. He had read and kept to himself the near-lifetime of what Sophia had written my mother. It had been a gift more than worthy of the wait. The voice in the letters has helped him set loose this written story of their early lives. He told me they prove women are finer and stronger than men. Two women, in their own way, had cared deeply and without war for the same fellow — had shared their lives and proven intimacy needs no closeness to thrive. Each woman had done so, living with the parts of him mortal love will allow. Days before he died he told me where to find the letters. I had his blessings to see them. He wanted me to know the Sophia behind them.

A woman so deep in her nineties should stoop more. That was my thought at first seeing her in the holiday-lighted foyer of the crowded house, two hours before Daddy's funeral. She came with her son, Dr. Matthew Thompson, a professor of music whose father she had divorced years before. My parents' lawyer met them at the plane, and they became far from the only people of color to bring a condolence. My father had a reputation about him. A man and a jurist always far outreaching his times. There is no doubting that grew from the few weeks he spent in 1929 with this Sophia I am getting to know.

When I introduced myself, drawing near because of her years and the noise of the house, a knowingness came over her almost-creaseless face. The smiling eyes instantly possessed me as her own. Both arms, thin but seeming strong as bamboo, pulled and nestled me to the black velvet dress. She whispered, "I wanted so to come when your dear mother died. Will you forgive an old lady? Let me hold you up now. It is finally our time."

In my eulogy to the overflow church that afternoon, I put my gaze to hers down on the family pew. Out loud, as well as my brokenheartedness would allow, I thanked Sophia Proctor-Thompson for helping give my mother and this world a gift. For helping yank a beautiful man out of a backwater boy. I showed the church this lady in its midst, one who dared see the best a broken and poor boy could become, and who found no sin in hoarding thoughts and love of him. Mother years ago told me that long before Dr. Martin Luther King, Junior had his day, a boy and girl of differing colors had shown each other a way out of the darkest swale. I told that congregation the boy had been my father, and that the girl sat with us that day on the front row. I had her stand, and the room erupted in a leap of applause Daddy might have said, "would wake the deepest dead." I was glad, for it gave me some good weeping time. When it quieted, over Daddy's casket I told that congregation I believe God makes his finest home in a selfless life. And that we celebrated more than one that day.

Later in the cemetery's mild December shade, she begged some privacy. Lingered with a hand to the casket and a stare off toward an egret in the sun, where he pranced in silence on the marsh. My brothers and I stood with Matthew, learning of his mother's marks on the world. Her stowing of immense cash, auctioning off the entire Newport legacy — mansion and all — facing down gun threats from thieves, and seeing a good deal of the fortune through the worst of the Depression. I wiped her son's tears while he looked at her and told us of his mother's generosity — even to the bitterest who refused to tolerate a rich black woman re-creating the times around her. The funding of Freedom Riders, the schools for the arts, and clinics for children in places far from where so many philanthropists make their way. All that, and even a rocky and fallen run for the U.S. Congress, had become her life. She even earned a college degree at Columbia, teaching her classes as much as she learned from them, and giving scholarships to the younger students who struggled to pay their way. Matthew was proudest, though, of her reach. More than letting the greenbacks — Mr. Jefferson and Mr. Franklin — do her bidding, she had stirred the dust of the worst poor with her own hands. She had given God-only-knows how many meals to gaunt children all over the world — often traveling with a small piano to feed some joy into souls starved for some fully human life.

My brother, Dr. Ebenezer Locke (Doc Eb, to his liking), thought to ask how she and my mother found one another. How Mother came to befriend this remarkable life. Matthew believed it came from Sophia's early writing to Lew after she left the Proctor home. He had secretly given up the address of Mary Lizbeth Hunter at Queens College. Thus began the sharing of lives. The trust of two young women, set down into scores of lettered feelings — the best and worst of their times open to one another in friendship for years.

We soon would know more. From that little piece of ground that holds the reminders of my mother and father, this other woman they both knew how to love turned a step or two our way. Long and dark, in her fragile grace. We surely failed at pretending we had not stared at her quiet time with Daddy's remains.

Sophia came halfway and motioned us to the now empty chairs at his graveside — shouting words strong as a man's that the funeral home people would just have to wait, for she had some things to say. My George, God love him, agreed he'd take squirming Elizabeth in the limo on to the house. It was to be only we grown-up children and this living matriarch. She seemed more alive than any of us.

The day had begun its recline into balmy gold — in what's been a spell of warm December. All of us took our seats this one final time at Daddy's casket — near enough so he might have heard through the wood. Sophia gave a bending touch to the engraving of Mother's headstone and talked as if she were alone. She began with a longing to see the old Proctor house, figuring any crimes committed by her deceit there lay long settled in the clay. Before he died, Lew had left the great home and mountain farm to the Presbyterian Church, which had turned it into an orphanage.

She spoke of the blessed thought that her parents' own stone markers echoed the sound of playing children. Lew wanted the place to give them love without any binding of blood relation. Kneeling there, she thought out loud of missing the mountains to which she had never returned. Their indigo and topaz and shades in between — quiet in the smoky fog of a good rain draping over their place in the world. Their immovable place.

She lingered awhile, then asked Matthew's help to stand on the little black cane. With a smile tottering to the outer edges of her face, her right hand came again to Daddy's box, and she began.

"Children, the woman in this grave and the man taking his place beside her shared a mostly silent life with me. If this gentle man ever longed for me as I did for him, I am sure he lived mostly in a noble quiet with it. For he loved your mother so very well. It takes an old woman to know this for sure. And of this I am sure: There is beauty in loving someone from afar. If there is sin in such a way — such a love — then I am acquainted with the wrong God."

She gave a pat to the casket and a long heavy sigh to the still afternoon, whose only sounds were of birds and the poorly stymied cries of four grown children. She paused — gathering strength for the memory we were about to hear.

"None of you knows this. Though I believe the soul of my dear friend, The Reverend Mary Locke, will bless the telling of it. Eight months after she died, I saw your father — my dear Frank — again. He never wrote to me. It was just like him to appear at the door of my apartment in New York unannounced, wet to the skin with rain, taking his own chance. Not much unlike he was when I pulled him from that piece of river in '29. Children, you can think it indecent if you wish. Think it a betrayal of mourning or of marriage or good taste. But when you get so close to the end of your life, you'll lock up less of your living it in the vaults of caring what people might say. I am not ashamed to say I put my arms around that man and I held him to me. I loved him, and he loved me, for the six days he managed to secret himself away from the life he made here. I helped him carry the grief of burying your mother he so adored, and he loved me so well in return. I played piano for him again, we danced and talked of old things we knew. And we made love. You'll snicker to think of it. But he said we had not one thing to feel ashamed of. Your father lay beside me in my bed and said, 'Well, I guess we just showed the sheets what the ground feels like at a tractor pull.' I believe your mother's soul — from the fine place they now share — laughed as loudly as I did. I believe she celebrated as he then read to me out loud from the lovely, happy parts of *Jane Eyre*."

An unstoppable laughter poured from my brothers and me. Our father's irreverent way survived him. The sound of our joy lit out into the air and somehow settled back to me. I felt I could hear his unmistakable voice say, "Love is too good to waste. Your mother and I know it well. Especially now, we know it so well."

We all hugged this matchless woman nearly to suffocation, then sat with her awhile in the soft shade where I will visit my parents' graves. We spoke of the outrageous things Daddy was prone to say, even in court. *Especially* in court. And we laughed more, watching the lowering sun draw rain from the wetland out beyond. I spoke of my dad always wondering where the drawn up rain would go. Remembering out loud how Daddy used to say the rain has more courage than a million men. It trusts in the way it is shown. Knows not to waste itself. Never afraid to go its way. Nor to fall.

As we stood to go, Sophia leaned the first kiss to the casket top, lingering there, her hands taking rest on it.

"Go with God, dear boy. Our dear boy. Give my love to my sweet friend. My Lizbeth. I trust she still forgives my loving you so."

A pause. Still as the nearly windless day. Her head stayed bowed to the wood.

"Father, Mother, Yahweh, Elohim — our God beyond measure of name — hold to them. Hold the souls you've let me love, my Lord. Hold them all. I'll be along. Soon enough."

On soft breath, her face rising to look away — out toward the sun-strewn marsh and water and the beach homes far beyond — came aloud just a piece of what I later found in Psalm 139. I suppose it a part of Sophia's common prayers, whispered many days and nights before. Her chosen reach to the hem of the ageless divine.

"Even the dark is not darkness to thee. The night is bright as the day."

—The End—

Acknowledgments

I dedicate *She-Rain* in portions.

First to my mother, Polly Cogdill, who held a nearly life-long secret about a beautiful act of love she committed as a child. Thank you, Mother, for revealing it, finally, with shockingly good timing to give this story the character of Mary Lizbeth. I can never speak words of love and gratitude enough to match what lives in my heart for you. In your shared faith and your extravagant love, I live to this moment.

To my father, George Lloyd Cogdill, who gave us all the loving gift of his sobriety from the brink of death. If your spirit can see these words, Daddy, thank you for fully becoming the beautiful man who taught me the strength of humility, the boundless value of learning, and the curative force of forgiveness. Thank you for believing in me. I am so deeply grateful, too, for your gift of words — especially sayings that draw laughter and blushing from people to this day. Through them, you live in these pages.

For others in my family who gave form to me as a man, who helped inspire *She-Rain*, and whose remains rest on little clearings tucked in the blue fabric of the North Carolina mountains: To my grandfather, Ernest Keys, whom I know only in stories — may heaven keep surprising you with the beauty and comfort your soul deeply longed for in this life. To my grandmother, Dovie Ella Crowe Keys, who worked in cotton mills as a child — your *joie de vivre* inspires me to live a big life each day. Your humor is my lasting gift. To my great-aunt, Kitty Parker, so brilliant were your hands and so deep your sorrows in this life — I live in your open heart to this day. To my great-uncle, Woodfin Parker, a World War I veteran and gentleman farmer — the tears of joy I shed for you best speak of the character and grace that are your gifts to me even now. Somehow in these pages, I am granted that one last conversation with

346

you for which I so dearly long. And to my uncle, Harvey Keys, whose Huck Finn boyish ways lasted a lifetime — your soul and mine live in Frank, Junior, rising from troubled times to a great storehouse of love on earth.

To dear friends I love to the marrow: The Ray family, thank you for your welcome, boundless fun, and for helping prove differences of race are no match for a lifelong, soul-altering, man-improving love. The late Julia Fitchett Cooke, attorney at law, for sharing a life that shone with the seismic strength of womanhood. Julie, I whisper to your spirit and to our God a thanks for the extraordinary gift of your mind, your tail-kicking inspiration, and for letting me dwell as the son you longed for in this life. You and your sweet mother, the late Olivia Fitchett — a lady of soaring Southern charms — grace me. The Reverend Bob Lawrence, who so beautifully helped inspire Rev. Lew — your friendship (so often given in a language anyone can grasp) is the stuff of the best fun on earth. Your brilliant voice given to divine work blesses the world. You are a voice of God. I have heard another divine voice in that of the late Mildred Glass — whose spirit of driven compassion salts the pages of She-Rain cover-to-cover. Dr. Cheryl McClary — you adopted me as your brother, you read She-Rain long before "The End" and you blessed me with the passion to keep going. Thank you for allowing me to love you as family. And Mr. Bill Cannon — my thanks for your stunning knowledge of steam trains. On these pages, those grand old steam engines move souls I dearly love.

Here's one I adore off the page: Jill, whose love keeps making me a better, stronger, more resolute man. For enduring my coming to bed at 4:30 in the morning on the heels of writing, for trimming my heart with a love I didn't think possible, and for passionately working as the editor of She-Rain, I am grateful beyond words. I could never have achieved this without your brilliant hand to my back. Nor could I have done it without loving you. You blessed my life with the brother I never had — Doug Kremer. Doug and Sue, I have felt your support through this long journey. I love you both. Jill, thank you, too, for sharing even your own mother, Jean Spiess — my coastal muse and a great woman of letters. The love of you both, and the caring you show to the people of She-Rain, renew me. In you resounds the voice of our dear Bob Spiess, who taught us to get after some abundant joy in this life each day. May we all soar as he did.

In the sixth grade, a caring teacher infused a terror into me, demanding that I stand and read a writing assignment out loud. At the end, she gave a long look and pronounced in her own caring way: You are going to be a writer someday. To Miss Walker, I am neck-deep in gratitude for that boyhood terror. In She-Rain, I have loved every moment of trying to live up to your prophecy.

Teachers show us the way to great minds. I salute here every educator who did
so for me. And to great minds of our past, I offer honors here as well — thanking
the spirits of Frédéric Chopin, Charlotte Brontë, F. Scott Fitzgerald, Oscar Wilde,
Carlisle Marney, and Alfred Lord Tennyson. Your brilliance alluded to on these
pages inspires across generations.

And without finality, I dedicate this book also to the great Savannah — our
golden retriever who adored and improved the humanity around her for thirteen
too-short years. With a beauty, a humility, and that unconditional love that comes
uniquely from a sweet dog, Savannah inspired the birth of Byron. In *She-Rain*, he
carries her to immortality. Many of the people mentioned here knew and adored
Savannah, and watched her live fully, serve humanity, and die far beyond any fear. In
She-Rain, I honor her contagious courage — and the extravagant love of her.

······>·●————·●————●<·······

About the Author

Michael Cogdill is blessed as one of the most honored television storytellers in America. His cache of awards includes 24 Emmys and the National Edward R. Murrow for a broad range of achievement, from live reporting to long-form storytelling. His television credits as a journalist include CNN, CNBC, MSNBC, and *The Today Show*, and Michael's interview history crosses a wide horizon: The Reverend Billy Graham, Dr. Mehmet Oz, Dr. Henry Kissinger, Abby Hoffman, Senator Hillary Clinton, Senator John McCain, Howard K. Smith, James Brown, Keith Lockhart of the Boston Pops, and many other newsmakers. His coverage credits include Presidents and Vice Presidents of the United States.

Michael spent ten years writing *She-Rain*, letting it evolve into a world of fiction drawn from his upbringing in western North Carolina but reaching far beyond. His other writing credits are *Cracker the Crab and the Sideways Afternoon* — a children's motivational book available at CrackerTheCrab.com, and a self-help volume, *Raise the Haze*. Michael makes his home in South Carolina with his wife, Jill (a children's book publisher), and their golden retriever, Maggie. He's currently working on his second novel and works of non-fiction as well.

BUY A SHARE OF THE FUTURE IN YOUR COMMUNITY

These certificates make great holiday, graduation and birthday gifts that can be personalized with the recipient's name. The cost of one S.H.A.R.E. or one square foot is $54.17. The personalized certificate is suitable for framing and will state the number of shares purchased and the amount of each share, as well as the recipient's name. The home that you participate in "building" will last for many years and will continue to grow in value.

Here is a sample SHARE certificate:

HABITAT FOR HUMANITY

THIS CERTIFIES THAT

YOUR NAME HERE

HAS INVESTED IN A HOME FOR A DESERVING FAMILY

1985-2005

TWENTY YEARS OF BUILDING FUTURES IN OUR
COMMUNITY ONE HOME AT A TIME

1200 SQUARE FOOT HOUSE @ $65,000 = $54.17 PER SQUARE FOOT
This certificate represents a tax deductible donation. It has no cash value.

YES, I WOULD LIKE TO HELP!

*I support the work that Habitat for Humanity does and I want to be part of the excitement! As a donor, I will receive periodic updates on your construction activities but, more importantly, I know my gift will help a family in our community realize the dream of homeownership. **I would like to SHARE in your efforts against substandard housing in my community!*** *(Please print below)*

PLEASE SEND ME _____ SHARES at $54.17 EACH = $ $_____

In Honor Of: _____

Occasion: (Circle One)   HOLIDAY   BIRTHDAY   ANNIVERSARY

     OTHER: _____

Address of Recipient: _____

Gift From: _____ *Donor Address:* _____

Donor Email: _____

I AM ENCLOSING A CHECK FOR $ $_____ PAYABLE TO HABITAT FOR HUMANITY OR PLEASE CHARGE MY VISA OR MASTERCARD *(CIRCLE ONE)*

Card Number _____ Expiration Date: _____

Name as it appears on Credit Card _____ Charge Amount $ _____

Signature _____

Billing Address _____

Telephone # Day _____ Eve _____

PLEASE NOTE: Your contribution is tax-deductible to the fullest extent allowed by law.
Habitat for Humanity • P.O. Box 1443 • Newport News, VA 23601 • 757-596-5553
www.HelpHabitatforHumanity.org

LaVergne, TN USA
12 April 2010
178973LV00002B/36/P